PRAISE FOR *STUMBLING IN THE PUBLIC SQUARE*

Nobody knows the sordid history of political corruption in the United States better than James Merriner, who has done deep dives into the subject in several nonfiction books. In Stumbling in the Public Square, Merriner applies his investigative talents to the art of fiction and to the administration of one of America's least respected presidents, Warren G. Harding.

To many people, Harding may appear as one of the blander figures of the colorful period we know as the Roaring Twenties. In Merriner's novel, Harding is the nexus and (sometimes unwitting) abettor of some of the worst, most blatant corruption in our history. Yet as a character, Harding frequently evokes sympathy: he is portrayed as a man possessing well-meaning instincts, but too weak and compromised to resist and control the vipers that infest his administration.

Around this poignant, equivocal figure, Merriner has fashioned a grand entertainment, richly evocative of that period of high crimes and high living. A large cast of adventurers, schemers and thieves – most of them real historical figures – populates the story. While Stumbling brings the past to vivid life, Merriner makes it clear that the real culprit is something that never gets old: human nature.

— Scott Spires, Author of *Abandon All Hope*

MORE PRAISE FOR *STUMBLING IN THE PUBLIC SQUARE*

In Stumbling in the Public Square, James L. Merriner blends investigative journalism and historical fiction into a page-turner. The stumbler in question is Warren G. Harding, 29th president of the United States; the public square, the America of Harding's era (c. 1908-1923). But it is the presences lurking in the shadows of his administration that make this novel so compelling a read. Merriner is fair to Harding. Yes, the man may have been a drinker and a womanizer, a self-described "lightweight" in the office of presidency. But with his wife "the Duchess" beside and sometimes leading him, he advocated such causes as civil rights and a post-World War I Veterans Bureau. To what extent was Harding aware of the seeds of graft an corruption within his administration that would sprout into the Teapot Dome scandal? Only history knows. Thanks to James L. Merriner's tireless research and skills as a writer, we don't just read of Warren G. Harding's life and times. We are imbibed in this sad and seedy saga from beginning to end.

— Herry Ringel, Author of *Shemhazai's Game* and *The Phantom of Skid Row*

For Pat -
a true bookaroo!

Stumbling in the Public Square

James L. Merriner

James L Merriner
1/20/23

www.auctuspublishers.com

Auctus Publishers

Book Design by Colleen J. Cummings
Cover Design by Itala Langmar
Cover Model: Anna Strojek

Published by Auctus Publishers
606 Merion Avenue, First Floor
Havertown, PA 19083
Printed in the United States of America

ISBN 979-8-9868429-1-2 (Print)

ISBN 979-8-9868429-2-9 (Electronic)

Library of Congress Control Number: 2022952148

To the artist Itala.
My inspiration, my love.

Contents

Justice is pushed aside; righteousness
stands apart, at a distance; for truth
stumbles in the public square,
and honesty can't enter.
—Isaiah 59:14 (Common English Bible)

Prologue

May 30, 1923

He had seen it happen dozens of times in the movies and always wondered how it would feel. Would it sting like a wasp or smash like a hammer? Bullets travel, what, hundreds of feet per second. So the impact must be a blow, not a sting or a burn. Unless it was just a .22, maybe. Getting gut-shot probably hurt most of all, any caliber. Movies didn't have sound and so you didn't even hear the shot, smoke just burst from the muzzle, then guys clutched themselves and fell down. At least the bad guys did. Good guys somehow just got grazed or maybe injured a little. Obviously, villains needed training in marksmanship. But as to how it felt, that was something a man could not know in advance. A man did not go around asking gangsters, how did it feel when you got shot?

When the moment came he felt nothing at all. The bullet entered his left temple. He was right-handed. They found him on the floor of his hotel room with his head partway in a metal wastebasket.

Roxy was irked that they told President Harding before they called her. But then, you can't fight city hall and you certainly can't fight the Oval Office. If she opened the door of her suite at the Hotel Washington and walked to the window at the end of the corridor, she could see the White House. But the view held no interest for her.

Jess Smith's death was registered as a suicide but Roxy knew better. A lot of people must know better, come to think of it. Not even they could keep this crime quiet forever, for all their experience in doing so. She cried because crying was supposed to make you feel better but it didn't, not for her.

To calm herself, she imagined the scene when Warren Harding was told that Jess was dead. He would be sitting up on pillows because he could not sleep lying down any more—hell, he could hardly breathe. His pajamas would be smartly pressed. His colored valet would check to make sure the Duchess was not nearby, then he would enter softly and tug at the presidential sleeve.

"Begging your pardon, sir, but there is some news. Very sad news it is, sir."

"Goddamn it, what is it now?"

"Mr. Jess Smith is—he's dead, sir. Dead by his own hand." He looked into the president's eyes to judge whether he should go on or let the news sink in.

At this point a normal person would exclaim, "What!" or "You can't mean that!" or some such outcry. But Harding would just tighten his mouth and thrust his jaw forward a bit while calculating the implications. He would try not to wrinkle his long forehead because the Duchess had told him they both were getting too many age lines. Roxy liked to think that Harding's eyes would moisten. The first thing he would say would be, "Get me Mr. Daugherty."

"Yes, sir, he's right outside, sir."

Of course Attorney General Daugherty was already there, seeing as how his roommate and best friend was dead. My God, so many secrets. With Jess gone, who would pick out the Duchess's clothes for her?

Roxy had encountered death before. Grief wants to turn to anger, and then anger wants to turn to nostalgia. Jess went around with this chin tucked down because he thought it made him look humble, but the effect was merely to balloon his double chin. He was a big man, but he wore a Chesterfield coat even on warm days because he thought it made his shoulders look larger. People said his big round spectacles with black frames made him seem "owlish." Now all these once-annoying traits had become endearing.

Was it the last time he came to visit her that he looked at that pistol through a store window and actually blanched with fear? No, that was the time before last, when they stayed in that awful hotel in Columbus that he thought was swell. And then after turning white at the sight of that gun in the window he seemed to turn, really, kind of green.

Jess recently had made a practice of sitting in the rear of restaurants with his back to the wall and facing the entrance. She thought it was something he had picked up from cheap novels. On their final weekend together he leaned over the restaurant table and said out of the side of his mouth, "See that man over there? How does he look to you?"

Roxy knew how to glance furtively and size people up. "Oh, he's all right."

"I don't like his looks."

"Well, don't look at him. He's all right. He's just a traveling man."

"I still don't like his looks."

"Jess, for Christ's sake."

His response was odd. "Yes, for Christ's sake," he said as though it were something he had just thought of.

He had sent a telegram from Washington telling Roxy to make any plans she wanted for Saturday night.

"What do you want to do?" Jess asked.

"Dinner and dance at the club as usual, sweetie."

"No, let's go home."

"Already? But I made reservations at the club."

"Oh."

"You told me to. Remember?"

"I know. Well, will you do me a favor?"

"What?"

"Will you come on home?"

"All right, yes, of course."

"Let's go home before dark."

So they took the afternoon train from Columbus to their hometown of Washington Court House. Another odd thing, he asked Roxy to carry his briefcase. In the train she sat facing forward while Jess sat across from her, facing backward. She tried and failed to interest him in the spring landscape scrolling past the coach windows. Then she tried to calm him by jabbering about hometown stuff. He said, "Don't talk too loud. He'll hear you."

"Jess, please. And anyway, I'm not saying anything of importance. Just yak-yak."

"He's already looking at you."

"Men always look at my hair and my bosom. I'm a stacked broad, remember?"

No smile, no chuckle.

"And they always want to tell me I have beautiful eyes."

"I don't like the looks of that fella."

"Oh, stop looking at him."

"I don't like the looks of that fella."

"Okay, but stop looking at him."

When they got off the train, Jess kept peering over his left shoulder.

"Don't do that! Stop that!"

"Well, I wanted to see if that fella got off the train."

"Don't you do that again."

"All right." He seemed relieved, so that fella must have stayed on the train.

When they got home he said, "I am afraid."

"I can see that, but why, honey?"

"They are going to get me."

She knew better than to ask right away who “they” were and what “get me” meant. In good time she asked and he said only “they passed it to me.”

She played dumb. “So they’re going to try to pin all the blame on you, huh?” Like his life wasn’t in danger.

He did not reply.

“Tell me all about it, Jess. I know so much already.”

“No, just cheer me up.”

When he took off his pants she saw that he was not wearing his customary money belt. He used to carry a stack of thousand-dollar bills in that money belt. She had never seen a thousand-dollar bill or even imagined that such a thing existed. She wondered whose picture was on it.

“Alexander Hamilton.”

“Alexander Hamilton? Isn’t he on the ten? Or is it the twenty?”

“ I guess they ran out of founding fathers to put their faces on.”

Roxy remembered that grief comes in waves. No more money belt. Now she really did cry, hard.

Part One: Ohio

June 16, 1908

Roxy as a little girl was everyone's darling, with large, intelligent, wide-apart blue eyes. She lived with her mother Eldora in an apartment over Jess Smith's store. Their antecedents were uncertain. Eldora said she was a widow who had moved to Washington Court House, Ohio, from Memphis. Roxy could remember living in Memphis but not South Dakota before that. When she shut her eyes and tried to visualize her father, the outlines of his face seemed to dim and blur while the sad eyes grew more distinct. That was what she remembered, the sadness.

Eldora rented rooms on the second floor to give music lessons in what she called Mrs. Stinson's Music Conservatory. Jess's mother Opal had left an upright piano there and Jess said she was welcome to it. She taught piano to local kids for twenty-five cents an hour. Not prejudiced, she even taught Catholic kids—and even transplanted Kentuckians, the "brier-hoppers." Her room faced south with six-foot double-hung sashes and plenty of sun, so Eldora did not have to burn much coal for heat.

Jess ran the biggest store in town. A banner over the shop windows, stretching from street corner to street corner, blazed EVERYTHING FOR EVERYBODY. SMITH'S MARK DOWN SALE ON NOW. The sharpest dresser anywhere, Jess shambled over the sales floor with something between a waddle and a swagger. His late father had said "his legs are hooked on funny." Jess took the most interest in ladies' fashions.

When Roxy was ten or eleven Jess bought new-fangled cash registers and showed her how they worked. He lifted her up to sit on the counter to see the contraption. He pressed keys and small black rectangles with white numerals appeared in an oblong window. It showed $4.98 and he pulled a polished wooden crank. The cash drawer magically opened and a bell rang, ding!

"I like the sound of that bell but what's it for? I think some people might find that it startles them, don't you think, Mr. Smith? Well, it did me when I first heard it."

"Oh, my dear child, that's to alert me, or whoever is in charge here, that there was a sale."

"You need to know every time there is a sale?"

"No, child, it's so the customer doesn't hand over the money and then the clerk just puts it in his own pocket."

"You mean they don't put it in the cash drawer like they're supposed to?"

"No."

"The clerks did that? A lot?"

"Oh, child. Well, sometimes they used to, let's say."

"And why do y'all charge numbers that are so uneven, that just slow people down, like, you know, $4.98? Or $2.49?"

"My, my, but you are a bright little girl. Let's say a lady hands over a big, five-dollar bill. Well, now there's no hidden cash drawer and the clerk can't just pretend to open that drawer and then put that fiver in his pocket. He has to open the cash register to make change, give the lady two pennies, see? I don't permit my clerks to carry any change on their persons, see?"

After that, Roxy watched the clerks make change. She saw that they fumbled with the pennies, nickels, and dimes, sometimes moving their lips in calculating the correct change. She knew the correct change instantly.

When Roxy went to school the other kids made fun of her Memphis habit of saying "y'all," so she said it even more. On the first day of school one year the teacher unfolded a note from the principal. She rose from her desk and read in a flat tone: "All coloreds and Kentuckians report to the principal's office for delousing." Two Kentucky girls and one Negro boy sat looking stunned. They waited, looked around the room, then slowly stood and walked out. They would not look at one another. Roxy had never heard the words "coloreds" and "delousing" together before.

"Mr. Daugherty was behind that," Jess Smith explained when Roxy asked. "He even offered to pay for it. He is very interested in public health and wants all the kids to be clean."

Harry Daugherty was the most prominent lawyer in town and looked the part. He was thick-set with a high forehead, dark brows, straight black hair and, unfashionably, no mustache or beard. Jess and Harry were often seen together—in fact, outside the store, if you saw one you saw the other. Roxy did not like Mr. Daugherty because he called her "Punkin." "My name is Roxanne, but you may call me Roxy," she admonished to serial failure. Eldora noticed that Harry never flirted with her or any other women, although he looked prosperous and distinguished and easily could have. His wife Lucie was sickly, poor man.

Meanwhile, Eldora pursued Jess without success. He was pudgy and awkward but he was one flamboyant dresser. He had money.

Some years passed and Roxy said, "Mama, I got my period." Eldora waited a week and said, "I've got something very serious to say to you." Roxy sat on the edge of her bed while her mother stood before her with the air of a constable about to make an arrest. "You've become a young woman now and there's something you should know before you go out in the world." Eldora put her hand over her crotch. "This here? Men build Taj Mahals to that." Eldora lifted her hand. "Just be sure that you get something for it. Don't ever give it away. Make sure you get something for it. Don't give it away. Get a building."

Roxy was impressed by this news but was not sure what the Taj Mahal was. Some big temple in Japan or some place like that. At school she asked her teacher. The teacher took a geography book from a shelf and after trying three different spellings found a halftone picture of the Taj Mahal in India. Roxy marveled. Men build Taj Mahals for *that?*

She was sixteen, practicing the piano, when Jess entered, bowed to her without speaking, and sat on a plush armchair by the wall, his usual throne. She scarcely nodded his way, wrapped up in a mazurka by Chopin, Eldora's favorite composer. The piece actually was beyond Roxy's talent. But Jess, who was unmusical, found her playing exquisite. Had Roxy taken notice, she would have seen that Jess was a man sitting in ambush. His breath was rapid, his eyes vigilant.

Roxy did not hear him approach the piano bench. Standing behind her, he placed his hands on her shoulders. She stopped playing, annoyed by the interruption. But she did not resist when he placed his hands on her upper arms, stood her up, and turned her around. She looked at him without expression. He looked directly at her and yet seemed focused on something far distant. With the piano bench between them the man had to lean awkwardly over it and drop his chin to kiss her.

Years later, Roxy wondered if that had been her first kiss. You are supposed to remember things like that but she was not sure. She was certain, however, that it was his first kiss. Audibly breathing, he kissed hesitantly and softly. He had saliva at the corners of his mouth and smelled of talcum powder. Roxy calculated instantly—she was sixteen, it was 1905, so he would have been thirty-three.

Back then, he quickly retreated a half-step and said, "Forgive me, sweetie, I should have asked permission. I am not in the habit of taking liberties with young ladies."

She said "Mr. Smith, you are a damn fool," leaned far over the bench herself, pulled him down and kissed him properly.

Jess started crying. Roxy moved to make her way around the piano bench but Jess held up his big, chubby hands. "No, no, it's all right, it's medical. The doctor says I am borderline diabetic and I have high blood pressure and those, those what, those conditions can cause me to cry sometimes." That sounded like nonsense to Roxy but she went and put her arms around him while he blubbered.

Harry Daugherty told Jess, "If I'd have known you were going to fall in love with her, I'd have strangled her for you out of common decency."

Jess, who never wanted to offend Harry, offered only a lame comeback. "You don't have any common decency and you know it."

Harry was active in Republican politics in Ohio and Jess tagged along with him. The two frequently traveled from Washington Court House in southwestern Ohio to Marion in north central Ohio. They directed the political career of a genial newspaper publisher there.

Roxy was nineteen when she married Jess. It was a small wedding because, as the prettiest and smartest girl in Washington Court House, she didn't have many good friends. Her mother did not attend either.

The Marion publisher, Warren G. Harding, sent the newlyweds bouquets of delphiniums and free passes good for one year on the Baltimore and Ohio Railroad.

January 7, 1894

Warren Harding was twenty-eight years old, married less than two years, when he had his second nervous breakdown. Warren was a creature of disorder, his wife Florence a creature of order. These types must marry each other so that they can make each other miserable. Florence was a morning person, Warren a night person. These types likewise must marry. Iron laws of society.

With his wife's blessing Warren took the train north to treat himself to another stay at the Battle Creek Sanitarium in Michigan. Despite his robust, six-foot-one frame and square-shouldered stride, Harding was an unhealthy man. He suffered from painful attacks of indigestion, especially at night, along with headaches and signs of depression. These symptoms worsened after he married Florence, who offered many helpful suggestions for how he should run his *Marion Star* newspaper.

Many famous people took the cure at Dr. John H. Kellogg's sanitarium. It was known for innovative treatments such as vegetarian meals, hydrotherapy, and a clinical obsession with stool samples. Kellogg had so many patients that the Michigan Central Railway built a line to the sanitarium with a train station there. "The San's" carriages, with drivers in green-and-white livery, awaited Harding when he got off the train. He had barely unpacked in his bedroom in the men's wing of the complex when Dr. Kellogg himself knocked on his door. The men exchanged greetings and Kellogg welcomed Warren back.

"I trust," the doctor said, "that you are still familiar with our philosophy and our program. We require that you ingest no tobacco, no alcohol, and no meat." He paused to await a nod. "Also that you refrain from all forms of sex, including masturbation. But these—"

"I shall strive to do my best to honor those principles," Harding lied.

"But these are just the 'thou shalt nots,' " Kellogg continued. "The positive aspects of your stay here are at least equally important. You will enjoy the utmost in personal hygiene, exercise for the body and the mind. What is more, all the benefits of fresh air and Christian fellowship."

Kellogg, in his early forties and only five-feet-four, sat in a chair deliberately carpentered low so that his feet comfortably reached the floor. He was dressed in white linen with a white hat and white shoes. Harding said, "I have only the fondest memories of my previous visit to your excellent facilities."

Kellogg obviously had something on his mind and Harding waited for it. The doctor shifted in his chair, removed his hat, cleared his throat and said, "Mr. Harding, as a newspaperman, I trust that you are what they call a man of the world, am I correct?"

"The first part of your observation is certainly true, at least. I like to think that I am the only newspaper publisher in the country who started out by setting his own type. In fact, sometimes I still go down to the shop and set the type myself. It gives me a good feeling."

"Excellent, excellent. And now forgive me for raising a matter that is most delicate." Another clearing of the throat. "I ask you frankly and ask you to answer in the same spirit, is it true that there is Negroid blood in your ancestry?"

"No. That is a gross calumny that is being spread by my beastly father-in-law, Mr. Kling."

"So the allegations are untrue?"

"I tell you they are lies."

"I am gratified to hear it. But you mentioned Mr. Kling and now forgive me for raising another matter of the utmost delicacy. There are reports, and you need not inquire as to my sources, of Jewish blood in Mr. Kling's heritage."

At this, Harding seemed amused. "Mr. Kling has made many enemies who would like to do him in the eye. No, the Klings came from a part of Germany where there are many Jews, but they themselves were not Jewish, I assure you."

Kellogg all but clapped his hands in delight. "Oh, that's all very well, Mr. Harding, I knew that you would be a man who would support modern science." He unbuttoned his jacket and reached inside to withdraw a magazine with a sky-blue cover: *Good HEALTH. Conducted by J. H. Kellogg M.D. Published Monthly*. Harding recognized the curlicued style of the newfangled typeface. He took the volume, flipped open the cover, and read the headline over the lead article: "The Race Betterment Foundation."

Harding, a man who loved to talk, stayed silent.

"As you see," Kellogg said, "we are establishing a foundation to serve the cause of protecting the race. The white race is being mongrelized. All the best scientific minds tell us that we must take serious steps to improve the health and quality of the human race. You have heard of the new science of eugenics?"

"Yes, I have heard the word," Harding said.

"Good, good. No, I am not asking you for money to support the foundation at this time," Kellogg said as Harding shifted uneasily in his chair. "We are seeking just now to enhance the public's knowledge of this vital matter through the popular press. I believe the *Star* would be an excellent exponent of our cause, don't you agree?"

Harding leaned forward and assumed an earnest air. "Doctor," he said, "the only causes I promote are those of a free press and a free people. Let me give you an example," he added, seeing disappointment droop over Kellogg's face. "The Anti-Saloon League is based in Ohio, as you probably know. Many of my readers and subscribers are members of that worthy organization. Many of my readers and their families are fine Baptists. But for every dry, there is also a wet. So, again, many of my readers are fine Methodists and Presbyterians and they believe just as strongly that Prohibition would be an unjust abridgment of their freedom. So, you see, I present the news faithfully and honestly and I try not to take sides on social issues that just divide our people. I'm a booster, not a knocker."

Kellogg had listened solemnly. He said, "My dear Mr. Harding, I am afraid that you have misunderstood me. We are presenting not a social or a political issue. What we advocate is sound science, pure and simple. The quality of the human race is declining before our eyes, don't you see? But by taking the science of inheritances into account, we can improve the health and strength of the race."

Harding fell back on an aw-shucks, country-boy routine. "Ah, doctor, I'm afraid that the science you speak of is over my head. I am a small-town newspaperman. I could not advocate something that I myself do not understand. Nor would I wish to offend any of our Negro readers." He tried and failed to think of a single Negro subscriber to the *Star*.

"Oh, pish-posh, I think you understand it perfectly well. And if not, we have experts here that can tutor you. By the way, we would plan to take out a significant amount of advertising in the *Star* in the interest of educating the public. And I am sure the board and I could make an adjustment in your fees here."

If this had been an outright political bribe, Harding might have taken it. But because it threatened to taint his own sacred realm of journalism, he scrupled. "Of course," he said, "we always welcome all our advertisers. But as for my care and treatment here, I always insist on paying my own way, wherever I go." (Not true. Harding took free passes from the railroads and free concert tickets.) Kellogg left in good humor after inviting Harding to dine with him that evening. He actually did place an ad, though just a quarter-page, in the *Star*.

And so the weeks passed in monochrome as Harding endured the San's privations. Even the dinners with Kellogg and his brother William, who had invented corn flakes, had no charms for an epicure. Within a month Harding was seeking out the nearby Red Onion tavern, where beer foamed, cigars glowed, dice rattled, and ladies danced.

Harding encountered Susan Hodder as they both, dressed in white linen robes, waited outside the San's massage rooms for their rubdown appointments. He knew Susan from Marion—in fact, she had lived next door to Amos Kling and was a childhood friend of his daughter Florence, now Harding's wife. Susan had been a good-looking girl with some spark and a little glamour. She had moved out of her father's house upon getting married, but the marriage soon soured and she moved back in. She was at the San seeking treatment for "nerves," a catchall for any illness for which doctors found no physical cause.

When Harding said hello she looked at him with a frankly appraising gaze. Polite chitchat turned to comments about the barbarous personality of Amos Kling. With that in common, Harding ventured,"You know, the people who work here call the Red Onion a dive and a gin joint. Now, I don't think that's fair. It's actually a classy place. They've got a mahogany bar and a dance floor. With a five-piece band. Anyway, ahem, that's what I've been told. Did you know I used to play the cornet in the Merry-Roll-Round?"

"Oh yes you did, I remember you there. You were so young and handsome and all the girls wanted to go with you. But you never even looked at me."

"Now there you're wrong, dearie. I used to watch the boys line up to see if you might consent to take their hand and let them skate you around. 'Oh, please, Susie, just once around.' And if you did not wish it you would say 'Oh, no, these skates are killing any feet.' And then the boy would weep in despair."

The laughter of women is one of God's graces, Harding reminded himself. Susan's had the sound of finger cymbals. After a long laugh she said, "That's nonsense and you know it but I like to hear you say things like that. Have you really been to the Red Onion?"

Joy filled Harding's heart. "Well, um, maybe once or twice when I was here for a brief cure a few years ago. Say, why don't we go dancing there? Surely the good doctors here do not forbid it. Dancing is good exercise, after all."

His calm grey eyes and regal brows implored her. "Warren—I can't call you Mr. Harding, we've known each other since we were kids—I would love it."

That night they met under the high stone archway that formed the San's gate. She wore a demure white chiffon with ruffled sleeves and appliquéd white rosebuds. Harding—although the Duchess sometimes scolded him for his slovenly appearance around the Star's offices—had a knack for putting himself together when it counted. He admired his image in the mirror wearing a light-blue serge coat and white linen trousers. It was summertime casual so he had no waistcoat.

They met outside the gate where clumps of the San's patients waited for the Red Onion's buggies. The crowd giggled like naughty children playing hooky from school. The tavern sent buggies to carry its patrons a little over two miles down a dirt road. In the early summer dusk the June bugs buzzed around the buggy lanterns. Warren entered the buggy first, sat on the left, and extended his hand to help Susan step up. In the warm night her small hand was cool.

The buggy driver snapped the reins and the horse plodded. "I assure you, miss," he said, looking over his shoulder, "we shall have you back in good time." The tavern promised to return its patrons to the gate before the San's eleven p.m. curfew. He wondered why he did not feel guilty about cheating on Florence. The answer, or a big part of it anyway, was that he resented how she had pressured him into marriage. Their union tested his forbearance—Florence had had a child out of wedlock and never married the father, although she later claimed to be divorced and even altered public records toward that end.

Warren stopped thinking about it. He did not like to think ill of anyone, especially himself. He turned his thoughts and his eyes to Susie.

She was more than a head shorter than Warren and at first an awkward dancer. The band played a sentimental song in three-quarters time that anyone could slow-dance to. She hummed the tune and even softly sang some of the words, surprising Harding. Where did she learn that song? This was not her first visit to a night club. "Oh, dearie," he said, "tell me it isn't hateful to you to have me kiss you." She answered, but not with words.

Well before the curfew they walked slowly outside, arm in arm. In the ride back they held hands but were too decorous to kiss when those in other buggies might see them, even in the dark. They waited three days, then took horses from the San's stables instead of a buggy. Susie was awkward in sidesaddle but she thrilled to the animal's power. When they arrived at the Red Onion and Warren helped her down from the mount she contrived to fall into his arms. Inside, Harding had a couple of beers but Susie did not drink. "I have seen what alcohol can do to families," she said. "A wise resolution," he said. Both were impatient to leave. He raised his eyebrows and dipped his chin to ask a question. She nodded and stood from the table. Walking out, they did not bother to keep their hands off each other. A colored servant brought their horses from the stable.

Warren kept a blanket folded in his saddlebags. Back from the tavern, they spread the blanket on the grass in one of the spa's parks. "Oh, I'm so glad!" she said. Warren was grateful for her lack of feigned reluctance.

It was a guiltless time of lust. A pregnancy resulted. She did not blush or stammer when she told him. Just about Warren's first thought—he had had mumps as a boy and feared it might have left him sterile—was "at least now I know I can do it." When Susie did not plead with him to divorce Florence and marry her he fell in love with her even more. So much so that he actually considered a divorce.

"I could never hurt Flossie like that," Susie said. "She and I grew up together. But I am carrying your child, Warren, and I am going to treasure it the rest of my life." He interpreted that to mean he should not hint at an abortion. "And no, I'm not going back to my husband. I have been single before and I can be single again."

"Oh, dearie, you are so brave. So much braver than I have ever been. You are too grand a soul for me."

"You will write me? You will come to see me when you can?"

They decided that she would go home to Marion only to pack her things to move to another city. She would claim to be a widow. Warren would send money to support the child. They were sitting on the grass where they had held their trysts, leaning against a tree, weeping.

*

Shortly after Harding had gone to Battle Creek, the business manager of the *Marion Star* resigned. At once, Florence rode Warren's bicycle to the newspaper office. She told herself that she would help out just for a few days.

She knew she must make her way by force of will, not by her looks. Florence was one of those almost-but-not-quite pretty girls whose name is legion. A matter of millimeters. Florence was a bit tall, five-foot-six, with blue eyes, high cheekbones, and a long, thin, straight nose. Her lips were of normal, even attractive, size and shape, yet they always seemed pursed in disapproval. She bobbed her hair and had it fashioned into short curls with a curling iron, a style known as marcelled. A pince-nez had replaced her spectacles.

"I am going to build a circulation department," she declared to the man behind the counter where copies of the afternoon paper were sold. "How many subscribers do we have?"

"I don't rightly know, ma'am."

"Well, how many boys do we have delivering newspapers?"

"We ain't got none, ma'am."

Soon they did. Florence gathered boys from working-class families badly in need of the extra cash they could earn. "Here is one of my boys," she would say, patting his shoulder, "he will be famous some day." Florence mapped out the town's streets and assigned routes for door-to-door delivery. Hard workers were paid fifty cents but if a customer complained about anything, payment was in pennies. She spanked or even slapped truants and miscreants. But if one of her boys got sick, she sent food and a visit by an eminent doctor.

The town was surprised that Florence showed such maternal sentiments. "It's because you miss Marshall so much," her younger friend Carrie told her. Florence's illegitimate son Marshall was now a teenager in Amos's house. "Marshall is Papa's boy to raise," is all she said. When the boy's father, a no-account tubercular alcoholic, died, she did not attend the funeral. Neither did Marshall.

Florence did not mention that death in her journal. In her writing her eyes were clear and dry. "I do not like to cook," she wrote. "I hate fussing with food. I can clean out the garret or even the cellar if I must and I like to decorate and care for rooms. But I'd rather go hungry than broil steak and boil potatoes." She made the newspaper so prosperous that the Hardings never worried about going hungry.

After creating a circulation department she took over the business side. Scanning the account books, she found that the interest owed on money borrowed for new printing presses was more than the remaining debt itself. She went to bankers she knew through Amos and negotiated short-term loans at lower rates. Meanwhile, if a *Star* subscriber's account was delinquent for three weeks, she cut it off.

A couple of fellas quit, unable to tolerate taking orders from a woman. Others snickered that she not only ran the paper, she ran Warren too—she was five years older and bossed him around. But the workers were grateful for higher wages and big Christmas bonuses. Florence wrote, "I believe the womanly way to get what we want or what we know belongs to us is by gentility and firmness minus militancy." Minus militancy or no, Florence hired the first woman reporter in Ohio.

Warren came home after nearly a year in Battle Creek and gladly let Florence manage the business while he wrote folksy editorials. He asked his readers, "Why is February like a woman?" Answer: "Because it never reaches thirty." Most of his time was spent making speeches and running for public office. He was elected to the state Senate despite the opposition of Amos Kling, who stumped the district warning that his son-in-law was "a Negro."

September 2, 1908

The Hardings planned a celebratory dinner for Harry Daugherty and the newlyweds Jess and Roxy Smith. It was a thank-you to Harry for running Warren's political campaigns as well as a salute to Jess. The Hardings were relieved that he had finally married. Maybe that would squelch the noxious rumors about him and Harry.

Harry Daugherty had a new Cole motorcar which his butler kept polished. However, no car was reliable enough to make the eighty-six miles from Washington Court House to Marion, mostly over unpaved roads, without breaking down. So Roxy, Jess, and Harry, whose sickly wife could not travel, took the train.

Jess was proud when he saw other men ogle his wife, which was often. At five-foot-seven she was nearly as tall as Jess. Her face did not have a flaw, including the flaw of being too nearly perfect. You could say her face was a little too long, her jaw a little too strong. Or you could say she was a bit short in the leg relative to her long torso. Whatever you said, you admired her thick, wavy strawberry-blond hair that seemed to change color according to the angle of light. She had the kind of phosphorescent blue eyes that men wanted to keep looking into.

Roxy, accustomed to having men stare at her, spent her time observing Jess and Harry. Once again she noticed something odd about them: They never exchanged jocular insults the way that men do. Indeed, although they called each other "Harry" and "Jess," they spoke to each other in a rather formal way, as if both were attorneys in court. And aside from shaking hands, they never touched each other, at least not in public. But that could just be their inbred Midwestern Protestant reserve—although Harry had been raised Catholic, hadn't he? Maybe the stiffness was an effort to foil the rumors about them, or maybe that was just the way they were. Jess could be quite formal even with his wife. Some day, Roxy thought, I will ask him about it.

Harding sent a carriage to meet them at the Marion station. The Hardings' three-story house was notable for its huge, elaborate front porch topped by an equally long widow's walk. Inside, Florence had hired Tiffany and Company to paper and stencil the walls and ceilings. She had ordered the stained glass windows on a trip to Germany.

As usual, Florence, in an ivory dress of crepe de chine, was a bit overdressed. Roxy wore a green velvet dress, certain that Florence could distinguish real velvet from velveteen. Jess wore his favorite grey suit with a lavender waistcoat, lavender tie, and lavender handkerchief. In this effulgence, nobody noticed Warren's silk grey suit and dark blue satin tie.

They gathered in the parlor for before-dinner drinks. Regrets were expressed about the absence of Harry's wife Lucie, crippled with arthritis although only in her forties. Warren offered a toast to her return to health.

To compliments regarding the house, Warren said, "the Duchess deserves all the credit for the decor." He claimed he called her the Duchess after a character in a comic strip in a New York paper. That was a fib. He called her the Duchess because she was imperious.

"Yes, the windows came from Germany," Florence said in answer to somebody's question. "We got them on a trip with my dear friend Carrie and her husband. I'm sorry, I should call her Mrs. Phillips now. Jim Phillips runs the big dry-goods store here. I'm so sorry they were otherwise engaged today."

Roxy saw the briefest flicker of light flash in Warren's eyes when the name "Carrie" was spoken. Did anyone else see it? Did I imagine it?

Then Roxy noticed something else. Mrs. Harding did not wear a wedding ring. Was this her idea of a declaration of feminine independence? Was she a suffragette?

Jess offered, "Yes, it's too bad your friends are not with us, because I would have liked to talk business with Mr. Phillips. We're in the same racket, you know."

The Duchess turned toward Roxy. "Well, Mrs. Smith, I understand that you and I can talk about music in Cincinnati! It is to my everlasting regret that I had to discontinue my studies at the Cincinnati Conservatory. You know, I once practiced so long and so hard that my fingers bled."

Warren leaned toward Harry and whispered, "That's how the ladies always like it, long and hard."

The ladies pretended they didn't hear. Florence removed her pince-nez and softly rubbed the little red marks inscribed on the sides of her nose. She replaced the spectacles and ventured, "Exactly what are you studying, Mrs. Smith?"

"Well, mostly they are still trying to decide whether I am an alto or a contraalto. My instructor, Mr. McPeek, said that if I could learn to sing alto perfectly, I would never be out of work. Seeing as how they are so rare, in women, I mean. Anyway, everyone at at the Music Hall says my deep voice sounds sexy."

This observation was unappreciated by Mrs. Harding. The look from her cornflower-blue eyes could have frozen a hot chocolate. She swallowed and then asked, "You're at the Music Hall?"

"Why, yes."

"Oh, goodness. I was always afraid to go there unless I was with at least one friend or maybe two. That huge building. It's haunted, you know."

"Haunted, the Music Hall? Is that so? I never dreamed."

"Why, yes, by ghosts from the old burial ground that it was built over. You haven't heard them? Or heard about them?"

"I'm afraid not. It's so haunted that you were afraid of it? Really? Did you ever see any ghosts?"

Roxy hoped that she kept any hint of mockery out of her voice. She bit her lower lip, something she did when concentrating on something. Jess and Harry wore vacant looks. Warren showed the face of a husband who tolerates his wife's peculiarities.

"No, my dear," the Duchess said, "but it wasn't just me. The stars told me to avoid it and the stars never lie."

Roxy made a note: This woman believes in the occult. Useful information. She said, "But the Music Hall is where you go for the symphony and the opera and the ballet, even. Didn't you want to take advantage of them?"

"As I said, my dear, I enjoyed those evenings very much, but only if I was with friends."

Warren put in, "Cincinnati really is the Queen City, isn't it? It really is the most cultured city outside of New York." He was planning to run for governor and talked up the state of Ohio every chance he got. Harry and Jess added their high regard for the arts in the Queen City.

When the the servants served supper, Florence made sure that Roxy was not seated at Warren's right or left, lest he place his hand on her leg under the table or at least play kneesy with her. Thereafter, Mrs. Smith was not invited to the Hardings' social functions if the Duchess could help it.

Jess had planned to spend a few days in the area doing political errands for Harry and Warren. But the next morning, the desk clerk at his hotel handed him a night letter from his mother Opal. DO NOT BE SURPRISED WHEN YOU COME HOME IF I HAVE GONE WHERE THE ROSES NEVER FADE AND TEARS NEVER FALL.

November 13, 1913

Roxy decided to divorce Jess after she was kicked out of the Marion Hotel for the sin of being a married woman traveling alone. "Mrs. Jess Smith, Washington C.H., O.," she signed the registry with a flourish.

"And what time will your husband be arriving, ma'am?" the desk clerk asked as he turned the guestbook around so he could read the name.

"Oh, he's not coming on this trip. He's home sick, he's a diabetic, and he's taking care of his mother, she's a diabetic too."

"Oh, that is a pity, ma'am. Now, I'm sorry, ma'am, but married women who are not accompanied by their husband are never registered as guests in this hotel."

"What!"

"Yes, ma'am, this is a respectable establishment. I'm sure you can understand our restriction in this regard."

How could this scrawny kid put on such an unctuous manner? Roxy took a moment to count slowly to three while she looked around the lobby. "Now look, sonny"—she knew that would offend him—"I am the headline singer at the Marion Opera House tonight. My manager made this reservation three weeks ago. So give me my room key and we shall forget this little unpleasantness."

He swallowed hard, Adam's apple bobbing on his long neck. Tall and gawky in an ill-fitting suit, he was probably just out of school. Aw, maybe she was being too hard on the kid. He made a show of manly resolve.

"I am really sorry, ma'am, but that is our policy. I cannot allow any exceptions."

"I will speak to the manager about this!" Well, no, she hesitated. The manager would just tell her that if he made an exception for her he would have to make an exception for everyone and then he probably would try to flirt with her. "No, never mind that. Just give me your telephone."

He reached under the counter for the phone and placed it in her hands. "I am going to call Mr. Warren Harding." At that, the kid took a step back in dismay and nodded his head in respect. Roxy lifted the earpiece and told the operator to connect her to the Harding residence. A maid said that Mr. Harding and Mr. Daugherty were at the Star. She reached the newspaper and talked with Warren and Harry in turn. They said they did not want to make a fuss but did not say the real reason why—because Florence's father Amos Kling was a major owner of the hotel. It was decided that Roxy would sleep in a guest bedroom at Warren's home while Harry took Roxy's room at the hotel.

Roxy would have preferred a hotel room but she was too tired and cranky to argue. She and Harry Daugherty had traveled to Marion on the bumpy Columbus and Toledo Railroad (Amos owned a piece of that, too), Harry to talk politics with Warren and Roxy to get paid for singing. Her instructor at the Cincinnati Music Hall had told her she had the talent to star on the opera stage but lacked the "moral stamina," as he put it, to devote years of her life to the necessary training. She did not disagree. She liked the big city and had gone there largely to get away from her mother-in-law Opal. But she did not welcome the rigors of voice training.

So the instructor became her manager, booking her in nightclubs and music halls around Ohio and in the "sin cities" of Kentucky across the Ohio River from Cincinnati. The Marion Opera House was one of the most prestigious appearances for her so far. She sang popular and ragtime songs with two or three arias thrown in to bring culture to the yokels. Usually she could count on local musicians to accompany her with better than adequate skill.

On the trip up to Marion, Harry did not make even an oblique pass at her. Harry might be a crooked lawyer as everyone said, but he surely was devoted to his half-paralyzed wife. "You know, Mr. Daugherty, I admire you," she said. "I hear that Mrs. Harding has been very sick. I could only wish that Mr. Harding would be as devoted to his wife as you are to your Lucie."

Harry noticed that Roxy's throaty voice had taken one of its sudden, serious drops in tone. These shifts were part of her charm. "My dear Roxy, Warren Harding is an exemplar of rectitude, a paragon of manly devotion, even, I daresay, uxorious."

"Damn it, Mr. Daugherty, I keep telling you and I keep telling Jess, too, don't talk so high-falutin with me. You don't fool me. As my mama used to say, you're gettin' above your raisin.' "

"Ah, but it's kind of a mockery, don't you see? It's like, secretly making fun of all the snooty people we have to deal with by imitating them, outshining them, even. You know how they look down on us all because we're hicks." He pondered a moment. "And then it impresses the judges when I argue in court, too, and the jury as well."

"Well, my experience is that if you try to fool people and play tricks on them, it comes back to hurt you in the end. And anyway, I'm not snooty, and neither is Warren Harding. His wife, I won't say."

"Warren will be president some day."

"Mr. Harding? *Warren?*" She laughed.

"Mark my words."

The subject of this prophecy met them at the train station that afternoon in his new Stevens-Duryea. He said that Florence still was housebound but was steadily getting better. After Roxy's call from the hotel he appeared there to drive her to his home. "The maid will look after your things," he said. "Please don't disturb the Duchess, she's probably asleep. And I'm coming to your concert tonight, wouldn't miss it for the world."

Roxy dressed carefully that evening, for she had planned a new sensation for her act. Back home the previous week, she had taken off her girdle and resolved not to wear it again. It was uncomfortable and her figure did not need it. So she reached for a garter belt, then spurned it too. This decision raised the problem of how to hold up her stockings. She opened her cedar trunk—the one that Opal believed contained wicked things—and removed a couple of garters. She rolled down her silk stockings to just above the knees, then rolled up the garters. She stood up from the bed and tentatively tried out a few dance moves, then a twirl. Inspiration struck her. She donned her white concert dress, the one with black embroidery and a wide skirt, and her long white gloves with silver stitching. If she stepped or twirled just so, her mirror confirmed, the skirt swirled and garters peeked out.

In the living room Jess was reading in his grey leather chair, which he had selected in the belief that it complemented his grey suits. "Honey, look at this," she said. Putting a polka on the Victrola, she sang and twirled. "What do you think? I'm going to do this in my next show!"

"I think that you will gain a well-earned notoriety with that particular maneuver. I believe that all the gentlemen will love you and all the ladies will despise you."

"That is my intention exactly!" They giggled like children.

Roxy went back to her trunk in search of garters that would match her hair, or maybe a pale lavender instead. All she could find was black, red, and white. She picked red.

Roxy pioneered this innovation years before rolled-down stockings became a national fad for so-called flappers. Indeed, she claimed to have launched this fashion trend but was ignored. But then, all fashion trends and catch sayings and slang terms must begin with somebody somewhere, don't they? Why not garters with Roxy in Marion?

She performed that night under the name Roxanne Smith and filled nearly every one of the hall's thousand seats at seventy-five cents a ticket. It had helped that Harding offered an advertising discount to her agent, who had placed a half-page ad in the *Star* featuring a halftone photo of Roxy looking sultry in an evening gown. Halfway through the program, she first flashed the garters. Some men gasped; their wives frowned and tsk-tsked. At the curtain call she received enthusiastic applause, mostly from the men.

After the program it was cold and rainy but fortunately Warren had a landau waiting for them at the curb. The carriage was Florence's but Warren had borrowed the horse and driver from Amos. "What'd y'all think?" Roxy asked Warren and Harry. When she was excited the "y'all" of her Memphis childhood might surface. The two men praised her performance throughout the short ride to the Harding home. She could accept compliments gracefully—an uncommon skill.

Upon stepping into the Hardings' entrance hall Roxy instantly sensed the presence of serious illness, a kind of vapor of decay that can infect the most well-kept houses. What was it? Not a smell, exactly; she did not detect antiseptics or medicines or even see the sickroom upstairs. But there was a kind of unmistakable thickening of the air, an impression that Death had been skulking about. No, on second thought, there was indeed an odor—camphor was the dominant note. Roxy had a clammy feeling and wondered whether the smell would permeate her clothes. The men did not seem to react. They must be used to it.

For all her energy, Florence's health was no better than her husband's. She was born with a "floating kidney," abnormally small and hence not stationary. If it shifted just a bit, the tubal outflow was blocked and toxins built up in the bloodstream. The condition quickly could turn lethal.

In the parlor Warren expressed the Duchess's sincere regret that she was as yet too unwell to receive visitors. The kidney ailment had knocked her down again. Several years back, she had been hospitalized for five months. Doctors decided that her heart was too weak to permit an operation to remove the bad kidney, so she was wrapped in hot towels and blankets so that heavy perspiration might remove some of the toxins in her body. She wrote in her journal, "I have reason to think I am not a great way off from, if not very near to, the great occasion of eternity. The time may not be long before I embark on the last voyage." She grew fatalistic and did not ask to see either a pastor or a fortune teller.

Warren went upstairs to look after his wife. He looked grim coming downstairs and whispered to Harry, "Her face doesn't have any more color than wax paper. But she insists that I take care of our guests."

Warren and Harry drank highballs and smoked cigars while Roxy smoked cigarettes. The men talked politics, which Roxy had always ignored as another thing that men did without women, but now she paid attention to try to discern why men took it so seriously. A nurse entered.

"I beg your pardon, lady and gentlemen, but Mrs. Harding has sent me down with a request. She has asked that Mrs. Smith sing my lady's favorite song, 'A Perfect Day.' I opened her door a little so that she can hear you better. She said that this song always lifts her spirits and then she will sleep peacefully."

They looked at one another in surprise. Warren had not even known "A Perfect Day" was his wife's favorite song. They rose without speaking and left the parlor for the music room, leaving the doors open. Roxy knew the song and the sheet music was open on the piano. She sat at the keyboard and played and sang loudly.

I want to tell you something
It's not a secret or anything
You're not alone in being alone
At the end of a perfect day
And if you leave all your dependents
Then they will gain their independence
Don't make a martyr of yourself
It's just the end of a perfect day
And it's never how it seems
The rain may fall on the best laid schemes
But in a written testimonial I'd say

I never really knew you anyway
Now don't go crazy or anything
Just want to tell you that it's over
It's the end of a perfect day.

The men had been expecting syrupy lyrics about flowers glowing golden in the sunset and children's laughter and stuff like that. Why, this song was not sentimental, it was not even bittersweet, it was sardonic, resigned, almost mournful despite the peppy melody. Warren, pondering, realized that he had never fully understood the soul of his Duchess. Harry, who had long been trying to ingratiate himself with her, had much the same kind of thought. And Roxy, who had regarded Florence as just a bossy older woman, felt a wave of sympathy. Yes, this was a song to appeal to a woman who had lost her first husband and given away her son, a woman who had looked death in the face and grasped the vanity of human wishes.

Part Two: The Senate

February 9, 1915

For his first junket the newly elected senator from Ohio steamed to Hawaii with his wife. In Honolulu they met Charles F. Forbes, who headed the board that oversaw construction of the naval base at Pearl Harbor. Forbes was a red-faced, red-haired hustler, an all-around kidder, backslapper, con man, and flirt. He even flirted with Florence. ("He actually makes passes at her," a Washington socialite remarked to her friend. "That must be a unique experience for the Duchess," replied the friend, Alice Roosevelt Longworth, in her sweetest voice.)

Charlie Forbes escorted the Hardings to all the sights in Hawaii. He also took them for a cruise on a new navy submarine, an unusual privilege even for a senator.

"Welcome to the *USS K-8*," Forbes said, taking Florence's hand to lead her down the gangplank behind Warren.

"The *K-8*? My, such an unimaginative name for a ship flying the American flag."

"So named because it replaces the H class, Mrs. Harding. But you're right, it does betray a lack of imagination. I shall petition the navy to rename it the *USS Florence Harding*."

"Oh, don't be silly, Mr. Forbes, now you're just making fun of me."

Warren bounded down the gangplank, feeling the gladness that sings through men upon boarding a conveyance to take them fast over land or sea. As it toured the harbor the Hardings rode with the boat's officers on an open bridge atop the conning tower.

"You know," Warren said, "the Germans have just announced that they will conduct unrestricted submarine warfare in the European war."

"Let the Europeans fight it out in the Atlantic," Forbes said. "The Pacific, this is our natural sphere of influence. America's future is based right here at Pearl Harbor."

"Well, I don't speak for President Wilson, but the Senate is afraid that there will be attacks on our shipping even though we are staying neutral."

"I wouldn't worry about that, senator. The Germans are too afraid that we would enter the war ourselves."

Warren asked questions about the *K-8's* speed and armaments, then descended to tour the interior. Florence stayed topside lest she show immodesty by climbing up and down steep ladders in a dress. To her the boat looked like a long, narrow box balanced on a bulbous hull. She wondered how it stayed afloat, let alone how it traveled underwater. She stood with her feet apart, swaying adroitly to the pitching and rolling.

"Why, Mrs. Harding, where did you get such sea legs?" Forbes said. "As far as I know, Ohio is a landlocked state."

"Oh, well, I grew up riding sidesaddle. To ride sidesaddle you have to have a good sense of balance."

"Marvelous! Permit me, then, the honor of at least naming one of my thoroughbreds at Saratoga after you." (There were no such thoroughbreds.)

"Mr. Forbes, usually I disdain flattery, but you are such a dashing gentleman that I forgive you." Florence, normally more hardheaded than Warren in her judgments of people, fell for him.

Meanwhile, her husband was fretting to the point of lost sleep over fights with his mistress. Carrie Phillips was angry because Warren had taken the Duchess first to Florida, then to Hawaii to convalesce from her near-fatal illness—instead of secretly meeting Carrie in New York or Toronto as they had planned. Carrie was Florence's closest friend, had been so since childhood.

Supposedly, the affair had ended for good after six years. It had started in heartbreak for Carrie and her husband Jim. She was taller than Jim but still wore the stylish big, tall hats that seemed to dwarf her husband. Jim did not mind. He was proud to be seen next to the town beauty.

They had a daughter and a son but the son died at age two. While both parents were house-bound with depression, Jim appeared close to a total breakdown. Warren insisted that Jim go up to Battle Creek for a cure. "Don't worry, Jim, I'll look after your daughter and your wife while you're gone." From her hospital bed in Columbus, Florence urged the same course of action.

Warren had bought a new 1905 Stevens-Duryea, a motorcar that looked like a buggy except that it had small woodenspoked wheels, headlamps, and a crank in back to start the gas motor. With this conveyance he called on Florence's lifelong friend. She was alone at home on South Main Street when Warren knocked. At once each was shaken by a gust of sexual desire capable of uprooting trees—something that, for all the love poetry in the world, rarely happens between a specific man and a specific woman.

Afterward, they talked and wrote to each other in code. In Italy, Warren brought a statuette of the naked goddess Diana and told Carrie it looked like her. He called his penis "Jerry" and her vagina "Seashell." She signed her letters "Constance."

Gossip of the affair inevitably started to waft through Marion. Even Roxy heard about it and she told Jess, who already knew because Harry knew. Yet the Duchess remained willfully blind, maybe because Warren always treated her with proper respect in public and at home.

Carrie wearied of Warren's years of unfulfilled promises to divorce Florence and marry her so that they could retire to a farm and raise children together. A devotee of German *Kultur*, she threatened to leave both Jim and Warren and take her daughter to school in Germany. When she actually booked passage, Warren broke down. "I stand more than willing. If, after trying and seeking, or pondering and measuring, you think I can give you my love to nearest heaven and you want me then I'm yours now, any time—for all time," he wrote. Whatever that meant, Carrie rejected it and sailed for Europe. "Zu spät. Zu spät. Auf wiedersehen," she wired his office at the *Star* from aboard ship. Too late, goodbye.

While in Germany Carrie gathered the paperwork to apply for permanent residency. She returned home during her daughter's summer school vacation and took decisive action. She sent an erotic letter to Warren at his Mount Vernon Avenue home, confident that Florence would open and read it. Which she did.

Enraged and wounded, the Duchess marched Warren to a lawyer's office to seek a divorce. Right away, Warren sent Carrie a letter about this misfortune. Carrie reasonably concluded that the Hardings would divorce, the Phillipses would divorce, and then she and Warren would marry.

After her best friend had betrayed her, Florence had no intimate friend to turn to, even if she could have swallowed, in seeking a consoling friend, the social stigma attached to adultery and divorce. That barren truth, though, was not one that she explored in her journal. Instead, she wrote about the misery of her sex: "Most of the pain in this world is located in the hearts of women." Not only that, but "passion is a very transient thing. To me, love seems to have been a thing of tragedy."

She could remember only one time that Warren yelled at her—she had been nagging him about his clothes or his chewing tobacco or something. Now, in this time of mutual hostility, he never raised his voice. Their relationship became a kind of monotony that one tries to tune out like background noise. At length, Florence reasoned that only a "big soul" could change her mind once the rage had cooled. She was such a soul—who could deny it?—and so she told the lawyer not to file for divorce after all.

However much either of them wanted their freedom, they both wanted respectability more. She could not let Warren go. He could not make up his mind to leave. So they settled into a kind of a partnership, or more like a fellowship, or even a kind of love, the love expressed in shared forbearance. Florence Harding was not the first or the last political wife to patch up her marriage for the sake of her husband's career—and her own social status.

Warren told Harry about the reconciliation, who told Jess, who told Roxy. "It's obvious," she said. "If he left the Duchess, one of two things would happen. One, she would fall sick into bed again and the state of Ohio would never forgive him for abandoning her. Or two, the Duchess would plot her revenge on Carrie. Gosh, I shudder to think what forms that might take."

"See, Roxy, you're so smart, that's why I married you."

The secret affair resumed the next year. Warren could not stop himself from writing Carrie, blithely unmindful that the letters could be used for blackmail or to blow up his marriage. "You know my love is all your very own, that there isn't one iota of affection in my home relationship," he declared. To stoke his jealousy, Carrie paraded another lover in front Warren. She even sent Warren copies of that lover's letters. When next they met Harding pulled a long face and sniveled.

"Warren Harding, you're just talk. All talk and no action."

"Now, dearie, you know that I have to travel all over this damn state. I have a good chance to become a United States senator. And if the voters do confer on me that high honor, well, then I will perform my public service. And then we will be together," he said, attempting an embrace.

"Oh, bah! You know I have spent years now trying to talk you into getting out of politics. It's Flossie who keeps pushing you into it. I don't know whether you even really want it for yourself. I think you just like to travel and run off at the mouth."

"Oh, dearie, how sharper than a serpent's tooth is your anger. You know I can't divorce the Duchess now. It would not only ruin my career, it might even ruin the *Star*. Not to mention that it would absolutely destroy her."

"Fiddlesticks! Do you think that Flossie loves you? She spent all her time in Rome looking for Gypsies so she could have those tarot readings. She wanted to know if you would be elected senator. And then she wanted her own fortune read. She didn't even ask about you. Listen, Warren, I know Flossie better than you do. I've known her longer!"

Carrie and her daughter went back to Germany.

November 2, 1915

The guests at Nick and Alice Roosevelt Longworth's poker party at their mansion in Washington, D.C., were surprised when they heard piano music and loud singing from the drawing room downstairs. They identified the voice, not an entirely pleasing one, as Florence Harding's. Evidently she had tired of mixing drinks for the guests when she was not even their hostess and slipped away. Besides the Hardings, Congressman Longworth's guests included Ned McLean, the owner of the *Washington Post*, and Ned's wife, Evalyn Walsh McLean. Evalyn was Alice's best friend.

Florence had gone to the party because, whenever possible, she did not let Warren out of her sight. She did not approve of gambling and hardly tolerated drinking but she politely mixed drinks on request. When Warren, or even Nick, said,"Duchess, you are lying down on the job," she obediently mixed a whiskey and soda.

Evalyn McLean went downstairs. "Mrs. Harding, you play and sing wonderfully," she lied. Florence looked up with a sour smile. In her handbag on the piano bench was a small notebook bound in red leather. In this notebook she wrote the names of people in Washington who had snubbed her. The first name entered was that of Alice Roosevelt Longworth. Florence noticed that Alice always stood straight as a ruler, with her long neck and upswept hair emphasizing her height, and with her shoulders held slightly back as if showing off her breasts, which were unexceptional. "You're very kind," Florence said to Evalyn.

Although Washington was the seat of a democracy, it had a queen. Her name was Alice, the daughter of Theodore Roosevelt. Alice held a grudge against the Hardings because she thought that Nick, not Warren, should be the new Ohio senator. A famous mimic, she imitated for Ned's and Evalyn's amusement Florence's Midwestern twang. She was especially good at the grating way that Florence called "Wurr'n!"

Later, Alice informed Evalyn that Florence was home sick, in fact near death, with kidney disease. "Oh! I will go to call on her tomorrow," Evalyn said. Alice was surprised. She would never call on the Hardings, who had moved into a two-family building on Wisconsin Avenue. Why was Evalyn, a millionaire married to another millionaire, calling on such a poseur, such a parvenu, who lived in a two-family home?

At the Hardings' door Evalyn said to the maid, "Tell Mrs. Harding I want to see her." She found Florence in bed, her face that waxy pallor that had so alarmed Warren during her previous illness in Ohio. "I am very sick," Florence said. "I have sent for my physician." Her doctor was Charles E. Sawyer, a Marion homeopath, a quack-a-doodle. But Florence was convinced that only he could save her life.

"You must get well soon so that we can enjoy ourselves at the Longworths again," Evalyn said.

"Oh, no, I'm afraid that poor Mr. Longworth is an alcoholic. He told me himself that he has blackouts."

"Well, of course he's an alcoholic. And so is my Ned. I almost am one myself. I am a morphine addict, you know."

"What!"

Evalyn told her story. She grew up poor in Leadville, Colorado. When she was twelve, her father struck gold and they were wealthy overnight. The family moved to Washington and Evalyn was sent to Paris to study music. When she was nineteen she floored the accelerator of her motorcar, a Mercedes. It overturned and killed her seventeen-year-old brother. Evalyn's leg was shattered "and that," she said, "is when I started drinking that horrible black liquid stuff. Godfrey's Cordial." Florence's eyes said, what? "You know, laudanum." A mixture of morphine, codeine, and other opioids. "Pretty soon I was taking ten grams of morphine a day. So that's the fight I have, going on and off it."

"My goodness, Mrs. McLean, you surely are straightforward in telling me about your troubles."

"Oh, phew. I'd rather tell you to your face than have you hear it from all the gossips in town. I have no secrets, not even from Ned."

Evalyn's calling on her was really, Florence thought, one of the largest kindnesses anyone had ever shown her. Amazed that a high-society lady would be so intimate with an upper-middle-class person she hardly knew, Florence's defenses fell like a column of eggs. She told her own story—about papa Amos, about her son, about the boy's lout of a father, about Warren, about Carrie. She hoped that confessions would give a sense of burdens lifted, as the Papists believed. Mostly, though, she still felt sick.

Obviously in pain, she sat up. "I know you must love this town," she said, "but I think it is an awful place, the most awful place I have ever lived in."

"Really, Mrs. Harding? I am saddened to hear that. Why don't you like it?"

"Well, because—I'll tell you. Every woman in this town is after Warren. You know it's true. So I'll keep him close to home until I'm on my feet again."

"Oh, an attractive man like Mr. Harding? He can go out after dinner, can't he? I do hope so. I certainly want to see more of him."

Florence glared at Evalyn's deadpan face until she realized that Evalyn was joking. At that moment the two became best friends. Alice Longworth, for her part, resented that Florence was taking her best friend Evalyn away from her. Florence's glee at that circumstance was enhanced when Evalyn said she had married Ned mostly to prove that she could steal him from Alice. No wonder, Florence thought, that people call Washington a small town.

The quack Dr. Sawyer's homeopathic purgatives must have worked, or something did, because Florence recovered. Evalyn, almost thirty, and Florence, in her mid-fifties, became an odd couple seen at concerts and movies and boutiques around town. Evalyn was conventionally pretty with a heart-shaped face, wide shoulders and, despite her hard living, a nice figure, while spidery blue veins were starting to appear on the back of Florence's hands. The younger woman was wildly unconventional; the elder was prim. Yet they became inseparable.

All the while, the names of people in Florence's red notebook multiplied. At a reception for Senate wives under the Capitol rotunda, everyone knew she was a hick from the Ohio sticks as soon as they heard her say "chimbley" for chimney or "bresh harbor" for brush arbor. Anna Cabot Mills David Lodge, the wife of Senator Henry Cabot Lodge of Massachusetts, did not even try to hide turning her chin up and her face away from Mrs. Harding.

Nor did Florence grasp the sacred rites of calling. A respectable woman knew the labyrin-thine rules for making and receiving calls or else was an outcast. So Evalyn tutored her. "First of all," she explained, "you have to pick a day to be at home. That is when people may call on you."

"But I'm always home except when I'm back in Marion. Oh, I know what you mean, that was a joke. Okay, I'll take Tuesday."

"No, take Thursday. Tuesday is for calling on the wives of Representatives and Wednesday is the day for calling on the wives of members of the Cabinet."

"I will remember that."

"I'm sure you will. Now, let's say you're calling on Senator Borah, who has a wife and a daughter under the age of twenty-one, you leave five cards—two of your husband's, one of your own, and two of your own daughter's."

"But I don't have a daughter. I have a granddaughter but nobody here knows about her."

"Yes, yes, I am just giving you the rules that you should know. Now, a simpler case. A man and a wife alone, you leave two cards of your husband's and one of your own . . ."

"Uh-huh." Usually Florence relied on her memory but in a matter of this importance she took notes. Not once did she say it was asinine for Washington, which after all was just a sleepy southern town, to have such pretentious ideas of high society. But she asked, "You don't go around leaving your own cards with people's butlers, do you?"

"Oh no, honey, I am too rich and established for that. Hostesses seek me out. Well, not just me, they want the publisher of the *Washington Post*. But even Ned and I are country cousins compared to Alice. When Alice wasn't even married yet she canceled her day at home because these carriages full of tourists used to pull up just to gawk at her."

"How horrible for her," Florence said, startling herself with her tone. Look at me, Washington is already making me a worse person. Back home, I was never sarcastic.

"You worry too much about it, Flossie. Why, the hostesses will seek you out, too. They like to show that they are bipartisan and broad-minded. You know, Yankees and cowboys, kings and commons, that sort of thing, all together. They'll use you to show how tolerant they are."

"Really? Oh, well, the hell with all of this, then. I think I'm just going to put up a big sign in our front yard: Rent a Hick by the Day, Week, or Month."

"A joke! Florence Harding made a joke!" Evalyn laughed until her sides hurt. Florence was surprised at her own wit. Warren always said she had no sense of humor.

*

Roxy and Jess remained good friends after the divorce was granted. She did not even move out from his home above the store for several weeks. Jess was so domestic, it was as good as having a maid, which they had anyway. When he had lived alone, people would come over and say with some wonderment, "You know, for a bachelor, you really keep this place neat and clean." Jess was, as far as he knew, the only white man in America who could successfully fold a fitted sheet.

He bought a nearby building with three apartments and gave it to Roxy to move into. "Well, mama, I finally got a building for it," she said quietly.

"What?"

"Never mind."

Jess believed that Roxy left him because his illness kept him from performing his manly duties in bed. "Oh, honey, you know that's not it," she consoled, uselessly. "You know I'm just not wifey material. You knew that when we got married." Jess cried.

Roxy did not tell him that mostly she was bored. War in Europe was making Americans jittery; the economy slowed down and so did Roxy's singing career. The only times she got excited was while volunteering for Warren's Senate campaign. He was a blowhard and yet he was blessed with that exceedingly rare talent of achieving instant intimacy with strangers. He made crowds feel good about him—and themselves. Not even Jess or Mr. Daugherty could explain it. They just plotted the maneuvers of politics. Warren won the votes.

Roxy decided to get a job. She would work for Senator Harding and not just as a stenographer. She and Jess falsely checked into the Hotel Washington as a married couple. They smiled at the irony—the Marion hotel kicked her out because she was a married woman and now that she was a fake, this Washington hotel welcomed her.

One call from Jess got her an immediate interview with Harding. The senator's bodyguard, Leland Jackson, met her in the antechamber of Room 134 of the Senate Office Building. He was of middling height and muscular. Roxy disliked him. He wore a cowboy hat and carried a gun and wanted everyone to know it. His hair was a little too long and a little too carefully combed. Harry Daugherty, who employed him as an "investigator," had foisted him on Harding. Roxy was prepared to spurn Leland Jackson's flirtations for the umpteenth time when Harding came bounding into the room with expressions of joy at seeing her. He steered her into his office, shaking her hand so vigorously that she wondered when she would be invited to sit down.

Roxy dressed practically as a nun with an ankle-length black dress but she did wear a smart white hat with a broad black band. Harding gazed frankly at her form, though he said nothing untoward. Roxy asked after Mrs. Harding's health and they chatted about back-home matters until she said, "Mr. Harding—senator—I don't know if Jess told you, but I came her today because I want to work for you."

Harding wore sincere puzzlement on his face. "But surely Jess left you well fixed?" He meant that a woman would not need a job unless she was poor.

"Oh, yes, Mr. Harding, that's not why I'm here. I don't need the income, I mean. I want to help you represent the people of Ohio and the nation too. I want that to be my major purpose in life."

Still perplexed, Harding gave no sign of encouragement or its opposite.

"Mr. Daugherty and Jess both said they couldn't have done without me in the Marion office. You know I practically lived there. I hardly ever even saw my place in Washington C.H. So now I know about how financing campaigns works"—she ticked off points on her fingers—"I know how to run a team of volunteers, I talked with people, especially at your campaign rallies, to find out what the voters really want." At this, Harding could nod in agreement.

"Mr. Harding, I would be of great assistance to you. Not as a stenographer, I can't even take dictation, but you could call me a stenographer on the payroll if you like."

"Mrs. Smith—I'm sorry, Miss Stinson—you are a very bright young lady and I'm sure you would be a great asset to this office. Unfortunately, though, I have already exhausted my budget for Senate staff." A lie.

"Well, you could put me on the Republican payroll, then. I'm sure Mr. Daugherty could arrange that." Still the stone face. Roxy decided to drive her pitch home. She had thought a lot about how to put the next points delicately.

"You see, senator, you have a great many friends. I mean that as high praise—I should have so many friends. But I can see, I'm sorry, but I can see that sometimes some of them try to take advantage of you. It would help if you had someone outside your inner circle to alert you about those people, don't you think?" With his hands folded on the desk, Harding dropped his chin and raised his eyes in a gesture that might have meant anything. Roxy looked him in the eyes and played the queen of hearts. "And then, especially, you know, sometimes your women friends. You know, they might try to take advantage of a famous man like you." Implied message: I know about Carrie Phillips. A silence ensued until Harding said without expression, "Go on, Miss Stinson."

"Well, look, Mr. Harding, you know women are going to get the right to vote soon. It's just a matter of time, isn't it?" Harding had avoided taking a firm stand on this issue but gave a slight nod. "They may well have the vote in the 1920 election. So you will need to have a woman on your staff to understand women's concerns. A women's intuition, you might say." She laughed; Harding did not. "That would make Mrs. Harding happy, wouldn't it? It's in the stars, she might say." Implied message: I know your wife is a stargazing fool. So you need me.

Harding rose and walked around the desk with his hands in his pockets. Leaning against the front of the desk, looking down at the seated Roxy, he lavishly praised her intelligence, her grit, her invaluable assistance in the campaign. Jess was a lucky man and a damn fool for ever letting her get away. He would look for room in the budget to hire another assistant and would stay in touch. In the meantime, many women found fulfillment in volunteer activities. Please don't hesitate to call if I can be of any service. And so on.

On the way out, Roxy did not acknowledge Leland Jackson's greeting or presence. All her energy was devoted to refusing to cry. She had expected that Harding might demur but not that she would be treated like a dizzy dame. Harding's thought was almost audible: Why does this rich, pretty girl want a job? Suddenly she heard in her head: *All coloreds and Kentuckians report to the principal's office for delousing.* Now she better understood what those kids heard. *We know your place and it ain't with us.*

Outside in the November rain she judged that nowhere else in the world is rain as damp and cold and miserable as in Washington. The temptation to walk up Delaware Avenue to Union Station to take the next train back to Ohio was strong. But she needed to tell Jess how the interview went.

*

Harding attended a reception for freshman senators held in the Capitol office of Henry Cabot Lodge, the titan of the Senate. Warren took him for a pompous old bore. His bushy mustache was still sandy but his white goatee matched his white linen suit. Though short of stature, Lodge's clothing, gruff bearing, and severe manner all said: I Am a Statesman.

But then the pillar of ice melted; Lodge's eyes twinkled and he grinned."Say, senator, I bet you have observed that there are many comely wenches in this town, are there not? I understand that you have already selected one of them for your personal secretary." Warren thought that Lodge might actually elbow him in the ribs but of course the Brahmin was too dignified for that.

"Yes, I always admire the fair sex, but my wife keeps me on the straight and narrow. When you meet her you will understand."

So his reputation had proceeded him. He stood in confusion, took a swig of his whiskey and soda, until Lodge gave him a manly clap on the shoulder. "Eh, senator?"

"Well, Cabot"—that was audacious, assuming familiarity with Henry Cabot Lodge—"I like the companionship of comely females as much as the next man. And are you the next man?" Another daring maneuver. Nobody joshes with Cabot Lodge.

He bought it! Warren's instinct for people had not failed. Lodge chuckled and withdrew his hand from the shoulder. "Now, senator, we both know that gentlemen never kiss and tell." Warren got the jab behind the joshing: Lodge knows everything that goes on in the Senate. Someone else approached to shake Lodge's hand and Warren took the opportunity to move on.

Warren found that being a senator was tougher than he had expected. Many politicians suppose that U.S. senators are indolent, comfy in the security of their six-year terms and three-day-a-week Senate sessions. But Warren wrote Carrie, "Honestly, never was my time so pressingly filled in all my life." But "the engrossment from toil" saved him from depression, he added. Despite four different stays at Battle Creek he still felt depressed at times.

Warren seated himself in the Senate early each afternoon so he could hear the chaplain's opening prayer. "I need it," he told Carrie. "God help us all." The chaplain, a Baptist like Harding, "humbly beseeches his guidance, even as I inwardly supplicate him now." The irony of expressing piety to his adulterous lover did not tag Harding's attention. He kept a harem, not the Sabbath.

Still, Harding was spiritually unmoored and studied his mother's Seventh-Day Adventist faith. She had joined the denomination after two of Warren's siblings had died of jaundice on the same day. His sister Carolyn grew up to serve with her husband as Seventh-Day Adventist missionaries in Burma. Their faith asserted that Negroes have every right to join whites in church and Harding appreciated that. Of course the church remained as segregated as any American institution but at least it adduced the equality of races, at least before God. Dr. Kellogg's racism back at the sanitarium still rankled Harding, for reasons he could not explain.

Harding's complexion was slightly darker than those of most white people. He knew of no personal African ancestry, but each time he had to deny accusations from Amos Kling and others that he was "a colored man," Warren saw the look on the doubters' faces. If he was indeed partly African, their expressions telegraphed, how dare he run for public office? Then, what about people who really were Black? How could they put up with such looks on white people's faces all their life? Amos Kling unwittingly had made Warren Harding a progressive on racial issues.

During this time, Harding faced the freshman senator's rite of making his first major speech on the Senate floor. Listening to the chaplain one day, he knew what he wanted to say. He wrote his own speeches and went straight to his office to put thoughts on paper.

Even though as a junior senator from the minority party Harding's words carried little weight, he was regarded as a Republican rising star. He rose in favor of an antilynching bill. "Democracy is a lie if our Negro brethren are denied the protection of the laws," he said. Southern senators always killed such bills, but Harding had made his point. Cabot Lodge nodded at him in austere approval.

Harding had relied on his silver tongue since he was a boy. Despite his size, he was poor at sports—growing up in a culture in which male popularity pretty much equated with athletic talent. He soon learned that he could get his way by talking. That and his bonhomie. He was not nervous at all before his first Senate speech.

His bodyguard Leland Jackson warned him that he might face political or even personal reprisals from Southern senators. Jackson also tried to caution Warren against another of what Harry Daugherty called his "woman scrapes." Warren wondered how in the hell Lodge and Leland already knew about his "personal secretary." Harding had gotten himself involved with a woman who was even nuttier than Carrie.

But Carrie remained the love of his life. Unsympathetic with his claims of overwork, she made a demand. She demanded that he accept no visitors from Marion, or even from the state of Ohio, at his home in Washington. If Florence would not let *her* in there, she could not let *anyone* in. Warren consented: "No Marion friends, no Ohio friends can be invited to our home, until you can be welcomed here," he wrote. He did not discuss this directive with the Duchess.

One of the visitors thus shut out of the home was Roxy Stinson. The Duchess would have kept Warren from giving her a job even if he had wanted to.

March 24, 1917

A German submarine sank a French passenger ferry in the English Channel. President Wilson threatened to sever diplomatic relations with Germany unless it stopped sinking civilian ships. A resolution in the Senate would endorse Wilson's stance.

"Warren Harding," Carrie wrote, "if you vote to cut ties with Germany I will send your letters not only to Jim but to the press. I will start with the *Columbus Dispatch* and they will be on the wires the next morning for the *New York Times* and the *Washington Post*."

Warren was horrified—exactly the effect that Carrie intended. He went to see Henry Cabot Lodge.

"You know, Mr. Leader, I would like to support the party on this resolution but you know I have many Irish in my state and you know how the Irish hate the British.

They don't want to see us backing up Wilson on the side of England. I'm getting lots of Irish letters."

"Yes, yes, it is a dilemma." Both men took thoughtful puffs on their cigars. "I always tell every senator who seeks my counsel, you can vote your conscience, you can vote your constituents, or you can vote your party. Very rarely"—harrumph, harrumph—"will it fall to you to vote for all three of these interests at once. These are the hard choices that we take the oath to make as public servants. Now, indeed, this may be a time for you to vote in support of your Irish constituents."

Damn, Cabot was being difficult. "Of course, the Irish are a minority in Ohio and most of them are Democrats anyway. But where does my statewide constituency lie? I really can't tell. You know I also have a lot of Germans in my state and they don't want us fighting their fatherland. Cincinnati is all German, but you knew that, didn't you? You know something, I could be much better informed on this issue if I had a seat on the Foreign Relations Committee."

Lodge looked at the ceiling as though deep in thought. "I believe that that prig Wilson is such a damn fool that we Republicans will take back control of the Senate this November. Then there will be more of our seats to fill. Yes, I think the junior senator from Ohio would make an outstanding member of the Foreign Relations Committee."

So the deal was cut, Warren's vote for the resolution in exchange for a place on a powerful committee. That left Carrie's threat hanging. A gambler all his life—in poker, he always drew to an inside straight—Warren took the chance that Carrie was bluffing.

"All right, you oaf, I will keep the letters. But never ask me again to send them back to you and if Wilson ever asks for a declaration of war and you vote for it, I will release the letters. You know I will."

Thus ended once again the affair between Warren Harding and Carrie Phillips.

As the temperature of war fever rose, Harding made speeches assuring that the best way to maintain peace was to prepare for war—a chestnut going back to presidents since Washington and dictators since Caesar. On April 2, the inevitable came. Wilson asked Congress to declare war on Germany.

For a turning point in history it seemed rather flat, thought Florence, watching from the House gallery. The speech sounded more like a sermon than a call to arms. The United States had a sacred mission because "the world must be made safe for democracy." The president looked angular and grave, wearing a pince-nez and appearing like the former college professor that he was.

Florence had a seat in the reserved section because she was the wife of a senator. Alice Roosevelt Longworth had a reserved seat because she was Alice. Afterward as the crowd shuffled out Florence kept her seat to watch Warren conferring with other senators on the House floor. They all looked grim. Alice ambled over and took the empty seat next to Florence.

Alice smoothed the floor-length dress in the pale azure tint that she had made famous as "Alice Blue." Her hat resembled a man's straw boater. She had to duck slightly under Florence's own broad-brimmed hat to speak softly to her. Florence could smell her perfume.

Florence wore a dark grey dress and a black silk neckband, a fashion accessory that she herself had made popular in Washington. She feared that she looked dowdy next to Alice.

"Were you ever once inspired during that whole speech?" Alice asked. "Christ, we aren't fighting them to make the world safe for democracy. We are fighting them because their U-boats keep sinking our ships. My father would have had them all on their feet cheering and saluting."

Theodore and Alice Roosevelt despised Wilson for lacking the balls to have led the country into the war a year ago. Wilson had won reelection in November 1916 on the slogan "he kept us out of war."

Florence looked at Alice with what she hoped was a reassuring smile. "Well, your father might have the opportunity to serve his country again, and even more grandly this time," she said. She meant that Theodore would seek the Republican presidential nomination in 1920, as everybody in Washington expected.

Alice misunderstood, thinking that Florence alluded to Theodore's efforts to persuade Wilson to let him take a new batch of "Rough Riders" to fight in Europe. Roosevelt had become famous as a colonel over a volunteer cavalry of Rough Riders in the Spanish-American War in 1898.

"That fathead, that sour pickle will never let Father gain any more glory," Alice said. "Of course, I don't say that to Father. He lives in hope." Alice had become candid with Florence. She still held resentments against Warren but had warmed to Florence in admiration of her brains and her backbone.

"You know," Alice continued, "if there were some way for the whole country to listen to Wilson's speech today I bet he would not have roused them. Too many long sentences with too many dependent clauses." As the daughter of Theodore Roosevelt, she knew something about rhetoric. "Doesn't he know that most Americans don't go past the eighth grade? Hell, most of them still don't have running water."

"I just feel bad for our boys who have to go fight over there," Florence said.

"Are you confident about your husband's vote?" Alice wanted to know.

Her grievances against Warren Harding went back to the Republican National Convention in 1912. After a political tussle between Warren and Nick, Alice called Warren a crook to his face. A most unfair charge.

Theodore Roosevelt ran for president on a third-party ticket in 1912 and lost. Nick Longworth had supported his fellow Cincinnati politician, the losing President William Howard Taft, over his father-in-law Theodore. That election effectively ended the Longworth marriage. Both Nick and Alice happily carried on affairs. Meanwhile, Harding kept trying to make it up to Alice. He led an unsuccessful effort in the Senate to send the Rough Riders overseas but Alice was unmoved. Warren called every beautiful woman "dearie" and Alice was the only one who forbade it.

Good Lord, Florence thought, does everything in politics come down to personalities? She had expected public issues to turn on class conflicts or competition among interest groups but instead they seemed to depend on who likes or dislikes whom. Warren kept telling her that politics is a matter of shifting alliances, that your friend on one issue is your foe on the next. But that, Florence thought, gives politicians too much credit for caring about issues. They were moved by vagrant enthusiasms. Either that, or their votes votes already had been purchased.

Warren also said that you could always tell the amateurs in politics: They took it personally. Maybe so, but most of the politicians Florence knew were awfully good at carrying grudges. So they were all amateurs? For public men they were thin-skinned, although they all claimed to be clothed in rhinoceros hide.

"I asked you, how will Warren vote on the war?" Florence, interrupted in her thoughts, looked at Alice in surprise. She said, "Warren Harding prays for guidance. I am sure the good Lord will lead him to see the justice of our cause."

Alice sniffed at this pomposity; Florence regretted speaking with such sanctimony. In fact she often felt a bit abashed around Alice. It seemed that Alice had discerned the secret of living well and scorned everyone who could not. Florence admitted to herself that Alice had a severe beauty, with a perfect complexion, wide-apart, all-seeing eyes, and a kind of magnificent hauteur.

Those haughty eyes now were trained on the legislative floor, where Florence turned her gaze as well. Knots of legislators still stood in the aisles, gesturing and talking. Their voices floated up to the galleries as a low steady drone. The air in the room seemed heavier, the law of gravity stronger. It held those senators and congressmen in the chamber and the two women in their seats. Florence and Alice fell silent. The United States was going to fight a war in Europe. For long minutes, nothing else mattered.

Harding said time and again that he supported the war only to defend American shipping against German submarines, not to make the world safe for democracy, in his mind an asinine ambition. Four days after Wilson's speech he joined a large Senate majority in casting his vote for war. He once again called Carrie's bluff, for she did not release his letters. But his Germanophilic mistress never again spoke to him with affection.

December 2, 1917

"The thing that really gets the Duchess's goat," Harry Daugherty said, "are the McClellan saddles."

"What are McClellan saddles?" Roxy asked.

They were at a banquette in the Hungry Workman diner in Washington Court House and Roxy was perplexed that Harry had arranged this coffee with her and Jess in the first place. Usually he tried to avoid her company, keeping Jess to himself. All three of them were in grumpy moods. Snow had sat on the ground for a few days, enough to make slush on the sidewalks and muck in the yards. Worse, the snow everywhere was speckled with soot from factories and coal fires and steam locomotives. Even the surrounding hills, low and steep at the edge of Appalachia, looked washed-out somehow, a milky white punctuated by the bleak and black bare trees. Jess thought the skeletons of trees could seem haunted, menacing if you looked at them against the grey skies long enough. It was the kind of wintry day that makes Midwesterners think about going south.

Roxy and Jess sat together on one bench and looked across the table at Harry on the other. Harry was stone-faced as usual, yet he seemed tense about something. Roxy thought maybe it was family woes—his son and daughter were alcoholics. Anyway, he was going on and on about corruption and waste in the government's war effort. "The McClellan saddle," he said, "was a saddle designed for the cavalry back in the Civil War. By General McClellan, you see."

Jess raised his right eyebrow to ask, And so?

"The Duchess says they're too light and too narrow, the soldiers don't like them, but they're the official cavalry saddle. The Duchess knows horses, you know."

"Wasn't McClellan the top general until Lincoln sacked him? Well, there you have it. He was the boss and so he got to pick the saddle. Probably made a profit on them," Roxy said.

"No—well, yes, probably, but you don't understand," Harry said. "We've ordered thousands and thousands of them! Tens of thousands!"

Again Jess with the raised eyebrow.

"We're not sending any cavalry overseas! None! It's a boondoggle, that's all."

Roxy raised both her brows. "How do you know this, Mr. Daugherty?"

"Ahem, I am not at liberty to disclose my sources. But I can tell you that the Republican committees in the Senate are investigating procurement issues in Mr. Wilson's War Department. And I will take the liberty, Miss Stinson, of telling you that Mr. Leland Jackson is one of our most able investigators. But you must not ask him about it."

"I won't."

"But why don't they take scandals like that to the press?" asked Jess, who answered his own question at once. "It's too early. They would be accused of disloyalty, if not outright Bolshevism."

Harry nodded gravely. Roxy looked at Jess with new respect. I am getting an education in politics, she thought.

"How do you think the war is going, Miss Stinson?" Roxy was surprised that Harry asked her opinion about anything. She would remember the look of set purpose on his face.

"I just feel so bad about our boys who have to go and fight over there. I went to the train depot here when the first boys went to go off to army training camp. They looked so young, even to me, and I'm still young. You could see, some of them had bought new shoes just for this trip. So they walked kind of awkwardly, the leather was still stiff. And they carried these cheap carpetbags. Or maybe cardboard suitcases and their mothers were all crying. It just about broke my heart."

"Didn't they know the army would give them shoes?" Jess asked.

"Ah, but the shoes, that's the point!" said Harry, stubbing his cigar in an ashtray. "See, even after ordering millions of shoes there was still all this leather left over, so the War Department ordered all of those McClellan saddles so that the saddleries could get rich too."

He paused with a look of strained patience, of a man trying to keep his temper. "Or mosquito netting! They ordered forty million yards of mosquito netting! Forty million yards! Mosquitoes aren't a problem in France, for Christ's sake! Beg pardon, Miss Stinson."

Roxy and Jess shook their heads at this extravagance but Roxy said, "I'm sure there is profiteering in every war, Mr. Daugherty. I remember hearing stories about the Civil War. I still say the worst thing is the boys who have to fight. Mr. Jackson told me that he lied about his age to avoid the draft and I didn't blame him at all."

(Roxy did not report the fullness of that conversation. After Leland had driven her to a singing gig in Dayton, she had called him:

"Hello, Mr. Jackson. You know they passed a law saying that all men have to register for the draft up to age thirty-five. How old are you, anyway?"

"Why, it's sweet of you to worry about me, darlin.' "

"I'm not your darling. I asked you a simple question."

"I'm thirty-four."

"Ah, that's too bad. Now you might have to go and fight."

"Naw, the draft will never get me."

"Why not?"

"I lied about my age."

"Oh, good. I just didn't want you to go and get your ass shot off in France."

"Why, darlin,' that's the sweetest thing anyone's ever said to me."

She hung up.)

"Do you think we are making the world safe for democracy?" Harry asked. He had a habit of staring hard at his interlocutor when raising important matters. Roxy supposed that was how he addressed the jury in court. What had gotten him so wound up about the war?

"Hmpf. Well, I remember when we had civics class back in high school. The teacher kept saying that democracy was the best form of government. So I said, 'How come everybody has an equal vote when they don't have equal abilities to think?' "

Jess laughed and after a moment Harry chuckled. Jess gave her a playful poke in the arm. A waiter came up to refill their coffees. Roxy looked out the storefront windows at the thin, evanescent December sunshine. The coffee was stale and bitter and she sent it back with orders to brew a fresh pot. The men nodded to the waiter as if they were just going to say the same thing but she beat them to it.

"Huh. What did your teacher say?" Harry asked.

"He just laughed and then all the kids laughed too. It was that mean kind of laugh when they don't like you, you know. I wasn't very popular in high school."

"The girls were all jealous of you and the boys were all afraid of you," Jess observed.

Harry looked around and then lowered his voice a notch. "Democracy?—Bah! We make a fetish out of freedom but name me one nation on earth that is free. Name one?" Roxy and Jess looked as though they were trying to solve a puzzle. "You think we're free here? People are being arrested just for talking down the war. Just because of Woodrow Wilson and his goddamn war. Beg pardon again, Miss Stinson."

"I'm with Senator Harding on that," Jess said. "He says it's none of our business to go around imposing democracy on other countries. If Germany or even France, for that matter, don't want democracy, why should we care?"

"Well, I don't know, but I can tell you one thing we're no longer free to do," Roxy said. "We're not free to buy coal, not at almost any price. Everybody's complaining. They sent all the coal to the navy to carry our troops overseas. So now we have to buy stove wood for heating and now you can hardly even get firewood anymore. So people are cold." She pulled together the unbuttoned jacket that was draped over her shoulders and made a little shudder.

"It's even worse than that," Harry said. "Would you believe there are two hundred ships tied up at the piers, waiting, in New York? Two hundred. Because the coal cars have tied up all the train lines so much that they can't get through."

With a jerk, Harry picked up a Hungry Workman menu and slapped it on the table. "Just look at this! 'Side dishes. Liberty Cabbage.' What the hell is 'liberty cabbage'? Sauerkraut! But you can't call it sauerkraut because that might show partiality to Germany." He shook his head at the human capacity to err.

Jess said, "I think our only hope is to elect a Republican president next time."

Roxy almost shrieked: "Oh, please God, this war will be over before then!"

"I wouldn't be sure of that," Harry said. "You know how people thought early on that this war would be over soon. If for no other reason, just because the countries involved would run out of money and resources. But of course the bankers figured out how to keep the money flowing. By selling debt, mostly. Over in Europe they're liable to run out of fighting men before they run out of borrowed money."

Roxy groaned. Jess looked doubtful. The waiter appeared with fresh coffee.

The men lit cigars and Roxy lit a cigarette from the silver cigarette case Jess had given her when they got married. Harry leaned back and gazed into the distance. When he leaned forward he said quietly, "This war is not being fought over any fixed principles. Hell, I don't believe there are any fixed principles. If there were, countries would not keep changing them as often as we change our shirt collars."

There seemed to be little to say after that. As they exited the cafe into the December chill, the sky the color of dirty dishwater, Harry said, "I thank the both of you for your candid views. I shall convey your sentiments to Senator Harding."

Roxy had an unkind thought: The reason Harry is so upset is that he was not cut in on any of the boondoggles.

Harry went immediately to the bank owned by his brother Mal. (Somehow this bank held the funds of the Ohio Republican Party instead of any of the big banks in Columbus.) Harry dictated a letter to Mal, who wrote in longhand and then gave it to his secretary to type. It was addressed to Special Agent Calvin Weakley of the Cincinnati office of the Bureau of Investigation of the United States Department of Justice.

> Dear Mr. Weakley:
>
> I have the honor of serving as the chairman of the American Protective League in Washington Court House, Ohio. I also am president of the Midland National Bank here.
>
> I bring to your attention the activities of Miss Roxanne Stinson of 126 Court Street. Miss Stinson is a young divorcee with a "fast" reputation. She openly advises our young men to lie about their age so as to evade conscription to fight for their Country.
>
> Further, Miss Stinson disparages our Democratic form of Government and publicly states that the United States should not attempt to bring Democracy to Germany or to any of the Central Powers or even of our Allies. She states that she has opposed our Democracy ever since she was a student in high school.
>
> She further accuses the suppliers of Coal to fuel our American Navy and other of our Industries of corruption and profiteering.
>
> Accordingly, we believe that Miss Stinson should be investigated for violations of the Espionage Act of 1917 (50 USC 37), to wit, conveying false reports or false statements with intent to interfere with the operation or success of the military or naval forces of the United

States or to promote the success of its enemies when the United States is at war; or to cause or attempt to cause insubordination, disloyalty, mutiny, or refusal of duty in the military or naval forces of the United States, or to willfully obstruct the recruiting or enlistment service of the United States.

We also request that Postmaster Barrow of Washington Court House be interviewed for possible impoundment of mails received by Miss Stinson.

The American Protective League continues to stand proud and ready to serve as the civilian auxiliary of the Department of Justice. Together, we will root out the spies and traitors in our midst as we continually beseech the Almighty to bless the arms of America.

With Faith in our Victory, I am

Mal S. Daugherty

Three days later, a truck parked on Court Street and a man wearing the work uniform of the Central Union Telephone Company got out, buckling his tool belt. He entered through a basement door and found the box containing the phone lines. Only the line to Roxy's apartment was connected; the other two apartments still did not have phones. With a knife, the workman scraped the insulation off the two wires, then snapped alligator clips on them. Attached to the clips were wires connected to a receiver. The receiver was secreted in the box and the door to the box closed. The job took less than five minutes.

A central switchboard was set up in an upstairs room over Mal's bank, with taps running into it from Roxy's phone and those of other suspects in the town. A red light blinked on this board when Rosy lifted her receiver. A stenographer with a headset took a record of the conversation. The government paid her wages.

January 27, 1918

Evalyn McNeal's driver picked up Florence at her home and drove her and Evalyn to nearby Walter Reed Army Hospital across from Rock Creek Park. They used to go riding in that park but gave up that luxury for the rest of the war.

A nurse recognized the two ladies from their frequent visits and opened the door to the ward. They looked out over what at first glance appeared to be a blaze of white—acres, it seemed, of beds on which lay white sheets covering disfigured men. The hospital had eighty beds when the war started and now there were 2,500.

The eyes of the first soldier that Florence encountered were bandaged, so he could not mind if she stared. Large blisters covered his wrists, upper arms and parts of his face. Mustard gas, Florence knew. Apparently this man had gotten his gas mask on in time to save his life but the gas seeped through woolen uniforms to raise painful blisters. He sensed the women's presence and reflexively tried to raise his head.

"Good morning, soldier, just lie still. I'm Mrs. Harding."

"And I'm Mrs. McLean. We're here to make sure you boys get all the care you need."

"Thank you." The voice was thin and wheezy and Florence thought he probably had some lung damage. Best not to ask questions.

But Evalyn said, "Your country is proud of you, son. Where are you from?"

"Parkersburg, West Virginia, ma'am."

"Why, I've been to Parkersburg!" Florence said. It was true. Parkersburg was a stop on the train to Columbus. "A lovely place." Not true.

"Where were you serving, if I may ask?" Florence shook her head and waved her hands to signal Evalyn not to ask questions, but too late.

"The Third Battle of Ypres, ma'am."

He pronounced it Epress. This little thing, this country boy's ignorance of how to say the name of a French town, where he had been sent to fight in a war he never wanted, touched Florence as much as anything. What a silly thing to get upset about, she thought, stifling sniffles. Taking another look at the man, she saw the army had not cut his hair. It was dark and wavy above a handsome face.

"Is there anything we can get you?" the irrepressible Evalyn asked.

"No, thank you, ma'am. The army takes good care of me."

"Would you like some cigarettes"—Evalyn looked at the name on a chart hanging over the foot of the bed—"Daniel?"

"No, thank you, ma'am." Florence wanted to kick her. Did she think this man could smoke?

Moving down the aisle to other beds, the ladies took dictation for letters home from soldiers with mangled hands who could not write. When they left the ward a doctor told them the Parkersburg man would lose a lung in surgery that afternoon.

The hospital visit had taken all morning and Florence asked Evalyn's driver to hurry so she could make her appointment at Union Station in time.

"Oh, the hell with the canteen," Evalyn said. "You're too tired, physically and emotionally. Believe me, I know it when I see it."

"After what we just saw at Walter Reed, how could you say that we should slack off?" Florence said. "And why in the world did you ask that first soldier if he wanted cigarettes? He had lung damage, he couldn't smoke!"

"Oh, I knew that, Flossie, for heaven's sake. I thought he might trade them to get other things from the other boys or even from the nurses."

The Duchess frowned and slumped in her seat and said nothing more. Evalyn knew she had lost the argument about Union Station. That is where her driver stopped.

Inside the station Florence joined a group of wives who had been organized by Lois Marshall, the wife of the vice president. They handed out coffee and sandwiches to throngs of soldiers who were leaving by train for seaports. Helping out on this day was Eleanor Roosevelt, the wife of Franklin Roosevelt and a distant cousin of Alice's.

"Good afternoon, Mrs. Roosevelt," Florence said. "Will we see Mrs. Longworth with us today?"

"I don't think so," Eleanor said coldly. "To my knowledge Alice has only been here once. She said she got 'canteen elbow.' " Several of the women suppressed smiles. The two branches of the Roosevelt family, Franklin's and Theodore's, detested each other. This remark by Eleanor would make the gossip circuits by nightfall.

Florence filled cups with coffee, making sure to smile at every soldier. She could not get the blind soldier from Parkersburg out of her head. When as a younger woman she was hospitalized for five months with a bad kidney she had vowed to make things better for hospital patients. But, really, did we do that mutilated man any good?

After a three-hour shift at the Union Station canteen she walked four blocks down Delaware Avenue to the Capitol. Inside a caucus room, wives of senators and Cabinet members had formed a Red Cross unit. First Lady Edith Wilson had put it together. The women wore white uniforms and caps to make sweaters, caps, socks, scarves, whatever, for our boys at the front.

"Do you know I never ran a sewing machine in my life before I came in here?" Florence asked one of her friends, the wife of a senator from a Western state. "It's true. My maid did all the sewing back home."

"Well, you know," her petite friend said, "my father was the governor of Idaho but we didn't have a maid. I always did all my own sewing."

"Really, you didn't have help? Who looked after you?"

"There was this one state trooper who sort of took a shine to me. He used to tell me stories about fighting in the Indian wars."

Never would I meet such interesting people back home in Marion, Florence thought. I just wish this war would end. Her hands ached and her legs were tiring from the treadle of the sewing machine.

The *whirr* of the sewing machines was still in her ears when she got home. She told the cook just to fix her a scrambled egg but then she changed her mind and went straight to bed. Florence stretched out on the cool sheets. She was physically and mentally tired. It was a good tired. She had not felt such a satisfied fatigue since she had taken control of the *Marion Star*.

March 6, 1918

Leland Jackson sat in the lobby of Room 143 of the Senate Office Building ("the SOB"), a recently built, art deco grey fortress across the street from the Capitol. As a government employee, an investigator for the Republican members of the Senate Committee on Military Affairs, he had swapped his cowboy hat for a boater. His one good suit, old-fashioned and double-breasted, did nothing to slim his bulky frame, not that he wanted it to.

Obviously in an agitated mood, he twirled the boater in his hands and looked around Senator Harding's anteroom. On the left-hand wall was a large framed poster: OHIO GAVE FLIGHT AND LIGHT TO THE WORLD. It featured drawings of the Wright Brothers' airplane and Thomas Edison's light bulb.

When called into Harding's office, he endured with patience Warren's booming welcome and joshing. "How are you and the lovely Miss Stinson getting along now? You make such an attractive couple. If you are in fact a couple now, hmmh?"

"Actually, senator, Miss Stinson is the reason for my visit." Harding, puffing a cigar behind his desk, motioned for Jackson to take the nearest seat facing him.

"As you know, sir, the Bureau of Investigation is investigating German sympathizers and spies. Well, I have come to know that Miss Stinson is being investigated."

"What!" Harding's look of surprise was genuine. "Who told you that?" He placed the cigar in an ashtray and let it rest there while staring at Jackson.

"Sir, I am bound by honor not to disclose my source. I will only say that in my work for the committee I am called upon to make inquiries of agents of the Justice Department."

Harding tilted back his head and closed his eyes. "Whatever is she being investigated for?"

"I don't know, but somebody turned her in to the American Protective League. All I can say is, she is an acquaintance of Carrie—of Mrs. James Phillips. And she's a known German spy."

Harding snorted and shook his head before remembering to assume an impassive face. Damn it, he had sent repeated letters to Carrie warning her of the investigation and begging her to be more circumspect. She not only did not care about being shadowed, she made a point of raising German shepherds in the batty belief that the kennels demonstrated her support for the Kaiser.

"Does the investigation involve the usual—taps on her phone, visual surveillance?"

"Yes sir."

"You have not told Miss Stinson any of this, have you?"

Jackson looked offended and waited a long moment before deigning to grunt "nossir."

Harding had started to regret contributing to war hysteria. Just a few days before, he had given a speech to a patriotic group in Baltimore. When wound up he could get orotund. He urged "pitiless" treatment of spies. "We must be for America first!"

The speech got a rousing ovation but for once the cheers did little to gratify Harding. He felt he was trying to convince himself of something he did not truly believe. Oh, sure, flag-waving was part of being a politician. But then why did he feel so hollow in his innards?

"Tell me this, Mr. Jackson. Have they discovered any incriminating evidence against Miss Stinson?"

"They ain't found anything that I know of for sure. The taps have been, what they say, unproductive. Hell, sir, you've known her longer than I have. You know she ain't a German sympathizer."

Harding rose, put his hands in his pockets and paced behind his desk, frowning. He looked up and said, "No harm will come to Miss Stinson. I will see to that. You may take my word for it, Mr. Jackson."

"Thank you, sir, I am most grateful."

Neither man could know that on that very day, agent Weakley in Cincinnati had received a letter from a Bureau of Investigation official in Washington.

> Your referral of the case of Miss Roxanne Stinson has been reviewed by this Office. Miss Stinson is the former wife of Mr. Jesse Smith, who is known to be a friend of Senator Harding. Surveillance of both persons yielded no instances of either party attempting to undermine the patriotism of the Senator. Neither has Miss Stinson undertaken activities to interfere with the operations or success of the military and naval forces of the United States under the Espionage Act.

> Accordingly, we are suspending our investigation of Miss Stinson. However, a reliable Informant assures us that he has first hand knowledge of Miss Stinson's publicly expressing disloyal, scurrilous, and abusive language about the United States government and its prosecution of the War. The investigation may be resumed after the new Sedition Act is passed as expected.

After showing Leland out, Harding continued pacing in his office. His hatred of Woodrow Wilson grew as his anger rose—how could that man sic his Justice Department on an innocent girl from Ohio? OK, Wilson personally was not to blame, but he was the one who had jacked up this war fever, this national scourge of suspicion and accusation. If they are tapping Roxy's phone, they probably are investigating Harry and Jess too. In fact, they are using her to get to them. And then to get to me? He already lived in fear that the investigation of Carrie would reveal his love letters.

So—how to get Roxy out of this scrape? He could invoke his senatorial authority to deputize somebody to ask the Bureau of Investigation to drop the case in his name. Just to keep his skirts clean, he could do so through the lawyers on the staff of the Committee on Military Affairs. Regrettably, though, the Democratic majority controlled every committee. Plus, Wilson's Democrats ran the Justice Department. Democrats were likely to leak his name to the press with a smear that he was protecting a suspected German saboteur, a young beauty. The damage would be done even if they never named Roxy. No doubt they would insinuate a romantic interest on his part. Then his Republican colleagues would have to waste their time defending him. He did not want to generate resentments among his fellow Republicans.

Well, letters had not done any good with Carrie, but Miss Stinson was a sensible girl with a good head on her shoulders. Although I still can't understand why she wanted me to give her a job. Harding sat at his desk again. He deliberately did not use Senate stationery, choosing instead paper printed only with his monogram. By his lights, the letter was short and to the point.

> Dear Miss Stinson,
>
> Mrs. Harding and I have always enjoyed your company and we are proud to call you our friend. I am writing to you about a serious matter and I hope and trust that you will take it in the spirt of friendship in which it is offered.
>
> It has come to my attention that you have been accused of disloyalty to the United States and that therefore you are under surveillance by Governmentagents. Of course such an accusation is preposterous and of its origin, I have no idea. Nonetheless it is advisable that you speak with caution on the telephone and even with your friends. I further advise you not to plan any trips to Washington with Mr. Smith in the near future as your movements here would be monitoredunder a cloud of suspicion.
>
> It makes me very disgusted that we must consider these things but my conviction is very solemn. Really, this war problem has distressed me infinitely more than you can guess. I know for a certainty that you are a loyal and patriotic citizen but passions and prejudices are not at my command. A difficult situation cannot be defied, it has to be met with tact and prudence until the mists are cleared away. Remember your country is at war, and things are not normal, and justice is not always discriminating.
>
> I pledge to do everything I can to lift the burden of this execrable calumny from you. In the meantime if I can be of any assistance, please wire my Marion office or write me at Post Office Box 1920 in Marion.

I have no doubt that I can rely on your discretion in keeping this matter strictly between us.

With all very best wishes,

WGH

Roxy's first thought was: So that's why I've been hearing those strange clicks on my phone. Her second thought was: God damn them! Third: Who the hell turned me in to the government? And for what?

Her hand was shaking as she picked up a cup of coffee from her kitchen counter. So the feds are tapping her phone? She was never one to chat on the phone. With effort of the mind and body she tried to remember every call of the past several months. She didn't have a boyfriend. Her manager had proposed a couple of singing gigs but she was no longer interested. With a couple of girlfriends she made dates to go to the PhotoPlay theater. With Jess she would arrange to meet for coffee—they never even mentioned the war on the phone that she could remember. She had seen Leland a couple of times in Washington but they just shared news of the war, nothing that was not in the papers.

She felt vulnerable and then frightened. Then she was enraged, not just at being placed in peril herself but at the realization that her own government was spying on people. Here was this new technology, many people didn't even have a telephone yet, and already the sons of bitches were using it to screw people. She was no naïf, not some kid who had just found out that life is unfair. Indeed, she had thought she was unshockable. But she was shocked.

And why did Mr. Harding send a letter to warn her? Despite all her work on his campaign she never knew him well. That old biddy the Duchess obviously disliked her. Could she have been the one who accused her of "disloyalty" just to be mean? Maybe so, and then rather than confront the fearsome Duchess, Mr. Harding had decided to write her that letter?

And the way he said it—you're being spied on but don't make a fuss about it, and you shouldn't go to Washington with Jess any more. And all because we're over in Europe fighting their wars for them. Why? Already one of the boys she liked in high school had come home a corpse.

In the sixth grade all the kids had to memorize the Gettysburg Address. Her teacher had made a point of saying that in just the first two sentences of that speech, Lincoln had explained and justified the Civil War. She had never heard two or any number of sentences from President Wilson or anyone else that explained the Great War.

It was the kind of thing, the more she thought about it, the madder she got. As the shock and confusion cleared, her defiance increased. Thinking of school reminded her of the dimwitted boys who seemed to be awed in her presence and too scared to talk, but she knew they made fun of her behind her back. *She thinks she's so smart.* And the girls were just as bad. *She thinks she's so pretty she's too good for us.* All those kids, they seemed to think the most important thing in the world was to be liked, never ever to be seen as "stuck up." And for what? She tried to think of one of her adolescent rivals who might have reported her to the feds out of spite. But none of them followed politics at all.

Mr. Daugherty had told her that democracy was a farce and the war was corrupt. A residual school-bred patriotism led her to regard Daugherty as extreme, as a bitter middle-age man. She set her coffee cup down, picked up Harding's letter between her thumb and forefinger and shook it as though she could make the truth fall out of it. The government spies on innocent people. Now, she thought, I see that Mr. Daugherty was right.

Wait! He was the one who directly and unexpectedly asked her about the war. Looking back on that strange conversation . . . was he baiting her so that he could turn her in? Did he hate her that much just because she was close to Jess? Jess had kind of played dumb that morning. But he could not possibly have been in on this!

That afternoon she walked to the Carnegie Library, carrying with every step her sense of having been violated. She looked up back issues of the Washington newspapers. She wanted to know when the Espionage Act she had heard about was passed and just what it said. She found the text of President Wilson's State of the Union address:

> There are citizens of the United States, I blush to admit, born under other flags but welcomed under our generous naturalization laws to the full freedom and opportunity of America, who have poured the poison of disloyalty in the very arteries of our national life; who have sought to bring the authority and good name of our Government into contempt, to destroy our industries wherever they thought it effective for their vindictive purposes to strike at them, and to debase our politics to the uses of foreign intrigue.

Roxy read that long sentence twice. She never thought that a president would utter such invective against his own "citizens of the United States." She read on: "They are not many, but they are infinitely malignant, and the hand of our power should close over them at once."

Walking the block and a half along North Street back to Court Street, Roxy reflected, well, that's one thing that Wilson got right for sure. The hand of their power has closed over my insides, that's just what it feels like. I can just see his bony Presbyterian finger poking at me.

Then she thought of something else that Harry Daugherty said. He said Prohibition is coming and it will be the best opportunity ever offered to make quick and easy money.

Well, if the United States is dumb enough to outlaw the sale of alcohol, I am not dumb enough to stay poor when I could get rich. Whatever bootlegging schemes Jess and Mr. Daugherty are cooking up, I am getting in on them. I not only will join them, I will think up some of my own.

And when I talk on the phone, I am going to say vile things just to give the sonsabitches who are listening in a thrill.

While Roxy made this resolution, wiretapping had become such an exciting new indoor sport—with no referees—that Alice Roosevelt Longworth took it up. She volunteered to plant bugs in the home of a high-society friend who was the mistress of a moneybags named Bernard Baruch, the head of Wilson's War Industries Board. Alice and army intelligence agents shared many laughs, listening to sounds of the couple having sex. But sex, at least, did not violate the provisions of the Sedition Act.

Harding rose in the Senate to speak against the Sedition Act. He put his hands in his waistcoat pockets and looked around at the senators. How many of them even gave a shit about the First Amendment, he wondered. "Our citizens have learned that the federal dog will bite and so they take care to stay outside the length of the dog chain. My friends, that is not the way of a free Republic, even under the passions of a world war."

Harding added that the president's officers "speak contemptuously of Congress. An assistant secretary had the effrontery to say the other day that the administration could get along very well in the conduct of the war if it were not for the interference of 'numbskulls on Capitol Hill.' " Now he had their full attention. An insult to the Senate!

The Sedition Act made it a crime, in time of war, to speak in a disloyal or profane way about the United States' form of government, its military, its uniform, its flag, or its sale of bonds. Harding was one of a small minority that voted against the bill. His stand provoked talk among Progressives in his party that he should run for president in 1920.

The truth was, Harding was falling to pieces under the strain. "Frankly, I am in the depths," he wrote to Carrie. "I am half-sick, and blue, and half sensible, stupid, glum, depressed. I can't sleep." He took off for a fishing vacation with a Senate buddy.

October 14, 1918

Jess knew that he was staring up at the skyscraper like a bumpkin in the big city for the first time but he did not care. The New Yorkers could laugh at him and then go screw themselves. He was on East Forty-Second Street admiring the new Hotel Commodore across from Grand Central Terminal. Twenty-five stories of fawn-colored brick surmounted by three-story-high flagpoles with gigantic American flags flapping in the wind. Jess saw this edifice as a symbol of America's rising imperial might. We are beating the greatest powers of Europe. England, Germany, France are ruined, laid to waste, while we're standing taller than ever. Just look around at all the motorcars here, hardly any horses to be seen any more. The new colossus of the world, the prolific maker of automobiles and grand hotels and battleships, the United States of America. How could it be dumb enough to outlaw the sale of alcohol?

Roxy stood fidgeting on the sidewalk next to him with the air of requesting his attention. She was not sharing in his sentiments. "OK, let's go in," he said, taking her hand to cross the street.

The lobby inside was big enough to hold a circus in, with an artificial waterfall and vaulted ceilings to rival a cathedral's. Jess asked for directions to the Dining Room. William J. Burns had wanted to meet him in the Men's

Restaurant, but Jess told him that Roxy had to be part of the meeting.

Harry Daugherty's plan had been that Billy Burns would appear to stumble upon them. Just a businessman from Ohio visiting New York and happening to meet a couple from back home. Nothing sinister going on. This charade was prudent in case somebody recognized Burns. He was a minor celebrity.

Billy Burns had become famous as a police detective and private investigator who nabbed the anarchists, labor thugs, and Bolsheviks who planted bombs in public buildings. He was from Columbus and even though Harry Daugherty had defended in court a couple of the crooks that Burns had caught, they were pals. Burns had arranged to meet Jess because he wanted in on Harry's rum-running racket.

After the waiter brought drinks, Jess leaned over the table to light Roxy's cigarette. That was the signal. Billy ambled in from the entrance doorway and bumped against Jess's chair from behind. "Why, Jess! You old son of a gun! Fancy meeting you here! And this must be your beautiful wife that I've heard so much about!"

He might be a great detective, Roxy thought, but he's a lousy actor. She blew smoke out her nose, smiled, and said, "Actually we're divorced but we're still good friends." She held out her hand for him to shake while Jess all but shouted, "Billy, old sport! Here, please join us," pulling out a chair, "I insist!"

Burns sat and snapped his fingers for a waiter. After ordering a drink he said in a low voice, "It's just a matter of a few months now, a year at the most."

"Yes, Massachusetts, of all places, just ratified. I didn't think they had that many Baptists out there," Roxy said. Burns looked at her in apparent surprise that she was taking part in the conversation. Roxy saw a handlebar mustache pasted on a well-fed face over a neck that was almost as wide. Another middle-age beefy man in a baggy suit. His hair was short, thick, and black. From experience with Leland Jackson she noted the telltale bulge of a shoulder holster under his jacket.

"But they've still got all those Puritans out there, don't forget," Burns said, thinking this was a clever remark. "How did Harding vote on Prohibition, anyway?"

"Senator Harding voted yes," Roxy said. She did not add that he did so in a typically Harding way. He said, "I do not claim to be a temperance man. I do not approach this question from a moral viewpoint." However, there were too many Baptists and Anti-Saloon League members in Ohio to risk voting no.

Congress had passed the Eighteenth Amendment and sent it to the states for ratification. The three at the table speculated on which states would be next to ratify. Once Burns had his drink in front of him, Jess looked around to see that no adjacent tables were occupied, then got down to business.

"Harry's very happy that the two of you might become business associates," Jess said. "But there's a thing you've got to understand. We sell honest product. Our liquor is never watered down or adulterated with any other substance. We never poison anybody. If you sell any product with the Lynchburg label, it has to be the straight stuff. Of course, if you want to rebottle it with different labels, that's your business and we couldn't stop you anyway."

Burns scooted back his chair and made as if to rise and leave. "I can't negotiate in an atmosphere of mistrust," he said.

Roxy said, "Well, why can't we have a relationship based on mutual mistrust?"

Burns narrowed his eyes and clenched his teeth without looking at her. Jess said, "See? I told you she was sharp."

After a moment Burns had to grin and nodded to Roxy in salute. He scooted his chair back in and said, "I agree that delivering honest goods is a sound business practice. In fact, we might get top dollar by establishing a reputation for top quality."

"Right, that's Harry's thinking," Jess said.

With Prohibition looming, distilleries were closing down, selling out cheap. Harry had bought the distillery in Lynchburg, Ohio, and others in the area for a song. He secreted their barrels of liquor in barns and warehouses.

"I admire Harry for getting in on the ground floor of this," Burns said. "You know, you bet on the horses, you'll probably lose. Bet on people wanting to drink, you're sure to win."

"Another thing to understand," Jess said, "is that you will not pick up product at our places of inventory. We will deliver at a mutually agreeable entrepôt. At night, or course. Really, Harry doesn't have to sell to you or anybody yet. He's doing this really as a gesture of goodwill to you." Actually, Harry wanted Burns's investigative skills and law enforcement contacts.

After some dickering they settled on a price of three dollars a case. Once the amendment passed, Burns could resell at triple or quadruple that amount. He and Jess toasted "easy money and quenched thirsts."

Roxy said, "I would think the people in place to make the most easy money from this are the district attorneys. They can take payoffs from the producers, or they can take payoffs from the wholesalers, or then they could turn around and take payoffs from the distributors. From the truck drivers, from the gunsels even. Of course they'll have to bring some cases to court for the sake of appearances." She took a drink of soda water and regarded each man with an artless, sincere look. "But they'll only have to put up a half-assed case. Or bribe the judge. Or no, take a payoff from the bootleggers who want to have the judge put away one of their own competitors."

She stubbed her cigarette in an ashtray. "Really, they'd have to think of ways *not* to get rich from this."

Both men looked at her with unblinking eyes. Roxy looked right back, her eyes brilliant, alert, and yet relaxed. Since she was a child she had known that a grand fate would come her way, one that would enable her to exploit both her intelligence and her beauty.

February 26, 1919

The Duchess took a streetcar lest somebody notice the license plate of the Hardings' car if her driver parked at her destination. She got off at Dupont Circle and walked through wet, blowing snow up New Hampshire Avenue to 1509 R Street Northwest. How did the cold northwest wind off the Potomac penetrate so far inland, she wondered.

In the parlor of the three-story town house, "Madame Marcia" Champney carefully brushed snow off Florence's coat and hung it on a hall tree. She doesn't overdo it, noted Florence, who was aware of her own trait of overdoing things. The only paraphernalia in the modestly furnished room were candles, a brass dish holding burning sandalwood incense, and a garish diploma on the wall to certify that Madame Marcia was a minister of the Spirituality Church. That diploma had cost her three dollars.

She had earned her fame by predicting that Mrs. Norman Galt would become the first lady. The widowed Mrs. Galt laughed it off but in the fullness of time Ellen Galt became the second wife of President Wilson, whose first wife had died recently. Now it seemed that every other grandee in Washington, even Supreme Court justices, consulted Madame Marcia. It was Evalyn who had recommended her to Florence.

Marcia grew up in New York tenements with, she claimed, some Gypsy blood in her veins. She ran errands for "a dirty old woman who looked like a witch." Assigned to take the old woman a pack of tarot cards, Marcia studied the goblins and knights for hours, then sat in a corner to watch the "witch" tell fortunes. Her father and later her husband abandoned her. Marcia danced in a vaudeville troupe, then worked in a millinery sweatshop where she read palms during the lunch break. On the Coney Island boardwalk she wore a black wig and fake gold earrings to pose as "Little Olive" as part of a "Gypsy Camp." Her readings were so popular that soon she hung out her own shingle. She had established herself in Washington ten years ago.

She steered Florence through a curtain of dyed black chiffon into a back room. "I can read tarot, palms, tea, and the zodiac but the zodiac is the best," she said. "The stars never lie."

Many years ago Florence had attended a spiritualism camp in Indiana. "The stars never lie" was the very slogan she had repeated there. Florence nodded and took a heavily upholstered seat at the table. No crystal ball, she noticed, that's good.

Marcia wore a simple black dress with a string of pearls. To Florence's eye, trained by Jess, the pearls looked real. Marcia was in her early fifties and obese. Her long, tinted hair was of a shade something close to apricot. For some reason Florence felt a need to pat her own short marcelled curls.

Florence gave Marcia the date and time of day of the births of Warren and herself—but not their names. Marcia insisted on her customers' anonymity even if they did not.

"I close my eyes and turn all my thoughts within," Marcia said. "I throw my mind into an infinity where there is neither time nor space. I become oblivious of externals." A long pause. "Pictures begin to unfold before my inner vision."

She read the horoscopes. "Jupiter is dominant with you," she told Florence. "Hereafter I shall call you Jupiter." Florence nodded. As to Warren's birthdate, Marcia said, "I hope this person is a man. No woman could be strong enough."

Florence took offense. "Don't say that, Marcia. A woman might be found who is strong enough to play that part. But you are right. This is the chart of a man who is prominent in public life."

"Oh my. Oh my." Mars, Mercury, and Saturn were in conjunction with the Sun under Scorpio in the eighth house—the house of Death. Uranus was in the fifth house, Karma. Marcia told Florence, "There are strong signs of earthly love and of gambling for the highest of stakes. This gentleman extends complete confidence to his friends. He tends to be enthusiastic and impulsive, does he not? His fate will depend largely on the influence of love, presumably in a marriage. But there appear to be many love affairs of a clandestine nature. He is highly perplexed about matters of finance but he will gain money through the employment of many people or in public service."

Florence thought, how could she say such disturbing things in such a flat voice, as if reading a story in a newspaper? And in some kind of foreign accent that nobody can place?

Seeing the alarm on Florence's face, Marcia said, "Do not be frightened, my dear Jupiter. The signs of earthly love will prevail."

"Don't sugarcoat it," Florence said. "I wish to know it all. I am not afraid."

Marcia closed her eyes and lifted her chin in a posture of seeking enlightenment from the heavens. Then she cleared her throat and said, "If this man runs for the presidency, no power on earth can defeat him."

"He is in the running," Florence conceded.

That was true. Theodore Roosevelt had just died. Common opinion, worth what it usually is, held that if President Wilson succeeded in creating his League of Nations, he would run for a third term. With Teddy gone, Harding would make a plausible Republican candidate. This prospect did not altogether thrill Mrs. Harding. She always worried that something would happen to her Warren.

Marcia continued, "But you must know . . ." Ahem. "You must know . . . he will die a sudden death, perhaps of poison. Or that he will sacrifice himself for his friends. . . . This person will be the next president of the United States, but he will not live out his term. He will die in a sudden, if not violent death. The end, when it comes, will be sudden after an illness of short duration."

She looked to see how "Jupiter" was taking this. Florence's face was as stark and grey as the February sky. She was stroking her black neckband as if that ritual might help her breathe.

Marcia soldiered on. "Poison or its effects is indicated. It is written in the stars. Following the splendid climax in the House of Preferment, I see the Sun and Mars in conjunction in the eighth house of the zodiac. And this is the house of Death. Sudden, violent, or peculiar death."

Of course she knows, Florence thought, so I might as well say it. "This man is my husband."

"Yes. Does your husband believe in astrology?"

"He just laughs at it. Like he's doing me a favor by humoring me. But I believe, Marcia, and I must guide him. You must tell me how."

"You, Jupiter, are a child of destiny. You must be strong, take a firm stand and hold to it." Whatever that meant, Florence did not look consoled.

Florence's mind, always quick to process information, now shut down. In some layer of the subconscious she recognized that there were only two possibilities. Don't let

Warren run. Or Marcia is mistaken. The stars don't lie but Marcia might have read their signals faultily.

When one is informed that a family member has died the response is always "it doesn't seem real." That was Florence's feeling as she walked through the snowfall back to the streetcar line—at least the wind was at her back this time. Marcia's words could not be assimilated, absorbed, incorporated. It was unreal, unthinkable.

Then a third possibility popped up. Maybe the prophesy would apply in 1920 but not if Warren waited until 1924 to run.

Florence never considered that Marcia might have deduced her identity from information she had gotten from Evalyn McLean. Evalyn knew all the gossip in Washington and anything she didn't hear was conveyed by Ned from his sources at the *Washington Post*.

The sorceress haunted Florence's thoughts and dreams for the next four years. Eventually, Marcia was paying secret visits to the White House.

March 1, 1919

Carrie was answering Warren's love letters with bitter recriminations. "SOME VICTORY!" she sneered after the armistice was signed on November 11. "Our 'great victory' will level us. 35 billions of debt and a hubbub of crap heaps, for instance just aeroplanes alone, not mentioning the four pounds of poison gas that each of these twenty thousand planes were to drop on Germany to extinguish the race."

My Lord, Harding thought, she's sounding worse than Harry Daugherty.

Carrie turned to their relationship. "It's appearances, *not love*. I'd dearly love to write of love if love could write—no one in this world today can read the language if any one in the world could write it." The insight was clumsily worded, but Carrie understood the global spiritual desolation wrought by the Great War better than Harding did.

"Your polite little frigid note received," he wrote back. "It is all right. I had no reason to expect more. Probably it is all I deserve. Let it go at that. I am always disappointing everybody and you in particular, even when I do the best that I know how."

"Spare me your self-pity, Warren," Carrie thought when she read that. When Warren later sent her a very affectionate Christmas note she replied by proposing to meet him in Washington. Warren was overjoyed—he had promised to "make amends" and maybe they would be lovers again.

She appeared in his lair in the Senate Office Building. She sat but did not remove her coat and hat. Warren paced uncomfortably, thrusting his thumbs under the arm holes of his waistcoat.

"Warren, I know you are having affairs with other women. Now don't deny it."

There was a scratchiness in her once-sugary voice he had never heard before. "But, dearie, when have I ever denied it? You know that I can't see you very often. Or else I would. No other woman compares to you. And then I have not objected to your affairs with other men."

"I won't let you change the subject, Warren. I am here because I deserve to be compensated for all I have done for you. Well compensated. And tangibly." Her eyes glistened with contained high-class rage.

Warren stopped pacing and stared at her. She had never asked for money before. Well, she had asked him to buy her a Cadillac, but that was during balmy times many years ago.

"Oh, dearie, is that a threat?"

"You know, Warren, that I have about two hundred and fifty of your letters."

Warren went behind his desk and sat in the leather chair. If this was going to be a business meeting, then he was going to assume his seat of authority.

"I sent those letters with a loving heart and I believed that you kept them out of love."

"Yes, that is why it would be such a shame if those letters became public. You not only couldn't run for president, you couldn't even be reelected to the Senate. Also, as you know, I long ago told Jim about our affair, so that would not be a consideration."

It was true. Her husband not only took the news with equanimity, he still considered Warren a pal.

"Now, Carrie, you know that I am being mentioned as a possible candidate for president. If that should happen, I—"

"That's my fucking point!"

Warren was impressed but not shocked. A respectable woman never said *fuck* unless she really wanted to place emphasis on something.

"You don't really want the office, you're just mad about collecting honors. Like some people collect butterflies or something. And then you're just afraid to say no to the Duchess, too. And you're both just small-town people who think you're too big for your small town!"

"Well, hell, you think you're too big for the United States of America!"

"Maybe I am, but let's get back to the matter at hand. You owe me, *Senator* Harding," she said with venom.

Warren detested scenes, abhorred confrontations. He felt he had but one card left to play. He pleaded with her to wait to see if he actually won the presidential nomination, in which case he would be in a much better position to pay her. She agreed to that condition and walked out without a kiss or a handshake.

Two nights later, the couple in the apartment under 578 Wardman Park Inn in Washington heard loud, disturbing noises—shrieking curses and the sounds of objects being thrown about—from the apartment above.Then they heard a scream and it sounded like a man's. They called the cops.

A tall, blonde, beautiful woman answered the knock on the door. Her hair was a mess, her makeup was smeared, and she held her white terrycloth robe closed tightly against her sternum.

That was the first thing the two cops saw. Then they spotted a paunchy middle-aged man in his pajamas on his hands and knees, muttering something.

"Ma'am, we're going to come in," the taller, beefier cop said.

"Come right in and arrest the son of a bitch," she said.

As they entered the man put his right hand on the arm of a chair and leveraged himself to his feet. He looked woozy and there was a liquor bottle on the coffee table. "Sir, what is the problem here?" the big cop said. Then the other one saw the reflection of the man's back in a mirror over the fireplace. He was bleeding from below the left shoulder.

"Christ, Eddie, look at this," he said, grabbing the man's shoulders and turning him around. There was a rent in the pajamas and a clean, open gash that would require stitches.

"It's nothing, it's nothing," the man said. "She'll bandage it up." He tried to look dignified, an impossible ambition in the circumstances. "I am Senator Harding. This lady is my legislative liaison."

"Senator! I thought I recognized you from your pictures in the papers. Sir, you have been injured. We'll gonna take care of you. Sit down and bend forward with your head between your knees. Lady, will you bring me a towel?"

"Why not let him bleed to death?"

"Please, ma'am."

She brought a kitchen towel. Eddie sent the junior cop out to the police call box on the corner to summon a nurse.

"I guess nobody is gonna wanna press charges, huh?" the cop said as he held the towel against the cut.

"I cut him with a broken champagne glass. That's the kind of charge that I press," the woman said, flamboyantly tying the sash around her robe.

"Ma'am, I have to have your name, you know."

"She is Grace Miller Cross," Harding said. "She is my employee. There will be no charges filed."

Grace, the "legislative liaison," was the "personal secretary" whom Henry Cabot Lodge had kidded Harding about back when he first went to the Senate. That blonde hair isn't real, both cops thought. She's a tough cookie, all right, both thought. She's not that young, she's starting to get fat, the younger one thought.

A young nurse came and took four stitches to close the wound. She was primly professional but as she left she smirked at the people in the room.

"We need to take your statements now," Eddie said.

"Miss Cross and I were having a disagreement. I guess you could say it was an altercation," Harding said.

Grace Cross now was sitting in an armchair and smoking a cigarette. She crossed her legs and gave the junior cop a thrill by baring an expanse of thigh. She did not look at him as, pencil and notebook in hand, he tried to ask questions.

"You will find no mention of Miss Cross in the Senate records," Harding said. "I employ her personally. Therefore, I see no reason why this matter cannot be confined to this room. Officers, I thank you for your assistance."

"Sir, you understand that we have to file a report," Eddie said. "We'll just write it up as a domestic disturbance with no charges or arrests. It will just be put in a file and forgotten."

"This must never appear in the press."

Eddie looked as though Harding had insulted him. "Of course not, sir. Reporters never go through those files. And just to be sure we'll sit on it for a while."

"Thank you, thank you. May I get you gentlemen a drink?"

"Get them out of here," Cross said.

"Miss" Cross was actually the wife of James E. Cross of Findlay, Ohio. Like many Ohioans, they had come to the wartime capital city looking for jobs. Harding found nothing for James but hired Grace right away. Senate personnel rosters were full so he paid her salary out of his own pocket, not an uncommon practice for senators.

Grace told the cops they had argued over money. More likely, she was upset because Harding was still writing to Carrie and still screwing Nan Britton and who knows who else. Maybe she should not have felt so slighted—when Warren was out of town, he sent love letters to her too.

A few days later Warren went to Nick Longworth's mansion on W Street for a poker party. Alice was away and it was a stag party with Nick, a couple of other Ohio congressmen, Harding, and Daugherty. Nick had invited a couple of showgirls to serve drinks and generally improve the scenery.

When the butler showed Harding in, Nick practically bounded across the room to greet him. "Don't worry, Warren, I'll shake your hand but I'll be sure not to slap your back!"

Goddamnit. So much for the discretion, the honor of cops. Well, I suppose this gossip was just too delicious to keep on ice. But I can trust these guys not to spread it around. A private joke, okay, let them have their laugh at my expense. Thank God the Duchess hasn't seen my bandage.

"Why, Nick, what are you talking about? My back is still as strong as when I used to drive mules on my daddy's farm."

"Of course it is! But just in case you've got a little backache, have a drink."

Hard wooden ladderback chairs, rather cheap ones, actually, were placed around the poker table. When Warren took his seat Nick called to a showgirl, "Honey, bring this man a pillow to put behind his back. He's been working too hard and I think he pulled a muscle."

Warren observed carefully and Nick was the only one who chuckled. So he hadn't told the others and he surely had sense enough not to tell his wife Alice. Harry obviously knew, though. His gloomy face across the table told Warren, I'm not even going to bother to scold you any more, go ahead and fuck the world.

Grace Cross kept her own mouth shut. But the next year, she told the chairman of the Republican National Committee, by way of demanding blackmail money, that she could identify a "birthmark" on Harding's back.

June 28, 1920

The Republican bosses had to sell their war bonds because Warren Harding could not keep it in his pants. They had regarded Harding as a compliant mediocrity, a senator who looked good enough and talked well enough to be elected president. Then his longtime mistress demanded hush money. And then they learned of multiple current and former Harding girlfriends scattered across half the country.

"Put all those dames together, you'd have a field hockey team," one boss said.

"Hell, two squads of them," said another.

So they cashed in the Liberty Bonds they had purchased during the Great War and sent the money to Harding's campaign office in Marion, Ohio. It would be used to buy the silence of who knows how many dollies.

If the bosses had known that a girl was in charge of their blackmail fund, they would have stopped payment on the checks at once.

Roxy Stinson did not mind that her former husband, Jess Smith, carried the title of campaign treasurer while she was not even listed on the payroll. The divorced couple remained friends, occasional lovers, and partners in crime. She was planning to get her reward after Harding was elected president in November 1920. She told no one of her scheme, not even Jess.

Roxy opened the mail and tallied the checks in a bedroom converted to a makeshift office in the Harding home in Marion. She sat at a card table, the desk—a battered, scuffed antique donated by the local high school—reserved for Warren Harding alone.

Jess straightened his tie, pulled down his waistcoat, and patted down his hair in the ritual he performed before entering any room. He wore a light-grey, summer-weight suit with a purple tie accented in lavender. But the expensive tailoring did not conceal his chubbiness. Nor did the circular spectacles in heavy black frames make him look as intelligent as he wished.

Roxy's outfit was a simple cotton house dress in a muted plaid, suitable for her tedious work.

As Jess sat down on the opposite side of the card table the couple nodded to each other but did not speak. Jess reached for the pile of checks already logged by Roxy. They checked each other's work and kept separate records, one for them, one for the Harding campaign, and another for the Republican National Committee.

When they were finished Jess asked in his high tenor, "What time are you seeing the paramour?" Jess and Harry, who was Harding's campaign manager, had determined that Roxy should negotiate with Harding's most importunate mistress, Carrie Phillips.

"It takes a dame to dicker with a dame," Daugherty opined. "Men don't have the balls to stand up to a woman when she starts crying. Turn on the waterworks, a man's knees start to buckle."

"Yeah," Jess said, "but then it might take forever. Women

believe that if there are two people in a room, one of them has to be talking. They can't stand it being quiet."

"So what? We got lotsa time. Roxy's a tough broad, she'll do fine."

Actually, Daugherty resented the campaign's reliance on Roxy, his competitor for Jess's affection.

Roxy said, "It's supposed to be this afternoon but I've got to see Mr. Daugherty first. Where is he?"

"In the prefab, I reckon."

Reporters, photographers, and visitors seeking the green Harding home with its suddenly famous, broad white porch were sent to a white wooden house, a prefab ordered from Sears & Roebuck, that had been set up on the lawn. Daugherty, jowly and looking gravely vacant as usual, stood on the stoop, spouting off to reporters. Roxy tugged at his sleeve and drew him inside to escape the photographers. They were always on the lookout for beautiful women whose photos would be favored for the front page.

"Mrs. Phillips and I should meet somewhere out of town," Roxy said. "There are just too many people here. People are lined up just to say they stood on the porch."

"Yeah, I've already thought of that. You're booked in the Deshler Hotel."

Roxy wanted to drive the fifty miles south to Columbus—she was proud of knowing how to drive—but Daugherty insisted that she take the train the next day. As she entered the hotel she felt reassured. The place was so big that nobody would notice that she and Carrie Phillips were there at the same time.

The Deshler strived for the monumental look of all the new luxury hotels with a big lobby, a high tin ceiling, fluted columns of fake marble, and murals with classical themes. Roxy strolled across the lobby with the wordless authority of beauty. She wore a cloche, the close-fitting, bell-shaped hat that was now *de rigeuer* even though Roxy disliked them because they concealed the bounty of her strawberry-blonde tresses. Under a knee-length skirt of black chiffon was the audacious novelty of rolled-down stockings. Roxy believed she had pioneered that fashion trend back when she was a professional singer.

She took an elevator to Carrie's suite on the twelfth floor. At least Carrie was not a forty-seven-year-old woman trying to look like a twenty-seven-year-old; Roxy gave her that. Even so, Roxy knew, Carrie looked in the mirror every morning for new wrinkles around her eyes and mouth. (Roxy was thirty-one and had just started the practice.) Another thing, Carrie had not plucked her eyebrows to attain those fashionable thin arcs. But then her brows had a naturally pretty arch. Her ivory drop waist dress was too long for the current mode. Instead of a cloche, Carrie wore a black hat with a high crown and butterflies and roses around the flat brim.

"How nice to see you again," both women lied. Carrie called the front desk and asked for a pot of tea. Roxy chose a burgundy-colored leather armchair cater-corner from the couch, where Carrie sat facing a coffee table. Each woman remarked on the view out the window of the LeVeque Tower, the tallest building in Ohio. Small talk seemingly exhausted, they waited in silence for the tea to arrive.

"Please allow me," Roxy insisted when it arrived, and tipped the bellboy a silver dollar, making sure that Carrie noticed her generosity. That should show her that I am here to talk serious money, she figured. As for the bellboy, he could hardly believe his luck.

"May we proceed to business?" Roxy asked, crossing her legs and turning her face toward her adversary. Each woman took a three-quarters-profile view of the other. "Mrs. Phillips," she said, "I am authorized to offer you a very substantial consideration of ten thousand dollars. However, this offer is contingent on you and your husband leaving the country for the next year. And of course you will surrender the letters in question."

She waited for whatever version of it-will-cost-you-more-than-that that Carrie had prepared. Instead, Carrie sat silently and looked bored. This is the woman that Mr. Harding was crazy about for fifteen years? Roxy wondered. And both Mrs. Harding and Mr. Phillips didn't suspect a thing for, I don't know, how many years?

Actually, those two had not suspected anything even when the couples toured Europe together for six weeks—not even when they toured Europe together again for two months—and Warren and Carrie had carried on the whole time. Carrie considered herself to be a highly cultured person and attributed Florence Harding's blindness to lines from Lord Byron:

Whether it was she did not see, or would not,
Or, like all very clever people, could not.

The silence perplexed Roxy because Jess and Harry Daugherty had described her as a chatterbox. After a long while Roxy asked, "Are you not feeling well, Mrs. Phillips? Is there something I can get you?"

"Miss Stinson, Warren Harding has wasted a lot of my time, and a lot of my youth, over many years. There is no reason for you to waste my time here today."

"The offer is not satisfactory? It's very generous."

"You know that I require an annuity in addition to a grant of cash, which is inadequate as you also know."

"Oh, Mrs. Phillips, I had hoped that we could come to an agreement this afternoon, but I am not authorized to discuss the matter of an annuity with you." Not true.

She studied Carrie's impassive face. It was squarish with a long, thin nose and thin lips. There was something regal in her perfect complexion, bright eyes, and air of hauteur. Men probably called her, not beautiful, but striking.

Carrie opened her hand-tooled leather bag, withdrew a pack of cigarettes, and languidly lit one. Then she reached in and pulled out a letter, unfolding it carefully and holding it up to make sure that Roxy could read the embossed legend in an upper corner: UNITED STATES SENATE CHAMBER. My God, Roxy thought, the son of a bitch was dumb enough to send love letters on official Senate stationery.

Carrie cleared her throat and read in a monotone:

I love your mouth, I love your fire
I love the way you stir desire.
I love your sins and daintiness
Love every thread in which you dress.
I love you garb'd, but naked MORE!
Love your beauty to thus adore.
Robed only in your tresses gold . . .

"Please, Mrs. Phillips, that is really not necessary," Roxy interjected, though she was fascinated.

"Oh, but I think the press would be delighted to learn that Senator Harding is possessed of literary gifts," Carrie deadpanned. "Some of his letters go on for thirty-five or forty pages and I have over two hundred of them. Every sentence is eloquent. He's not just a gifted orator, you know. He—"

"Please, Mrs. Phillips, I don't need to know the contents of the letters, they are not at issue for us here today."

Carrie replaced the letter in her bag, snuffed out her cigarette, sipped her tea and said nothing.

They finally settled on $20,000 up front, $2,000 a month while Harding was in office, and a year-long, 'round-the-world trip for Carrie and her husband Jim. Thereafter, Jim would be considered for an ambassador's post, but an appointment was not promised.

"Miss Stinson, there is one more item that I require. It is not monetary in nature." She paused to let Roxy's curiosity rise. "I demand a written apology signed by Mrs. Harding."

"What!"

A favorite ploy of coquetry is to tilt one's head to the side and brush a lock of hair away from an eye or ear. Roxy never did that: it was beneath her. But now she tilted her head, fingered her hair, and stared at Carrie in open amazement. She needed a couple of seconds to recover a poker face.

"I demand a written apology for the brutal way she treated me at the Marion train station in 1917."

Roxy bit her lower lip. She thought Jess and Harry had told her everything known about the affair. A poignant dimension was added to the scandal by the fact that Carrie and Florence had been inseparable childhood friends—Carrie the prettiest girl in town, Florence the richest. Wealth and beauty tend to stick together. But something had happened at the train station that nobody had heard of?

For the first time she could remember, Roxy felt inadequate, unequal to the task. How can I negotiate with somebody who is willing to destroy a presidency just to appease her hurt feelings? What did Mr. Harding do to this woman, anyway?

"Mrs. Phillips, why in the world should you desire an apology from Mrs. Harding? It would seem to me, forgive me, but it seems to me that Mrs. Harding is the aggrieved party in this matter. She has not required an apology from you, is that not correct?"

"She called me a traitor. She must withdraw that slur against my name."

As Carrie told the story, Warren and Florence went to the station for a ceremony honoring the first detachment of hometown boys going off to the Great War. Florence reveled in the pageantry of small-town patriotism—flags flying, bands playing, folks cheering—but Warren seemed oddly subdued; he even declined the mayor's invitation to give a speech. When a politician—when Warren Harding—sloughs off the opportunity to speak to a crowd, something is wrong. As for her part, Carrie said, she merely was warning the boys that the German army was the most powerful in the world when Florence accosted her, screaming that she was a traitor.

Huh, Roxy thought, I would like to hear Florence's side of this story. She said, "Mrs. Phillips, you know I cannot agree to such a demand. I must submit it to those whom I represent."

"Yes, do so."

In the end, Florence signed an affidavit stating that she had never accused Mrs. Phillips of treason and moreover had never accused her of conducting an adulterous affair with Warren Harding. The lawyer Harry Daugherty carefully worded the paper so that the words "apologize" and "apology" did not appear. Florence exacted her own price for this humiliation. The blackmail fund paid her $5,000 for her signature. Meanwhile, Florence now had another reason to detest Roxy for sticking her nose into the Hardings' private affairs.

June 30, 2020

The next item on the agenda was to locate the daughter whom Harding had fathered back in the Battle Creek sanitarium, who would be about twenty-five years old now. Daugherty's investigator Leland Jackson found that Susan Hodder's last known address was somewhere in Nebraska and that her daughter had married and moved to New York.

"Take the next train to New York," Daugherty said. Roxy had spurned Leland's constant efforts to seduce her, but she gave him a hug and wished him luck before he left. Within three days Leland found that Marion Hodder, named for the town, had married a man named Flynt. They had lived at West 101st Street and Marion had a daughter of her own, Priscilla. Then Marion died of tuberculosis at twenty-two. Fling took Priscilla to live with his parents in Elmira, New York.

Leland was so excited that he called Daugherty long-distance, reversing the charges, instead of sending a cheaper night wire. "She's been dead for years! There's no exposure at all," he said, meaning exposure to blackmail.

Daugherty next sent him to look for Susan Hodder in Chadron, Nebraska, which as far as gossip in Marion was concerned might as well be the moon. She lived in a white two-bedroom frame house with wood siding and a concrete foot stoop, a type that populates the Midwest by the millions. Leland removed his cowboy hat when she answered his knock.

"Good morning, ma'am. You don't know me but I am here on behalf of a very good friend of yours. I think I can do you a good turn."

"Come inside."

She's still not bad-looking, he thought. She motioned him to an armchair as she sat on a sofa. Leland noted that she did not offer him tea or lemonade or anything. This is not like an old lady's home, he thought. The parlor is not stuffed with useless objects like those of his parents' generation. No antimacassars on the furniture. No family photos, not even of her daughter. On the wall behind her was a framed—Leland squinted—cover of a recent *Vogue* magazine. On the beige sofa was a single round blood-red pillow.

As he looked around she said, "Mr. Jackson, you are welcome here but I am busy. Please state your business."

Leland leaned back and crooked his right boot onto his left knee. "Mrs. Hodder, my client is the next president of the United States." Just what Daugherty had told him to say.

"You're here for the letters, aren't you?"

At least Mr. Harding always went for smart broads, I'll give him that. "Yes, ma'am. I am prepared to offer you a substantial amount"—he patted his waist as if indicating a money belt underneath—"for the release of any and all correspondence between you and my client."

"Mr. Jackson, you are trying to sound like a lawyer but I can tell that you aren't. They're still taking advantage of Warren, aren't they?" Shaking her head. "I used to try to tell him about that."

"But you haven't heard my offer!"

"Mr. Jackson, I have lost my only daughter. Not all the money in the world can make up for that. I am left with my memories. And your client's, as you call him, expressions of love."

"Ahem, ma'am, it is for that very reason, his love for you, that I am here. It is his wish to provide for your old—for later on in your life." A pause for effect. "I can offer you five thousand dollars."

"*Acch!*" He had heard that *acch!* from Ohio Germans all his life. "Did Mr. Harding really think he could buy me off? He's not behind your trip today, is he?"

"No, ma'am," which was technically true. Harding left these matters up to Daugherty. Leland thought of searching the house for the damn letters but she let him know they were in a safe deposit box.

"Mrs. Hodder, will you give your word of honor that you will never tell anyone about your association with my client or make any private letters public?" Another line from Daugherty that he had rehearsed.

"Mr. Jackson—if that is your name—if I have kept to myself all these years, you don't need any promise from me. You can tell Mr. Harding I said that."

Leland uncrossed his legs and leaned forward with an air of confidentiality. "Ma'am, if you will forgive me for asking, since it seems our money does not appeal to you, how have you lived here all these years?"

She fluttered her hand at an unimportant question. "I was a seamstress, a midwife. Things that ladies can do. And Mr. Harding sent us checks until a few years ago."

Leland liked her and in the end gave her a thousand dollars out of general principles. There was so much money floating around.

Roxy asked, "How did it go with the old woman?"

"Not so great. I'm not used to being nice to people."

"Yeah, you sure aren't nice to me. I never even hear a compliment from you."

"Why, darlin,' you're such a tough broad, I never even thought that you needed compliments."

"Why, Leland, what a sweet thing to say."

That night she went to bed with him for the first time. She disdained her girlfriends who fell for dangerous "bad boys" who would only hurt them in the end. But Leland isn't so bad, she thought. And the cowboy act isn't all fake. As a boy he spent years on a ranch in Oklahoma. Sometimes his grammar is bad. That bothered her.

Afterwards, as they both silently smoked cigarettes in bed, Roxy thought, it wasn't desire that put me in this bed. It's the damn campaign. Long hours of tedium every day but with thrilling moments now and then. People get so wound up they have to do something to unwind. Like drink too much. I've seen people sacrifice their free time, their lovers—hell, even their marriages—just so that one politician could replace another. It was ridiculous when you thought of it like that. So . . . what's the payoff? For Leland, it's a job. The big lunkhead, he isn't even a good lover. Few men are and yet they all think they are Casanovas.

She stubbed her cigarette in an ashtray and said, "Leland, why don't you talk to me? Aren't I talkable to?"

" 'Talkable to.' See, that's why I'm crazy about you, the things you say." He took the last drag on his cigarette. "Anyway, I thought dames were supposed to go for the strong silent type."

"Maybe, but nobody goes for the strong *mute* type. You know, you have nice muscles because you exercise. Maybe you should try exercising your vocal cords. It might change your life."

He rolled on his side and placed his arm over her breasts. "I want you to be my second mistress."

"What! Who's your first mistress?"

"It ain't important for you to know that."

"Is she prettier than me?"

"No."

"Is she smarter than me?"

"No."

"Well?"

"Well, see, we been together eight years now."

"Eight years, really? That's it? Longevity? If that's your reason, how come you buy a new motorcar every year?"

Leland had a secret fantasy of inventing some kind of device that would get women to shut up. Probably it would involve electricity somehow but that was as far as his thinking had gone. It would earn him millions of dollars and the gratitude of every man in the world. He tried kissing Roxy to shut her up but she got up, got dressed, and left.

July 7, 2020

With Carrie Phillips appeased and Susie Hodder silent, Grace Miller Cross was the next unpredictable box of fireworks for the blackmail fund. She was considered so dangerous that Harry Daugherty went to

Washington to handle her himself. The first thing he wanted to do was destroy her credibility. He went to see Ned McLean at the *Washington Post*. Harry's first idea was to have Mrs. Cross smeared in a gossip column but not even Ned was that sleazy. Or rather, he thought the maneuver would not suffice.

"Is this about that dolly that Warren's got working for him out of his Senate office?" Ned asked.

"That's her. She's going around letting people know she's got the letters. Do you know, Warren's crazy enough to write these girls on Senate stationery."

"Jeez-us. That man just thinks with the wrong head. But I always say, if you want to get something out of a dame, send another dame to talk to her."

"Yeah, that's what we say. Got anybody in mind?"

Ned thought of his women's page editor but she wasn't tough enough. "Give me a little time."

Harry didn't wait. He called his new bootlegging partner, the famous private eye Billy Burns, to town. He was told to break into Grace's apartment. At first Burns botched the job. He invaded the home of a Mrs. George Cross at an apartment on G Street, not Mrs. James Cross at the Wardman Park Inn. Burns took some papers from the latter place but found no Harding letters.

Back to the *Post* at Fourteenth and E streets went Harry. Ned poured both of them two fingers of Scotch. Ned was short but he would be handsome if he didn't look half-soused most of the time. Ned had a nice mustache, dark hair with just a dignified swoosh of widow's peak, and a sincere-looking, earnest face.

"Jess tells me you've got a girl working for you, his ex-wife," Ned said. "She's got brass balls for a dame. Why not use her?"

Harry did not want to give Roxy any more standing or credit in the Harding campaign but Ned was right, they needed her. He sent a wire telling her to catch the next train to Washington.

The gag was, Roxy would pretend to be Ned McLean's agent, seeking to buy the love letters so the paper would score the scoop of the year.

Roxy checked into the Hotel Washington and took Grace to lunch at the Ebbit House on "newspaper row" on Fourteenth Street near the *Post*.

"Are you a reporter?" was Grace's first question.

"Oh no. Mr. McLean insists on the utmost secrecy. If I were one of his reporters, this would be all over the newsroom by this time tomorrow and then one of the other papers might pick up on it."

"So how do you know him?"

"Let's just say that I handle business matters for him."

Grace gave a slight shrug. She obviously thought that Roxy was one of Ned's girlfriends.

With little prospect of small talk to establish rapport, Roxy said, "Miss Cross, listen, you're missing the big picture here if you insist on keeping those letters secret. You know the Post will pay you very well for them. And even more, you'll be famous after they write you up. This will be the biggest story of the year by far. You can go anywhere, go into show business if you want."

Grace showed no flicker of interest. "And now, let's be blunt, what is even more important, you will bring down that man, that four-flusher. You can tell by the way he's treated you, he's doesn't have the makings of a president. It's practically your patriotic duty."

Grace did not yawn but tried to give the impression she was stifling one. "Oh, I think I'll just hold on to the letters for a while. Cash, you know, cash is worth a lot more to me than publicity. You newspaper people, getting on the front page is all you think about. Me, I think, wait until Warren is elected. And then these letters will be worth, who knows how much more."

Roxy removed the napkin on her lap, wadded it, and put it on the table with a gesture of pique. "You know something, Miss Cross? I think you're bluffing and I'm going to call your bluff. I don't think you have any letters at all, you just want the attention." Then she gave the smile you give people when you want them to think you have seen through them.

Unruffled, Grace reached for the handbag under her chair. She unclasped it, withdrew an unmarked brown envelope evidently containing papers, and brandished it like a pistol.

Roxy, who was young and lithe, snatched the envelope from Grace's hand, rose, turned, and sprinted out of the restaurant, nearly colliding with waiters twice. She left Grace screaming at the table.

Sure enough, the envelope contained a few of Warren's love letters—but were they all of them? Roxy had the desk clerk call Harry in his hotel room. He came down, glanced at the envelope and nodded to Roxy with an expression that said, "I expected no less." They went to see Ned McLean at the *Post*.

Ned read a couple of the letters and whistled. "This man missed his calling," he said. "He should be writing romantic novels. Really, he has a way with words."

"Yeah. You of course will keep this matter confidential," said Harry, reaching for the loose pages on Ned's desk. He kept the envelope with the other letters clutched in his left hand.

Ned looked at him with disbelief. He said, "Only the goddamnedest, biggest fool in the world would ever expect a newspaper publisher to keep anything confidential."

Harry looked stricken. Ned maintained a hard poker face, staring at Harry for a minute before breaking up at his little joke. Roxy already was laughing.

Grace had to be compensated for the theft of her letters, so Ned sent her on a tour of Europe with his society editor. The blackmail fund paid for it.

So the Grace Cross problem appeared solved, at least until after the election. Billy Burns put a tail on her but he was called off after a couple of weeks. That left the blackmail squad to enforce the silence of Augusta Cole, who had aborted Warren's baby, and who boarded Warren's sister Carolyn in her home. In his own research, Leland Jackson found Ruth Cecilia Hoyle, who had an illegitimate son by Harding, who had arranged for the boy's adoption. These women were paid modest amounts to sign affidavits denying any rumors of an affair with Harding.

As for Gertrude Knisley, a New York woman whom Harding had helped to buy a cabin in the Adirondacks and had promised to marry—Burns discovered that she had committed suicide.

That apparently completed the mission of the blackmail squad, which disbanded with a party for the occasion.

Ah, Warren thought, but nobody, certainly not the Duchess, knows about my darling Nan. She doesn't want money, she just wants to be with me. And she says she takes the precaution of burning my letters. And our baby daughter is eight, nine months old already.

Nan Britton, Harding's twenty-three-year-old mistress, had nurtured a crush on him since she was a schoolgirl in Marion. He set her up in Asbury Park, New Jersey, where she gave birth to Elizabeth Ann "Christian." The father supposedly was Lieutenant Christian, serving his country overseas. Next, Nan moved to Chicago and hired a nanny. Warren provided sufficient money.

August 24, 1920

Eddie Rickenbacker buzzed the town of Marion in a Spad S.XIII, the model he had flown into glory as America's ace of aces in the Great War. It was painted in its war colors of olive drab with a bright red cowling over the engine. Rickenbacker found the Harding house below him right away, as thousands of people were jammed into the yard and the streets. He made two low passes over the crowd, waggling his wings. The folks cheered and waved and he waved back. On two more passes he dropped tiny sandbags attached to little red-white-and-blue paper parachutes.

They rained on the largest crowd Marion had ever seen. The parachutes were printed "The Harding Theatrical League Salutes Our Next President Aug. 24 1920" or "America Wants Mrs. Warren Harding for First Lady Aug. 24 1920." Rickenbacker was a Republican.

The so-called Theatrical League was forty Hollywood stars. They stood on the now-famous front porch behind its tall white columns. The Duchess had organized this extravaganza with the help of the Republican national chairman, who had movie industry connections. Florence had married politics with show business, inventing the celebrity endorsement. She did so with a panache that Harry Daugherty, who held the title of campaign manager, never had.

Every boldface name in Hollywood was there, including Al Jolson, Ethel Barrymore, Mary Pickford, Douglas Fairbanks, Lillian Gish, and even the notorious singer and actress Mary Louise "Texas" Guinan. Florence had wanted to exclude Guinan, who had falsely claimed to lose seventy pounds in a weight-loss scam, but the Republican chairman was smitten with her and sent an invitation.

Al Jolson, the biggest star in the country, bounded to the front steps to snag a paper parachute from the air. Inspired, he climbed back to the top step to sing the Harding campaign song, which he had written. "We're here to make a fuss / Warren Harding, you're the man for us!" Accompanied by a jazz band imported from Chicago, Jolson waved his arms in time, then doffed his hat to wave above his head. The crowd cheered so lustily that Jolson segued into his biggest hit, "Swanee," followed by "Avalon," the first national hit record based on jazz. The other stars came down and stepped into the crowd, helping to lead a singalong. The Glee Club of Columbus asked the band to play "Flo from Ohio" for them, their tribute to Florence. Thousands of people swayed and sang together. Rickenbacker did a couple of loops in the sky and flew away.

I'm not starstruck, Roxy told herself, these actors are people just like us. She was elated nonetheless—not by Hollywood glamour, but by the excitement that falls to a very few lucky presidential campaigns: the conviction that they cannot lose. The crowd, the reporters, the newsreel cameramen, they all felt it. They were with the winner. The war was over but the country remained fed up with Wilson and his war and his war rationing and his postwar inflation. And the Democratic presidential nominee, James Cox, was as inspiring as a gnawed bone.

This is it, Roxy thought, this is how I am going to be the first female presidential adviser in history. Besides first ladies, that is. Mr. Daugherty and the Duchess are against me, but I am making myself indispensable to Mr. Harding and he has to know it. She edged herself close to Jolson by way of looking for Leland Jackson, who was on the porch behind the Hardings as their bodyguard. Florence and Warren were clapping in time but then Warren stopped, withdrew a pack of cigarettes from his waistcoat pocket, and proceeded to light up.

Florence turned around to face her husband to hide him from the newsreel cameras. She yanked the cigarette from his lips and tossed it to the floor. "Warren Harding, don't you ever smoke a cigarette in public. Cigars and pipes are all right but cigarettes just seem to infuriate lots of people who have a prejudice against them. Many men think they are sissified." Warren said nothing. He gently pushed Florence back to his right side and smiled for the cameras. Florence said, "Let's move to the other side for the photographers over there." Actually, she had spied Roxy near Jolson and did not want Warren to get anywhere close to that young and beautiful woman. Slow, measured steps and a chin held high expressed her disdain.

Charles Forbes, the man they had met at Pearl Harbor, who had spent the last four years befriending the Hardings, shook Warren's hand and kissed Florence on the cheek. Then Florence bumped into the Republican chairman. That man had chewed Harry out about the wastrel blackmail fund but now was so thrilled that he clasped Florence in a bear hug. At first a stone, she softened and hugged him back. Party bosses had been troubled because both Hardings would go into funks during which it seemed they didn't really want the White House.

"Don't worry about the Duchess," Warren told the bosses. "No woman ever lived who objected to becoming, if possible, the first lady of the land."

"Don't worry about Warren," Florence told the bosses."There isn't a United States senator who does not believe that he should be president."

The concerns of the bosses were warranted. Flossie's soul was rent between her conviction that the White House was their destiny and her fear of Madame Marcia's prophecy. Warren's soul was battered by the fear that he was too small for the biggest job. Plus, the danger that his philandering might surface.

All of them should have worried more about Warren's health. He was up to 220 pounds with high blood pressure, a weak heart, occasional spots of blood in his urine, and unhealthful habits.

But nobody could hold dark thoughts on such a festive day. A reporter had written that delphiniums were Florence's favorite flower, so she posed with bouquets of delphiniums for all the photographers in turn. She had her silk neckbands dyed the saturated blue of delphiniums so that "Harding blue" was rivaling the old "Alice blue" of Alice Roosevelt's as a fashion statement.

As the newsreel men moved back to capture Warren's speech, Al Jolson ambled among the folks on the porch, offering swigs from a silver flask. Prohibition against making or selling booze had taken effect the previous January, but drinking from your personal stock was legal. Everyone, especially the Hollywood crowd, drank through the afternoon. The Hardings did not imbibe in public but Warren, Harry, and Jess had started the day with eye-openers.

Florence tried a few times to straighten Jolson's tie but then gave it up. "This is our farewell to alcohol," Jolson said as he presented his flask.

"No, it isn't," replied more than one reveler.

Warren gave a typical "front porch campaign" speech. "We need citizens who are less concerned about what their government can do for them, and more concerned about what they can do for the nation." Harding's political antennae sensed that nobody was in the mood to listen to a speech. He cut it short and invited the movie stars to autograph Harding for President posters for the townspeople.

As the sun lowered in the August haze the town followed the Hollywood folks back to the train station, where they boarded their chartered Pullman sleeping cars for the trip west. Al Jolson, though, stayed behind as the Hardings' guest because he was judged too drunk to travel. The

Hardings also put Charles Forbes up for the night so that he could catch the next day's train to his job in Oregon.

That evening after the hubbub was over Warren, still aglow from the marvelous day, said, "Duchess, let's go out to a moving picture just like we did when we were young." They started to walk out the door for the PhotoPlay with Leland and Roxy when Jolson shouted, "I'm coming too." Nobody said no to him but before getting up he passed out on the couch again.

The show on the bill was *Why Women Sin*. "Men don't wonder why women sin," Warren cracked. "They wonder why they don't do it more often." Florence and Roxy showed no reaction; Leland barely chuckled.

The film starts. A man neglects his wife because he is obsessed with being elected governor. A political boss opposes the candidate. The boss frames the man by setting up a phony tryst that captures the man in a compromising moment. All is lost until the hero, a detective, arrives to arrest the conspirators. The man, realizing the error of his ways, begs his wife's forgiveness for neglecting her. She forgives him.

It was not the best choice for a night out for Warren and Florence Harding.

September 6, 1920

Warren interrupted his front porch campaign to attend a meeting of Republican leaders in Chicago. Harry had not scheduled enough time to hold a rally at a Chicago arena, so they just planned a speech from the rear platform of a train car at Union Station. Florence had wanted to visit wounded vets at Cook County Hospital but Warren asked her to stay with him because she was popular with the crowds. Also, she could assay crowd reactions as well as anyone aboard.

The mostly Irish crowd, waving green placards, cheered. If even Irish Democrats are for us, the Hardings concluded, we're in.

Jess did not get to hear the applause. He had been sent to Woodlawn Avenue on the South Side to placate Nan Britton in the apartment she shared with her sister. Jess disliked Warren's young mistress but even so, before knocking he performed his ritual of adjusting his tie, yanking down his waistcoat, and patting down his hair.

"I waited and waited for him but he never came. But, but he promised!" Nan pouted.

"Miss Nan, believe me, he is as sorry as he can be, but there just is not enough time today. We have to get to the Wisconsin State Fair before it closes."

"But I thought he wanted to see baby Elizabeth!"

"Um, ahem, Miss Nan, you know that he has said he never wants to see the child, although he will willingly, full-heartedly even, support her." Jess made a show of looking at his watch. Time to go.

"But I wanted to tell him something that will help him win the election!"

That got Jess's attention. He raised his right eyebrow in that quizzical look of his.

"Mr. Cox once made a pass at me. Really. I was sitting in the front row when he came to give a speech. He was giving a talk about trust. And he walked by me and leaned over and he put his hand on my knee. And he said, 'Let me tell you, young lady, I'd trust you anywhere in the world.' "

"Permit me to ask for clarification. You are talking about James Cox, the Democratic candidate for president?"

"That's right."

"No, no, no, Miss Nan. We have a deal with them. We don't spread stories about his skirt-chasing and they don't spread stories about Warren's Negro blood."

"Warren doesn't have any Negro blood!"

"Yes, I know, but what difference does that make? The rumors are going around but we have the Democrats' word that they aren't propagating them."

"But what does Warren say about these awful rumors?"

"He says for all he knows, one of his ancestors might have jumped the fence."

Nan commenced an admixture of laughing and crying, dabbing at her eyes with a handkerchief. This girl can cry without smearing her makeup or mussing her hair, Jess observed in admiration.

He barely made it back to Union Station in time. He stepped aboard the *Superb*, the Hardings' private car. Evalyn and Ned McLean were in their own private car, the *Enquirer*. Evalyn, talking with Florence in the *Superb*, told Jess, "The boys are next door playing poker."

Actually, next door the boys had put aside the cards to talk politics. Roxy was fixing the drinks. She still had no official position with the campaign.

"What do you think of our slogan, 'Back to Normalcy'?" Harry asked as she handed him a bourbon and water.

"Better than back to abnormalcy."

Leland laughed louder than the quip merited.

"You should have seen all the micks out there," Harry told Jess, who was sitting on a bench apparently just watching the scenery roll by. "Without the ethnic vote in the big cities, the Democrats don't have a chance."

Harding nodded cheerfully. Jess opened a briefcase and handed him a folded copy of that morning's *Chicago Tribune*. Its political columnist speculated on who would fill Harding's Cabinet. Harry Daugherty would have a high position, although of course no president would ever install his campaign manager as attorney general. That would be unseemly.

"The main reason I want to be in Washington is to protect Harding from the crooks," Harry had told the

Tribune. "I know how trustful Harding is and I know who all the crooks are, and I want to protect Harding from them."

Jess, Roxy, and Leland expected at least some kind of mild rebuke from Warren. What presidential candidate wants his closest advisor to call him naive in the public prints? But Warren and Ned McLean were amused. Ned said, "Warren, that means you've got to put Harry in as attorney general and myself as his deputy. Then I'll print all those crooks' names in the *Post*."

Warren said, "Are presidents exempt from libel and slander laws? Harry, you're the lawyer here, you tell me. See, I want to name all those crooks myself and get the credit for it."

As Harry took a second to think of a retort Jess concluded that this conversation was unfruitful. He went back to the *Superb* to see if the Duchess needed anything. She relied on him more every day. At least he told himself that.

Jess had stayed in expensive hotels but he had never seen a hotel room as swank as these private Pullman cars. The leather armchairs and sofa looked plush enough to seat the fat man at the circus. The ceiling was forest green and cream; the carpet and window dressings were a softer, embracing green while the window frames were accented in gold. The windows in this rolling palace were of beveled glass.

Florence and Evalyn sat in armchairs with an oval pedestal table between them. Both women were smoking but only Evalyn held a drink.Extending her arm with an elegant flourish, Evalyn said, "Jess, dear, get me another Scotch, won't you please?" He took the glass and went to the fully stocked bar of polished mahogany.

"Do you know what Alice said?" he heard Evalyn say. "She said that you want to be first lady so you can get back at all the people in Washington who have slighted you."

"Oh, you know, I can't help liking Alice," Florence said insincerely. "I just wish she wasn't so brittle."

"But she's right, you know. You can kick all of their asses. Revenge is sweet."

"No, I want to devote my position to helping our poor veterans."

Jess wondered as he handed the scotch to Evalyn, why is the Duchess being so righteous? Just then Roxy came in from the vestibule to the *Enquirer*, looking determined. She had concluded that the only way to get to Warren was to go through Florence first. At first she had asked Jess to serve as an intermediary but he begged off, afraid to offend either Florence or Harry.

"Good afternoon, Mrs. Harding. I have wanted to have a chat with you for quite some time. May I?"

The Duchess pursed her lips even more than usual but she indicated that Roxy should take a seat on the sofa with Jess.

Roxy smoothed her skirts and said, "Mrs. Harding, I have always admired the ways you have advocated for women's rights. Why, in a couple of months, you will be the first woman in American history to cast a vote for your husband for president!"

"Yes, as all the reporters keep reminding me." The implied message: Why are you wasting my time?

"Well, you can't imagine how much it pleases me that we have finally won the right to vote. Can you believe that the Nineteenth Amendment was not even ratified until just three weeks ago?"

"Yes, it was a long struggle." Meaning: Get on with it.

Roxy's claim of support for women's suffrage was not entirely accurate. It bruised her ego to admit it, but she had never marched for the cause. Instead, she had accepted the "blood tax" argument as reasonable. Only men paid a "blood tax." Women never had to go to war and shed their blood for the flag, so how did they deserve to vote? Now Roxy believed that if women had a voice they might prevent such outrages as fighting foreign wars and spying on innocent citizens.

Envy and guilt had been feelings foreign to her soul, but she had come to envy the marchers, some of whom went to jail for their insurrection, and to taste a pinch of guilt over having let her side down. She was unsure how to handle these novel feelings, except that there was one door she might push open to bring women further into the twentieth century. She could join the Harding White House as a counselor to the president. The first woman in the White House who was not a maid, cook, stenographer, or first lady.

"Mrs. Harding, may I ask, did you read the column in this morning's *Tribune*?"

The Duchess removed her pince-nez to rub the red marks on either side of her nose, an infallible sign of limited patience. "Yes. I do wish that Mr. Daugherty would not speak so freely to the press. The very idea that Warren needs protection from crooks!" Frowning, she shook her head.

Damn, this is going badly. Roxy took a moment to gather her thoughts. "Actually, Mrs. Harding, if you will forgive me, Mr. Harding does have many friends and he tends to be too trusting of those friends. That is not a criticism, you understand. I should have so many friends.

"But I believe he could benefit by having somebody in his circle who could warn him about those no-accounts who might try to take advantage of him and his position. And I think this should be a person with actual authority and a person who serves on his staff. And"—she leaned forward and executed one of those shifts in tone that telegraphed something serious on the threshold—"I believe that I am that person."

The Duchess stopped rubbing the red spots but did not move her hand or raise her face. Roxy glanced over at Evalyn. She was staring at her in astonishment. Jess was studying his shoes.

"I believe I am qualified because I understand the financing of a presidential campaign"—a tactful, she hoped, allusion to the blackmail fund—"and because I know all the people involved, the people who think they should get something just because they know Mr. Harding. And I believe that Mr. Harding trusts me and respects my views.

"But it's more than that," she continued more briskly. "It would be a great advance for women's rights, don't you see? To have a woman serving in the White House at a level above a stenographer. Of course my duties would not need to be spelled out for the press. They could just put me down as an assistant to the president or something."

The Duchess replaced the pince-nez and looked at Roxy without expression. "Miss Stinson," she said, "I do not presume to advise my husband about personnel matters."

Roxy tried hard not to show her deflation. She had expected contrariness from the Duchess but not an outright, obvious lie. She had anticipated at least an acknowledgement of her audacity, or at the very least an endorsement of the advancement of women. "Well, I hope you at least will think it over, Mrs. Harding." They shared a few meaningless remarks for the sake of politeness and then Roxy returned to the *Enterprise*.

Jess did not follow her but continued his study of the floor. When at length he looked up he was surprised to see Florence put her hand over her eyes and make choking sounds.

"Oh, Evalyn, I had a conviction that Warren Harding would be nominated and he was. Oh, Evalyn, I see only tragedy ahead."

September 7, 1920

Harry Daugherty got off the Harding train at Milwaukee to head south to Oklahoma. Warren owed the oil millionaire Jake Hamon a big favor. To pay him off, Harry would offer an appointment as secretary of the interior. It wasn't too early to make up a Cabinet, was it?

Hamon's wife, Georgia, had left him after he launched an affair with nineteen-year-old Clara Smith. He arranged for Clara to marry one of his nephews so that he could hire his "niece" as his "secretary." Jake Hamon was Florence's cousin by marriage, so his wife, Georgia, was able to make an appointment with Harry Daugherty in Chicago. Georgia Hamon wanted Harry to carry a message to Jake: He had to dump Clara if he wanted her to live with him as his wife in Washington. Harry would keep his word, he would deliver the message, because he didn't want any scandals involving the Harding Cabinet in the press.

Harry opened the door to an empty train compartment, stowed his suitcase overhead, and sat on a bench, not happy about his errand to Oklahoma but relieved to get away from the hubbub of the campaign too. Another man opened the door but Harry gave him such a malicious glare that the man closed the door to continue up the aisle and leave Harry by himself.

As the train huffed out of the station he stretched out his legs and heeded the clackety-clack of the wheels. That background noise always helped him to think. As did a cigar, which he lit with full ceremony, shaking the match and placing it in the ashtray built into the arm rest. Harry leaned back, clasped his fingers behind his head, and ruminated:

Well, the *New York Times* called me a third-rate lawyer. Screw them. When I become attorney general they'll see what kind of a lawyer I am. Warren will make me A.G., I'm sure of it. So then I will be in charge of enforcing the

Volstead Act. The law that says a free people can't slake an honest thirst. So to get a drink they will have to deal with crooks.

Yeah, I've known crooks all my life. I could tell them all the real reason why people aren't honest, why it looks like every politician is a crook, every cop is on the take. The fact of the matter is, most men are mediocre. That's a horrible thing to have to face up to. No man wants to admit it. But if you counted deeds instead of pretty words, crookedness would win by a landslide. (The corners of Harry's mouth turned up in pleasure at this epigram.) Actual, real talent, real brains, that's as scarce as hen's teeth and so taking dough on the sly . . .that's how the mediocre men . . . it's their weapon against the society that they think is not giving them their due. What a cruel fate, to know you are only average. So what a swell consolation, that they would be great if only they had got their rights. But the trouble is, most of them are dumb enough to get caught.

And now they're saying I was crooked, the way I got Warren the nomination. I guess the most famous thing I'll ever say, I was spouting off to some reporters and I said the convention would be deadlocked and so the party bosses would sit around a hotel room about two o'clock in the morning and pick Warren Harding. But I never called it a "smoke-filled room." Some reporter put that in. But now that it's a press cliché it will live until the end of time.

And then the dumbest thing of all, there's a rumor going around that when Cabot Lodge asked Warren if he wanted to be president, he said, "I don't know, I'll have to ask my wife." What a crock of shit. Any man who is surprised to wake up in the White House is a fool and Warren Harding is no fool. What Lodge actually said was that Warren shouldn't be nominated because he's of such a lower class that he lives in a two-family house.

Well, some men are born great, some achieve greatness, and some are born in Ohio. We've had, let's see, McKinley, Garfield, Hayes, Grant, four Ohio presidents since Lincoln died. Republicans can't win without carrying Ohio. And Warren will attract the women's vote now that they can vote for president. The Duchess will be an asset, too. They actually touted her for first lady at that Hollywood rally. I can't remember any campaign ever doing that before.

The Democrats went ahead and nominated their own newspaper publisher from Ohio, James Cox of Dayton. He can't work a crowd for shit. And his running mate is some young bureaucrat nobody ever heard of, Franklin D. Roosevelt. So Warren should win unless he gets in trouble with all his women scrapes.

I can't get over how all the smart people could not see our strategy. Don't they know what a gift it is, to be always underestimated? And they never perceive that Warren *wants* to be underestimated. Another thing, the delegates were exhausted as the convention dragged on. They didn't settle on Warren until the tenth ballot and by that time everybody's hotel bill was piling up. Warren might be the first president to be installed because of high hotel bills.

And now all the smart people are saying Warren is dumb because he gives these speeches that are just blasts of rhetorical trumpets that really don't mean anything. How can they not see the wit behind it? Don't they imagine that Warren knows what he's doing? He even made up his own word for it, *bloviating*. How dumb can he be if he makes up his own word for it? He knows that political rallies are a form of entertainment, just like all the photoplays coming out of Hollywood now. And you have to think that some people in the audience get the joke behind the oratory, we're all in this together, it's a farce and we choose to call it democracy.

It's funny how people like to play make-believe in politics, come to think of it. Like Jess, he goes around like a gangster, a real bruno, but he's actually quite a sensitive fellow. Well, who doesn't wear a mask, come down to it.

*

Harry did not sleep well in the Pullman and was less than exuberant when Jake Hamon picked him up at at Oklahoma City. Jake looked the part: cowboy hat, fringed leather jacket, cowboy boots. A worn and weathered face—this man is an ambulatory stereotype, Harry thought. I wonder why so many people are stereotypes? As Jake drove them to his ranch on a dirt road the flat barren landscape gave Harry an unexpected sense of nervousness. How could people live without trees and hills around them?

Jake's cook prepared an elaborate wild duck supper. Harry admired the head of a bison on the dining room wall. "Teddy Roosevelt shot that buff'lo," Jake said.

"That's bullshit, Jake, and you know it's not a 'buff'lo' but a bison," Harry said.

Jake grinned. "Well, that's what I like to tell my Republican friends, anyway. And Teddy really did spend a night here. I was just a young man but I gave him a handsome contribution to his campaign."

Harry pointed his cigar at the bison as if offering it a smoke. "You know, Jake, you're right, Oklahoma is still the Wild West in some ways. And because you are so familiar with western issues, Senator Harding is considering you for Interior."

"I would be de—" At that moment his "niece" Clara stormed in. The strap of her bright red dress hung off her left shoulder and down her arm. Funny the little things you notice, Harry thought. Not a real blonde. She was barefoot, too.

"Jake, goddamn you, you son of a bitch! What, are you ashamed of me? I'm not good enough to sit down with you and your high and mighty friends? Fuck you!"

She picked up the carcass of a duck off the platter and flung it at Jake. It hit him above the right eye. A good aim, Harry thought.

Jake calmly took a napkin and wiped his face. He dabbed at the spots of grease that had fallen on his shirt and brushed the duck off his lap onto the floor. He slowly rose, went to Clara and slapped her, knocking her against a sideboard. He picked up the empty chair at the end of the table and clubbed her in the ribs. She howled and ran out, clutching her side.

"Please forgive that most unfortunate interruption," Jake said, sitting back down. "Why don't we have some coffee? I will call the cook."

"Um, Jake, wouldn't it be better if we resumed our discussion tomorrow? You obviously need to attend to some domestic matters."

"No, we were—" There was Clara again. She had gone into the bedroom, opened a chifforobe and a drawer. Therein was a Smith & Wesson .38 Special, which she now held in her right hand. Her left hand pressed on ribs that might be broken. She was gasping and crying.

Again Jake rose without a word and approached her. Clara did not speak either. She fired twice. The first round missed and the second got Jake in the liver.

With Jake supine and bleeding on the floor, Harry knelt beside him. "You're gonna be okay, you're gonna be okay." He could barely feel a pulse. Jake did not try to talk and his pupils were dilated. Probably he was going into shock. The Mexican cook ran in, grabbed a napkin and pressed it to Jake's midriff. Harry grunted "call a doctor" as he rose and left. He did not look at Clara, who had dropped the gun to the floor and was still screaming as though she would never stop.

Jake had a new Nash Touring Car, silver-gray with a black top and fenders and red wheel spokes. It was unlocked. Harry did not note its beauty as he sat behind the wheel and forced himself to calm down enough to remember how to start the damn thing. Spark advance, then throttle, then choke, then the ignition button, then delicately pull back the choke.

As he drove the forty-five minutes to Oklahoma City he sometimes had to steer into the prairie wind, it was so strong. The canvas top of the car fluttered noisily. The sun was kissing the horizon behind him, casting the landscape into a dry, sickly tawny as Harry cursed this desolate country. Harry's mind was running faster than the car:

Jesus, I've seen some things in my time but I never saw a dolly plug her man in the guts with a .38. Women. They make a scene so they can shed their tears. But for chrissakes they don't shoot the sonofabitch. What did Jake think he was doing with that crazy bitch anyway? Something was cracked in that man's headbone.

What are we doing all this for, for the sake of electing Warren Harding president? A man who can't keep his pecker in his pants. And that's not even the biggest problem. The biggest problem is that he is not ruthless enough to be president. All great men have a killer instinct. However much they try to hide it. Warren wants to be everyone's pal.

Okay, I've got to settle down and think this through carefully. The Mexican didn't know my name, he'll just say that some gringo was there with Señor Jake. If Clara's ribs are broken she can plead self-defense and get off. Probably even if she's just bruised. But I was never there. She's got to say that . . .

Harry parked the car at the train station. He used the stationmaster's phone to call the chairman of the Oklahoma Republican Party. He had joined Jake in delivering the state's delegation to Harding at a critical moment at the convention. The chairman would have somebody pick up

Jake's car and otherwise would know what to do. Harry caught the last train north that night.

Warren Harding said when he heard the news, "Too bad he had that one fault, that admiration for women."

Harry stared into Warren's face in a futile search for the slightest hint of self-deprecating irony. No, Warren really meant it as an offhand observation. Is he that lacking in self-awareness? Admiration for women. Harry would never forget that phrase. He turned and left Warren alone.

Jake died a week later with his wife Georgia holding his hand. Clara received one final expenditure from the blackmail fund. She was acquitted at trial. Harry Daugherty was not called as a witness because he was never there.

*

On the train back to Ohio, Leland Jackson pulled the brim of his cowboy hat low over his forehead, hoping that nobody would see his red, wet eyes. He sat half-crouched and made odd gurgling sounds. Roxy wanted to comfort him but did not know how. "When it hurts," she said, "don't try to hold it in, let it out."

Leland seemed to hiccup, twice. "Jake was better'n a pa to me," he said. "I'm gonna go down there and strangle that bitch that shot him."

"Come on, that won't bring Jake back," Roxy said. "He's gone and there's nothing you can do."

"He was like a pa to me. He took me in when I was just a no-account runaway kid. He's the one who taught me to ride and shoot, all that cowboy shit."

"Really? How long did you stay with him?"

"It was just gonna be a summer but it ended up four years. I left 'stead'a graduating from high school."

"You left? To do what?"

"Just bummed around until Mr. Daugherty called me in Omaha."

"Because Jake recommended you to him."

"Yeah."

"So you owe a lot to this Mr. Hamon. No wonder you are grieving."

"Aw, leave me alone, will ya?"

That night Roxy sneaked into Leland's sleeping berth, careful lest somebody spot her. She did not care about conventional morality but she did not flaunt her transgressions either. The compartment was so cramped that, standing, she contorted herself to get undressed while Leland watched her with something close to religious awe.

When she crawled into bed he said, "You know you're my only girlfriend now. I want you and nobody else."

"Do you think I'd be here otherwise?"

" 'Otherwise.' See, that's why I'm with you. You're so smart that some of it is bound to rub off on me."

Part Three: The White House

March 4, 1921

Warren Harding worried about Woodrow Wilson. In October 2019 Wilson suffered a major stroke. He had undertaken a punishing whistle-stop tour of Western states to sell his League of Nations. Wilson held the delusion, common to presidents, that if he could just speak directly to the American people, then all the obstructionists, all the fools and knaves in Washington would fall away. Wilson ignored his doctors and as a result now lay incapacitated. For seventeen months his wife Edith in effect had acted as president, though she denied it. What Harding worried about: that Wilson would not be able to sit up by himself in the car to the inauguration.

By tradition, the president-elect and the outgoing president ride together from the White House to the Capitol for the inauguration ceremonies. President-elect Harding and President Wilson were to be the first to take a car instead of a carriage. But how could Woodrow walk out from the North Portico, let alone maneuver himself into a limousine? Harding fretted that the ceremonies might be hampered by an invalid, deflecting attention from the star of the day, Warren G. Harding.

His courtesy call on Wilson after he was elected president in a landslide had not been encouraging. Ike Hoover, the chief usher, took him up to the Yellow Oval Room. Woodrow looked ghastly. Seated in an armchair and propped up by pillows, Wilson had that wax-paper face that reminded Harding of the Duchess's when she nearly died in that Columbus hospital.

"Senator Harding, I congratulate you on your victory. I pledge to you the utmost cooperation from my administration for a peaceful transfer of power," Wilson said. The left side of his mouth was frozen and he talked out of the right side. A blanket covered the left side of his body.

The dreary scene prompted a sober observation in Wilson's visitor. Well, Harding thought, a president is just a man after all, and not usually a fine example of one either. Harding uttered the usual pieties, including his prayers for the president's swift recovery.

"Sir," Wilson said in something that sounded like a plea but with his impaired voice Harding could not be sure, "be kind enough to permit me one more time to urge you to support the League of Nations. Generations of peace or war rest on the outcome." His rheumy eyes turned to Harding, expressing an almost scary appeal.

"Mr. President," Harding said, "that is the business of the United States Senate. As president, I will have little influence myself."

Wilson smirked—if that twist of his mouth was a smirk—at this sophistry and did not deign to reply. Harding felt rather abashed himself. "Mr. President," he said, "you fought a noble fight for your ideals. Nobody could have worked harder than you did."

Edith Wilson broke the ensuing silence. She had a broad face with a wide, full mouth. Cut her hair, Harding thought, and she would look like a man. She addressed the question Harding could not ask. "Our enemies are saying that I sign the president's papers for him. I assure you that I do not," she lied.

"Ask Ike," Wilson said, feebly raising his right arm to point at the chief usher. "He would know. I make every decision that is needed. But without my dear wife, my helpmate, I do not think that I would survive."

"We both got better than we deserved, Mr. President," Harding said. He thought that was a good line, one to end this interview on a note of courtesy. As Harding took the elevator down, he reflected that Wilson had not specifically denied that Edith signed his papers.

*

Florence previously had paid a courtesy call on Edith Wilson and that had not gone well either. When Edith had extended the invitation, Florence replied that she would be pleased to come with Evalyn McLean. Warren suspected that the Duchess intended a deliberate insult, for the Wilsons loathed the McLeans, but he did not ask his wife about it. Evalyn's and Ned's sins included spreading the joke all over Washington: "What did Mrs. Galt do when President Wilson proposed to her? She fell out of bed."

Soon Florence received Edith's handwritten note on White House stationery. "Come alone." In the Red Room she had tea with the first lady. Edith's first impression: the Duchess is over-rouged and affects a sense of grandeur which she has not earned. Florence, sensing the condescension, overreacted. She knew she was overdoing it but could not help talking too much and too loudly.

Edith interrupted. "I am certainly grateful that Mrs. McLean did not accompany you. News of her presence in this house would no doubt distress the president and his doctors have forbidden any unnecessary distress."

Florence straightened her posture and squared her shoulders. "Mr. and Mrs. McLean have been friends of

Warren Harding and myself for years. They showed us friendship when many others did not, including the occupants of this house."

Edith rose. "I am very much fatigued. My housekeeper will be pleased to give you a tour of the house. I am sure you will be happy here. Goodbye, Mrs. Harding." She turned and walked out twenty minutes before the scheduled end of the tea while also breaking the tradition of a tour by the first lady. *We'll see who can insult whom in Washington, Mrs. Harding.*

"We had a very pleasant visit. I liked her very much," Florence told reporters later.

On the morning of the inauguration, March 4, the Hardings left their rooms in the Willard Hotel to be driven two blocks to the White House. Once there, Harding saw that he had worried too much. Wilson shuffled out on Ike Hoover's arm, using a cane. With Ike's help Wilson laboriously but with dignity arranged himself in the back seat of the open Pierce-Arrow limousine. In front rode the president pro tem of the Senate and the Speaker of the House. *I wonder if we all look ridiculous in these top hats,* Harding wondered. Then, *what a thought to have on your way to becoming president. The kind of thing a small-town boy would think.*

Wilson looked so grim, maybe he wanted to ride in silence. But as the car crept up Pennsylvania Avenue he said, "My friend, you are about to have the greatest moment of your life. Most of what follows will be disappointment and gall. That is my advice to my successor. Seize and savor this moment."

"Thank you for the advice, Mr. President."

"You know I did not have an inaugural ball after my first swearing-in. Didn't think it was appropriate on such a solemn day. I took a lot of criticism for that."

Yeah, Harding thought, *that is just the kind of tight-as-sed thing you would do.*

Wilson huddled inside his black wool overcoat. "Cold today," he said. "Barely above freezing. It was much warmer when I took my first oath."

So, Harding thought, we're reduced to talking about the weather now. He ventured, "At least there are no suffragettes clamoring along the sidewalks as there were in your day. Thank God that our ladies have received the vote now."

"Yes, that was one of our Progressive projects that bore fruit," Wilson said. Actually, his support for female suffrage had been late and lukewarm.

He leaned toward Harding with an air of telling a secret. "I am going to presume to offer you one more piece of advice, my friend. Beware the weak men much more than the strong men."

"Again I am in your debt for your advice, Mr. President."

Neither spoke for the rest of the ride. At the east front of the Capitol they exited the car by protocol: first the Speaker, then the president pro tem, then Wilson, then Harding. The sun broke out of the clouds to shine on the quadrennial rite.

Wilson was helped to a seat in the front row of the temporary inaugural platform high on the Capitol steps. Florence, who had ridden in a second car with Edith Wilson in utter silence, was already standing there holding George Washington's Bible. She wore a blouse and skirt of Harding Blue; blue ostrich feathers poked from her wide-brimmed blue hat. A diamond sunburst selected by Evalyn adorned her black neckband. The white gloves were elbow-length.

At this moment, as so frequently in the past years, Florence thought: If only my father could have lived to see this. She held the Bible for Warren's left hand as the chief justice administered the oath. As Warren spoke the words, she mouthed each one along with him.

Jess sat in the fourth row, prominently displaying his badge as vice chairman of the inauguration planning committee. Harry sat on Jess's left, Roxy on his right. Some congressional magnifico, one of Nick Longworth's pals from Ohio, had tried to evict Roxy from her seat on the ground that she had no official status. Severely chastened by Jess and Harry, he retreated.

The two men had the same thought during Harding's inaugural address: No president has said anything memorable in his inaugural since Lincoln. They could hear every word clearly because the inaugural was the first to be carried over a public-address system. Typical "bloviating" but his voice still has an undeniable allure, Roxy thought. And: if only my mother could have lived to see me here. Opal Smith, too, for Jess. Imagine, a girl from Washington Court House at the inauguration of a president! Who's a friend of hers! Well, not a friend exactly, but . . .

During that celebratory noontime, Roxy, most unusually for her, felt a wave of memories and regrets, a mercurial parade of associations. Her mood perplexed her. At the very pinnacle of success, why do I feel a letdown? I know deep down that the White House is closed to me?

Warren's private luncheon with the Senate and parades occupied most of the afternoon. Then came the climax of years of toil. The Hardings entered the front doors of the North Portico of the White House as president and first lady for the first time.

Florence halted her husband for a moment. "Well, Warren Harding, I have got you the presidency. What are you going to do with it?"

Warren swallowed before answering. "May God help me, for I need it."

His prayer was heartfelt. Harding knew he was a lightweight and was too much of a patriot to want to saddle his country with a lightweight.

July 2, 1921

Roxy squealed with a stirring in her blood over something she had never seen before. An unearthly singing surged up her torso. In a heavyweight championship fight the challenger had just staggered the champion with a pile-driving right to the jaw. Roxy half-rose to her feet and clenched Jess's forearm so hard that he yelped in pain. Their cries were unheard in the roar of 90,000 people.

Jack Dempsey, the champ, regained his footing and threw an astounding twenty-five punches in the next thirty-one seconds. The bell saved the challenger, Georges Carpentier, who managed to waddle to his corner. Everyone in the outdoor arena in New Jersey cheered and screamed after the second round of the "fight of the century."

Roxy had bet $100 on Dempsey because he was an American and because betting is what one does at boxing matches. Just to be contrary, Jess had bet the same amount on the Frenchman, who enjoyed a better press. The promoters had painted Carpentier as a dashing hero in the Great War while Dempsey was falsely called a draft dodger.

As she sat and caught her breath between rounds Roxy said, "My God, Jess, look at that! Look to your left!"

There sat, of all people, Vice President Calvin Coolidge with Alice Roosevelt Longworth. Alice flourished a long black cigarette holder while Coolidge looked as he always did, like a stone-faced undertaker. Roxy saw Leland seated behind Coolidge and added, "It's true what they say, Washington really is like a small town, isn't it? Even here in Jersey City, it seems."

Harding had been in office just a few months and Leland had been rewarded with a cushy job in the Secret Service, assigned to protect Coolidge. The vice president was so anonymous and so boring, who would take the trouble to shoot him?

Anyway, Roxy often preferred Jess's company to Leland's. Jess was always a gentleman.

With another squeeze of his arm to show appreciation, she surveyed the crowd. Lots of women here—was that normal? Surely not. At ringside, a pompous announcer sat before a microphone. It was the first radio broadcast of a title fight. Here and there were movie cameras operated by men in the employ of (in Jess's name) Attorney General Harry Daugherty.

Ding! In round three Carpentier, fifteen pounds lighter than the champ, was so clearly outboxed that Roxy started to cringe for him. *Ding!* In the fourth round Dempsey followed a left jab with a right hook. His opponent sank to the floor, out cold.

The excitement left Roxy breathing hard and the asthmatic Jess breathing even harder. For the third time she grabbed his arm. "Jess, let's check into the nearest hotel!"

"You sure?"

"When have you ever seen me not sure?"

Jess told their driver to find the best hotel in Jersey City. The car was courtesy of Harry's Justice Department. The hotel was booked full but Jess showed his Justice Department badge and got a room.

"Thank you, sweetheart," Jess said afterward as they smoked cigarettes. "You know it's been a long time. You are still a comely wench. You made me feel twenty years younger."

Roxy had never believed the ugly talk about the relationship between Jess and Harry. Here, she thought, he has just proved it wrong. She said something complimentary and took a drag on the cigarette as her mind went back to the fight. Turning on her side and propping her head on her left hand, she said, "Jess, I want to see the films of that fight. When can we see them?"

"Harry's having a movie made, I think it's just for private showings in the White House. Something for Warren to show so people will owe him a favor."

"That's nuts. Why don't we distribute it and rake off the proceeds?"

"Can't."

"Why not?"

"It's against the law."

"What! Why?"

"Because of Johnson and Jeffries."

"Who or what are Johnson and Jeffries?"

"That was the 'fight of the century' back in 1910. A colored boy named Jack Johnson beat the shit out of a white man. Jim Jeffries. Well, come on, you can't have a movie showing a black man whupping up on a white man for heavyweight champion of the world. So the states in the South said it's illegal to show fight movies. And then Congress passed the same law a few years later, I forget just when."

A light dawned, first in Roxy's head and a few moments later in Jess's.

"How can you pass a law against showing a movie? What about the First Amendment?"

Jess shrugged and tried to blow smoke rings. "You can show it, you just can't take it across state lines."

"Uh-huh. What's the penalty for breaking this law?"

"I don't know. Probably just a fine. I don't think it's a felony."

Both smoked in silence for a minute.

"You know, when I was a little girl and had just moved to Washington C.H., I heard about the time the town almost hung a colored boy. 'Cause he had raped a white woman."

"Yeah, I was there, I remember it too." He was not going to tell her that was the day he met Harry. There was a violent race riot with multiple deaths and Harry had comforted the panicked younger man.

Another silent minute.

"Let's take the movie across state lines and pay the fucking fines. The ticket sales have got to be more a lot more than the fines," Roxy said.

"Tell me again why we ever got divorced," Jess said.

The next week, acting Attorney General Daugherty called the U.S. attorney in Cincinnati. When the movie was ready it was first shown to an American Legion post there for free. Ned McLean, who owned the *Cincinnati Enquirer* as well as the *Washington Post*, published an article about what a great film it was. Then it was shown in regular theaters. Movie-goers stood in long lines to buy tickets.

An exhibitor was indicted and presented before a U.S. district judge.

"You are charged with violating"—Jess, taking notes in the courtroom, did not catch the section of the U.S. Code. "How do you plead?"

"Guilty, your honor."

The gavel came down. "You are hereby fined the sum of one thousand dollars." By arrangement, this was the maximum fine. Without a pause, the defendant reached in his coat pocket for an envelope containing ten $100 bills.

This scam then was pulled in other cities—movie distributors, theater owners, U.S. attorneys, Republican-friendly newspapers. Because the scheme was all Jess's and Roxy's idea, Harry demanded only a 20 percent cut. He said he needed money to pay back the Republican National Committee for the blackmail fund.

Sometimes Roxy and Jess met resistance. The U.S. attorney in New York was a Democrat, not inclined to do Republican grifters any favors. Roxy was sent to see him. She had long ago learned how stupid men can get in the presence of a beautiful woman. The prosecutor had the authority of professional status but she carried the authority of beauty.

She dressed conservatively, no rolled-down stockings or short skirt. For important occasions she wore a headband, not a cloche, better to display her strawberry blonde hair. Her top was sleeveless with a modest V neck. She wondered whether U.S. Attorney Adalberto Migliore could tell that her pearls were real, not fake. Admiring herself in the mirror, she thought, any man who's not a fag and under the age of eighty will succumb.

Migliore sent a car to take her from Penn Station to the courthouse in lower Manhattan. He sat behind his desk in a suit with bold stripes, which he thought made him look taller, and with the jacket fully buttoned, which he thought made him look impatient and in charge. His appointment with an out-of-town nobody was resented, granted only after a call from some flunky in Daugherty's office.

When Roxy arrived Migliore motioned for her to sit down but she stayed upright in front of his desk. "Mr. Migliore, we wish to honor our veterans by giving them the opportunity to watch our movie of the heavyweight title fight. It's really a marvelous movie, the only one of its kind. We've shown it to the American Legion and other patriotic organizations in other cities—always free of charge. Now, we are told that we can't bring it into New York. Why? Because of an outmoded and misguided federal law. Surely your office has better things to do than to prosecute such a *de minimus* matter?"

"A nice try, Miss Stinson, but I am the judge of what is worthy of prosecution in the Southern District of New York. Please sit down."

She did so with a smile. "Oh, but our veterans are so excited to see this film of the fight. Our veterans deserve to be provided some free recreation, don't you agree? We would be happy to arrange a screening for the Regular

Democratic Organization as well." (A rookie mistake—the Regular Democratic Organization was the name of the political machine in Chicago, not New York.)

Migliore had been fingering a jade letter opener on his desk. He put it down and steepled his fingertips together, leaning forward in his chair.

"Please, Miss Stinson, I was born at night but I wasn't born last night. You and your associates intend to make money by showing the film commercially."

"Why, yes, Mr. Jess Smith owns the rights to this film, as you know, and he is my former husband, as you also know. He does not control the distributors and he does not control the theater owners. He just provides the reels of film and the distributors take it from there."

"Uh-huh. And what is your role in this endeavor, Miss Stinson?"

"I am Mr. Smith's assistant. I work for a salary and for a percentage of the receipts." She chose this moment to cross her legs.

"Bully for you. Miss Stinson, do you understand what you are asking me? I am sworn to enforce the law. You are asking me to go against my oath and to ignore an egregious violation of the law."

Okay, the man was being stubborn, forget the charm-school act, it was time to roll out the artillery.

"Oh, believe me, I respect the law but again this matter is *de minimus*. And now, speaking of law enforcement, you must be working very closely with the attorney general, prosecuting all those awful bootleggers. They are selling rotten liquor and people are dying! Mr. Smith and I are old hometown friends of Mr. Daugherty, and he has often spoken to us about how he will crack down on illegal alcohol—especially"—she lowered her tone just enough for him to catch it, spoke each syllable distinctly—"especially in New York."

Migliore lived in dread of the day when Attorney General Daugherty would hand a paper to President Harding to sign. That paper would fire the U.S. attorney in New York, who would be replaced by a deserving Republican. Such would be the end of Migliore's payoffs from bootleggers. He needed to buy some time.

He leaned back and unbuttoned his suit coat. Suddenly he was all surely-we-can-reach-an-understanding. Soon the people of New York were not denied the opportunity to watch the fight in theaters.

By late that fall, the fight film had provided Roxy and Jess $20,000 each. Roxy refused to put her money into Mal Daugherty's bank even after Jess asked her to, even after Jess assured her that she had not been under federal surveillance since 1918. Harry had told him so.

As a wartime measure, the Sedition Act lapsed as soon as the peace was signed. But the Espionage Act remained in force. Roxy asked both Jess and Leland to obtain her Justice Department file to see who had reported her for disloyalty. Both men said the files had been lost in a warehouse fire in Maryland. Roxy went back to the Carnegie Library to check the back newspaper stacks and found no report of a federal warehouse fire. One thing she had learned for sure—Mal Daugherty had led the local American Protective League. She had never trusted Harry and now she equally distrusted his brother Mal.

Roxy was proud of her fight-film scam, a way of getting back at a government that had spied on her, that had whipped up hatred of German-Americans, that had suppressed a movie just because Southerners hated the colored people. She also had decided that to get a White House job she needed to approach President Harding directly. It was a matter of figuring out how and when.

July 4, 1921

Washington gossips said that Evalyn's pet marmoset had spilled red wine on President Harding's white suit during the McLeans' big Fourth of July party. The story was false—the delinquent monkey actually had misbehaved at an earlier party. There still were enough antics to make that Independence Day party of 1921 talked about for years after. It really was the time that Evalyn took off the Hope Diamond she was wearing and hung it around the neck of her dog, who pranced around the estate.

Ned McLean had bought her the Hope Diamond in Europe even though it supposedly carried a terrible curse that afflicted its every owner. "I don't worry," Evalyn explained. "I had it exorcised by a Catholic priest. In Latin, too."

Ned had inherited the eighty-acre estate in northwest Washington from his father, a brilliant businessman who sired a feckless son. Not only was the estate, called Friendship, a playground for the rich, it became tantamount to a satellite White House for the Harding administration.

Inside the salon, Warren was on his way to Friendship's eighteen-hole golf course, Florence on the lookout for Evalyn, when they were greeted by the ubiquitous Alice Roosevelt Longworth. She stood in front of a Barberini tapestry from the sixteenth century with a drink in one hand and a cigarette holder in the other. "Warren," she said in a scolding way, "I am most disappointed that you did not take my advice."

She had sent a note to their home in Marion after the election: "Nick and I implore you not to nominate Harry Daugherty as attorney general. Harry is a crook. If you don't believe me, ask Nick. Ask any other Ohio Republican in the House. Please don't let your personal and professional relationship with Harry deafen you to them."

Now Alice looked coldly at Florence. "Duchess, didn't you try to talk your husband out of appointing Harry?"

"No, Mrs. Longworth, unlike some people I do not presume to try to control the president of the United States."

Alice laughed—not a derisive snicker but a full-throated roar. After a few moments Warren joined in and after a little more time even Florence had to smile.

As Warren cleared his throat to speak, Senator William Borah of Idaho approached, put his arm around Alice's waist, and all but yanked her away. "Come, my dear, let's stroll these magnificent grounds." He mumbled the barest of respects to the nation's first couple and turned away with his paramour.

Evalyn spotted them and called out, "Alice, you're a fool. You're hurting your reputation."

Alice looked back over her shoulder to say, "I'm a Longworth. I can do as I please. You ask Nick if I can't."

Nick, in a corner being served another drink by a waiter in a tuxedo, overheard. "God damn the day I ever married you," he all but yelled. "I have succeeded not because of you but in spite of you." Borah and Alice exited without turning their heads.

The room hushed and the sorceress Madame Marcia silently counted off the beats—one, two, three, four. Then the buzz of conversation resumed and Madame Marcia walked up to Evalyn and Florence, who had quickly adjusted their frozen faces. The three ladies went up to the huge screened-in porch on the second floor. Warren sought the links with gladness, relief, and a resolution to keep away from Alice whenever he could.

A light breeze through the screens was just enough to moderate the muggy July afternoon. Marcia praised the view from the porch of the gardens and fountains, the tall cedars, the duck ponds, the swimming pool. Children played with llamas, goats, and donkeys. "It is an idyll, a heaven," she said.

Florence stood next to Marcia, looking down on Alice and Senator Borah, the "Lion of Idaho." Borah had a square, senatorial-looking face and was considered handsome despite his hard eyes and a thin-lipped crease of a mouth. His clean-shaven chin presented a deep vertical groove.

Alice was known to dislike children but there she was, helping a little girl climb upon a burro while Borah stood stiffly a pace away. People back home were right, Florence thought—Washington really is a wicked place. Of course some people have extramarital affairs, but nobody back there is ill-bred enough to flaunt it, to taunt their spouses in public, rub their noses in it. Florence had become friends with Borah's wife, Mary, a gentle soul, when they sewed clothes together for the Red Cross during the war. Her heart sank for Mary and then for all wives whose husbands betray them. Melancholy overtook the first lady: We should never have come to Washington and if our fate is malignant it will serve us right.

She and Marcia joined Evalyn at a table under a lazily spinning ceiling fan. Marcia continued looking out the screens but Florence and Evalyn were indifferent to the view. Marcia turned to say,"I almost laughed out loud when you told Alice she was hurting her reputation. You, Evalyn McLean, worried about a woman's reputation? And Alice's, of all people?"

"I would say the magic has gone out of their marriage," Evalyn deadpanned.

Actually, Evalyn upheld at least one safeguard of her own reputation. She would not permit in the McLeans' homes Ned's mistress, Rose Davies, who was the sister of William Randolph Hearst's mistress, Marion Davies.

Marcia turned to Florence. "You've lost a little weight, haven't you, dear?"

"Oh, Marcia, I am worrying myself to death. Is the White House really worth it if Warren is to leave me before his term is out? Are you still certain about that?"

"It is not I who am certain, Florence, dear. It is destiny. You must hold firm."

Florence flung out her arms, then clutched her sides. Her eyes were dry but seemed to see nothing. "Power, glory, hah. They make slaves of us. That's too high a price to pay. Slaves. I mean it."

Evalyn said, "You poor dear, I think you need another glass of wine." Florence shook her head no. Evalyn summoned a servant. "Another Scotch and water for me, Terrence."

For his part, Warren knew nothing about Marcia's dire prediction. He was getting up a golf foursome with Senator Lodge, Harry Daugherty, and Florence's buddy Al Jolson.

"I saw Jess but where's Roxy?" Warren asked.

"She wasn't invited," Harry said.

"Why not?"

"Well, frankly, Warren, the Duchess doesn't like her and I have to stay on the Duchess's good side."

Warren shrugged at the inscrutable ways of women and teed up.

After eighteen holes Jolson went to find female company—an orchestra was playing in the ballroom. The other men took a table on the patio beneath the porch. Two waiters appeared at once to take drink orders. If anybody at the party thought about Prohibition, it was not mentioned.

"You're getting good press so far, Mr. President," Lodge said.

"Yeah, but my Cabinet is getting even better press." It was true, at least for the jurist Charles Evans Hughes as secretary of state, the banker Andrew Mellon as secretary of the treasury, and Herbert Hoover, who had organized food relief for Europe after the war, as secretary of commerce.

"I guess I'm the exception," Harry said. "Nobody puts in a good word for me except for Ned's *Post*."

"That's because they don't appreciate the value of loyalty in politics," Warren said. "If you're loyal to me, I'm loyal to you. And they will go after you because they can't directly go after me. And that makes me want to stand up for you. Loyalty has to go both ways."

"Now, speaking of loyalty—and respect—let me give you a piece of advice," Lodge said. "I've seen presidents come and go for thirty-five years. Insist that they call you Mr. President. Not Warren. The office must carry a sense of elevation, of dignity, at all times."

"But they've known me for just about those same thirty-five years and have always called me Warren."

"As you wish, Mr. President. But keep in mind what I said."

Warren turned to Lodge with an air of earnestness, as if grateful for the opportunity to explain himself. Harry noticed that his eyes were bright again, as in the old days. Often in the White House his eyes were dull. Harding said, "Let me tell you where I want to take this presidency. Andy Mellon came in the other day to talk to talk about the pound sterling. What do I know about the pound sterling? I don't understand the European stuff." (Treasury Secretary Mellon had lent $500,000 to the Republican Party and some of that money dropped into the blackmail fund.)

"So he says, Mr. President, we are coming out of the depression. We had to have a depression with the transition from a wartime economy to a peacetime economy. And he says, I'm not a politician but the depression probably was enough to defeat Wilson all by itself.

"Now, the war has left Britain crushed. The pound has been the reserve currency of the world for a century and more. So, he says, we have to keep the dollar strong, stronger than ever. Pay down the national debt. Cut government spending. Pretty soon we will replace the pound as the world's reserve currency and we will be the greatest power in the world for generations to come.

"I said, Mr. Secretary, that's why I hired you, to look after these matters. And now let me tell you what only a president can do. I am putting together the Washington Naval Conference. The first international disarmament conference in the history of the world, gentlemen! And it has nothing to do with the League of Nations. It—"

"I am honored that you included me in the delegation to that conference, Mr. President," Lodge broke in.

Harding had put Lodge on that panel, mindful of President Wilson's blunder in deliberately snubbing Lodge and Borah, shutting them out of negotiations for the Versailles peace treaty. Since they had no personal stake in its success, they took a straight shot against it in the Senate, wrecking Wilson's dream of a League of Nations.

He barely nodded to Lodge and said, "For the first time, the great powers might well come to an agreement to limit the number of capital ships. Or their total tonnage, at least.

"Let me tell you, the Duchess and I were there in Marion when the first boys were sent off to war. It about broke my heart, they were so young and fresh-faced. I knew that probably some of them would never come back. So my goal is, never again will American boys have to get on those troop trains and those troop ships to go and fight a foreign war."

Harry looked bored. Lodge said, "Blessed are the peacemakers, Mr. President."

Just then the dusk had turned dark enough for the McLeans to launch the first of many volleys of fireworks. Following the fireworks would be a showing of the raw footage of the first reels of the Dempsey-Carpentier film in Friendship's private theater.

August 13, 1921

It was the happiest time of Jess Smith's life. Each morning he stood at the northwest corner of Fifteenth and

H streets in front of the Shoreham Hotel, his clothes perfectly tailored and color-coordinated, his dark eyes behind round black spectacles, darting about in search of supplicants. Without fail, grifters, mugs, bootleggers, and influence peddlers approached looking for favors from Harry Daugherty's Justice Department. Jess stood with his thumbs thrust in the armholes of his waistcoat, welcoming one and all. If asked a question he was not ready to answer, he said, "You tell me and I'll tell you." If asked a question he liked, he reached into a silver cigarette case and said, "Have a smoke on me." He might or might not light up himself, depending on the state of his asthma.

Jess and Harry had moved in together at 1509 H Street. Jess's bedroom was decorated in pale pink taffeta. A door opened to Harry's bedroom because, each man said, he could not sleep comfortably without another person in the room. Harry's wife Lucie was cared for by a nurse in Ohio or at Johns Hopkins Hospital in Baltimore.

The men lived rent-free in a house owned by Ned McLean and decorated by Evalyn. A tinted window in the first-floor office allowed those inside to watch the street without being seen by those outside. Fine liquors were delivered regularly by a Justice Department courier under armed guard. Best of all, the place was just two blocks from the White House and one block from the Justice Department.

In the Justice building, Jess had an office adjacent to Harry's on the sixth floor even though Jess held no official position and was not paid. He was given a Justice Department badge and codes and enjoyed access to all files. In an anteroom was installed a stock market ticker machine to help Jess and Harry play the market.

In fact the market caused the first rift between them. Harry schemed to have Harding announce that the Justice Department would launch antitrust investigations of the oil companies. With their advance knowledge, Harry and Jess could short the oil stocks and mike millions.

"Harry, I am telling you, that's a bad idea."

"Why?"

"The Progressives are already bitching all the time that the oil companies put Warren in there. Do the antitrust thing, Jesus, that will set all the hounds to baying."

"Fuck the Progressives. We'll snooker them by calling it a crackdown on the oil trust."

"Come on, Harry, you're a better politician than that. You really want every Democrat in the country saying that Warren is just putting on a show? That's it's all a scam to manipulate the stocks to benefit the Rockefellers? And meanwhile all the Republicans are saying, what the hell are you going after oil for?"

"That's why it would have to be done carefully and with a lot of subtlety."

"Yeah? Try running it by the Duchess first. See how subtle she'd be. Then you tell me and I'll tell you."

"Oh, we wouldn't necessarily have to involve the Duchess first."

"Yeah, and then we'll both go floating out to sea on the same shit list."

That stopped the conversation, but Harry never gave up on plotting to deploy such a swindle. When he was young he thought he sought wealth to provide the best possible care for his crippled wife and alcoholic son and daughter, but he soon quit trying to kid himself. His greed was of a noble purity.

He made Ned McLean a dollar-a-year special agent of the Bureau of Investigation. The publisher of the Washington Post, the poker-and-booze buddy of the president, the husband of the first lady's best friend, was granted the authority to investigate and spy on people.

The McLeans' in-town mansion was on I Street across from Harry's and Jess's place on H Street. Ned was a frequent visitor to H Street, as was Warren Harding, for whom Ned brought in showgirls. Harding called the place "The Love Nest," although Ned was credited with the motto,"where the deals are made and the girls are laid."

As Ned's boss and chief of the B of I Harry named Billy Burns, who was allowed to keep his private-eye business. Burns had been cut into Harry's bootlegging business after meeting with Jess and Roxy in New York. He was so crooked that his B of I deputy, a young J. Edgar Hoover, was embarrassed to tell people where he worked.

Burns more than repaid any debt owed to Jess by introducing him to George Remus. Al Capone in Chicago got most of the publicity but Remus was the country's biggest bootlegger. Evalyn and Alice were not the only ones who wondered why Harry and his cronies all looked so much alike—big head, broad face, coarse features, thick neck. Remus fit the pattern except for one mark of distinction. He wore a derby that was too small for his head.

At the Federal Reserve Bank in Cincinnati, Remus wrote checks to cash, withdrawing neatly wrapped stacks of $100 and $1,000 bills. On each check he wrote the initials "J.S.," indicating Jess Smith. He carefully placed the money in a black leather briefcase and took the train to Washington.

Remus met Jess in the lobby of the Hotel Washington. Both men looked around for anyone who might recognize them or be tailing them. Satisfied, they went to an upstairs suite.

Jess admired Remus's diamond stickpin. "Thanks," Remus said. "You're pretty well turned out yourself. Now let's proceed to business. You know that I was a criminal defense lawyer. A damn good one too." True—he had pioneered the "insanity defense" in a murder trial.

"I know that. Hell, I've read your file. You came from Germany and you started out as a pharmacist."

"Since you read the file, you know exactly what I'm here for."

"Yeah, you're under indictment for about a thousand violations of the Volstead Act. Even you aren't a good enough lawyer to get yourself out of this one."

Jess, who hated confrontation, saw too late that his smart-ass remark made Remus angry. Remus got red around the collar and slammed the satchel on a table.

"There might be a conviction before a jury," Jess hastened to say. "But when the case goes to the appeals court, it will be reversed."

"Shit, for this kind of money I want an acquittal at trial."

"Sorry, we can't guarantee that. What's the difference? It'll drag out for years and you're a free man. Now let's say the impossible happens and it goes all the way to the Supreme Court. In that case the president would pardon you. There is no likelihood of you going at any time."

Remus grunted. With his left hand—probably leaving his right hand free to reach for a gun—Remus snapped open the briefcase. He held it open for Jess to see inside. The neatness of the blocks of cash pleased Jess almost as much the money itself. He nodded.

"The first quality of a gentleman is neatness," he said.

"We have then a gentlemen's agreement?"

"It is done." They shook hands.

Jess caught the late train to Columbus, toting as usual two leather suitcases holding his clothes and bottles of illegal alcohol (he favored Harry's own Lynchburg Whiskey). Jess met Roxy at the Deschler Hotel. In their suite he solemnly, without cracking a smile, hung up his coat and pants. Then he unbuckled a money belt, held it up as though regarding a snake. Why is he putting on this mime show, Roxy wondered. Frowning, Jess unzipped the money belt and withdrew sheafs of bills between his thumb and forefinger. Then he flung seventy-five $1,000 bills around the room.

Both Jess and Roxy screamed so loudly that a bellboy was sent to knock on the door. Jess cracked the door enough to tell him to scram. He and Roxy laughed and cried so much that they fought for breath. Roxy bounced on the bed, sweeping up thousand-dollar bills in her arms and tossing them in the air again. Jess sang:

My father makes book on the corner
My mother makes second-hand gin
My sister makes love for a dollar
My God, how the money rolls in!

Roxy joined in the second verse, to the tune of "My Bonnie":

My granny's a bawdy house keeper
Every night when the action begins
She hangs out a little red lantern
My God, how the money rolls in!

Then together:

Rolls in, rolls in, my God how the money rolls in, rolls in!

"There are about twenty more verses but I don't remember them any more," Roxy said, catching her breath and stepping down from the bed. "Oh! I never dreamed I would ever see so much money at once."

"Sweetheart, we'll sing one verse every time we get together. And when we get to the end we'll start over again. Because how the money rolls in." Then, neatness being the hallmark of a gentleman, Jess meticulously gathered and counted the bills, placing them in a perfect rectangular pile.

Roxy hesitated to introduce a sour note, but said, "You and Mr. Daugherty might get caught some day, you know."

"Nah," Jess shrugged. "It's our turn, see."

"Our turn?"

"Yeah, see, we saw how all the Democrats got rich on crooked war contracts. Then the Republicans got back in and so now it's our turn. See, that's the beauty of the two-party system." Roxy looked quizzical. "That's how we attain parity in getting rich. With us it's Prohibition instead of war, but, you know, as long as things stay roughly equal, nobody gets too upset."

"Democracy in action," Roxy said sarcastically. Then she asked a question that had been perplexing her. "What about Mr. Harding, is he getting pieces of this pie?"

Jess pondered a second and said, "No, Warren doesn't steal. Or if he does, he does it in such small amounts that, like I said, nobody gets too upset."

"Such becoming modesty."

"Heh heh. Baby, let's go home."

They went to her home in Washington Court House, planning to spend the weekend. But on Saturday morning Jess got a telegram from Harry: RETURN AT ONCE. LONELY HERE. MISS YOU.

September 30, 1921

The first thing Florence did as first lady was to open the White House gates. Edith Wilson had kept the place locked down so that nobody could see how disabled her husband was. On Harding's inauguration day, crowds swarmed into the White House in numbers and unruliness unseen since Andrew Jackson's inauguration in 1829. In the months to come, Florence liked to lead tours of the public rooms herself. "It's the people's house. They should see it," she said.

Warren not only agreed with her, he decreed that between noon and 1 p.m. every weekday, anybody could walk in and shake his hand. When Harry suggested he might find better uses for that time, Warren said, "I love to meet people. It's the most pleasant thing I do; it's really the only fun I have. It doesn't tax me, and it seems to be a very great pleasure to them."

Harry looked at him a little harder and saw how bright were Warren's eyes during that hour, how in contrast they seemed wary and a bit frightened the rest of the day. Maybe Warren should somehow be the head of state but not the head of government, something like the king of England. That way the Duchess, who already saw herself as queen of the White House, would be the royal consort. She'd like that.

Contrary to Harry's musings, Florence was building a reputation for modesty and wifely frugality. She renounced the first ladies' tradition of buying new White House china. "Hard times are still afflicting our country. The Wilsons' china will serve perfectly well for the Hardings and their guests," she said to applause from the press.

Florence got on well with reporters and tried to use those contacts to get publicity for the needs of Great War veterans. However, she did not allow reporters to cover her visits to army hospitals. Those were for her soul alone.

Accompanied only by a Secret Service man, she asked a wounded soldier at Walter Reed Hospital if she could get him anything.

"Thank you, ma'am. The thing I want most of all is just some sunshine."

"What! They don't take you out in the sun?"

"No, ma'am, I ain't seen no sun in twenty-three days."

She stormed down the hall to get a nurse, then personally pushed the man's wheelchair out to the grounds and sat with him for forty-five minutes.

Soon the president persuaded Congress to create a Veterans Bureau. To run the new bureau, both Hardings believed, they knew just the man: Charles F. Forbes. He had built the Pearl Harbor naval base and delivered some Western delegates to help Warren win the nomination.

The Hardings decided to go to Chicago with the new veterans chief to scout a potential site for a hospital. The care of wounded veterans in private and institutional hospitals was pathetic, a national disgrace, and Warren promised to build new government hospitals.

At a suburban racetrack called Speedway, Florence stepped off about twenty paces. She returned to Forbes and said, "That's just about fifty feet."

"Yes, dear lady? And?"

"If the hospital is only about fifty feet wide, then every room can have windows. When I visit the hospitals so many of the boys are in rooms that are so dark. I want to make sure that every soldier gets some sun in his room."

Forbes agreed. Later when people asked why Speedway Hospital was only fifty feet wide and over two thousand feet long, he said it was Florence's idea.

But it was definitely Forbes's idea to meet the contractor Elias H. Mortimer at a room in the Drake Hotel in Chicago. Mortimer gave him a $5,000 bribe for millions in construction contracts. Also, the taxpayers bought the Speedway land for more than twice its value; the owners kicked back part of the price to Forbes.

Harry and Evalyn both saw through Forbes. Evalyn, for one, tried to do something about it. Rather than approach Harding at one of his poker nights at H Street—when alcohol diminished his clarity of mind—she waited for a White House luncheon.

"He is not loyal to you," she told Warren. "He is only out for himself and he will get you in a lot of trouble. I'd call him a four-flusher except that he's much worse."

"Evalyn, I can't believe it. Anyway, I won't turn on a friend because of gossip. God, I can't be an ingrate! Now, can I? This stuff you've heard—forget it."

Undaunted, Evalyn took her case to the Duchess. "You don't know what you're talking about!" Florence yelled, so angry that she did not speak to Evalyn for eight days.

Back home, Evalyn quietly smoked a cigarette. The Harding administration has already started downhill, she thought. It will descend into squalor.

October 24, 1921

The death of a woman at a "Love Nest" poker party on H Street prompted Harry and Jess to move out of there. Jess had just finished leading a singalong of "My God, How the Money Rolls In." Ned had thoughtfully provided showgirls for the night's entertainment. Warren Harding leaned indolently against a white enameled mantel, smoking a cigar while guests cleared a large table for use as the showgirls' stage. Impatient for the show, some guests began flinging bottles and glasses off the table. A bottle struck one of Ned's "sporting ladies" in the temple and she collapsed.

Within seconds one of Harry's thugs fronted Harding, grabbed his shoulders and started hustling him out. "Get the Secret Service out of here too!" shouted the thug, Gaston Means.

By now Warren was scurrying out the back door himself. "There's no Secret Service inside," he said. "I hate being followed around all the time. I told them they can wait out front. I'm going to a private party with my friends, nobody's going to shoot me in there."

"Yeah, but this might be even worse than getting shot," Gaston Means said with a sneer as he pushed Warren into a White House car.

Friends of the victim, Summer Walsh, laid her on a couch but could not revive her. She was taken to a hospital where she died. A potter's field received her remains.

Her brother Sebastian started threatening to blackmail Harding. Warren told Harry to take care of the matter and Harry told Billy Burns, the new head of the Bureau of Investigation. The Justice Department railroaded Sebastian into St. Elizabeth psychiatric hospital until he learned some manners. "Don't tell Mrs. Harding and don't tell Christian," Warren said, referring to his personal secretary George Christian.

Since there was no Secret Service report or police report, the woman's fatal accident at 1509 H Street never happened. Even so, Harry and Jess abandoned the place for the Wardman Park Inn. But Gaston Means continued to use H Street as the office for his rackets.

So now Harry Daugherty had Billy Burns, Gaston Means, and those men's agents as official government investigators. Leland Jackson called them "the deviated septums" because they all looked as though they had had their noses broken in alley fights. Gaston Means was a deviated septum, though the only one who favored bow ties. Means had been accused of looting a widow's estate and then killing her, but he beat both raps and so he must be okay. Burns had employed Means in his private-eye agency and considered him a savvy investigator and extortionist. "You'll not only take orders from me," Burns told him, "but from Jess."

Soon, Jess met Gaston at H Street. "It's got to be done in New York," Gaston insisted. "Too many people know us here. You ever been to the Vanderbilt Hotel? You know how to get there?"

Ah, Jess thought, so Gaston is going to treat me like a bumpkin-come-to-town. Fine. Like Warren, he knew the value of being underestimated.

"Had you ever imagined how much alcohol is needed in manufacturing? And to produce pharmaceuticals? Truly an amazing amount. Why, we can hardly keep up with the demand," Jess deadpanned. Gaston just grunted.

Jess went to New York and walked into the Vanderbilt. In his briefcase were Treasury Department forms allowing the purchase of bonded government liquor for medicinal or industrial purposes. Jess had forged the signatures on the forms. He entered the lobby with his hat pulled down over his eyes. He also removed his black-rimmed round spectacles, despite his bad vision, because many people recognized him by them.

Gaston had rented adjoining rooms on the fifth floor. Jess opened the unlocked door to one of them. On a table was a large, empty glass fishbowl. Jess pulled from the bowl an envelope, counted the cash. Fifty $1,000 bills, neatly wrapped. He deposited an envelope containing the liquor certificates. The cash was tucked into Jess's briefcase. Gaston watched the transaction through a peephole in the door to the other room.

Jess left the room and took the elevator down, feeling wretched. He felt—not insulted, exactly—demeaned. This was not how men do business, he thought. A man does not hide in another room like he is afraid or, worse, ashamed. A man looks you in the eye, shakes your hand. The ancient rite of money changing hands—that meant you were men, doing something serious. Money in one hand, alcohol permits in the other, a swap: honest and clean. Otherwise you were just a bruno, a four-flusher. Put them in a fishbowl, for chrissake.

And we deal only in high-quality stuff, too. We don't blind people with bathtub gin, we don't poison them, we don't kill them. This is bonded booze from official government inventories. We can be proud of how we do business. We pretend to hijack the liquor trucks, everybody's in on it, nobody gets hurt. We don't rub out other gangs like they do in Chicago and Detroit. What did Gaston think, I was going to barge in there with a bunch of cops? Okay, I might do some more deals with him, but only on my terms . . .

Jess was supposed to return to Washington to help Harry move into the Wardman Park, but he changed his mind and went home to Ohio instead. This time there was no celebration with the money belt. He just put it on Roxy's dresser.

It was at the tail end of the fall colors, the end of their favorite time of the year, and Roxy had expected that they would take a ride to enjoy it. But Jess took off his glasses and lay on the bed with his hands clasped behind his head, looking dejected.

"All right, sweetie, what's wrong?"

First he told her about the woman's death in the Love Nest. Roxy hesitated a second before asking, "Was Leland there?"

"Hell, no. He wouldn't have been there unless Coolidge was, and Coolidge don't play poker or chase girls."

"Well, good for him."

"You know something, baby? I am not cut out for this. This intrigue is getting me crazy. If I could just come home, but I am in now and I have to stand by Harry."

"But just a little while ago you were having the time of your life. It's only been a half a year or so and already you're feeling so low?"

"I just had a deal in New York, it wasn't on the square, I didn't like it. It's the whole scene. Hell, even the Duchess is pulling a long face. Do you know what the Duchess says? Evalyn and I pick out clothes and stuff for her and take them up to her room. Sometimes she's all excited but other times she looks like her dog just died and she says"—he mimicked a thin, sepulchral voice—'I see only tragedy ahead.' "

"Oh, you know she listens to that mumbo jumbo, those fortune tellers. They've probably got her all upset, told her Warren's got the clap or something."

Jess just puffed his cigarette.

"What does Warren say about the Duchess running her life according to those star charts?"

"I think they pretty much agree just to let each other run their own lives."

"Yeah? Maybe if we had had that kind of arrangement, we wouldn't have gotten divorced."

She knew at once she should not have said that. Jess started to cry, as she knew he would. She consoled him in her own way, a bit maternal, a bit erotic, tracing circular designs on his stomach and rubbing his scalp. Jess found her ministrations both comforting and disturbing.

In the morning Jess took the cash to Mal Daugherty's bank. He and Mal kept meticulous records of one account in particular, "Jess Smith—Extra No. 3," the remaining blackmail fund. Harry, through Jess, was slowly paying back the Republican National Committee.

October 26, 1921

One of the perks of being president is that you sometimes get to know in advance when history will be made. On the train heading south President Harding made final revisions to his handwritten speech with his fountain pen. There are things that need to be said, Harding thought, that sometimes only the president can say. He was going to amaze everybody—North and South, Republican and Democrat, everybody—by going to Birmingham, Alabama, and calling for civil rights for Black people.

Alabama has sixty-seven counties and every one of them sent a "county queen" to greet the arrival of the Harding train. Harding stepped down to the platform, followed by his wife, and lingered for happy minutes exchanging well-wishes with the beauty queens, his grin broad, his eyes twinkling. He knew the Duchess would scold him for it later but he did not care. The Alabama National Guard fired a twenty-one gun salute and then all the factories in the city sounded their whistles. Red-white-and-blue bunting hung from every storefront and lamppost along with banners bearing Harding's portrait. The Duchess's mood improved—this was much better than the campaign; this is how a president should be received all over the country.

A gleaming white automobile actually manufactured in Birmingham, a Premocar, led the parade. The Hardings sat in back while up front was a local dignitary and the Negro driver, a popular barber selected for this honor. Tens of thousands, the largest crowd in the city's history, showered flowers on the Hardings. There were no Negroes in that crowd. They were cordoned off separately.

Harding was both fronted and backed by patriotic bunting when he spoke from a platform in a park. He really did "look like a president," as both his friends and his critics said of him. Even the low fall sun seemed to flatter him, with half his face warmly lit and the other half dramatically shadowed. He bloviated for long minutes about the industrial and economic surging of the South. Then: "If the Civil War marked the beginnings of industrialism in a South which had previously been almost entirely agricultural, the World War brought us to full recognition that the race problem is national rather than merely sectional. . . . It is common knowledge that the World War was marked by a great migration of colored people to the North and West."

Florence sensed, and wondered whether Warren did, a tension stiffen the crowd. Everybody knew about the great migration, but where was he going with this?

"A high-grade colored soldier told me that the war brought his race the first real conception of citizenship—the first full realization that the flag was their flag, to fight for, to be protected by them, and also to protect them."

Harding now was skating on very thin ice. Over in their segregated corner the blacks cheered, but the whites in Capitol Park and on the bordering streets clenched their jaws and hardened their eyes. Harding continued, "Let the black man vote when he is fit to vote; prohibit the white man voting when he is unfit to vote." A collective shaking of heads ensued with a few scattered noes but the Southerners considered themselves too genteel to boo the president of the United States. Harding departed from his text to point directly into the white throng and say, "Whether you like it or not, unless our democracy is a lie, you must stand for that equality."

Now both his personal beliefs and his political instincts told Harding to reassure these folks that there were limits to the radical change he proposed. Southerners were most afraid of racial intermarriage but, simply as a practical matter, that would never happen. Time for some soothing words.

"I would insist upon equal educational opportunity for both races," he said. "This does not mean that both would become equally educated within a generation or two generations or ten generations." In the meantime, "I would mean equality proportioned to the honest capacities and deserts of the individual." But even given such equality, "racial amalgamation can never come to America."

Florence, seated behind her husband, studied the crowd. Many of the women nodded; some of the men unclenched their fists. When the speech ended the applause was a notch above merely polite, but the distant Blacks yelled and the men waved their hats above their heads. She feared the whites would turn and yell at them back, but they kept their gaze straight ahead. Whatever the coloreds felt was unworthy of attention.

On the train to Fort Benning, Georgia, where they would spend the night, Harding said, "Well, Duchess, are you prepared for the thrashing we are about to take?"

"Oh, Warren, I am proud of any criticism we would take for that speech." Silently she wondered whether her father's spreading stories about Warren's Negroid heritage formed part of his motivation.

Back in the White House, Harding had the Northern and Southern newspapers brought to him in the Solarium. He was especially interested in the *Birmingham News*, which had worked hard to entice a presidential visit in the first place. Harding had made an "untimely and ill-considered intrusion into a question of which he evidently knows little," the News huffed. A senator from Mississippi warned that "if the president's theory is carried to its ultimate conclusion, then that means that the black man can strive to become president of the United States." Just as horrifying, "it means white women should work under black men in public places, as well as in all trades and professions."

Commentary in the North was mostly positive, although some Democrats suggested that Harding was merely fishing for more Black Republican votes. The president was most gratified by letters of praise from two Negro intellectuals, W.E.B. DuBois and Marcus Garvey.

Harding put down the papers, sipped a morning coffee, and placed the cup back on its saucer with a satisfied sigh. Florence and George Christian, the man in charge of the White House staff, regarded him in expectation of a pronouncement. "I'll tell you something I've learned in this business," he said. "It's easier to move ten thousand people at one time than it is to move ten people. Duchess, our presidency will be remembered for the Birmingham speech."

Roxy thought so, too. She called Jess and said, "He's going to go down in history as the president who told those horrible southerners that they had to treat colored people like human beings." That grade-school directive, *All coloreds and Kentuckians*, still rang in her memory. So did her disbelief over the outlawing of boxing films just because a Negro had beaten a white man years ago.

"Yeah, but it was just a speech," Jess said. "Will it really change anything?"

"That's not the point. Remember when he stood up in the Senate and made that speech for a law against lynching? And now he goes to Alabama, that's like going to Timbuktu, to the ends of the earth. Don't you see he's making history? I mean, I want to be a part of that. Can't you be of any more help? I'm relying on you, you know."

"Baby, I'm doing everything I can."

"Have you asked Mrs. McLean to help?"

"Hey, that's an idea."

November 9, 1921

"Why does the Duchess hate me so much? I never even flirted with Mr. Harding." Roxy reached back in her memory. "Nor vice-versa either."

"Oh, it's because—do you want to know Harry's theory?"

"Harry has a theory?"

"Sure. It's because you're not part of the family."

"The family? The Duchess's only family is Warren. She had a husband and a son that nobody knows about and they both died, didn't they? Both drunks, according to what you hear from Harry."

Jess liked to time his visits when Roxy's maid had the day off because then he could bustle about her apartment doing domestic things. He came back to Washington Court House every third or fourth weekend while Roxy visited Washington now and then. Jess was brewing black tea from Ceylon while cracking eggs for French toast. Roxy took a quart of milk from the icebox.

"You've got to remember how the Duchess grew up," Jess said. "She had this brute of a father and her mother spent most of her time sick in bed. Mostly, you know, just to avoid any attention from Amos. Then when she started running after Warren, he had something she had never seen before—a big, happy family."

Roxy leaned against the archway to the butler's pantry, wearing an old dressing gown and an expression that said, Yeah? So what?

"Warren was the oldest child—in fact, he was something of a mama's boy—and he had six brothers and sisters. They were all crazy about each other, including the mama and papa. So the Duchess figures, oh, so this is what a real family is, I'm going to make my own family and I'll be the queen of it and not let anybody else in. That way, nobody can come in to hurt me."

"All right, then, so who's her family besides Warren? Evalyn McLean, and that sheep-dip of a doctor, what's-his-name, Dr. Sawyer, and then Mr. Forbes—you, Jess? Who else?"

"Huh. I'm maybe a kind of auxiliary or honorary member when I go see her with Evalyn. She likes me because Evalyn likes me. Even though she hates Harry, she likes me because Evalyn likes me. There's maybe one other guy, George Christian, you know, Warren's secretary."

"Yeah, I've met him. He's the Hardings' next-door neighbors' son up in Marion."

"Yeah, but don't hold that against him. He's really very good at his job."

Despite being a dandy, Jess's table manners were not the best. Now they were sitting at a table in the breakfast nook and Jess talked while chewing his French toast. Roxy long ago had given up trying to correct that defect.

"So the Duchess will fight the world to protect those four or five people. Everyone else is a threat, or at least potentially a threat. And you, my dear, you know why the Duchess sees you as a threat."

"But that's crazy, I'm not a threat. Harry and Mr. Forbes, they're the threats, and that's because they're crooks. Everybody in Washington knows it. The Duchess doesn't like Harry, I'm sure, because he takes the credit for Mr. Harding getting to be president. But that's not the same thing, that's not being a crook. Anyway, never mind Harry, what about Mr. Forbes? You know that scandals are going to break sooner or later."

"Maybe, but you don't have to worry about Harry getting caught. He's the smartest man I know."

Roxy sipped her tea and bit her lower lip. After a minute she said, "He thinks he can bend the world to his own will. You can't get dumber than that."

Jess looked perplexed, as though he had never thought of such a thing. He inclined his head and furrowed his brow.

Roxy pondered another minute and said, "Harry thinks he is this big political philosopher. I once heard him say that all politicians had unhappy childhoods. And so that's why they're always going after power and approval. The approval and love they never got as kids. Simple, huh? And you can never satisfy them. You know, if they lose, it's not just a setback, it's like the end of the world for them."

"Yeah, you know what else he says? The politicians, they'll take payoffs, sure, but they really aren't in it for the money. It's the applause, it's thinking they're so important," Jess said. He saw that he had caught up with her thinking. "But, look, the president of the United States had a happy childhood! According to Harry himself. So maybe Harry got it wrong. Or maybe Warren is, you know, the exception that proves the rule." Jess chewed and swallowed and said, "But maybe that's why Warren thinks the people around him can't hurt him. He thinks they're all part of a big family. And family won't hurt you. At least not in public."

"Just what I was going to say," Roxy said. "So Mr. Harding has this big family where everybody loves him. That's why he keeps people like Mr. Forbes around him. But then the Duchess has this small, tight family and everybody else is a threat. Ha! We'll call it the Harry Daugherty theory of marital relations."

"No, theory of politics," Jess said.

"They're the same thing, aren't they? Well, I don't care what the president thinks, Mr. Forbes is going to cause a big scandal."

Neither one added aloud that Harry Daugherty might do likewise. Or Jess Smith. Or his confederate, Roxy Stinson.

Roxy said, "Well, both of those families, so-called, the Duchess's and the president's, they're both going to be busted up. And sooner than you think. Then what?"

She put down her teacup with some force and the air of having made a decision. "Jess, I want you to do me a big favor."

"Name it."

"I want to write the president a letter and have you give it to Mr. Christian to make sure he gets it."

Jess said nothing but his eyes said, you still have this crazy pipe dream, don't you?

"Really, Jess, Mr. Harding needs me now more than ever. Somebody outside of his gang of grifters. Somebody who will tell him the truth about Mr. Forbes. Somebody who's not part of his gang—or one of the Duchess's 'family,' either—and so this person has nothing to lose by telling the truth. Like, telling him when his girlfriends are going to get him in trouble. Maybe, if that came from a woman, it would sink in."

They had bought off Grace Cross and got her to disappear but Roxy was sure that Warren was screwing someone else by now. Jess had not told her about Nan Britton.

He puffed out his cheeks and blew out the air. She was asking the impossible, to choose between his love for Harry and his love for her. Harry and the Duchess both wanted Roxy to go away and stay there. If he bootlegged Roxy's secret letter into the Oval Office and Harry found out—Jess didn't want to think about it. If the Duchess found out, he would blow his access to the White House.

Moreover, Jess was a frightened man. Billy Burns and Gaston Means—high government officials of the Bureau of Investigation—had had the brother of the dead show-girl committed to a locked psychiatric ward. Jess was so alarmed by that act that he couldn't sleep for two nights. Deep down, he knew he was a make-believe tough guy. Billy and Gaston and the other thugs, they were the real thing.

"Roxy, my dear, you don't know what you're asking. To go down in history as the first woman assistant to a president? Warren isn't such a flag-waver for women's rights that he has ever even thought of such a thing. And you know that the Duchess wouldn't allow it—she's the only woman adviser Warren could ever have. And besides, what do you know about government?"

"Oh, come on. Government isn't hard. If it were, there wouldn't be so many mediocre people doing it."

Jess half-smiled and nodded at that.

"And besides I think the president needs someone to tell him when what the government is doing is hurting ordinary people. They tapped my phone! And even after all this time I'm still careful about what I say on the phone. And all that bootlegging money—you know that money comes out of the pockets of real people in the end. Don't you see, sooner or later the people are going to rise up."

"You know what Harry says about that? He says that when the wolves are well-fed, the sheep are safe."

"Hmpf. Yeah, a real philosopher, isn't he."

"Like I said, I'm getting out next year and coming home."

"Come on, Jess, where are you going to be when the shit hits the fan?"

"There I'll stand, spic and span."

Roxy sighed; her shoulders slumped. "All right, look, I know I'm asking an awful lot but could you carry a letter to Mr. Christian for me? Maybe give it to him at his house? I know it's hard getting into the West Wing." She saw Jess about to raise another objection. "You don't have to tell me it's a really long shot. But it's a chance I want to take. And not only that, it's a decision for Mr. Harding to make, not his wife or you or anyone else. Look, maybe he secretly wants to get out beyond his Ohio gang, you know? Maybe he knows he needs someone like me."

Roxy had imagined such high-minded motives on Harding's part but had not carefully studied her own motives. The United States government was the biggest show on Earth and she wanted to be part of it. She felt she was on the outside looking in. She did not like that feeling, that she was missing out on the action. The government spends five billion dollars a year! That's billion with a *b*.

The main fact was that Roxy was bored, felt her life was going nowhere after the run of the fight film was over. She had little to do except keep track of their money, including Jess's bootlegging money. And she realized, at barely the level of perception where she would acknowledge it, that a job would bring order to the messiness of her life. A little deeper than that lay the understanding that she was lonely. Her pride kept that truth submerged.

She could see that she was putting Jess through an ordeal. She cleared the dishes from the table as Jess sat motionless except for wrinkling his forehead time and again.

"Sure, just give me the letter before I catch the train."

Roxy all but threw the dishes in the sink with a loud clatter and ran to hug him. Quickly she wrote a note—she had long thought about its wording. She especially praised Harding's courage in giving the Birmingham speech.

There was a major piece of the puzzle they were missing. Harding's secretary George Christian was not one of the Duchess's team. Part of his job was keeping the first lady in the dark when Nan Britton sneaked into the Oval Office.

December 2, 1921

President Harding wanted to free Eugene V. Debs. What was the point of being president if you could not correct an injustice, right a wrong done to one man? The government had arrested more than two thousand people for sedition during the Great War. Debs, a prominent socialist, was sentenced to ten years in prison for speaking out against the war. From his cell in the Atlanta federal penitentiary, Debs had run for president in 1920. As a felon he was ineligible to serve, but he promised "if elected, I will pardon myself." That kind of wit appealed to Harding. Another irresistible attraction was that freeing Debs would piss off Woodrow Wilson.

Harding had hoped that the Supreme Court would halt this rape of the First Amendment. But the court not only upheld the Espionage and Sedition acts, it did so unanimously with even the so-called Progressive justices voting yea. That ruling provoked Harding to seek the release of Debs and others but his attorney general was against it.

"The man's a Bolshevik and he was duly convicted," Harry Daugherty argued.

"Damn it, Harry, he still had his First Amendment rights."

"Yeah, but he still wants to overthrow the American government."

"Hell, he's sixty-six years old. And he's sick. Bring him up here and talk to him and then you tell me if he's a threat to this country."

So Harry had Debs put on a train in Atlanta without a guard, secretly hoping he would escape and run off to set up some violent radical cell somewhere. "I told you so!" Harry then would crow. But Debs showed up quietly, completely bald and looking like a high school math teacher.

"Mr. Debs, do you advocate the overthrow of the United States government?"

"Certainly not. Have you read any of my writings?"

"I'll ask the questions here. Would you be willing to sign a loyalty oath, expressing contrition for your criminal acts and pledging to obey all laws of the United States, in return for a commutation of sentence?"

Debs hesitated only a moment. "No, sir."

Out of politeness, Harry asked if Debs wanted anything. Debs asked for a bowl of fresh fruit. "Fresh food is one of the things you miss most in prison, you see."

After an all-morning meeting Harry went back to Warren. "He didn't flinch at anything. He looked every fact squarely in the face. He didn't apologize for anything—and he didn't ask for clemency. I'll admit that that surprised me. I can respect him as a man and he's not a threat. But even so, he was lawfully convicted and deserves to serve out his sentence."

He, Warren, and the Duchess happened to be sitting against a wall in the State Dining Room. Florence led them there to inspect the redecoration she had ordered. The mounted heads of moose, elk, bear, and Dall sheep—all shot by Theodore Roosevelt—were gone.

"Warren Harding," she said, "don't you dare pardon that man. You know that what he wants above all is to get you out of office. He'll just go out and stir up more labor trouble for you." Indeed, it had been a tough year for violent strikes.

Warren reached for his drink, only to remember that he restricted his drinking to the private rooms upstairs. Such a privation, he reasoned, honored the spirit if not the letter of the Volstead Act. He lost his patience.

"Goddamn it, I am the president of the United States! Most of the time you think you are, but I am!"

Laddie Boy, the Hardings' Airedale terrier, was so started that he yelped, jumped up, and ran around the room. Harry tried to remember if he had ever heard Warren yell at the Duchess before.

"Let's go upstairs," Warren said. They took the elevator, all stone-faced including Laddie Boy. They sat in the screened-in sleeping porch that President Taft had installed on the roof. The early winter day was just warm enough to sit outside and admire the view of the Washington Monument—the kind of day that reminds people in Washington that theirs is a southern city. A servant brought drinks to Warren and Harry.

Florence broke the silence. "You know who had the nerve to write and tell me that Debs should be let out of jail? Norman Thomas."

Thomas, the quadrennial Socialist candidate for president, had been one of Florence's newsboys for the *Marion Star*.

Warren nodded. "Norman's a good man."

"Yes, but Debs is a socialist traitor. The only good thing I'll say for him is that he spoke out for women's suffrage but that was years ago."

"There, you see, that's his problem," Warren said. "He came out for the women and then he came out against fighting a foreign war. In politics you can't be right too soon. Or too often."

Harry and Florence drew breaths, struck by the same thought: How could a man so brilliant at politics be so weak at governing? Harry had a further thought: Why aren't there any superb administrators who are also superb politicians? Teddy Roosevelt, maybe. I'm beginning to understand why there will never be another Teddy.

"Well, if you're sure that's what you want, Warren, I'll draw up a commutation paper. But he's got to swear a loyalty oath."

"No! Then it looks like we've negotiated with him for his freedom. I'm not negotiating, I'm releasing him."

"Okay, then. But a commutation of sentence, not a pardon."

"Right."

"And I'll say this, too. Even if he did sign the oath, I would expect him to go back on his honor. But then, on the plus side, letting him out will deprive the Progressives of a martyr."

Florence broke in. "Aha! As you like to say, Warren, leave it to Harry to get to the heart of the politics of it. You boys have another drink and I'll have a scotch and water myself." Both men saw that she had made her peace with the Debs matter. Even Laddie Boy yawned contentedly.

"Well, now, let's talk about the so-called political prisoners," Harding said, withdrawing from an inside coat pocket papers containing a typewritten list of names along with his own hand-written notes. "I am also declaring a general amnesty for these twenty-three people who are still sitting in jail for opposition to the war." He handed the papers to Daugherty, who received them grimly.

He looked over the names and muttered, "There are some anarchists on this list." Harding looked at him steadily and did not reply.

With a gesture of what-can-you-do, Harry folded the the papers and secreted them in his own jacket pocket. "But now, back to Debs," he said. "He's still in town, you know. I'll have Jess take him back."

A week later, Warren told Harry, "I'm going to release Debs on Christmas Eve so that he can spend Christmas Day with his wife."

Harry could not resist a sour look. "Doing so would desecrate Christmas. If you're so bound and determined, wait until New Year's."

"Don't argue with me, Harry."

Harry said nothing but his face said much. From that moment his relationship with Warren Harding cooled.

*

"You know what Mr. Debs misses most in prison? Take a guess," Jess said.

"A private bathroom?" Roxy ventured.

"Ha! No, quill toothpicks. Really. He said you can't get them in prison, you can't even get the cheap wooden ones. See, we happened to be just a block away from Union Station, where the F.W. Woolworth's on the corner? So I told the driver to stop, I went in and I bought a whole pound of quill toothpicks and came out and gave them to him. Really, I thought he was going to cry."

Roxy laughed and said, "It's too bad he had to go back to prison, even for a short time."

"That's what got me, he took it so calmly. I was in his place, I'd be looking around for the unguarded exits. To make a run for it. But he just climbed on board like he was going home or something."

"Well, I'm just glad that Mr. Harding did the right thing. Remember when he was in the Senate he spoke out against lynching, and then he came out for treating the coloreds better. In Alabama! That took some nerve. And now he lets Mr. Debs out of prison. Shouldn't he get a lot of credit for all that?"

"Naw, people just want to know where they'll get their next drink."

December 25, 1921

Christmas Day came, spent by Eugene Debs with his wife and by the Hardings with Evalyn and Ned McLean in their Washington home. Florence had been alarmed by a Secret Service report of an anarchist's bomb threat and demanded that they get out of the White House. This threat seemed to be serious—Florence was not overreacting.

Evalyn sat at the bottom of the carved staircase in their I Street mansion. She wore the Hope diamond against a black silk dress open-backed to the waist. Warren bowed and said, "I am grateful to my assassins for such a very pleasant Christmas."

"You're welcome here even when nobody wants to blow you up."

"Please, Evalyn, that's not funny," Florence said with real anxiety.

Evalyn nodded. "Both of you, if we don't see Jess first, please thank him for us for the wonderful present. He gave us corn-fed cattle, prize yearling cattle, for our farm in Virginia."

"Farm? I thought it was a small principality," Warren said.

It was indeed a huge estate, called Belmont, nestled against the Blue Ridge Mountains. The Hardings liked to spend weekends there. Dr. Sawyer forbade Florence to ride, saying it was too strenuous for her weak system, but she cheated a couple of times. She took a horse from the stables to ride up to a ridge line alone to watch the sun set over the mountains.

The McLeans also had places in Maine, Colorado, and Florida. Warren, especially, looked forward to their New Year's trip to Florida, as he said in greeting Ned.

Ned approached wearing a Santa Claus hat, put on to delight his kids and also because he just liked to appear pixilated. They went into the ballroom to see the eight-foot Christmas tree. It was decorated by lit candles, with a servant standing by full time to guard against fire. Something about the scene reminded Florence of the much more modest Christmas tree in Carrie's house in Marion when she had arrived there homeless and penniless with two-year-old, fatherless Marshall. She mentally scolded herself for thinking of such things and tamped the memory back into a cellar of her mind.

After drinks were served Warren expected Ned to talk about Debs, but instead he brought up the Washington Naval Conference.

"Three different treaties requiring all the great powers to give up some of their warships. Or at least stop building them. Warren, if you don't do anything else during your first term, that will go down as a great achievement."

"Thank you, Ned. By the way, you should have seen Cabot Lodge's face when I told him we were going to propose giving up nine of our capital ships. Nine! I thought he would have a stroke."

Warren looked the most relaxed and pleased he had in months, both McLeans observed. He must be delighted that something he did came out right.The Duchess had been nodding along. She now all but cheered and said, "They said Warren Harding couldn't be president because he didn't know anything about foreign affairs. I wish all those no-accounts could hear this conversation."

Warren, in a brocaded armchair, raised his glass to his wife, who sat on a sofa with Ned. "Anyway," he said, "I don't mind Lodge and the others I put on the American delegation trying to snag the credit. That'll just make it easier to get the naval treaties ratified next year."

At that point kids and dogs came running into the room with a roar to paw through the presents again. Warren gave each child a silver dollar, then the adults went upstairs for an early dinner.

The men joined a couple of male servants for poker while the women watched Mary Pickford in *Little Lord Fauntleroy* in the McLeans' private studio. America was in love with Pickford's curls and Florence flattered herself that her own marceled curls somewhat resembled them. Charlie Forbes had told her so, anyway.

A door slammed somewhere. The noise made Florence jump out of her chair and stifle a scream.

"Oh, Flossie, I wish you could relax. There's no way on earth that Warren could be harmed here."

The first lady nodded. She felt a bit sheepish but found it difficult to read the movie's title cards through moist eyes. From habit, she removed her pince-nez and rubbed the bridge of her nose.

Both women felt haunted, though Evalyn would not say so. Something lurking, something not quite discernible but ominous, infected the room. Evalyn knew a bit of Italian and a particular word came to her. *Presagio.* An omen, a sign.

January 23, 1922

"I've got a boring job," Leland complained to Roxy during their post-coital cigarettes. Leland had taken a room in the Wardman Park to be near the Coolidges, who had moved in there. She always booked a separate room in the Wardman Park for retreat in case she and Leland had one of their spats.

"Why is it boring?"

"All I do is follow the Coolidges around to parties and ribbon-cuttings. I never even get to see the White House."

"You don't go to the White House?"

"No. The Duchess doesn't invite the Coolidges."

"Why not?"

"Same reason she doesn't invite you. Grace Coolidge is younger and prettier. And nicer, too."

Roxy considered this while she drew up the blankets. The Wardman Park was a swell place but they didn't heat it enough. Jess always said he was cold there.

"I'm getting bored myself," she said. "Harry and Jess have their bootlegging running pretty smoothly now. And you know they have all those Volstead indictments to cash in on as well. All I do now is keep track of the money."

"Why don't you go out and sing again?"

"Nah, I don't sing any more. Too many cigarettes have spoiled my wind and my voice. In fact, finish this," she said, handing him a glowing cigarette butt.

"Jess gives me stock sometimes instead of cash," she continued. "So I'm playing the market now. It's kind of interesting and I'm pretty good at it. I'm better than Harry and Jess and they've got their own ticker-tape. And Mr. Harding. Jess says Mr. Harding's losing money."

'You'd think he'd have enough to do as president."

"You know something? I don't think he really likes being president."

"Yeah? Well, I can tell Calvin likes being vice president. Lots of attention but no responsibility." He rolled on his side and put his left hand on her midriff. "Okay, if you're bored, I've got a project for you."

"Yeah?"

"Find out who all the spies are."

"Spies? The war ended years ago now. Who needs spies?"

"The Harding administration is full of spies. Really, everybody's spying on everybody else. Actually, since you mentioned it, Gaston Means was a German agent. And Billy Burns was a British agent. But that's neither here nor there. I'll give you a hint. Gaston and Ned McLean are the only ones who hang out on H Street now. The new command post is a house on K Street."

"Oh, hell, Leland, I know about 1625 K Street. I'm Jess's ex-wife, remember?"

Leland chuckled, something he seldom did. "You used to call the H Street place the 'fornicatorium,' What are you going to call K Street?"

"I don't know, I'll think of something."

"Okay, another hint. Find out why Billy Burns sent one of his deviated septums to Montana."

"Montana? Is Montana even a state? Have you ever met anyone from Montana?"

"Yeah, that's why it's so strange and why you need to find out."

"Fine. Then when I find all the spies, what's my prize? A trip to Paris?"

Leland reached over to stub out his cigarette in an ashtray, then rolled back on his side. He was silent for a couple of minutes while caressing her bare stomach. Then he said, "I reckon we can think about getting married now."

"Why, Leland, that's the most romantic proposal I've ever heard."

Another period of silence. The room was dark with just enough light through the shades for Leland to study Roxy's features. He said, "You know, you can be a real bitch sometimes."

"You're not just saying that?"

"See what I mean?"

"Come on, Leland, do I look like wifey material to you? Be serious. Why spoil what we've got?"

Leland reacted as expected, with sullen silence. Damn it, Roxy thought, I've hurt his feelings. I'll try to make it up to him.

The next morning Roxy speedily solved the first mystery by going to see Jess in his office in the Justice building.

"Hell, Billy didn't send one of his agents to Montana, he went out there himself. There's a Bolshevik running for the Senate and he's running against the corruption in the A.G.'s office. He says there are many paths of corruption and they all lead straight to Harry."

"How do you know he's a Bolshevik?"

"I know what Harry tells me. He says the guy's an outright Communist. His name is Burton K. Wheeler."

Jess had two telephones on his carved oaken desk. One of them rang and Jess made a show of lifting the earpiece and then replacing it in its cradle, hanging up to show that Roxy was more important than anyone who might be calling.

"So what's Harry going to do about it?"

"He will neutralize the threat to the efficient functioning of the office of the attorney general."

"Is it to be, um, physical?" When she realized just what she was asking she repressed a small shudder.

"No, no. Billy will find that Wheeler's committed some crime that Harry can charge him with."

Roxy was dejected. The war ended three years ago but the government is still screwing people. How could the president not know? She looked at Jess. His face was blank. She asked him no more questions but put on her fox fur coat and left.

For her second round of sleuthing Roxy made an appointment with Dr. Charles E. Sawyer for a "female complaint." Roxy shared the consensus opinion that Sawyer was a ridiculous popinjay. Florence was convinced that Sawyer's pills and herbs kept her alive, so Warren made him a brigadier general in the army medical corps. Short and slightly built, Sawyer loved to strut in his new blue-and-gold uniform. One time the newsreel cameramen filmed him marching along the West Wing colonnade. They asked him to repeat it again and again until they got the shots just right. Sawyer complied until he was sweating and puffing in the heat, but nobody was filming. This practical joke was celebrated in the press corps for years.

Roxy knew Sawyer's wife, May Elizabeth, and his mistress, Berenice Blacksten, from Ohio. She also knew that the Doc was utterly jealous of anyone, in particular Charles Forbes, who might get as close to the Duchess as he was. At Sawyer's office in the State, War, and Navy Building across the street from the White House, Roxy, feigning embarrassment, said she suffered from painful periods.

After examining the patient—more thoroughly than Roxy believed was necessary—Sawyer said, "Take one teaspoon each of Guelder rose, black haw, and dong quai. Make a tea of each one separately. Have them steep in boiling water for a full ten minutes. You may take them throughout the day as you wish until you feel relief." From a magpie's nest of cubbyholes on the wall, Sawyer extracted the remedies, which Roxy had no intention of using, and measured them into separate containers.

Roxy put them in her handbag with thanks and began to chat about getting adjusted to Washington. She managed to drop a disparaging remark about Charles Forbes. Just for a second, Sawyer stiffened and frowned.

"Mrs. Blacksten works for Mr. Forbes at the hospital in Perryville, Maryland," he said. "She has told me of some distressing irregularities."

People back home wondered what Sawyer saw in Berenice Blacksten, who had been Florence's cook. She was quite plain and had only an eighth-grade education. Roxy, though, sensed the passion and intelligence bubbling inside that small frame. So Berenice was Sawyer's spy against Forbes.

"Irregularities? Really? Like what?"

"That information will be disclosed at the proper time to the proper authorities."

"Oh, of course, doctor. I really wasn't trying to pry, I was just making conversation."

"No offense taken, ma'am."

"Thank you, I'll be going now. I trust that Mrs. Sawyer is well?"

"Quite well, thank you."

Besides Mrs. Sawyer, Roxy also knew Forbes's wife, Kate. A journalist, Kate was given total access to the Duchess to write puff pieces about her for the newspapers. So Kate was Forbes's spy inside the White House. No doubt, Kate and Florence shared "girl-talk" confidences which got back to Forbes.

In a cab to Wardman Park, Roxy tried to draw a diagram in her head of the spies and counterspies, a geometry of espionage. My God, was every White House like this? The Duchess's doctor's mistress, Berenice Blacksten: She spies against Forbes in Perryville. Charles Forbes's wife, Kate: She sees the Duchess constantly, spies in the White House for Forbes. But meanwhile, there were rumors that Forbes himself was having an affair with President Harding's sister, Carolyn Votaw. Does Kate Forbes know? Does Warren? Charles Forbes probably knows more about what goes on in the White House than the president does. Harry Daugherty, of course, has his own Bureau of Investigation to spy on anybody. He had outright thugs like Billy Burns and Gaston Means, although he made particular use of Jess to get news from the Duchess.

The complexity of the intriguing gave Roxy, she was surprised to realize, a new appreciation of politicians. They must keep track, if they are both ambitious and competent, of scores, even hundreds of people and their interrelations. They must know a man's professed politics, his real politics, his family connections, what he hates, what he fears, who controls him, whom he thinks he controls, what kind of pork he wants for his constituents. He must keep a card file in his head of thousands of these combinations and permutations. No wonder great legislators and great presidents were so rare. For all her smarts, Roxy did not have that particular skill. You had to be born with it.

Or maybe it really didn't have much to do with general intelligence. Maybe it was an over-developed mental muscle, like a tennis champion's forearm.

Roxy reported her detective work to Jess, who seemed unimpressed. "The Duchess has her own spy in the whole government, namely, me. But nobody dares to say a word against Charlie Forbes to her. Or to Warren."

March 20, 1922

The lady's hat was old-fashioned, with a wide black brim, red roses around the crown, and two pale pink streamers down the back. It sat precariously atop Warren Harding's head. When Warren was drunk he didn't stagger but walked with a kind of prancing, mincing step. He pranced down the dock wearing the hat and one of Ned McLean's sporting ladies on each arm. He sang "Goodbye, Girls, I'm Through":

I'm the happiest lad in all the flowery kingdom
A miracle has come into my life
I've seen the girl I ever sought
The girl of whom I've ever thought
The ideal one, the one I mean to make my wife.

The one whom he actually had made his wife stood on the prow of the *Nameoka*, the McLeans' houseboat moored on the Intercoastal Waterway in Florida. The waterway's dank smell of fish and salt did not improve Florence Harding's mood. She screeched, "Warren Harding, you come in here this minute! I want to talk to you!"

Warren turned around and tipped his hat to the Duchess. Then he reversed and continued to stroll up the pier with Ned, Harry, Jess, and Harding's secretary George Christian. They had gone to Florida to celebrate a Senate vote in favor of the naval disarmament treaties.

When Warren got back on the boat, minus the showgirls, he said, "Well, Duchess, you look beautiful tonight."

"Warren, you have been drinking! And acting disgracefully!"

"Well, what of it?" He ordered another drink then and there. Florence raised her right index finger to start wagging it at him but before she spoke Warren said, "Don't lecture me! I've taken all I'm going to take from you!"

He turned to Ned. "Ned, old sport, we're going out tonight. We're going to Bradley's." It was a popular casino.

Florence, her chin high and her voice like a ripsaw, said, "I'm only going to say one thing. The reporters have given us our privacy because I asked them to. But they won't stay away forever."

It was Evalyn and not Warren who asked, "Is that a threat?" Evalyn wanted publicity no more than the Duchess did.

Florence said only, "Warren, you ought to be ashamed to let people see you in this condition. You are practically ruined now."

Ned said, "Warren, which one of those girls did you like best? I fancy the one who didn't wear any jewelry, myself. It shows a becoming modesty."

"Let's go, Ned." Warren, Ned, and and the showgirls got into the car that Ned had rented with a driver. The Duchess was left to sulk. Harry and Jess stayed behind with dim hopes of soothing the furies.

Ignoring them, Evalyn summoned her own car. She feared that if the president drunkenly stepped foot in a Palm Beach gambling den it really would ruin him. At Bradley's casino they drove through the parking lot three times but failed to find Ned's car. On the drive back to the boat Evalyn passed by the house of a friend. Florence spied, standing outside the door, Warren's favorite Secret Service agent. That man understood that keeping the Duchess away from Warren was part of his job.

"Stop! Stop! For God's sake, stop!"

"No, no, it wouldn't look right. The president's wife arguing with a Secret Service man to let her in the door?"

Florence glumly agreed. The boat had three double staterooms and, once back aboard, she kept peering into each to see if Warren had somehow sneaked in.

"Evalyn, do you know where to reach them?"

"No," she lied. "They'll come along without our searching for them."

"Well, we'd better send for them to that house."

"Oh, that would never do. Suppose they weren't there? It might get in the papers." Getting in the papers was a horror that neither wanted.

The delinquent husbands got in well past midnight. In the morning Evalyn said, "Now, Mr. President, you had a nice day yesterday. I want you to take some coffee and stay right here with me. You are leaving on the 12:30 train. You stay here and we'll play poker or bridge."

Harding, with a hangover unto death, lacked the energy to object, although he did muster the vim to bicker with the Duchess. He acquiesced about taking the train to Washington. At the Palm Beach station the men formed a cordon around the first couple, hoping they would pass unrecognized. Warren and Florence ducked into the McLeans' private car.

Several days later in the Yellow Oval Room, Harding tumbled from despondency into outright depression. I need another visit to the Battle Creek Sanitarium, he thought, but a president can't do that. A president can't do anything that normal people do; he must extinguish all hope of it. Outside, tiny pellets of snow were blowing around on a blustery March day. A low overcast obscured the top of the Washington Monument. Suddenly Harding wanted to go out and feel the cold, feel chilled to the bone. He called for his valet to bring the light leather jacket that he used to wear when riding in the Ohio countryside with the Duchess. The valet looked at him funny but said nothing as they rode the elevator to the sleeping porch on the White

House roof. Harding sat, ordered a drink, and then waved the valet away. He did not button the jacket. He did not feel cold. He felt nothing.

A sharp thought intruded: Carrie and Jim Phillips are back from their world tour and she wants me to make Jim the ambassador to Japan. Jesus, even for Carrie, that's a crazy idea. That's the goddamn thing about being president, everybody always wants something from you. It never stops, I can't even tie my shoes without Christian telling me the people lined up to get something from me. People spend their lives trying to get this goddamn job and then it's a misery. Our only true friends who aren't just out for themselves are Ned and Evalyn and I'm not so sure about Evalyn.

He stopped thinking and just stared at the snow pellets turned into flakes. He buttoned the jacket and turned up the collar but was not conscious of those actions.The next thought: I've got to start taking better care of myself. Doc Sawyer takes my temperature and blood pressure and looks at my urine every morning and he tells me I'm killing myself. He's probably right. Well, what of it. If I die in office I'll be remembered fondly, like McKinley.

And then some more glassy-eyed staring; he could not have told you how much time had passed when the valet patted his arm. "Begging your pardon, sir, but you have a guest. Mr. Forbes, sir."

"Show him into the Yellow Oval Room."

"Yes, sir."

Forbes wore a sealskin coat and as he handed it to a butler he said, "My God, Warren, were you sitting up there wearing just that jacket? You'll catch your death."

"If I do, so what?"

Forbes stared at Harding. Just a year in office and he already looked awful. Bags under his eyes, sagging jowls, a patina of fatigue. "Are you all right, Warren?"

"Just having a little trouble getting my breath recently. Just a winter cold. Nothing to worry about."

"You're working too hard. Don't let the Duchess push you so much. Take a week's rest. Just insist on it."

Harding shrugged. "You know something, Charlie? I'd rather be an ambassador than president. Being president is rather an unattractive business—unless one relishes the exercise of power. That's a thing which never greatly appealed to me."

Forbes thought, if you don't want to exercise power, why in the hell did you run for president? So you could hear "Hail to the Chief" and "Ruffles and Flourishes"?

Harding rarely expressed self-pity, but now it gushed. "You are looking at an unhappy man, Charlie. I told the Duchess before we moved in here, the demands upon my mind and body might be too much. And by God they are. I never find myself done. I never find myself with my work complete. I don't believe there is a human being alive who can do all the work there is to be done in the president's office. It feels as though I have been president for twenty years. It is hell! No other word can describe it."

Harding did not ask why Forbes had come to see him. Forbes quickly realized this was not the time to bring it up. Harding's sister Carolyn Votaw was the personnel director in Forbes's Veterans Bureau. She was a sincere advocate for social uplift and pressed her brother to create a Bureau of Human Welfare. She also was one of Forbes's mistresses. Charlie had come to notify Warren that he was dropping Carolyn from the travel roster for junkets to visit hospital sites. There had been too much criticism of the lavish costs of those trips.

Forbes's spies of course had told him about Warren's drunken antics in Florida. Now he thought, maybe Warren has some kind of sick wish to be caught. Maybe he has a secret or unconscious desire to have a scandal drive him from office.

He said, "Mr. President—I'm going to call you Mr. President so you might take me more seriously—what you need is complete rest. Congress is in recess now, the hell with them. Go home to Ohio if that's what you want. Go fishing. Go riding with the Duchess."

Harding made no sign of having heard him. He said, "You know I have not been intimate with my wife for so many years I have lost count. I have made a complete botch of my personal life. There was one love of my life and she hates me now." He turned in his chair to face Forbes. His eyes were lifeless. "Charlie, tell me you are my friend."

"Oh, Warren, you know I am your friend."

Harding stood up. "I want to be outside. This house is a damn prison."

Forbes retrieved his coat and the valet brought Harding a heavy wool overcoat. They put on wool hats and walked onto the South Lawn. Harding indicated a bench facing the tennis court where the old stables used to be. The valet with a whisk broom brushed snow off the bench and laid a blanket on it. The two men looked at the Washington Monument, ghostly in the snowfall.

Forbes did not know what to say when Harding began to cry.

June 22, 1922

Jess took Roxy to the notorious "little green house on K Street" but it was not little and not really green either. It was a three-story Victorian townhouse of limestone with a slightly green tint. One of Harry's cronies in Ohio leased it for the gang.

Gaston Means was playing poker with a Republican boss and a couple of what Leland called the "deviated septums."

The men all but ignored Roxy as she served them drinks. They gossiped about the Hardings and Gaston offered, "To visualize a love scene between the president and his wife is entirely beyond the imagination of man." Hearty laughter followed. Roxy was surprised that Gaston would say something so mean in her presence. He had to know that she was close to Jess and Jess was close to the Duchess. Then she understood: Of course, she was just the girl serving drinks. She was like a piece of furniture except for being ambulatory.

"Hey, girlie," said one of the deviated septums, "take your hat off and let down your hair for us." Silently, she removed the cloche, shook her tresses. Roxy knew that guy. He was the kind of son of a bitch who would pronounce "Bayer aspirin" as "bare assburn" and then behave as though he had cracked a hilarious joke. Women put up with a lot, she thought.

She had observed that men usually are uncomfortable around women, especially the beautiful ones. Well, maybe their scatology was a kind of bravado, a way to deflect the discomfort. That was a kinder way of looking at it, anyway. Meanwhile, how soon could she see Jess?

Jess was in an office upstairs running a racket. During the war, the government seized assets owned by Germans. Now a government board was deciding whose postwar claims to recover those assets were valid. Jess said that taking bribes for favorable rulings was even more profitable than bootlegging. And simpler. Roxy wondered why, unlike bootlegging, she could not take much interest in this form of boodle. Maybe because it was outright graft, whereas bootlegging provided something that people wanted. Or maybe she was just tiring of the constant parade of grotesqueries. Look at those men there with their cigars and their booze and their cards and their booming voices. Alice Roosevelt Longworth had said of the little green house,

"No rumor could have exceeded the reality." Yeah, Roxy thought, that's right.

She wondered, not for the first or second time, why Harding had so many crooks in his government when he was not crooked himself. Could he really not know what his poker buddies were doing?

She lit a cigarette in a futile attempt to counter the cigar smoke and pondered how to escape these oafs. "Hey, boys, why don't we turn on the radio?" she suggested brightly just to bring some diversion into the place. On a table was an Arborphone radio, the kind the Duchess had just installed in the White House, and Washington now had its own radio station, WJH.

Suddenly the men drew their cards close to their chests and studied them intently. Roxy guessed what was up. They did not know how to turn the radio on or dial a station and would not admit it. She sighed and walked to a window because she heard a truck backing into the driveway.

It was an armored car. There's so much graft that they bring the money in armored cars now? Two men in white overalls, with a third man in a suit holding a gun, carried a big metal box into the house. Opened, it contained twenty cases of booze. One man took a few bottles of vintage wine down to the wine cellar. The poker party got so raucously noisy now that Roxy almost cried out with relief when the clock on the mantel struck three p.m.

That was her signal to go through a sitting room to a side door and open it to George Remus. They nodded to each other but did not speak. Remus climbed the stairs to Jess's office. He was the industrial-scale bootlegger who had bribed Jess to keep him out of jail. Roxy waited in the sitting room until the meeting ended.

"George, I wish you'd take off that damn derby," Jess said. "Let me give you a fine Ponte Rialto boater."

"Mind your own fucking business."

Okay, so that's how this meeting would go. "Have a seat, George. Drink?"

"I never touch the stuff."

"Right, I forgot. Let's proceed to business, then. Here's the situation. There is so much money to be made in bootlegging that the price of bribery has gone up. You know Treasury Secretary Mellon? No? Well, he calls it price inflation because of excess demand. Everybody wants a piece of the pie."

"Jess, I'm not here today to talk about economic theory. I know what you're saying. I tried to corner the graft market myself, but I learned that there isn't enough money in the world to buy up all the politicians who want a piece of it."

That remark relaxed Jess; Remus understood. "Cigar? No? You know, George, it wasn't us that raided your 'farm' there in Cincinnati. That happened before Warren even took office. So now you're convicted on multiple counts and you might die in prison."

Remus glowered and twirled his diamond stickpin, such that in Jess's eye it caught and then lost its sparkle. "Dammit, Jess, I'm not here to talk about ancient history either."

"All right, let's consider. The case goes to a three-judge panel in the appeals court. That means you've got to bribe two judges. Or, God forbid, let's say it goes *en banc* to the whole ten-judge circuit. You see?"

"Since you won't get to the point, I will. Fifty G's and that's the last dollar you'll get from me."

"I appreciate a man who knows what he wants and comes directly to terms." Jess stood and reached across his desk to shake hands. Remus ignored him and placed an envelope on the desk. Jess did not insult him by counting fifty $1,000 bills under his nose. At the bottom of the stairs Remus nodded to Roxy on his way out. She was not surprised that the meeting was over so soon.

Upstairs, she asked Jess, "How can you stand to be around that man? He's an insufferable ass. And Gaston

Means down there. You know something, Jess, I've known crooks and I've known braggarts, but I never before knew crooks who bragged about their crimes like these fellas."

"You will be interested to hear that Gaston Means has been suspended from the Bureau of Investigation."

"Really? What for?"

"Somehow he got some blank forms from the Treasury Department and forged the signatures so that he could get bonded government liquor and bootleg it."

"Well? Isn't that what you do?"

"Yeah, but Harry don't like freelancers. It shows a regrettable lack of team spirit."

"Then why is he still hanging around?"

"He still runs his private-eye business here. And he's got those file cabinets down in the basement. There's enough in there to hang us all."

Roxy leaned back in the sofa and blew smoke toward the ceiling. Her hair was still down and she fingered the felt cloche in her hand.

"Jess, I'm getting awfully tired of this shit."

"Me too, sweetie. Like I said, I reckon we'll go through the winter and then next spring I'll still be with Harry but we're getting out of the extracurricular activities."

"I wish I could believe that," Roxy said with another sigh. She glanced at him and then noticed a strange, slight tremor in her right hand.

September 9, 1922

Doctors expected Florence Harding to die of uremic poisoning. Her right kidney was blocked again. Churches and synagogues across the country called for prayers for her. Theaters and movie houses paused their Sunday matinees to ask the audience for standing silent prayers. At the White House, a disabled Negro veteran hobbled up to the North Portico and hung a wreath. He told reporters, "I lost my leg. I didn't have a friend in the world who cared. But Mrs. Harding one day found me recovering from the operation in the hospital. She seemed interested when I told her I had no friends. Next day she came with a big bouquet of flowers."

Florence ordered the White House gates to stay open. Woodrow and Edith Wilson came in a horse-drawn carriage to offer their respects and prayers. Thousands of folks knelt and prayed on the driveway throughout the month of September 1922. Even Roxy and Jess, nonbelievers, knelt and prayed there. Alice Longworth, also a nonbeliever, did not.

After a few days of official lies, Warren ordered her doctors to issue an accurate daily medical report. "I won't be an Edith Wilson," he said, remembering her efforts to deceive the country about Woodrow's stroke.

Besides Doc Sawyer, Florence now had a real doctor. When she learned that Joel Boone had been awarded the Medal of Honor in the war, she named him as the navy doctor aboard the *Mayflower*, the presidential yacht. Dr. Boone had been called to the White House. He soon summoned the nation's most famous doctor, Charles Mayo of Rochester, Minnesota.

"Surgical removal of the kidney is her only chance of survival," Dr. Mayo said. "You see the indications of septicemia and she cannot maintain consciousness."

"No, no. Her heart is too weak to sustain an operation," Dr. Sawyer said. "The procedure would kill her. She is my patient and I must insist. I have seen her pull through this before."

"What is your opinion, Dr. Boone?" Mayo asked. Boone would not contradict "General" Sawyer, who outranked him. Boone was a mere vice admiral. He said, "Judging from her blood and urine tests, the surgery could wait overnight. In any case the decision should be Mrs. Harding's."

Warren spent every night at his Duchess's side. He knelt by her bed and recited his favorite verses from the 121st Psalm:

I will lift up mine eyes unto the hills, from whence cometh my help . . .

The LORD shall preserve thee from all evil: he shall preserve thy soul . . .

Florence was kept wrapped in blankets and hot towels so that perspiration might expel some of the toxins that her kidneys would not void. When her fever reached a life-threatening 105 degrees Warren told her that Dr. Mayo advocated surgery.

Her eyes opened and she said, "Don't worry, Warren, I'm not going to die," before slipping back into unconsciousness.

Evalyn arrived after midnight from the McLeans' estate in Bar Harbor, Maine. She looked awful—thin and unkempt. Her eyes bulged from a thyroid condition and she was developing a goiter. Warren asked her to try to reconcile the doctors.

"This man is going to kill her," Mayo said, meaning Sawyer. "Frankly, I am so disgusted that I am thinking of taking the noontime train home."

Sawyer told Evalyn, "I realize much more sharply than you just how the country will think of me if anything happens to her. But I know her constitution. I know what she can stand and what she cannot stand. I am gambling on my reputation. I am facing ruin, almost, just because I am convinced that if her heart holds out her kidney stoppage will open up."

Evalyn told Warren it was hopeless.

Besides Warren and the doctors and nurses, Evalyn

was the only person allowed in Florence's room. One night she looked at Florence and thought she had died. At that moment Florence was telling herself, "Stay awake! Stay awake! If you lose consciousness you will die."

She dug her nails into her palms so hard that they bled. Even so, she lost consciousness. Dr. Boone noted, "She had a very strange stare on her face directed right at Dr. Mayo and myself."

Florence saw those two figures become dim silhouettes. They shrank and receded into the distance, as though seen through the wrong end of an opera glass. She looked away and saw herself as a girl at her father's side in France. Amos had gone there to buy Normandy horses. Amos never looked at her, only the horses. Her favorite was a bay that she named Billy.

France faded from sight and and standing there at the foot of her bed was Amos Kling, now as an old man. He walked around to her side and looked down with apparent boredom. She had to tell him something.

"Papa, you just gave up! You gave up! That's why you died! I won't give up!"

Amos said, "You know you should have been born a boy."

Now her mother Louisa stood at his left. Amos put his arm over his wife's shoulders in an affectionate gesture that surprised Florence. Still, neither showed any expression.

"Mama, you gave up too! That's why you died! I'm not going to go with you! I'm not ready! I'm not going! Don't think that I will!"

Now Louisa smiled sweetly. Then both receded just as the doctors had.

Her son Marshall was at her bedside.

"And I know you gave up too! There was no reason for you to die like that, a drunkard. You gave up but you won't see me follow you!"

"Yes, my life was mostly a burden. Your scolding has no effect on me now, mama. Your judgment either. I just came to ask how you are taking care of my children. Jean and George. Your grandchildren."

Florence gasped in pain. She hardly ever saw her grandchildren. Marshall vanished and she expected her next visitor to be the boy's father, Petey de Wolfe. Or maybe her own father again. She had allowed Petey to impregnate her just so that she could get away from Amos. Deep down, Amos knew it. The whole town knew it. But nobody came for a long time. Florence started to blink and then realized that her eyes were shut. How strange, she thought. I can see with my eyes shut.

The smells of a sickroom gave way to a powerful odor of horse sweat. She saw a tall, proud horse running in the distance across a featureless landscape. It seemed to run in place without moving forward. Logically, the background should have been moving behind him, as in a movie. But both the galloping horse and the background—a cold white, a fish-belly white, with no shadows, no perspective—were stationary. Florence tried to sit up for a closer look. Now she discerned a teenage girl riding bareback and astride. She squinted harder. The horse was Billy and she the rider, but the only times she had ever ridden astride instead of sidesaddle was when nobody could see her. Billy slowed to a trot while staying in place. Florence whistled to him from her bed.

The horse stopped, looked her way, nodded and whinnied, and turned to approach the bed. "Billy, I must live! I must live!" Then a peace and calmness she had never known passed through her . . .

A nurse screamed. "Doctor, look!" Urine was flowing in such volume that the bedclothes were soaked. Dr. Boone wrote in his notes, "The pt. had spontaneously relieved the obstruction. She began to drain spontaneously from the kidneys voluminously, and began to clear mentally. Dr. Mayo and I observed this amazing episode. She demonstrated that, when death was on the threshold for her, she kept herself from dying truly by pure willpower."

The next night, when Florence was barely strong enough to write, she wrote in her journal, "The one thing that counts when you are down in the Valley of the Shadows is: What have you done for human beings?"

Dr. Mayo still advised surgery to remove the bad kidney. Florence kept saying, "I must not die, Warren needs me," clenching her fists. For the first time in a week, Warren walked out on the South Lawn. He looked old and worn out.

In her convalescence Florence thought a lot about how much had she done for human beings. She had helped a lot of veterans but maybe she had treated some people unfairly. Maybe one of them was Miss Roxy Stinson. Really, I should try to make it up to her.

Not until December did the doctors feel confident that she would survive. Sawyer remained worried that he might have provoked his patient's attack back in late August. He had presented to Florence undeniable proof that Charles Forbes was a crook.

August 28, 1922

Charles Forbes usually was called to the White House to cheer people up. He was the only one of Warren's poker buddies whom Florence really liked. He had a standard greeting: "Duchess, how about a little drink for a thirsty hombre?" Then he had a way of bouncing around the room with Laddie Boy, the Hardings' dog, that made even Doc Sawyer, who hated him, laugh. Forbes flourished a cane and a straw boater to dance a soft-shoe while evading the airedale's assaults on his pants cuffs. He had long arms and a long torso but disproportionate, short legs. His body type made his dance with the dog even funnier.

Florence was not blind to Forbes's failings. He ignored, did not even open, thousands of letters from veterans seeking help from his Veterans Bureau. When some of their complaints percolated up to Florence, she summoned Forbes to her sitting room on the second floor. He grinned like a cherub, fingered his bow tie, and said, "Duchess, I have the largest payroll and the largest personnel roster in the government. Of course there are going to be some bureaucratic mixups. We're working hard every day to straighten them out."

Forbes had used that excuse before. Florence responded as he expected. She took off her pince-nez and rubbed each side of her nose. Then she said flatly, "I had a long conversation with Carolyn."

That took the smile off Forbes's face. He had told Warren that he had bumped Carolyn Votaw, the president's sister, from his tours of West Coast hospital sites just to cut expenses. The real reason was that he was forced to break off his affair with her. Carolyn's husband, Heber Votaw, had threatened to throw him out a window unless he did so. Carolyn, a woman scorned, struck back by going to Doc Sawyer and dishing dirt on Forbes.

Doc remembered Carolyn as Warren's kid sister, younger by fourteen years. She had Warren's high forehead, soft eyes, and fine profile, yet she was not beautiful. Like Florence's, her features did not cohere in just the right configuration.

She had married Votaw, a Seventh-Day Adventist minister, and the couple served as missionaries in Burma for nine years. When they returned, her newly elected brother gave them government jobs. Carolyn headed Forbes's personnel division and Heber was named superintendent of federal prisons. "I've seen things on those hospital tours that you wouldn't believe," she told Doc. "And that's not even the worst of it."

Sawyer went to Florence's sitting room and told her about Carolyn's bombshells, along with some dirt, without disclosing the source, obtained by his mistress in Maryland. Florence agreed that he should inform Warren as well. In the Oval Office, Sawyer said, "Sir, I have evidence of serious wrongdoing in the Veterans Bureau."

"Yeah? Is it evidence or just rumor and slander? Show me evidence or you're wasting my time."

"The evidence is convincing, but what I'm really trying to do here, sir, I'm trying to impart a sense of urgency. You know that Mr. Burton Wheeler is likely to be elected to the Senate from Montana this fall and he is threatening an investigation of Mr. Forbes."

"What, Bolshevik Burt? I thought he had been taken care of."

"No, sir, Mr. Daugherty charged him with sedition for associating with communists and labor strikers. Violent strikers, I mean. But I regret to say the case was dismissed."

Harding grunted and tapped his cigar ash into a cuspidor by his chair. There is something strange about Warren's behavior today, Sawyer thought. He is pale, distracted, cranky; his eyes don't focus. The pallor was especially notable because of his dark complexion. He really doesn't know about Wheeler? Then Sawyer understood: My God, Warren is drunk. It's 2:30 in the afternoon.

When in doubt, Sawyer returned the conversation to Marion. "Warren, well, we both grew up in the country. And there we learned that all the frogs croak just before a storm."

"What of it?"

"Don't you see? Senator Wheeler is just the first frog to croak. There will be more and the storm is coming. There are other senators, they're saying that they will investigate the administration's oil leases."

"Tell Mr. Forbes to come see me."

So that was why Florence now said to Forbes in the driest of tones, "We have an appointment with the president."

"Ahem, Mr. President, I have nothing but the utmost respect for your sister. You know she is on the social welfare side, not the operations side, and I think she misunderstands the practicalities of running the largest bureau in the government. Also, maybe she has been given bad information. As you know, I have many enemies."

When Warren didn't speak, Florence said, "Is it true that you sell surplus government property at cut rates to your friends?"

"Dear lady, do you know how much war surplus material there is and how much the storage costs are? I'm actually saving the government money." Inspiration struck him. "Warren, have Mr. Daugherty send a couple of agents to my office. I would welcome an independent review of the books."

Warren merely nodded and said, "Do it."

Forbes arranged for his own investigators, who walked into his office and hardly turned around before reporting that nothing was wrong. Forbes knew that Daugherty was too sick to do anything.

It was a terrible year for sickness. Warren had been sick in bed for weeks with influenza. Jess had an appendectomy whose incision would not close and he had to wear a truss, which bothered him constantly. Harry sat at his desk, could not function, could not even pick up the phone, and called for his driver to take him home. Dr. Boone, now a member of the Hardings' inner circle, took a look at Daugherty and said, "You are about one half-inch away from a nervous breakdown. I insist that you get treatment at a sanitarium."

So Harry, his brother Mal, and Jess went to French Lick Springs, Indiana, for a month's rest. They bathed in the mineral springs and played poker and golf. Harry tried not to worry about Forbes. He already had assigned Gaston Means to investigate him.

Roxy came over from Ohio to keep Jess company for a weekend. Mal treated her with obvious dislike and Harry was more truculent than usual. Roxy was surprised by how old and tired Harry looked, how much more his jowls sagged. She had never seen a man look so sad and mean. Running rackets all day, every day, must be a wearisome profession, Roxy thought. Harry's hatred of humanity had made him sick. A sick soul contaminates the physical body.

Jess stayed off the links one day, blaming his inactivity on asthma and the truss. While waiting for a masseuse to come to his room, he told Roxy that Carolyn Votaw had betrayed Forbes to the Duchess. "And another thing. Billy Burns told me that Mr. Votaw asked him to cover up an investigation of a big narcotics ring down in Atlanta, the penitentiary there. He said it would make for bad publicity."

That last remark reminded Roxy of the air whooshing out of a ballon. She slunk down on the sofa, tried to take a deep breath and failed. Stretching her arms above her head, she managed to inhale deeply but could not ward off despondency. She left her arms upstretched with her hands resting against the wall and her bottom scootched down on the sofa. The posture was uncomfortable but it fit her mood.

"But the Votaws were missionaries in some foreign country, Jess. Religious people are supposed to be good people. Or at least better than us. Aren't they?"

Jess seemed unconcerned. He winced as he tugged at the truss belt.

Roxy said, "You remember the *Br'er Rabbit* stories we read in school? The tar baby? It's like the Harding government is just a big tar baby. Everybody gets stuck to it and gets tar all over them. Even religious people come here and even they get stuck."

Jess said, "Jeez, Roxy, it sounds like you maybe should be out preaching on a dusty road somewhere."

"There, you see, that's what I mean. You never used to make such smart-ass remarks like that to me. We're all being dirtied up by all this, everybody trying to do everybody else in the eye. All this, everybody shooting bank shots instead of straight shots. Isn't there anyone who's a straight shooter?"

Jess looked startled, did not know what to say. He cleared his throat and adopted what he hoped was a soothing tone. "Well, you should be safe, anyway, baby. What could they send you over for? You've paid your debt to society, right? By making timely payments of all those fines for showing those fight films. And then, as I've said, you don't need to worry about Harry, he's too smart to get us in much serious trouble."

"That's not the point!" she said, waving her arms. "All this spying and counterspying, everybody trying to screw everybody else. It's got to fall apart, don't you see? Mr. Harding's presidency is going to crash like an airplane and after just two years. And we're too deep in it to ever bail out. We're gonna go down with it, honey."

With that, she sat up straight and stifled a sniffle. Jess looked at her with a strange gaze, his eyes dim and watery. He thought of saying something snide about a tar baby and an airplane at the same time but suppressed the thought. "Oh, baby, the strain of all this is making us both morbid. Harry's sick as hell and I feel awful myself. We'll get rid of Charlie Forbes and maybe one of two others and then things will straighten out." Neither of them believed this. The crisis would outlast Forbes.

Jess continued, "Don't forget, Warren and the Duchess are both very popular with the people." Roxy left that evening.

October 26, 1922

The first lady could hardly refuse Alice Roosevelt Longworth's request to wish her well after her nearly fatal illness. Florence would not invite her upstairs to the living quarters, though. Alice always walked into the White House as though she still lived there. The Duchess would meet her in the formality of the Red Room. She sat in an pillowed armchair, wearing a dressing gown covered by a blanket. She was thin and pale with swollen wrists and ankles.

"I'm so glad to see you looking well," Alice said as she inserted a cigarette into a long black holder. "You gave us all quite a scare."

"Please don't smoke, Alice. The fumes do not agree with my condition."

For the first time, Florence saw Alice look amazed at something. Slowly and deliberately, she replaced the cigarette and holder in her tooled leather handbag.

"Why, certainly, Duchess. I appreciate your telling me so."

"Now tell me how are you, Alice? And how is Senator Borah?"

That was something of a low blow, even though Alice did not try to hide her affair with the Idaho senator.

Alice ignored the question and volunteered, "As you know, Nick is collecting pledges to be elected Speaker of the House next year. We do hope that he will have Warren's support. Oh, and that reminds me, wasn't it kind of Evalyn to let Warren use Friendship as a place to meet with friends from Marion? During your illness, I mean."

Alice, with a poker face, reflexively started to lift her arm to puff a cigarette, then remembered its absence. She turned her head slightly to look directly at Florence with the smallest hint of a smile.

It was Florence's turn to look amazed—exactly the expression that Alice had intended. "What on Earth do you mean?"

"Oh, you know, Warren likes to go to Friendship to play golf and sometimes there is a friend there from back home. You didn't know? Oh, I'm so sorry. Ask Evalyn, then."

For once, Florence was speechless. She understood that Alice spoke from malice because she still resented Evalyn for forsaking her friendship for Florence's. Alice must be lying, then. Was there any place on Earth where people lied more than in Washington? But still, she said to ask Evalyn about it.

Florence disdained to continue with a few more minutes of meaningless chitchat just to be polite. She bared her teeth in a simulacrum of a smile. "Yes, Evalyn and Ned have been very kind to us for many years. And now I'm afraid you must excuse me, Alice. I still get very fatigued about this time every day."

Alice grasped her handbag, rose, and surprising Florence again, bowed slightly from the waist. "You are absolutely correct, Duchess. It's important that you have complete rest. Soon you'll be your old self again." She wore a smirk as the White House doorkeeper showed her out.

Women from Marion? Florence ransacked her memory. Carrie was in Germany and anyway she hated Warren now. Recently Carolyn Votaw had given a personal tour of the White House to a young woman from Marion with a three-year-old girl. Florence had smiled and waved—tourists from back home. What was her name? Britton, I think. Jeanette Britton. Yes, the daughter of the coroner in Marion.

Actually, Jeanette was the sister of Nan Britton, Warren's young mistress, and the girl was their daughter.

Alice had told the truth about Warren's trysts at Friendship, although Evalyn did not exactly invite them. Warren and Nan simply showed up and walked upstairs. Evalyn shrugged—she was sick and anyway she was more concerned about Ned's philandering. She hired Gaston Means to keep a tail on Ned. She also advised the Duchess to hire Means to keep track of Warren. The Duchess did so.

Doc Sawyer was Florence's emissary in retaining Means. Doc then passed his findings on to Florence. "My lady, I am afraid that the miserable scandal is true. The girl was here for the last time last month. Mr. Means says that the president apparently has gotten tired of her constant demands for attention."

Florence's first question was "What does the little bitch look like?"

"Um, well, she's blonde and slender, not very tall. Cute, I guess, but not a great beauty. Kind of chubby cheeks." Florence raised her eyebrows and did not have to ask the next question. "Twenty-six years old."

"When did they have their bastard daughter?"

"Three years ago."

Florence started sobbing and Sawyer took his leave.

Florence became aware of her heart as a massive object, one that sank into her viscera and threatened to keep dropping. Idly, she wondered how it could keep beating down there in her abdomen. When her tears ran out she felt less grief than exhaustion. Somewhat to her surprise, rage against Warren and Evalyn did not rise to her throat. Numbly, she remembered what she had written in her journal as a young woman about betrayal as the theme of her life. Her first lover had abandoned her and their son; Amos had thrown her out of his home; her best friend Carrie betrayed her; Charles Forbes was double-crossing her and Warren both; Warren betrayed her with countless other women, and now her new best friend Evalyn was complicit in Warren's adultery.

Ah, but had she not betrayed her own son? One of her favorite childhood memories was of walking under the elms along East Center Street and kicking the fallen autumn leaves. But in the memory that stung her now, she was twenty-four and Marshall was four and she was marching him along that street to Amos's house. The street itself seemed to reproach her. Amos had offered to take the boy in, raise him as his own, all at his own expense. "I will give the boy my name so that he is not a bastard. That's the decent, Christian thing to do." Florence, nearly penniless at the time, agreed. Dry-eyed, she handed Marshall off to her father. Walking away, she mentally drew a schema of abandonment. Amos and the boy's father abandoned her, who in turn abandoned the boy. Which of them was the most heartless? She feared that the answer was herself. But no, Amos. Had to be Amos. He was the one who had whipped her periodically with a hickory switch.

Her mind leapt away from this sorrow and back to Warren and Nan. No, she realized, I was wrong about not feeling angry, I am damned angry and I am going to have it out with Evalyn when we go to Florida.

The first thing she did was to call Jess at his office in the Justice Department. Jess wired Roxy in Ohio: TAKE NEXT TRAIN TO DC. I WANT TO SEE YOU. SO DOES DUCHESS.

November 10, 1922

When Harry Daugherty got back to Washington he remained under a nurse's care. After comparing notes with Doc Sawyer and Billy Burns he prepared an informal brief against Forbes, then insisted on seeing Warren on "a gravely important matter" right away.

"Article One. Defrauding the government of the United States in real estate transactions.

"Count One. In Springfield, Missouri, Mr. Forbes's Veterans Bureau purchased land for a hospital. The land was valued at $35,000 but the Bureau paid $90,000, of which $25,000 was returned to Mr. Forbes."

Harry was not reading his document but speaking from memory while watching Harding closely. The president's eyes were hard and his jaw clenched. What impressed Harry the most was that Harding never reached for the cigar smoldering in an ashtray. Nor did he fumble inside a packet of Mail Pouch for a chew. His hands were clasped on his desk.

"Count Two. In Ukiah, California, Mr. Forbes's Veterans Bureau bought a parcel of land, recently sold for $19,257, for $105,000. Again, $25,000 was returned to Mr. Forbes, nominally as a 'commission.' "

"Count Three. In—"

"Goddamnit, Harry, stop it. I get the point. What else?"

Harry returned the hard stare before glancing at his notes.

"Article Two. Defrauding the government of the United States in the sale and purchases of goods and services.

"Count One. In the supply depot at Perryville, Maryland, Mr. Forbes's Veterans Bureau sold 72,000 brand-new bedsheets, purchased for one dollar each, for twenty cents each to private interests.

"Count Two. Mr. Forbes's Veterans Bureau, at the said supply depot, purchased 32,115 gallons of floor wax, valued at one-point-eight cents per gallon, for eighty-seven cents per gallon. Inventory specialists state that this supply of floor wax is sufficient to last one hundred years.

"Count Three. Mr. Forbes's Veterans Bureau, at the said supply depot, sold 98,995 pairs of pajamas, donated to the nation by the ladies of the Red Cross during the World War, for fifty cents each to private interests."

Warren rose and slammed his hands on the desk—something Harry had never seen. "Jesus Christ, don't tell the Duchess about that! She helped to make those pajamas and things during the war!"

"Certainly not, Mr. President. Count Four. Mr. Forbes's Veterans Bureau—"

"Stop it, stop it! These are all goddamned lies! You and Doc Sawyer have been out to get Charlie Forbes from the start!"

Harding started to walk around the desk and for a second Harry thought he might actually intend to throw a punch.

Instead, Harding turned around and stared out the south windows of the Oval Office. The drapes were open in the unrealized hope of getting some November sun.

"Warren, listen to me. Listen, please. I am speaking to you as your lawyer now. As your lawyer, I advise you to sit down and listen."

Once he had sat, Harding said, "As my lawyer, it was you and the Duchess who got me into such a mess as president of the United States. In which there is all grief and no joy."

"Let's leave that aside for now. Here's the thing. You might have committed misprision of felony. Which is a crime for which the Congress could, in theory at least, impeach you."

"What the hell is misprision of felony?"

"Concealment of felony. Having knowledge of crimes and doing nothing to see that justice is served. Especially in your case, nonperformance of office. You see, Doc Sawyer has been telling you these things for months and you did nothing. You didn't even reprimand Mr. Forbes. How do you think that's going to look to the Democrats on the Judiciary Committee?"

Harry could hear Harding breathing hard. We've both become old men in just two years, Harry thought.

"Let's be blunt, Mr. President. Ahem. The Republicans lost seven seats in the Senate in last Tuesday's election. Seven. Seats. And one of them goes to Bolshevik Burt from Montana. We still have a majority, yes, but some of the new Republicans are Progressives who would like to screw us to the hilt just like the Democrats would."

Warren looked down at his desk for several minutes. When he looked up he said, "Good afternoon, Harry."

Harry rose and hesitated. Always before, Warren had ended an afternoon meeting by asking Harry to stay for dinner. Today he had not even asked after Harry's health. When Harding stayed silent, Harry walked out without saying goodbye or shaking hands. The next day, Harry's direct phone line to the Oval Office never rang once. Another first.

Also on that day, Armistice Day, the soothsayer Madame Marcia called on the Duchess.

Except for being fatter, Marcia looked the same. She still glided with a former dancer's agility and still wore black with a string of pearls.

"Oh, Marcia, thank you for coming to see me on a holiday!"

"Oh, tut tut, madam, the stars never take a holiday. Why should I?"

"Marcia, I had to see you! I am surrounded by traitors! Terrible things are happening. I must know who are Warren Harding's friends and who are not."

Marcia noticed that Florence's illness had left her ankles and hands more swollen than usual. She twirled a strand of her apricot-shaded hair around a finger, then saw that such a gesture might imply that she was not taking the Duchess seriously enough. She portentously opened her book of readings.

"The president is coming under some very powerful influence and needs to safeguard his health. The opposition of the Moon to the Sun and Saturn in his horoscope shows that he cannot depend upon his friends. He should be suspicious of the ones he should trust and trust those he should be suspicious of."

Before Florence could interpret this gnomic pronouncement, Warren walked into the Red Room. Ignoring Marcia, he said, "I fired Forbes."

Florence, glowering, said, "Good!"

Warren nodded toward Marcia. "You will excuse us, madam." She left.

Warren remained standing. "I called him a goddamned liar. He said"—Warren sniffed; he still could hardly believe it—"he said, 'Ah, but Mr. President, lying is the only privilege that men have over all other organisms.' "

Florence could only shake her head.

"I've known plenty of liars, but never one that seemed almost proud of it," Harding said. He kept the stunned expression. "I told him he had to stop selling all that stuff out of Perryville and he promised that he would. Then I told him to submit his resignation. He begged me to let him take a trip to Europe first to save face. He made up some bullshit about needing to inspect the British veterans hospitals. He was crying. I let him go but first I made him sign the resignation letter."

"So you let him take one last junket?"

"Yeah. And I let him put off the trip until Christmas and New Year's so the press wouldn't pay much attention to it." He sat in a chair opposite the Duchess, still looking incredulous. He rang for a servant and ordered a drink.

"Be sure not to lose that letter, Warren," the Duchess said. Warren confidently patted his jacket pocket.

November 12, 1922

With one thing and another, Roxy's visit with the Duchess was delayed. Jess swore that he had given Roxy's letter to George Christian but she had heard nothing from it for a year. She thought that the president would have replied out of courtesy if nothing else, so evidently he never got it. Did one of the first lady's spies tell her about it? Roxy could not discern a purpose for the Duchess's invitation. Maybe she realized at last that Warren Harding needed an honest adviser, a troubleshooter? No, that was crazy thinking.

Oddly, Florence asked Roxy to enter with the usual line of tourists through the North Portico. In the East Room an usher would motion her aside and then escort her to the

Red Room. For reasons of her own Florence did not want Roxy's name on the Secret Service logs of visitors to the first family. This maneuver failed—the Secret Service kept two sets of records, one official and the other real. The latter inscribed Roxy's name. Besides, Harry had a deviated septum follow her whenever she came to Washington.

It was Roxy's first visit to the White House since Harding's inauguration day. The usher led her into the Blue Room first, then through its door to the Red Room. No doubt so that no tourists could peek through a door opening to the Red Room from the main hallway and spy the first lady therein. Roxy remembered the room as garishly red but in this dim light the walls were a nice burgundy silk velvet with the furniture upholstered in the same shade. Roxy dressed conservatively and wore a cloche lest she show off her magnificent hair. Florence wore a dress, no longer an invalid's dressing gown, but still looked pale and feeble. She managed a broad smile.

"I'm so happy to see you, Miss Stinson. You know how Mr. Smith is a dear friend of mine and he admires you so much."

Roxy said something of commensurate courtesy. They exchanged obligatory remarks about their health and personal appearance. The conversation turned to the election returns. Florence blamed the Republicans' showing on the lingering postwar recession. Roxy noted that the president was still personally popular.

Florence took a sip of mineral water and looked at Roxy as if weighing carefully what to say. "Thank you for not smoking, Miss Stinson, I didn't even have to ask you." She rang for a servant and asked whether Roxy wanted anything. Then she frowned, making a face to show she was about to impart something important. "Frankly, Miss Stinson, do you know something, I miss the people back home so much. People in Washington, they're all just out for themselves. Don't you find it so?" Roxy nodded. "But our old friends, you can still find the milk of human kindness in them. And that's why I regret so much that I haven't asked to see you more often."

Actually, Roxy thought, you haven't asked to see me at all. She offered a rehearsed comment: "Oh, Mrs. Harding, you know I always have profited from talking with you. You know I don't always agree with you but you always say something intelligent."

Florence smiled. "Thank you, my dear." She leaned forward as if to enlist Roxy in a conspiracy. "I'm going to tell you something I haven't even told Warren yet. You know this house gets many tourists, yes? And sometimes they are from back home in Marion. Or from Washington C.H., friends of Mr. Smith—and you. Well"—she batted her eyes and grinned as though offering a Christmas present—"I am going to give them all a personal tour of the White House! After all, it's their house." She leaned back and picked up her glass with a look of satisfaction.

"Why, that's so kind of you. Anyone would be thrilled to have a personal tour led by the first lady. But there are so many tourists, how will you know in advance which ones are from back home?"

Florence leaned forward again. "Oh, Miss Stinson, that's where I am going to ask you a very big favor. You were wise enough not to move to Washington, you still live in Ohio and Mr. Smith tells me you sometimes visit our office in Marion. Well, when you hear of somebody from Marion or Columbus or Washington C.H. planning to come to the White House, would you be good enough to let me know? Just give me a call or if I am not available call our Mr. Hoover." She meant Ike Hoover, the chief usher.

Roxy had trained herself never to wrinkle her forehead so as to prevent age lines; now she kept a placid countenance to prevent a show of surprise or disappointment. A couple of moments were taken to process the Duchess's words. Damn her, she wants me to spy for her. Somehow her network of spies is not enough and she wants me now. This must have something to do with Warren's philandering. He must be screwing somebody from Ohio.

"Oh, Mrs. Harding, I would be happy to do that. It's no trouble at all, in fact it would brighten my day to know I was helping to give people such a treat. Can I tell them in advance that they'll get a personal tour? That would add to the fun."

"Oh no, dear, I want it to be a surprise. That's part of my fun, you see."

"By all means, I see your point. But please tell me, how else can I be of service to you? And to the president?"

The Duchess seemed taken aback that she would ask such a question. "Please, Miss Stinson, just continue to be our friend. Please, you know I don't like to complain, but it can get awfully lonely here in this old house."

The rest of the interview was of no consequence. Roxy exited the North Portico to Pennsylvania Avenue and all but stomped her way to Fifteenth Street, too angry to feel the November chill. Rarely given to self-reproach, she cursed herself for a fool. "What an imbecile I was to think I could break into this administration as a woman assistant to the president. As if the boys were ever going to let a girl into their clubhouse. And what an even bigger imbecile I was, to ever think that the Duchess was going to give me the key to it." She was half a block past the Hotel Washington on Fifteenth Street before she noticed where she was and backtracked. What made her angriest was the feeling that she could not get people to take her seriously. *All coloreds and Kentuckians.* A small fly buzzed in the back of her brain, telling her that it might be her fault somehow. Even though she knew it wasn't.

She told the hotel desk to call her a cab to Union Station. She was going straight home, having no wish to see

Jess or Leland. But as she was packing in her room the phone rang with Jess on the line. For reasons he could not explain to himself, Jess had not told Harry about Roxy's meeting with the Duchess. But he was eager to hear from her how it went.

"It went fine. Jess, this is not something I want to talk about over the telephone."

There were three beats of silence before Jess understood. Even if there were no wiretaps, any of the girls at the hotel switchboard could listen in.

"Okay, baby, but give me a call as soon as you get home, okay? And write me a long letter."

"Yeah, okay, but first let me ask you something. Does our friend have a special friend from Ohio? Just say yes or no."

Another three beats of silence. "You know, you're right, this isn't a conversation for the telephone."

"Goodbye, Jess."

On the homebound train Roxy indulged in some revenge fantasies. She had it in her hands to destroy the whole government, pull down the temple like Samson. She would leak to the press that the Duchess got a $5,000 payoff from the blackmail fund. She would leak to the press that Harry Daugherty was there when Jake Hamon got shot. She would make it known that the Duchess ran her life by the stars. She would . . . Aw, the hell with this. She leaned back and tried to get some sleep.

December 19, 1922

When the Hardings arrived at the Flamingo Hotel in Miami they were whisked away by the McLeans to their rented 120-foot yacht. Florence was too spooked by Evalyn's appearance to confront her about Nan Britton or anything else. Evalyn had the pallor of sickness and a large growth on her neck. She was thin and, most surprising of all, had quit drinking. But she was back on laudanum, mourning another tragedy. Her nine-year-old son seemingly was unharmed when a car lightly struck him. He played the rest of the afternoon, then went to bed. He died that night. The boy was named Vinson in honor of Evalyn's brother who had died in the crash of a car that Evalyn was driving.

Evalyn and Florence, lounging on the deck wearing kimonos and pink mules, chatted and gossiped constantly. And yet, Drs. Sawyer and Boone noticed, an invisible screen seemed to separate them, a shared strain of some sort. Sawyer but not Boone knew the reason, whose name was Nan.

"I want to thank you," Florence said, "for putting up with Warren while I was so sick. You know, the White House really is a prison. If you hadn't let Warren get away to Friendship once in a while I don't know what we would have done. And I'm sure he had stimulating company there to distract him from all our troubles."

That hint was as close as Florence came to bracing Evalyn about Warren's trysts. Evalyn said something polite and noncommittal in reply. Otherwise, Florence repressed her pain. She had a lifetime's experience in doing so.

Their husbands understood that this trip could not repeat last year's bacchanals. Warren and Ned played golf and indulged in a few late-night poker parties, but neither was healthy and strong enough for the usual debauchery. The couples toured Miami, a small coastal city just starting to boom, and Warren issued a statement praising the promise of Florida. Ned printed it in full in the *Post*, which pretty much served as the administration's newsletter.

During a reception in a new Miami hotel a cardiologist happened to shake Warren's hand. He noted the president's labored breathing and sudden breaks in conversation. "This man will be dead inside of six months," he thought. Warren suspected the same, but Florence pretended not to know.

Or, as with Carrie's affair with Warren in its early years, she knew but chose not to know. She believed she had the answer for their travails.

Florence told the press, "We are particularly anxious to go to the territory of Alaska to see what could be done to bring the great national wealth of that vast territory to the door of the American people." She had desired this trip for years. It had been put off again this year because of her illness. Now she was determined to conduct a lengthy tour of the western states and Alaska. It would boost Warren's popularity with the voters and his health as well. In dreaming of an Alaska voyage the Duchess made a common error of judgment. She confused mere motion with actual progress.

In any court or convent or monastery since ancient times, its inmates develop an unspoken language. Subtle meanings can be conveyed without a word or even an open gesture. A nearly undetectable nod can communicate hard lessons. Language loses its necessity when people spend years together in close quarters. So when Charles Forbes entered the White House, Harding's secretary George Christian did not speak, scarcely glanced at him, did not blink. But one look at his face told Forbes that it was all over. Harding had returned from Florida to spend Christmas in Washington, only to learn that Forbes, despite his promise, was still selling inventory out of Perryville. Christian showed him into the Red Room.

Harding, standing, put his large hands around Forbes's throat and started choking. "You yellow rat! You double-crossing bastard! God damn you!" He walked Forbes back two steps and slammed him against the wall, still throttling him. Harding might be fifty-seven years old and sick but he was still big and strong. Forbes tried to gargle out, "You're killing me! I can't breathe!" Christian, hearing the commotion from outside, waited a satisfied minute before opening the door. He pulled Harding away.

Harding stared at the gasping Forbes's face, looking for contrition and seeing none. "Get out, God damn you," the president said.

The White House announced that the Veterans Bureau was being "reorganized" as Forbes sailed to England for a supposed hospital inspection tour. His trip did not go as planned. The developer Elias Mortimer had given Forbes his first $5,000 bribe back at the Drake Hotel in Chicago, the price of getting the federal contract to build the Speedway Hospital. Mortimer continued doing such deals while Forbes carried on an affair with Mortimer's wife, Kate. Meanwhile, in a sportsmanlike gesture, Mortimer had an affair with Forbes's wife, also named Kate.

Just before Forbes's departure, Kate Forbes emptied out her husband's bank account and ran off to Europe with Mortimer. When Forbes arrived in London, his resignation letter was released to the press.

Forbes's lawyer, Charles F. Cramer, also resigned. In the kind of coincidence that the press calls irony, he happened to live in the Hardings' old house on Wisconsin Avenue—they had sold it to him at a profit of $10,000. Cramer went into the bathroom, closed the door, and shot himself with a .45.

Cramer had spent the night writing letters, including one to the president. When he was late for breakfast the cook went upstairs and found him in the bathroom. The butler dragged his body to an upper back porch, then changed his mind and dragged him back to his bedroom and put him on the bed. When police asked why he did that, the butler had no explanation. The letters Cramer had written mysteriously vanished.

Days later the Senate voted to investigate Forbes and his Veterans Bureau. "Now all the frogs are croaking," Doc Sawyer could not resist remarking. A weekly newsmagazine, *Time*, had just been invented and its early issues described the mysterious suicide of Charles Cramer and the sudden aggressiveness of the Senate Judiciary Committee. Once again the Hardings fled to Florida with the McLeans.

May 1, 1923

President Harding's shot sliced into the woods on the seventh hole at Friendship. He told the caddy not to bother retrieving the ball. "I'm bushed, boys, let's go in," he said. "It's damned hot today"—it wasn't—"and since I'm ahead, aren't I?"—he wasn't—"I'll just declare that all bets are off."

Harry Daugherty, Dr. Boone, and a deviated septum named Barney Martin followed Harding to the clubhouse. The three noted that Harding looked old and drawn and that he had been grouchy all morning.

After drinks were served Harding said, "Harry, was Jess mixed up in any of that business with Mr. Fall?"

The press had just broken another scandal. Secretary of the Interior Albert Fall was guilty of issuing crooked leases for oil in a place called Teapot Dome. Both men remembered, but did not say, that Fall, one of Warren's old Senate buddies, was put in charge of Interior after Jake Hamon was killed.

"Why, no, Mr. President, why would he be? Jess knows that I've always detested Mr. Fall as much as I detest Mr. Forbes. If not more."

Boone and Barney Martin thought, but did not say: That's because Fall and Forbes would not cut you in on their deals. And both of those fellas were closer than you to the Duchess. Who hates you.

Harding grunted. "Well, Harry, I suggest that you tell Jess it will be impossible for him to go with us on the trip to Alaska. The party is already filled."

Harry made an uncharacteristic grimace. "Oh. Well, as you please, Mr. President, but you know he will be terribly disappointed. He has been feeling somewhat better lately, getting those new insulin shots that they've come out with, and he thought this western trip would be just the tonic he needs."

Boone said, "Mr. Smith's health is very poor. I would not advise his taking a long journey."

Harry snapped, "He's not your patient."

"Yes, that is why I can talk about him."

They glared at each other while Barney Martin enjoyed the show. Harding ignored them, raised a glass of Scotch to his lips, decided he didn't want a sip just then, and put it down. He said, "Jess keeps running with a gay crowd, going to all sorts of parties. You and I both know he uses the attorney general's car until all hours of the night."

Harry was amazed. After the Forbes and Fall scandals, Warren is worried about the unauthorized use of a government vehicle?

Harding caught Harry's look. "That might be a small thing," he said, "but in this current atmosphere of scandal everything we do is fair game for the Bolsheviks. And, yes, there's more. I know that Jess has interfered in cases in the Justice Department in irregular ways. Irregular and unseemly."

"Aw, Mr. President, you know that Jess loves to play the boulevardier, the man about town. He wants to feel important, he has to be part of the action. You saw how proud he was when they admitted him to the Metropolitan Club. I have him do errands for me, that's why he uses the car. You know that he's always been completely loyal to me and to you and the Duchess too."

Harding still did not pick up his drink as he said in a tired voice, "I don't question his loyalty, I question whether he is still of use to this administration. You tell him to go home and stay there for a while. And the Duchess and I regret that we will be deprived of his company on the Alaska trip."

Harry felt dizzy, the way he sometimes did ever since he got back from French Lick. He swallowed and said, "Very well, Mr. President, I'll take care of it."

Boone and Martin both started to say something, then thought better of it. All three men had a single thought: If the Hardings can dump Jess Smith, they can dump Harry Daugherty. Harry felt a chill settle over his heart.

Now Harding took a long swig of his drink. "Harry, I really appreciate that you came up here for this meeting." Harry, still recuperating from his illness, had been resting in Asheville, North Carolina, and working only half-days. "I want you to go back to Asheville and take all the time you need. Your health is more important than any damn job." Once more, his three guests had the same thought: Warren means that the presidency is not worth his own health.

"Thank you, sir. Actually, I think I'll go to Ohio for a few days, take care of some personal business." He turned to Barney Martin. "Barney, why don't you ride back to the office with me. I want to talk to you." Both men rose with impenetrably hard faces. Harry thought, Warren wouldn't do this on his own; the Duchess must be behind it. She never did like me.

The next morning, Jess went to the Metropolitan Club at 1700 H Street, pleased with himself because it was the most prestigious club in Washington if not the nation. He sat at the thirty-foot, beautiful arc of the polished mahogany bar and ordered a sling. That was code for a coffee with brandy. Jess sat alone at the far end of precisely placed parsons chairs of soft, butter-yellow leather. The club chamberlain approached. Jess took a sip from the cup with his right hand while tugging at the truss belt under his pants with his left.

"Mr. Smith, I regret to inform you that your membership privileges at our club have been suspended."

"What!"

"Yes, sir, it is most regrettable but I must ask you to vacate our premises."

Is that a real English accent or is he putting it on? Jess wondered. This city is full of frauds. Look at this man with his blue serge suit and his combed grey mustache and his chin in the air.

"I am a member in good standing, sir, and you can't make me leave. There obviously has been a mistake of some kind."

"I'm afraid not, sir. As you know, our bylaws provide that any member can blackball another member when allegations of moral turpitude are raised. That member's privileges are suspended while the board investigates the allegations. If the allegations are unfounded, the member is reinstated with apologies. You know this, sir, and so once again I respectfully ask you to leave."

"Who the hell brought charges against me?"

"Come, come, Mr. Smith, you know that information is confidential."

Jess offered commentary on the chamberlain's mentality, probable ancestry, and personal appearance. Then he walked slowly out of the club, head held high, and proceeded to the Justice Department. He stomped into Harry's office. Harry was expecting him.

When Jess was upset he tended to spray saliva when he talked (one of the reasons Roxy divorced him, though she never said so). "Goddamnit, Harry, somebody's kicked me out of the Metropolitan Club!"

Harry did not feign surprise. "Gee, Jess, that's a damn shame. Sit down. But you know, maybe it's for the best, as I'll explain in a minute. Go ahead, sit down. You're going to have to take some bad news."

Jess sat down and silently cursed his truss, his painful insulin shots, the Metropolitan Club, and the United States government. "Okay, Harry, level with me."

"Maybe you shouldn't be on the Metropolitan Club's rolls because you should leave here for a while without leaving any trace. As much as that's possible." Harry grimaced and twisted in his seat, surprised that he could not look Jess in the eyes. "Jess, this is the hardest thing I've had to do as attorney general: Warren has removed you from the Alaskan trip."

"What!"

"Yes, it's a damn shame but he says the party is full. If it makes you feel any better, I can't go either. Because of my health. But I'll go out to meet them when they get to San Francisco."

Jess was silent for a full minute until Harry said, "Jess, do you understand?"

"Oh, yeah. Opal Smith didn't raise no dummy. I'm the fall guy. I've been picked to take the fall for the Harding scandals. It's my lucky day," he said with a bitterness that Harry had not heard from him before.

"Jesus, Jess, don't be such a sourpuss about it. Charlie Forbes and Al Fall will take the fall—heh heh, Fall takes a fall." Jess was not amused. "All they're asking is for you to go back to Washington C.H. and lay low for a while."

Another minute of silence, both men shifting in their chairs. Harry burst out, "Dammit, Jess, don't you cry on me! Don't start crying now!"

"If I cry, it's because the diabetes and high blood pressure have that effect on me. That's what the doctors say. If we can't trust doctors, who can we trust?" Another bitter remark. And then, "Harry, we've always been honest with each other, so you can tell me straight out. Is it to be . . . is it to be physical?"

"What! What in the hell are you talking about?"

"You think Charlie Cramer really shot himself? Just tell me this. Tell me they won't put me in the loony bin like they did with that brother of that girl that died."

"Oh my God, Jess, you're going all the way around the bend. Look, just do this. Go home right now, get together with

Roxy, try to relax, go out to the Shack if you want."

"Is Roxy is any danger? She knows as much as I do."

Harry had thought about that, although he pretended that he hadn't. "Roxy? She'll be fine. Who even knows her outside of our little den of thieves?"

Jess made a production out of withdrawing a lavender handkerchief from his waistcoat pocket and wiping the lenses of his glasses. He replaced the handkerchief and glasses and then glared at Harry.

Harry said, "Jess, remember when they almost lynched that colored boy? And the militia opened fire on the mob? Years ago, yeah. You weren't there to see all the blood and guts. I had already taken you home. Well, that's how I feel right now, afterwards you feel horrified and empty at the same time. Kind of like washed out inside. That's what this is doing to me."

Jess reached for his hat and started to rise.

"Don't leave just yet. We need to talk about any cases left hanging."

Jess put his hat on but sat back down. "Okay. George Remus. King of the bootleggers. He's pissed off because his appeal was thrown out and he's been sentenced to Atlanta. He says he wants his money back. I told him we'd get his sentence commuted. But don't expect a pardon."

"All right, I'll talk to George. Anything else?"

"No. Goodbye, Harry."

As Jess walked out Harry called after him. "See you in Washington C.H. in a couple days."

May 4, 1923

This was the trip to Ohio that Jess spent in constant fear. On the train to Columbus he put one of his suitcases on the overhead rack and kept the other on his lap, clasped tightly against his stomach. He scrutinized every passenger, looked over both shoulders. He was so obnoxious about it that nobody sat next to him or across from him, which suited Jess fine. He had some experience with being followed—Gaston Means had put a tail on him as part of his sleuthing for the Duchess—and even though Jess felt no sixth sense about a tail just now, he could not shake a dread of imminent doom.

When he and Roxy went to the Deshler Hotel in Columbus she scolded him for being so jumpy. Jess had told her to make whatever plans she wanted, so she reserved a table at the Scioto Country Club for a dinner and dance. Roxy soon understood there would be no dinner and dance, no gaiety at all. She had never seen Jess in such bad shape. He was worried sick about something but she could not press him on it. He would tell her in his own time.

"Will you do me a favor?" he asked.

"What?"

"Will you come on home?"

"All right, yes, of course."

"Let's get home before dark."

He was just as close-mouthed on the train to Washington Court House. She tried to chitchat her way through the journey but could not deflect Jess from peering at everybody suspiciously. Patience was not her strongest point and she barked, "Goddamn it, Jess, stop that!"

"I'll be okay when we get home."

They went to Jess's apartment above his store because he said he felt safer there. His mother's old piano had been moved into Jess's suite but Roxy said she did not feel like playing anything. They sat across from each other in the dimness of the evening, smoking and watching each other's cigarette glow. There was just enough light for Roxy to see that Jess had not shaved. He sometimes shaved twice a day to maintain his gentlemanly persona.

This trivial detail alarmed Roxy even more. If Jess was neglecting his vanity, his whole world must be in peril.

Finally Jess said, "They're going to get me."

"Yes, you already said that once. What do you mean?"

He took a drag on his cigarette, exhaled, then repeated the process. He said, "I'm the fall guy. Harry is throwing me to the wolves to save his own skin."

Roxy drew a sharp breath. "Jess, you have to be wrong about that. What could you even be the fall guy for? The scandals are all about Charles Forbes and Albert Fall. That's who the newspapers are going after, not you. They like you! Come on, they've never even written up your hijinks around town. Just some of those hints in the gossip columns, you know how they are."

For Jess, his pause was brief. "Roxy, remember, you told me back at French Lick Springs that Harding was going to go down like an airplane. Well, the Senate is going to investigate Harry. Senator Wheeler is demanding it and the Republicans are such pussies that they won't stop him. So they're passing it to me."

"They're passing what to you?"

"The blame. I was out there freelancing all this shit that Harry didn't know about, so you can't blame him. That's how they'll put it on me, dead or alive."

Their cigarettes were stubbed out. Usually they would light another out of habit but in their shock neither had the presence of mind to do so.

Roxy saw a bright spot. "You can work all this out with Warren on the trip out west. Don't worry so much."

"Nope. He dumped me from the trip. Harry told me yesterday. That's when I knew."

Roxy's laugh was a cackle, irritating even to her. "That's what this is all about? That you can't go on a junket to Alaska! What a tragedy! And here you're talking about 'dead or alive.' "

Jess switched on a lamp next to his chair because he wanted to see her face. He forgave her when he saw that her laugh had been just a nervous outburst. She saw such hurt in his eyes that she went to sit on his lap.

"I'm sorry, sweetie. But listen. Harry can't be behind this. You've been his best friend for how many years now. I'll bet that if you traced this back to its source it's the Duchess."

"What difference does that make? I'm all through either way."

After another stretch of silence Roxy said, "Jess, I have to ask. Am I in danger too? I mean, I've kept all these records and I know just about everything you've been into. You haven't talked to me much lately but I know a lot."

Jess moaned pitiably. "Oh, baby, I wish I could answer that. I was going to go see Mal at the bank tomorrow to ask about the records but he's Harry's brother so now I can't trust him either. But you're not going to be in danger because of me. We'll figure something out."

They decided that what they needed most was sleep and they would cast fresh eyes on their predicament in the morning.

May 25, 1923

When Harry came to Washington Court House he worked a couple of hours each morning at the federal building in town before retiring to the Shack, his cabin in the woods. They called it the Shack but actually it was quite a luxurious lodge, set back from an old logging road. Jess was there with him but both men were sullen and spoke little.

They sat in rocking chairs on the screened-in porch, watching the Deer Creek flow. The woods were fully leafed out after a late, rainy spring. For the first time in almost twenty years, this verdant prospect did not lighten Jess's mood. The creek waters did not carry off his woes. The forest smelled of growth and decay alike. Like politics, he thought. He had had a miserable morning.

When he and Roxy got up, she was appalled when it took him a painful forty minutes just to get dressed.

"Oh, Jess, are you going to be any better today?"

"I don't think so. Every time I turn around I think I'm going to be either arrested or shot. I can't decide which is worse."

Jess was so buried in his own trouble that he did not hear Roxy's long, mournful sigh. She said, "Jess, you're taking this too hard. Look at it from Harry's point of view. Wouldn't it make sense that he thinks you should lie low for a while? Anyway, that's what Warren said and Warren is his boss."

"No, I've always known in the back of my mind that this was coming. I just didn't want to admit it. You said yourself, all this intrigue is grinding us down. The funny thing is, you know what all I did, most of the time? The only thing I did, mostly, was just to offer people guidance, telling them who to go to see about what." He was warming up to unload something bothering him. "They call us corrupt. You know what corruption is? It's just guys trying to get along and get ahead. Because they're loyal, see? They're loyal and they want to be part of the gang. You're a dame, maybe you don't understand the kind of pressure that loyalty puts on a man. See, you want to fit in. Who doesn't want to fit in? That's how you get ahead." Without looking in the mirror, he finished tying his necktie. He looked at Roxy as if expecting applause after revealing a truth.

She did not look interested. She said,"All right, but the thing you have to remember is, Harry's still on your side. He can't do without you."

Jess sat on the edge of the bed, willing to be soothed. At that moment Harry's driver had honked outside, summoning Jess to the Shack.

Once there, half-asleep, he noticed when Harry stopped rocking, stood and stretched.

"I'm going in for my afternoon nap. Don't disturb me for anybody except the president, understand? Nobody at all except for him."

"Sure, Harry."

Jess kept rocking slowly and dozed off. He was awakened by a sharp kick to the shin. He looked up into the menacing face of George Remus. King of the bootleggers.

"Where is Harry Daugherty, goddamn you?"

"Mr. Daugherty is asleep and he's not to be disturbed, George. He's been unwell. Why don't you sit down and wait a bit? And how can I help you?"

"I'm not talking to you, you damn pantywaist. For you I've got a sixteen-gauge choked down like a rifle. I'm talking to Harry. You go in and wake him up or I will."

"Oh, no, he left explicit instructions he can't be disturbed. Really, he's been very sick, worse than he lets on even to me. I'm sure he wants to see you but can't your business hold off a little?"

"You know I never carry firearms but my driver out there does. Now I want you to think about something. Think about how much pleasure it would give me to blow your fucking head off." Even under his silly-looking derby, George's face expressed pure malevolence.

Jess stepped inside and awakened Harry to a tirade of curses. George followed him and bellowed, "I've got to report to Atlanta in six weeks!" Without looking again at Jess he reached behind with his left arm and gave him a hard push backward. Jess stumbled and returned to the porch as George slammed the bedroom door.

Jess heard muffled shouts but could not make out the words. Once he heard something bulky thrown against a wall or to the floor. Jess lost track of time as his skin got hot and his head throbbed. At length George stormed out and without a glance or a word, stomped down the porch steps and across the yard. His driver held the door open for him and they sped away.

At least Harry, standing on the porch in his pajamas, did not have a mark on him. "That was George Remus," Jess volunteered, the dumbest thing he could have said. Harry let loose with a fusillade of curses against him. Jess was too shocked to move. Then Harry walked to the edge of the porch, leaned over the railing and vomited.

Harry wiped his mouth with the back of his hand and went into the bathroom. He came out dressed in a summer-weight linen suit. "You stay here. I'm going into town." Jess watched the car drive off, sick to his stomach himself, but nothing came up.

The rocking chair could not relax him; he stood and paced. Would Harry even send the car back for him? Finally it came. The driver squinted into his rearview mirror at Jess, who was mumbling to himself in the back seat. At the corner a block from Roxy's apartment on Court Street Jess commanded, "Stop!"

Jess went inside Brumgart's Hardware and asked to see a pistol. The young clerk lay on the counter a Savage Model 1917 .32-caliber. "It's a semiautomatic, carries ten rounds," the clerk said. "The barrel is less than four inches long, so it's very convenient for concealed carry. You want to carry, am I correct?"

He had never had a customer like Jess. He leaned forward with his hands splayed on the wooden counter, breathing hard while staring at the gun, wincing and opening and closing his eyes. Jess did not pick it up to sight down the barrel or even pull back and release the slide.

At last he said, "It's for the attorney general. Put it on Mr. Daugherty's account."

"Yes, sir. Should I wrap the box?"

"It's for the attorney general."

"Um, yes, sir. Are you taking it with you?"

Jess reached down to the floor, picked up his briefcase and opened it. "Put it in here."

"Very good, sir."

Outside, Jess waved the driver away and walked to Roxy's building. In her living room he opened the briefcase to show her the gun. She screamed.

"Jess, this can't be real! I've seen you faint at just the sight of a gun before. I mean, just faint, like *thunk* on the floor. What the hell is this?"

Jess affected a worldly-wise air. "Oh, I figured it was about time. Half the guys in Washington carry, you know."

"You don't fool me. You couldn't use this thing even if your life was in danger. Tell me what you were thinking." She couldn't say, are you thinking of killing yourself?

"I thought it might come in handy. I know lots of guys, they can teach me how to shoot."

Roxy would not cry. She stamped her foot and swallowed hard. She had heard Alice say, "Some women cry over card tricks," and she disrespected weepy women. But she broke down and cried hard. Soon she reached a crescendo, throwing pillows on the sofa to the floor, kicking them around the room. Jess watched until the storm subsided. Then they both sat on the sofa and held each other.

In bed in the morning Jess half-smiled at Roxy with a strange look—not melancholy or fearful but, Roxy thought, kind of wistful. She kissed his cheek and said, "Tell me what you're thinking."

"Oh, I was just wondering. You have a perfect body, so why can't I? I just wonder, what would it be like to inhabit such a thing as you?"

"Ha! Of all the mornings to say that to me. My hair is a mess and I'm wearing these ugly old men's pajamas."

"No mere attire could disguise such a comely form," he said. "But here I am, a sick, fat man. Somewhere I missed out."

"Oh, Jess. You know the door closes behind us when we're born and then we can't ask for any more gifts. And then we can't ask for a bigger helping of the ones we got, either. It's too bad but that's the way it is."

She continued with a rare bitterness, astonishing Jess: "You wonder, what's it like to inhabit me? Well, here's the news. People want to look down on beautiful women. Really. They think we're spoiled, that men always pamper us and that we can get any man we want, which isn't fair because we didn't do anything to deserve our looks, we were just lucky to be born that way.

"Well, what I want to know is, how come nobody says that about athletes? Jack Dempsey, Babe Ruth. Nobody says, aw, they don't deserve it, they were just lucky to be born a natural athlete. Nobody says that, instead, they're practically bowed down to. People name their kids after them. What's the difference, that's what I'd like to know."

These thoughts were novel to Jess, as was Roxy's pouting face. After a moment he chuckled, "You scare men away, baby. But you know what you sound like? You sound like a rich man who's bitching about having too much money. 'Why do people envy me so much, boo hoo hoo.' "

Roxy was done with this conversation. She didn't expect any man to understand. After a long silence Jess murmured, "God, I'm going to miss you."

"Miss me? But I'm going back to Washington with you. I can help you pack up things. Then we'll come back here for good."

She got out of bed and stood like a man, her feet hips-width apart and bending slightly backward while running her fingers through her hair. "You know something, Jess? I'm actually glad the Hardings kicked you off that trip. Yes, I'm glad. I'd say it was a blessing in disguise. Neither one of us every really liked Washington that much. Weren't you happier just running the store? We'll both settle in here back home. We'll live apart and visit each other like we do now. We've got enough money to be happy the rest of our lives."

Jess thought this over, staring at the ceiling with his hands clasped behind his head. Changing the subject, he said, "Harry says I need to check into a sanitarium. Doc Sawyer has one of his own in Marion, you know."

"Are you going to?"

"No. I don't like the Doc and I don't like Marion. I don't like his son, either. He's in charge of that place."

"Well, there are other places."

"My place is right here."

"Oh, Jess, that's the first thing you've said that's made the sun come out from behind the clouds."

She went into the kitchen to make coffee, surprising herself by taking delight in a simple domestic task.

May 29, 1923

While Jess was home he wrote to Evalyn. "Dear Evalyn, I am so happy and relieved that the operation for the goiter was a success. You have always been so nice to me and I have such a deep affection for you that I really get homesick for you. I want you to know how much I appreciate your kindness to me in every way. I probably will never be able to repay you but I am always willing and ready to do anything I can for you at any time."

Roxy was perplexed that Jess would seek solace from Evalyn; were they really such good friends? But then, she realized, Jess has no real friends except for me and Harry. He has no family, either, except for a sister-in-law and nephew he never sees.

She also was puzzled by Jess's moods. At times he looked like a man who had just thought up a private joke—the face of a punster. Mostly he looked forlorn, the hangdog face of despair. Other times he just stared into vacancy.

"I'm going back to Washington tomorrow," he announced one night over dinner at the Hungry Workman.

"Okay, I'll follow you the next day to help you pack. By the way, I'll be staying at the Hotel Washington instead of the Wardman Park."

"How come?"

"I like it better and it's in the city where I can shop. While you guys are almost out in the country. Anyway, Leland won't be there, he says he'll be in Boston guarding the Coolidges."

"Okay. Fine."

On the train, Jess again kept a suitcase on his lap and looked suspiciously at every passenger. In the Wardman Park suite that night he went to bed early to avoid Harry, who came in late. The next morning, Harry jovially invited him to a round of golf at Friendship. They played with Dr. Boone and the deviated septum Barney Martin. On the fourth hole Harry took Martin aside.

"Barney, will you look at Jess? He's in awful shape. I'm spending the next couple of nights in the White House, so I'd appreciate it if you'd take my room at the Wardman Park in the meantime and just keep an eye on him."

"Sure thing, general." (The attorney general liked to be called "general.")

On the eighth hole Dr. Boone took Harry aside. "Harry, I'm awfully concerned about Jess. Can you persuade him to have me examine him?"

"I'll try. Yeah, I'm worried, too."

Roxy, while changing trains at Columbus that day, went to a newsstand to buy the Washington and New York papers. She used to read them for information but now read them to note the current biases. Ned's Post of course touted the Harding administration. Other papers said Harding was still popular, the country was becoming prosperous, but "storm clouds"—unavoidable cliché—were gathering. She found no mention of Jess. Tired when she checked into the hotel, she decided not to call Jess until the morning.

Jess, after the round of golf, went to his office in the Justice Department but made no attempt to clean it out. In the Wardman Park that night he wrote a new will. It omitted Harry Daugherty as a beneficiary. Also he went through his desk drawers, selecting papers to burn in a metal wastebasket. He opened a window to let the smoke out. The smoke drifted steadily outside; the spring night was chilly and Jess put on a cardigan sweater. It had been a gift from Evalyn. At about 9 p.m. he called the McLeans at their estate in Virginia.

"Ned, thank God you're there. Listen, I've got to get out of here. Never mind why, it's a long story. Do you mind if I come and stay with you for a few days?"

Ned put his hand over the mouthpiece and asked Evalyn. She said, "I don't feel good, but tell him all right."

"You don't know how much I appreciate it, Ned."

"You're always welcome, Jess." Ned hung up with just a particle of irritation at the coming intrusion of a volatile guest.

At ten the phone rang again. "My God, Ned, there's a thunderstorm here in Washington like you've never seen." As if on cue, Ned heard a crash of thunder over the phone. "But, see, I've still got a driver on call here. He'll be able to drive me over in the morning with no problem, okay?"

"Why, sure, Jess. Just be sure, if the roads are still wet, tell the driver to take it slow."

"Don't know what I'd do without you, Ned."

At 1 a.m. the phone on the bedside table rang. Evalyn picked it up rather than wake Ned.

"I can still come to the farm," Jess said as if to allay their doubts.

"Jess, is there anything worrying you?"

"No, just scared to death." He tried to say that in a jocular manner but failed.

Evalyn heard a man—it was Barney Martin—say in the background, "Hang up, Jess, let the poor lady get some sleep." Jess did so.

Barney was staying there at Harry's direction but Evalyn assumed the gang was up late playing poker. "Sounds like Jess is getting drunk," she muttered to herself and went back to sleep.

Part Four: Testimony

May 30, 1923

It fell to George Christian, Harding's secretary, to call Roxy. "Miss Stinson, forgive me, are you awake? Fully awake now?"

"I'm sitting up in bed, what is it?"

"Miss Stinson, I'm afraid that I have very bad news. For all of us. Um . . . I will tell you straight out. Mr. Smith died this morning. Died by his own hand."

A scream. Christian waited. The first and natural reaction is always disbelief.

She stuttered, "Are you s-sure? H-how could it happen?"

Christian delivered the bare facts. Self-inflicted gunshot wound to the head. Body found by Bureau of Investigation agent Barney Martin. Bureau of Investigation chief Billy Burns, who lived in the apartment right underneath, called upstairs. Dr. Boone, summoned from the White House, pronounced death.

"Where is Jess now?"

"He is being, um, being, he is in the hands of a capable mortician."

"But shouldn't there be an autopsy?"

"Why, no, Miss Stinson, the suicide was obvious, no autopsy would be called for."

Roxy noted the curious hesitation in Christian's voice, like a man unsure of the truth of what he said. For herself, she was too stunned and hurt to know what questions to ask. She did manage, "What time did it happen?"

"Miss Stinson, Mr. Martin told the police that at about 6:40 a.m. he head a loud noise, like a door slamming. He said he went into Mr. Smith's room and found him lying on the floor."

"That's all?"

A clearing of throat. "Since you asked, he was found with his head partly inside a wastebasket. The wastebasket was partly filled with the ashes of burned-up paper. And I'm sorry, that's really all that we know right now."

A long period of silence.

"Miss Stinson, would you like me to call the hotel physician? He could bring you Nervine or laudanum if you prefer. Please let me know if there is anything at all I can do for you."

"I don't want any doctors or quack medicine."

"As you wish, Miss Stinson."

After she hung up Roxy sat on the edge of the bed trying to collect her thoughts or, rather, trying to have a thought. Her body seemed to hum to an internal piano chord stuck on the lowest C. Her first real thought was that, for the first time in her life, she felt old. She was thirty-two.

Self-blame was hardly known to to her but now it knocked on her heart. I should have been able to prevent this. I should have been more compassionate, more understanding, more alert to Jess's despair, more . . .

Her grief expanded to take in the world. People are ill-fitted for the lives they have to live, she thought. It's just too damned hard. At that she started to cry, for herself and for everybody—a howl that she had never heard before arose from somewhere inside.

Then she looked up, drew a deep breath in the conviction that Jess did not kill himself. He could never shoot himself—or anybody else either. They can call this a suicide but they can't get away with it.

Roxy accurately imagined President Harding sitting propped up in bed because he could hardly breathe lying down. In fact, he was awake when Dr. Boone entered.

"Mr. President, it is my sad duty to inform you that Mr. Jess Smith is dead. He shot himself early this morning."

Harding narrowed his eyes and stared at him. Not knowing what else to say, Boone recited the facts as he knew them.

Harding asked a single question. "Did he leave a letter or a note or anything?"

"No, sir. There were no papers in the room. Also I should say, both Mr. Burns and Mr. Martin said the body had not been moved. A .32-caliber pistol was on the floor near Mr. Smith's right hand."

Harding slowly and creakily got up. He put on a silk dressing robe and said, "We'd better tell Mr. Daugherty."

A wide central hallway runs the length of the second-floor living quarters. When Harding left his bedroom it suddenly seemed narrow and a half-mile long. He blinked repeatedly and leaned his right hand against the wall to steady himself. When he opened his eyes his vision was back to normal. He wondered if he was losing his mind.

Daugherty, two doors down, was out of bed and seated at a desk in his pajamas. He looked up quizzically. Warren said evenly, "Harry, Dr. Boone has some news for you and it's very bad news, so get ahold of yourself."

Boone did not even clear his throat before stating outright, "General, Jess Smith has shot himself. Fatally, I am afraid." He's staring at me just like the president did, Boone thought.

Harry next turned his gaze to Harding, who remained silent. Harry dropped his head into his hands. He turned red, then white, then red. The doctor feared that Harry might go into shock and went to take his pulse. Harry kept his face in his hands and leaned over so his head was between his knees. When he finally sat up he cried, "Why did he do it? My God, why did he do it? Why?"

"None of us has the slightest idea," Boone said. Harry then wanted details, which Boone provided.

They told the Duchess just before breakfast. She followed the pattern of expressing disbelief and then asking for details. "In the absence of knowing any other cause," Boone said, "he probably committed the act because of ill health."

"First Charles Cramer and now this," Florence said. "In just three months. Warren, there is a curse over us."

Warren nodded, then reflected that his wife probably meant "a curse" literally. Soon she would call Madame Marcia. Well, what harm could come of it?

If any official business was conducted that day, none of them could remember it later. Florence asked the cooks to fix Harry's favorite supper of rack of lamb but he hardly touched the food. He didn't even finish his drink. Harry's eyes, set deep under his brows, seemed to withdraw even further into glassy obscurity. Conversation proceeded in fragments of sentences.

"I think the times necessitate our watching a comedy tonight," Florence said. The servants often were called to set up a makeshift studio in the upstairs hallway. They watched a new Charlie Chaplin comedy, "The Pilgrim." The Hardings forced out chuckles now and then but Harry was silent except for occasional long, mournful, anguished, sepulchral moans.

Harry would not take Roxy's calls the next day as she packed to go home but he sent his public relations man, Ed Beiter. He was obviously a young man with a bright future and Roxy disliked him at once for the same reasons she at first disliked Leland Jackson—his hair was too long and too carefully combed and his drawl a little too patronizing.

"The general sends his compliments and his most sincere condolences," he said after bowing slightly. Roxy wondered how much hair gel was required to keep his sideswept waves in place. That style usually was complemented by a mustache but he was clean-shaven. When Roxy withdrew a cigarette from a pack on a table, he lunged forward with a lighter.

"Thank you," she mumbled. She did not ask him to sit and did not look at him again.

"The general has conferred with the town fathers in Ohio and they have determined to conduct the funeral on Tuesday," he said. Just three days after the shooting, Roxy thought. They must want to get him in the ground before anybody asks too many questions.

"The general regrets that he is too ill to travel to attend the services," Beiter continued. Roxy frowned but said nothing.

"You must understand, Miss Stinson, that Mr. Daugherty is personally devastated by this tragic event. I actually fear for his, um, his well-being."

He seemed to want to ask her something but, seeing no signal of permission, soldiered on. "The general asked me to inform you that the coroner was called to the scene and pronounced the death a suicide." She sat impassively. "The general did not authorize me to say this to you, but I feel I must. He called in his staff yesterday and he said—this is a direct quote—'How could Jess do that to me? It was the very worst thing he could have done to me. He has deprived me of a living refutation of all the charges and innuendoes that the communists are leveling at me.'

"And then he went on to say that Mr. Smith did not commit an act of cowardice, that what he did is traceable to sickness. He was a very sick man with diabetes—in fact he was in a diabetic depression—as well as high blood pressure and then also an appendectomy that wouldn't heal. And so the general said that his soul is safe and everything will be all right."

Even though Beiter was an official United States government spokesman, Roxy began to suspect that he was telling the truth. Jess really was a sick man, maybe all the pain really did drive him to take his life. And if he actually was murdered, surely Harry could not have been behind it. Suddenly a stray thought penetrated her mind.

"What happened to the .32 that he—that was used?"

"Um, Mr. Burns said that he, um, that he unfortunately has misplaced the weapon."

Roxy burst into raucous, brittle laughter. Of course the head of the Bureau of Investigation would "lose" the gun that killed the man who was closest to his own boss! Her time in Washington had produced a highly developed sense of the absurd.

Beiter now was in a hurry to leave. "Good day, Miss Stinson. Please don't hesitate to call on me for any service at all." He took a step forward to shake her hand but she was clutching her sides, laughing and crying at the same time. He backed away, turned, and exited.

June 2, 1923

By the time Roxy caught the 2:37 p.m. train she already had heard Alice Longworth's joke that seemed to spread over the city faster than telegraphy: "Jess Smith died of Harding of the arteries." Roxy had regarded Alice as an amusing relic of antiquity but now she hated her.

At the train station she once again bought all the Washington and New York papers. First stories on deadline were always wrong, or at best incomplete, but she hoped to resolve the conflicting details into a coherent narrative of the crime. She managed to get through a paragraph or two of each story but then the text started swimming. She closed her eyes and put the paper on her lap. Men cast their eyes to her even more than usual—a gorgeous dame with a stack of papers?—but if she noticed she did not care.

Once she reached Washington Court House she saw black bunting hanging from street lights and storefronts. The town was honoring its native son, its second most famous after Harry. Roxy went to Jess's store to buy a black dress and a veil. She was pleased to see that Mabel, her bike riding pal when she was a girl, now was manager of ladies' fashions. Mabel cried when she saw her. In fact the entire staff seemed to be mourning their former boss, moving about in a daze. Roxy took Mabel's advice and abandoned the veil. She was not Jess's widow, after all.

The First Presbyterian Church was jammed for the funeral. Mal Daugherty, seated in front of Roxy with Harry's children Emily and Draper, left before the choir's recessional. Maybe he wants to get to the gravesite early, Roxy thought. Actually, Mal went to meet one of Harry's assistant attorneys general in a black government sedan. The assistant gave him a sealed package. Mal broke the seal and looked at the contents. Jess's financial records, including even the little green notebook. Mal went straight to his bank to burn them in the bank's furnace.

For the traditional meal after the funeral the church ladies put out a dinner at a local fire house. Roxy skipped it. She went home to discover that nervous energy keeps you going through the funeral; after that comes the full realization of emptiness. She forced herself to think about her future. Maybe I will revive my singing career. No, I'm just saying that now because I'm bored and lonely. She now could admit her loneliness to herself. She tried to think of something, anything, she had to look forward to. The only thing she could think of was exposing Jess's killer or killers.

In the morning she called Leland, still in Boston (Leland never called her long-distance because it was so expensive).

Leland of course had sources inside the D.C. police force. He muttered the usual inadequacies of condolence. But he was unsympathetic to her murder theory.

"Yeah, some of the cops say the suicide was a put-up job, but what do they know? The coroner said suicide so the cops are happy to leave it at that. That's what I'd do, too."

A long pause. "I'll come out to see you next week."

"Can't wait, baby."

Roxy had inherited a roll-top desk from Jess's mother Opal. The next morning she sat at the desk, sharpened a pencil, and opened a looseleaf notebook. Her eighth-grade teacher had told her that when unsure of your course, an outline always answers. Having digested the conflicting news reports and Leland's information, she wrote in a small, precise hand:

I. Jess's body. Who saw?
  a. Gov't agent Barney Martin
  b. Billy Burns
  c. Dr. Boone
  d. coroner—when?
  e. police—when? names?
  f. Elmer Dwyer (Wardman Park mgr.)—?

So, she perceived, the first three people to see him were all high government officials with an interest in minimizing a scandalous death. What a coincidence that Barney Martin was there and that his boss Billy Burns lived right underneath and that Burns's boss Harry happened to be sleeping in the White House. And then Elmer Dwyer, assuming he was called into the room—the stories didn't jibe—would want no bad publicity for his hotel.

II. Who called Dr. Boone?
   a. Pres. H. after somebody (Burns?) called him?
   b. Billy Burns—before or after Pres. H. was called?
   c. Elmer Dwyer—before or after Pres. H. was called?
III. Inquest—lack of
   a. police inquest required by law? or coroner's ruling suffices?
   b. why no autopsy? Boone's decision? coroner's?
   c. why no gun? misplaced—who believes that?
   d. no dr.'s examination of entrance/exit wounds?

She added an afterthought:

   e. who else in the hotel heard the shot?

Scanning this tabulation of uncertainties brought a doubt to Roxy's mind. If there was a conspiracy to cover up a murder, wouldn't they at least have gotten their stories straight?

June 20, 1923

Warren Harding sat at the desk in his upstairs study, holding a fountain pen poised over a document. He changed his mind, recapped the pen, and slid the document to the side of the desk.

He rose, walked to look out the window, and returned to his desk. After ruminating a few minutes, he retrieved the document and uncapped the pen, but he still could not sign it. He lost count of the number of times this happened—damn it, I will sign; no, I can never sign. Finally he wrote "WarrenGHarding," his usual signature with the letters run together and an underline dashed off beneath "Harding." He had just sold the *Marion Star* for $500,000.

How can making half a million bucks cause such worry and sorrow? he asked himself, starting to reminisce. The happiest times the Duchess and I ever had were when we worked shoulder to shoulder putting out the *Star*. I know, a month or so ago I said in a speech to the newspaper editors that I would hold on to the *Star* and write columns now and then as an elder statesman. Bah, I would just be an ancient eminence telling the kids how real newspapers were run back in the old days. They would pretend to listen respectfully, wouldn't they? Well, whatever I might do, I have to provide for the Duchess if I pass on before she does.

He had bought a farm in Ohio and visualized retiring there while writing his memoirs. Looking out the window at the South Lawn, he somehow knew that this fantasy would never happen. Harding stood, clasped his hands behind his back, and tried to stretch by leaning backwards. The effort left him breathing hard. He tried raising his arms above his head with the same result and then sat back down. A good thing, he thought, that I left that farm to my brother George in my new will.

His sister Carolyn Votaw was astonished when she heard about a new will. "What on earth for?"

"Oh, I don't reckon I'll be coming back from Alaska." He said this in such a matter-of-fact way that Carolyn thought he was trying to be funny.

"Oh, Warren, don't be so morbid."

He merely looked at her. Why doesn't anyone believe that I'm sick? he wondered.

The Duchess remained sure that the two-month western trip would rejuvenate him. With her political adviser Harry Daugherty sick and in mourning, she laid elaborate plans by herself. Wealthy people in cities all over the country invited the first couple to stay with them, but Florence ruled out such visits lest the local folks resent their consorting with the rich. Warren would make whistle-stop remarks everywhere, with major speeches restricted to a few big cities. Otherwise, his appearances might become routine, humdrum. The press could not have that and the press must be appeased. Finally, she took the precaution of having a full-time nurse aboard. She hired Ruth Powderly, the nurse who had cared for President Wilson.

For all that, she felt compelled to summon the soothsayer Madame Marcia.

"You must take back what you predicted to me! You must! Study your charts again and be extremely careful!"

"Dear lady, the charts are invariable. We may not dispute them, only adjust our behavior in accordance."

"But Warren must serve a second term! He has to!"

Marcia put on her most sympathetic expression. "My dear, there is death stalking the air we breathe in Washington. Among the men in whom the president reposed unwise trust were some who dealt death." She closed her eyes and lifted her chin. "I see powder, a white powder in the astral plane."

What was this, an allusion to gunpowder burns on Jess's face?

"There are dark clouds around Mr. Harding, just as there were when I first consulted with you three years ago," Marcia continued.

"There will be cloudless blue skies out west," Florence said.

She knew that response was not just irrelevant but pathetic. Marcia's dress rustled as she stood, wished her well and murmured a cold goodbye, her voice mechanical.

Florence would have canceled the trip but for assurances from Doc Sawyer. "You and the president are both doing splendidly," he said. "In fact, I have never known the both of you to be better since coming to Washington." Well, Florence reasoned, the stars did not say that Warren would die *this year*.

Her husband, for once more hardheaded than the Duchess, wrote to a friend, "I cannot yield to one-tenth of the demands that are now being made upon me in connection with this trip. The grade is too steep. I need rest, but at the same time I want to see the country and its people."

That latter picture in his head pushed him to assent to a "voyage of understanding" in which he was to speak at eighty-five public appearances in six weeks (followed by a private cruise). For her part, Florence declared, "I have been wanting to go to Alaska for six years and they are not going to talk me out of it." To her the journey was mythical, a twentieth-century expression of the primeval American urge to head out west. And so on June 20 a ten-car presidential train departed Washington with twenty-two reporters, twenty-two guests, and twenty-seven staff members aboard. Nobody except Dr. Boone knew that he had secretly and prudently placed a coffin on the train.

Reporters noticed something peculiar. Ned and Evalyn McLean were not along for the ride.

June 22, 1923

When Roxy returned to Washington she went to police headquarters to see the police report on Jess's death. The desk sergeant told her it was confidential. She said he could hand it to her now or she would return with a lawyer because the report was public record. The sergeant conferred with the chief for twenty-one minutes—Roxy timed it—and then gave her a two-page document filled out with barely legible handwriting.

It offered no new information except the names of the cops who had showed up in Jess's suite. Roxy tried to talk with them. The chief grumpily informed her that the case was still under investigation and therefore nobody could discuss it. Roxy pointed out that on the contrary the case was closed, ruled a suicide. The chief said that the officers were on assignment and unavailable.

Angrily, she removed a paper clip to get to the coroner's statement under the police report. She gasped and swallowed hard upon reading: "Entrance wound: left parietal 0.4 in. above the sphenoparietal suture." Which meant the exit wound was on the right side. Jess was right-handed.

"Roxy, none of this will ever bring Jess back," Leland said.

"Oh, I know it, but I don't think I can rest until I know what really happened."

"You're serious, aren't you? All right, consider this. Any cop will tell you, in a murder situation you always look at the domestic angle first."

"The domestic angle? Jess wasn't married, you know that."

"Ah, but he practically was—and you know that."

Understanding came in a flash. "Harry? How can you say that? Harry could never do any harm to Jess. They were closer than brothers."

"Uh-huh, closer than brothers, that's my point." Seeing anger flush her face, he said, "Just speculatin,' darlin.' You asked me what the rumors were, well, that's one of them."

She stood up, seemed to reflect on something, and sat back down. "Leland, tell me how to go about hiring a private detective."

"Roxy, sweetie, you'll just be wasting your money."

The telephone rang. Evalyn McLean was calling. At the *Post*, Ned's police reporters got wind of what Roxy was up to. The reporters told Ned, who told Evalyn. "Miss Stinson, dear," she said, "you would do me a favor if you would come to see me at Friendship."

At the appointed hour, Roxy looked around with a higher appreciation of the McLeans' mansion as a bona fide guest than when she was just a girl serving drinks at one of their parties. A servant admitted her to the parlor and she had time to admire the tapestries, the paintings, the vases, the antique furniture. I really should be better educated in the finer things of life, she thought. Evalyn entered, pale and walking with a cane.

After the ceremony of greetings and inquiries after health, Evalyn said, "My dear, I want you to make me a promise. You are still young and beautiful. Don't waste your future mooning around here and trying to solve the mystery of Mr. Smith's death."

"Et tu, Brute?" Roxy said before she could stop herself.

Evalyn smiled in appreciation. "Yes, me too. And let me tell you why. I hired two private detectives to investigate the matter. It was a waste of money." Then she waved her hand as though the money was of no importance.

Roxy did not hide her surprise. "You didn't believe the suicide story either? But what was your interest in it? You were that close to Jess?"

She shook her head. "Ned knew about what Jess was mixed up in and he also knew about—and participated in, mind you—the blackmail fund. Which you so ably administered, my dear. So my interest was, first, to protect Ned, and second, to protect Mrs. Harding. And then also to protect the president, of course."

Roxy made an elaborate ceremony of lighting a cigarette. After a long exhalation through the nostrils she said, "Mrs. McLean, are you telling me that I am in danger?"

"Yes. But that's not the only reason why I am presuming to advise you. You would wear yourself out and waste a lot of time when you could be looking for a husband."

Roxy made dismissive gestures. "I'm not husband hunting, I gave that up years ago. But may I ask you—will you disclose to me what your private detectives found out?"

"Surely. There was a bellboy at the Wardman Park who spent the night with a guest, a lady, ahem. So when the sun came up he was sneaking down the fire stairs when who should he encounter but a big man who had dimples when he smiled. That was the entirety of his description."

"So—who is big and has dimples?"

"The only one I can think of is Gaston Means."

Roxy pondered through a puff on her cigarette. "If I were plotting a murder I would not pick Mr. Means as a confederate. He would be bragging about it all over town."

"Oh, don't think Gaston is as stupid as he acts. He puts on a show to create this big personality, it's how he attracts clients. But no, I don't think Gaston was involved."

"Then who?"

"That's my point, dear lady, we'll never know."

"You mean that's all the detectives found?"

"All that wasn't in the public record. I interviewed that loathsome man Barney Martin myself. He never told me the same story twice. He did say that Jess was not shot with the gun that was on the floor. So . . . then what?"

Roxy had known grief and loneliness the past several weeks; now she she was overtaken by profound discouragement. Finally she said, "You must have an opinion of why—why Jess was . . . "

"I will send a little Latin back at you. Cui bono? Who benefits from the elimination of Jess Smith and all his private papers? Who other than his patron? His roommate? His . . . his companion?"

At that moment a servant entered with a tray of tea. "Put it down and leave us," Evalyn commanded sharply.

After a sip of tea Roxy said, "I can never believe that Mr. Daugherty would ever do anything to hurt Jess."

Evalyn shrugged. "Probably not, but there are people around him who would be willing and able to do so on his behalf."

Another question occurred to Roxy. "Mrs. McLean, do you remember during the campaign when I talked to the

Duchess about a job with Mr. Harding? You were there in the car."

"Of course, dear. I never saw such grit. I wanted to give you a hug."

"Did Jess ever talk to you about talking to Mr. Christian or the Duchess on my behalf?"

Evalyn needed only a moment to search her memory. "No, never."

"Jess Smith lied to me," Roxy said as if reciting a proverb. She leaned forward. "Mrs. McLean, I am going to take your advice. I am going to go home and not stick my neck out anywhere."

"Bless you, my dear."

They then spent a happy half hour trading Washington gossip before Roxy said, "Mrs. McLean, you have been very kind to me and now I am going to ask another personal question. Why didn't you and Mr. McLean go out west with the Hardings?"

"We weren't invited. Or, rather, we were disinvited. The Duchess sent me very nice letters about how Doc Sawyer did not want to expose her to my illness. That was horse shit and I shan't ask you to excuse the expression. The real reason is that we are a famous couple and they did not want our publicity to interfere with their own. And then, well, there was a matter in which the Duchess was disappointed in me and that's enough about that."

"Mrs. McLean, you are the most honest woman I know. Certainly the most honest in Washington. I thank you with all my heart."

As Roxy took her leave Evalyn said, "Ned and I are going to Bar Harbor for the summer. Write us there as soon as you get back to Ohio."

July 13, 1923

Roxy was at her roll-top reading up on the rules of procedure for Ohio probate court. Mal Daugherty was threatening to contest Jess's will, which had left her $25,000. She dreaded having to go to court to fight Mal. It could only mean even more publicity.

She was tempted not to answer the ringing phone. She had tired of refusing requests for interviews. Reporters wanted her to talk about Jess and Harry. Reluctantly she picked up the earpiece. "Please, Miss Stinson, Senator Wheeler wishes to talk to you." Roxy had hung up on this call twice before, assuming it was another reporter using a fake identity to snooker her into an interview.

She knew that Burton K. Wheeler was from Montana. "What's the capital of Montana?" she demanded.

"What? It's Helena, why—oh, yes, I understand, yes," the secretary said. "Really, Miss Stinson, cross my heart, this really is Senator Wheeler's office and he really wants to talk to you."

"Very well."

"Miss Stinson, this is Senator Wheeler and I'm so glad we finally got in touch. I believe that you can be of tremendous help in a matter of great national importance . . ."

"I'm listening."

"Good, good. Look, this is an extremely sensitive matter which I don't want to discuss over the telephone, for reasons which I think you can understand. Now, I need to change trains in Columbus next Wednesday. Would that be a convenient time for us to meet? My office will provide all the assistance you might need."

"You know, for a Westerner, you talk with an Eastern accent."

"Ha! Now, see, that kind of skeptical mind, that analytical mind, is exactly why I think we will get along. And by the way, I was raised in Massachusetts. Please, Miss Stinson, you can put down your sword and shield."

"Okay."

"Now, might I invite you to lunch with me? You will be under absolutely no obligation except to hear me out. And my office manager, who is also my sister, will be with us. In case you are concerned about the impropriety of a single woman lunching with a married man."

"Mister, I have never been concerned about social proprieties in my life."

"Now I am even more sure that we will be partners."

Out of boredom as much as anything, Roxy assented to the meeting. "But listen, if I see, or as much as smell, a reporter within ten miles of there, I turn right around and walk out."

"Fine, I want you to hold me to that."

When they met at the Scioto Country Club Roxy was struck by how much Wheeler looked like Harry—in fact, so many professional men did. Wheeler was in his early forties and could only get balder and more jowly, his features more coarse.

He and his plain-looking sister, Maude Mitchell, were both perfectly polite as he pulled out a chair for her at a table in a private dining room. Maude was primly dressed in styles a little old-fashioned and wore her hair in a pageboy that went to her jawline.

Wheeler said, "By the way, I met your president on his western tour at the Anaconda Copper Mining Company up in Butte. He was—"

" 'My' president?"

"I meant your fellow Ohioan. He's everybody's president, or course. Anyway, he actually rode in one of the ore carts. The first lady was a big hit, too. She had on these long white gloves and shook all the miners' hands and laughed about it. 'Get them good and grimy,' she said. 'It's honest dirt.' "

"How did he look?"

"Um. Grey and worn out. Breathing hard. Frankly, the president looked like a sick man. And a minor point, I guess, his lips were swollen from sunburn. Sorry, didn't mean to be a Gloomy Gus."

Roxy did not reply. Almost the first thing she said was, "Don't think that I'm impressed just because you're a senator. I spent enough time in Washington to learn how much high titles are worth."

Burton smiled and nodded; Maude laughed outright. "Just so, just so," he said. "So now allow me to explain how you might help to deflate some of those high titles."

The pitch was, Wheeler was the ranking Democrat on a special Senate committee to investigate wrongdoing in the departments of Justice and the Interior. He wanted Roxy to testify before the committee in public.

"Well, as to the Teapot Dome and Mr. Fall at Interior, I don't know anything more than what I read in the papers."

"But you see, Mr. Daugherty is criminally liable for failing to prosecute Mr. Fall or at least his associates. And nobody knows more about Mr. Daugherty and his relationship with Mr. Smith than you do."

"But I'm sure you know that I administered, or what's the word, I was custodian of some of Mr. Smith's finances. That would make me an accomplice or an accessory or whatever the legal word is."

"I assure you, Miss Stinson, I would ask you to testify only under a grant of immunity from prosecution."

"Yeah, well, you might immunize me for whatever I say to the Senate, but would that immunize me from the Justice Department too? Isn't there still separation of powers? They could still go after me. Because Mr. Daugherty hates me. Really, it's personal with him."

Wheeler was surprised that a layperson would ask a legal question that shrewd. "But you see, Mr. Daugherty and his cabal are finished, washed up. Nobody at Justice would dare to touch you. Please understand, you would be of indispensable help in seeing that justice is done. We put some of these people away, the country might even have faith in its government again."

"Well, it might benefit justice, but it certainly would benefit the Democratic Party."

"Naturally so. Is that a problem? Are you a Republican?"

"I'm a cynic."

Maude laughed and said, "That makes you a citizen of Washington."

"No I'm not."

Later, after dessert was served, Roxy said, "Give me twenty-four hours to think about it. And at this point I would only agree to go to Washington to talk with your committee's lawyers. Nothing further."

"Fair enough. And now permit me to caution you. Please don't say anything sensitive over your telephone."

"Uh-huh. You mean it might be tapped. I am aware of that. I am not naive, Mr. Wheeler."

"Of course not. But another thing. Can you drive?"

"Why yes, I drove up here from Washington C.H. I'm a very good driver."

"Oh, I assumed that you took the train. Well, the point is, try not to drive alone and never drive alone after dark."

Roxy had not thought of that. "Now you're scaring me."

"Forgive me, but these are perilous times for our country . . ."

August 2, 1923

The Voyage of Understanding was a fifteen-thousand-mile smashing success except that it was killing Warren Harding. The crowds were large and happy at every stop. The Republican Party had hired "Hoorah

Harrys," men (and women) planted in the crowd to stoke the cheers, but they were pulled off as unneeded after just two days. The Duchess was as popular as the president. It seemed that everybody wanted to hand her delphiniums and roses. There was a craze for King Tut, whose tomb had recently been unearthed, and women gave Florence fashions in faux-Egyptian geometric patterns of black, blue, and bronze.

Wheeler had not told Roxy the whole story about the visit to Butte. As the Hardings drove to a lodge, a dozen young waitresses stopped their open car, throwing flowers and serenading them with ukeleles. Warren winked at each in turn, asked for another song, and then asked if he might see them again. Right in front of their entourage as they entered the lodge, the Duchess scolded, "Warren, it took you just as long to say goodbye to those girls as it did for you to run through three thousand tourists yesterday at Old Faithful!"

Dr. Boone took another view of the incident. Maybe Florence is right, he hoped—maybe this trip really is revivifying the president. He wrote in his journal, "The P. regarded the girls with his customary prurience."

The Hardings got their wish about seeing Alaska, spending two weeks touring the territory by train, boat, stagecoach, and mule. Doc Sawyer thought the couple had never looked happier. They returned to a 484-foot navy transport, the USS *Henderson*, to take them back to Seattle. Florence had insisted on the *Henderson* after learning that in the World War it sank a German U-boat by ramming it.

Warren spent most of the time aboard ship playing bridge and poker, but he also read *The Imperial Orgy*, a history of the tsars. He was concerned about the threat of communism and thought the United States one day might have to fight a war with Russia.

As the *Henderson* glided past the glaciers along the coast of the southeastern Alaskan panhandle, nearing Vancouver, the drone of a low-flying airplane prompted its passengers to look up. Boone, a navy man, recognized the type—a new Navy-Wright NW-2 floatplane. It landed, spraying salt water from its floats, cut the power, and drifted toward the *Henderson.* The ship sent a boat to secure the plane. The pilot opened the door and held out a diplomatic pouch; a sailor snagged it with a boat hook. The pouch was secured with a locked chain. Now Boone was alarmed. Secret intelligence? That couldn't be transmitted to the ship by wireless in code? Are we at war?

Harding, shoulders slumped, jaw clenched, carried the pouch below deck to his stateroom. From that moment, nothing could put life back into Warren Harding's dead eyes. Alone in his room, he read the handwritten note:

> Urgent. To be read by the President only. Miss Roxy Stinson is to testify under oath and under immunity before the investigative committee.
>
> Called by Senator Wheeler. Expected to testify as to illegal activities in executive departments. Parallel movement by Democrats to impeach Mr. Daugherty for malfeasance. Obvious implications for 1924 elections. I am at your service. Henry Cabot Lodge

Harding thought, of course Lodge, that old bastard, would know everything that goes on in the Senate, even in the Democratic caucus. What I can't imagine is what I ever did to turn that young lady against me. Or did they just buy her off? But with what? She's already rich. The Duchess never liked her, but she wouldn't turn traitor just to get back at the Duchess?

Harding searched his memory to recall whether he had ever flirted with Roxy. No—he did not even remember ever being alone with her—the Duchess was always there with her hawk's eye.

The more he pondered, the more he despaired. When he went back on deck it glowed softly in the opalescent twilight that hangs on so long in summer in the higher latitudes. "Sir, I bet you could still read a newspaper in this light," an officer remarked. Harding gave no sign of hearing him. He went to the rail, crumpled the note in his hand, and tossed it in the ocean.

After lunch the next day he summoned to his stateroom Herbert Hoover, his secretary of commerce and the most respected member of the Cabinet. Hoover was adept at running large organizations. Too bad, Harding thought, that he lacks political antennae and so he'll never be president.

He asked Hoover bluntly, "If you knew of a great scandal in our administration, would you for the good of the country and the party expose it publicly? Or would you bury it?"

Hoover did not hesitate. "Publish it and at least get credit for integrity on your side."

"Well, yes, but then that method might be politically dangerous," Harding said. He looked so nervous and distraught that Hoover said, "Please, Mr. President, may I call Dr. Sawyer for you?"

Harding suffered from painful "indigestion," which actually was heart disease, and insomnia. Sawyer dosed him heavily with purgatives such as aloe vera, olive oil, and flaxseed oil, and what he called "homeopathic eggnog." Among its ingredients were white baneberry, white arsenic, and belladonna—all of them toxic. Sawyer contrived to keep Dr. Boone away from the Hardings, "his" patients.

Then Warren got so sick that he could not hide it from Boone—or the press. Harding ate tainted crabmeat that had been stowed aboard from Valdez, Alaska. The abdominal pains were so sharp that he could not move and could not vomit either. Sawyer administered more purgatives and more "eggnog."

Sawyer said Harding might have contracted copper poisoning from crabs that swam in copper-laced water, or were stored in copper cans, or cooked in copper utensils. This notion was so ludicrous that reporters could not write it as straight news from a figure of authority. They tried to talk with Dr. Boone but he was tight-lipped and surly. General Sawyer still outranked him, even on a navy ship. And the Hardings still believed in him.

Just when Harding had recovered enough to stand and shave himself, a horrific jolt shook the *Henderson*. In a farcical replay of its World War heroics, the ship had struck one of the destroyers escorting it in heavy fog in Puget Sound. The *Henderson's* boiler room was flooding and the officers cried, "All hands on deck!" When Warren did not appear, Boone ran down to his state room. Harding was sprawled over the bed, a wet towel around his neck and half his face covered with shaving cream. He did not look at Boone. He said, "I hope this boat sinks."

The boiler was repaired, the smaller ship was towed to shore, no lives were lost. The fog stayed so thick that passengers could not see one another on deck, so entry into Seattle was delayed. The voyage remained snakebitten. Harding sent word to cancel half the Seattle events, but through a mixup he was scheduled to cram two days of appearances into one.

At the University of Washington stadium he spoke to the largest crowd ever gathered to hear a president—it also was the first to be broadcast by radio to both coasts. The microphones picked it up when his voice got husky and his breathing labored. He called Alaska "Nebraska." He leaned forward and gripped the podium as his manuscript fluttered to the floor. It was Hoover who lunged to the podium to gather the papers. Swaying and disoriented, Harding continued to speak. Neither Florence nor Sawyer nor Boone stopped him. Not only that, they took him to make another speech that night at the Seattle Press Club.

On the night train to California, Harding had a fever with a pulse rate over 130 and blood pressure of 175/100. Just seafood poisoning, Sawyer told the press, without "the slightest apprehension that the president's illness might end fatally." He explained that the president's "Anglo-Saxon race is the reason for his physical and mental strength." Reporters paid more attention to tree trunks laid across the tracks outside Roseburg, Oregon. Anarchists had placed them there to disrupt the trip.

Against Sawyer's advice, the Duchess canceled the rest of the trip. But she refused to put Warren in a hospital. The president's party checked into a San Francisco hotel. Warren angrily waved away a waiting nurse with a wheelchair. Florence and Sawyer supported him up to room 8064.

While Florence and Sawyer slept that night, Boone finally saw Harding alone. His diagnosis was quick. A dangerously enlarged heart. Boone sent a telegram to the president of Stanford University, a prominent physician. That doctor called San Francisco's top cardiologist.

Once they got past Sawyer's barrier of bluster, the two outside doctors determined that Harding had suffered a heart attack. They and Boone had to squabble with Sawyer over the wording of the next day's medical bulletin. "A temporarily overstrained cardiovascular system" was how the four doctors spelled "heart attack." "A digestive disturbance" was how they spelled "food poisoning." When a reporter asked Sawyer if Boone shared his opinions, Sawyer called him "a laboratory technician."

Back in Washington, a reporter remembered his 1920 interview with Madame Marcia, when she predicted that Harding would be elected president but "not live out his term." Does that prophecy still hold? The sorceress studied Harding's horoscope and pronounced, "It is the end. He will never recover. The crisis will come Thursday night. He will be dead by Friday."

Madame Marcia was correct. Warren Harding died on Thursday night, August 2, 1923.

August 3, 1923

Calvin Coolidge was staying at his father's farmhouse in New Hampshire, nestled against the Green Mountains. The phone there was so old-fashioned that it could not receive long-distance calls. In San Francisco, George Christian tried to call the store across the street from the Coolidge home, but its owner slept through the ring. Frantic, Christian sent a telegram to the nearest town: "The President died instantly and without warning and while conversing with members of his family at 7:30 p.m. His physicians report that death was apparently due to some brain embolism, probably an apoplexy."

The telegraph agent woke up Calvin's driver, secretary, and Secret Service man Leland Jackson. They raced to John Coolidge's home. John bolted up the stairs yelling "Calvin! Calvin!" and barged into his son's room. At 2:47 a.m., by the light of a kerosene lamp, John Coolidge, a justice of the peace, swore in Calvin Coolidge as the nation's thirtieth president.

At the Plaza Hotel in San Francisco, Florence Harding took no interest in when and how Calvin Coolidge was notified. People also noted how stony and dry-eyed she remained. The embalmers finished their work about 3 a.m. and placed the body back on the bed. Not much later, Florence came and directed them to put the body in a bronze casket along the wall. Harding was dressed in a formal black cutaway jacket and striped pants. Florence had the undertakers remove his tie and handed them another that she selected. Looking lovingly at her husband, she said, "He was magnificent in life but he is more wonderful in death." Others in the room exchanged glances—what a weird thing to say. Then Florence ordered that the coffin be sealed in glass.

She turned and snapped to Sawyer, "You keep me alive as long as you can. Don't let me go if there is a spark of life left in me!" For the next few hours she worked hard, greeting dignitaries who came to pay their respects and making travel arrangements for the funeral train, the whole time with an unspoken conviction: No newspaper can say that I broke down.

She made sure that Warren's casket was visible through an observation window on the train for its lumbering, 3,100-mile eastbound journey. Two soldiers, a sailor, and a marine stood at attention at the corners. At every station, and even between stations through empty miles of prairie, Americans gathered to salute their deceased president. A single bouquet was placed atop the casket. Its card, invisible to the onlookers, read: "Harry to His Old Friend Warren."

Calvin and Grace Coolidge and Evalyn McLean took special trains to speed south to meet Florence when she arrived at Union Station near midnight. The Coolidges told Florence to stay in the White House as long as she wished. She thanked them formally and even, Grace thought, coldly. Evalyn and the Duchess followed the hearse to the White House.

They were in Florence's bedroom when she said, "Evalyn, I want to see my husband." Evalyn took her arm as they walked slowly down the curving marble staircase to the East Room. Evalyn looked through the glass at the corpse. They had put lipstick on him so that he almost seemed to smile. That was a mistake, she thought. Warren was undignified in life often enough; in death he should look noble. Evalyn was surprised when she heard Florence call George Christian and say, "Open the casket lid."

Christian, befuddled but silent, placed a chair by the casket for Florence. She sat and leaned over so her face was close to his. Evalyn heard her say, "Warren, the trip has not hurt you one bit. No one can hurt you now, Warren."

Evalyn took a chair by the opposite wall to give Florence her privacy. Florence kept on talking but Evalyn could not make out the words. So many flowers were stuffed into the room that the scent hung in the air like dust after an explosion. Evalyn thought she actually might get sick. What did she mean by "no one can hurt you"? She had always feared that some lunatic might hurt him—after all, three presidents had been shot to death. But then, my brother who died, my parents . . . sometimes I feel grateful that they are now safe from all harm. That's probably what she means.

No, that's not what she means. She means: Now you are mine alone. For the first time I have you all to myself. After all these years, you are truly mine.

For two hours Florence kept up her macabre monologue. Evalyn shivered in the early-morning chill; she sneezed. Florence called for Christian to close the casket. She started wandering through all the floral arrangements, putting together a small bouquet of daisies and nasturtiums. These she place on the casket, then the women started back upstairs.

The next day, Harding lay in state in the Capitol and then a train took him home to Marion. Florence greeted old friends in the kitchen of her father-in-law's home. "Yes, it is too bad, but I am not going to break down," she told one who had grown tiresome with laying on the sympathy.

For the funeral Florence wore a black dress with a veil that reached to the ground. At the end, after the casket was carried into an ivy-covered vault, Florence went inside to be alone with Warren for one last time. She emerged dry-eyed, unflinching, and blinking in the sunlight. Looking up, she saw the tallest monument in the cemetery, occupying the highest point on Delaware Avenue. It was the gravestone of Amos Kling. Then came a thought so unexpected, so strange in the circumstances, that she thought she really might cry: *Well, papa, how do you like my black dress? I didn't have one so I sent a red gown and a yellow one out to be dyed. Saved us quite a bit of money, didn't it?*

August 6, 1923

Roxy read a wire-service report that Florence had been reading a *Saturday Evening Post* article to Warren that night. The article, "A Calm View of a Calm Man," praised Harding as a "stable" man for the times. "That's good, go on," Warren said on his sickbed. Then he groaned, dropped his head, and died. A fatuous myth propagated by the Duchess—Roxy sensed it at once. Her bullshit detector clanged in her head.

She went to libraries in Washington Court House and Columbus to read reports of Harding's death in the Washington, New York, and San Francisco newspapers. Just as she had tried to outline the circumstances of Jess's death, she tried to make sense of conflicting stories about the death of the president:

I. Who was with Pres. H when he died?
  a. Mrs. H.
  b. Dr. Sawyer
  c. Dr. Boone
  d. Miss Powderly (nurse)
  e. Miss Dausser (nurse)
  f. Mr. Hoover
  g. some combination of the above
  h. nobody

That roll call looked so ridiculous that Roxy attempted a summary:

a. Mrs. H: alone with H, ran out of the room to call drs.
b. Dr. Sawyer: taking H's pulse when he died, then ran from room
c. Dr. Boone: H was alone and dead when I entered
d. Miss P: Boone wasn't there; he'd gone to dinner with a friend
e. Miss D: Went to get a glass of water for H to take his pills, came back, Mrs. H had her finger in H's mouth, thinking he had merely choked on chewing gum
f. Mr. Hoover: Dr. Sawyer was there, lying across the foot of H's bed

II. Cause of Pres. H. death?
a. food poisoning
b. brain thrombosis
c. heart attack
d. pneumonia
e. apoplexy

III. Inquest—lack of
a. time of death? 7:00, 7:20, 7:35, depending on report
b. no autopsy—Mrs. H's decision
c. embalmers called to H sickroom within an hour

Roxy put down her pencil, sighed, and kicked the stack of newspapers on the floor. For the second time after a death she felt—she tried to find a word for it—vacant. Airless. Poor Warren, he had some outstanding qualities but they were not in sum the right combination of qualities to make a good president. Those scenes of his sickness and death, they were like somebody had written a satire to show how inept his administration was. Such a pity that now that his dying was so badly handled, he will never get to rest in peace in his tomb. Probably, rumors will start going around that somebody poisoned him.

*

Florence opened a wall safe in the Oval Office and removed its contents. She suspected that Warren kept his letters to Carrie Phillips in there. Actually, Carrie never had handed over those letters, but then she never revealed them either. Florence did not know that Christian had already emptied all the drawers of Warren's desk, which included letters from Nan Britton.

It was a hot, muggy August day but Florence ordered a fire in the fireplace. She started throwing "Private Office" files into the fire. Sometimes she took a break, watching the flames and stirring the ashes with a brass poker. She did this for five nights.

With help from the White House staff she went through all the closets. Except for one suit sent to the Smithsonian, she had the clothes boxed up for storage in Marion. With a scissors she snipped buttons from Warren's coats to be given as gifts for his friends and family.

Christian was going through all the offices in the West Wing, demanding every scrap of paper from the staff. These he crammed into wood crates, ten feet long and a foot wide and deep. Evalyn agreed to accept them at Friendship. She wanted redemption for having allowed Warren's fornications there.

Fifteen days after Warren died, the Duchess left the White House for the last time. In a cold rain she still wore black but without a veil. Evalyn's sharp eye noticed that Florence, who had never worn a wedding ring, now wore a mourning ring with a stone of jet. Evalyn helped her into one of the McLean limousines. Lined up behind was a convoy of empty cars to be loaded with Christian's crates.

Despite the rainy night the two women walked the gardens of Friendship. "Now that it's all over I think it's for the best," Florence said. "I would not wish him back to all that strain." Looking around, she said, "The grounds are so beautiful and it is all so peaceful. It does help me to carry my burden, as much as it is possible, to live in such an environment."

Fireplaces being small, Florence and the servants built a bonfire on a knoll overlooking the golf course. Soon Evalyn left to join Ned and their children in Maine but Florence diligently kept burning the contents of the crates. Some of the papers might be "misconstrued" by history, she explained to a gardener.

After three weeks on the job, Florence realized that not even she could scan and sort all the papers in a reasonable amount of time. She went home to Marion to take care of Warren's will, shipping the remaining crates there as well.

She fancied that there was a kind of poetic denouement in ending up back at the *Marion Star*. Every morning for six weeks she went to Warren's old private office and the potbellied stove they used to huddle around in the winter months. One by one she opened the crates and tossed the contents into the stove until the cast iron glowed red from the heat. Her face, hands, and blouse were covered with soot as she offered burnt sacrifices to the gods of forgetting so that *no one can hurt you now, Warren.*

March 11, 1924

Senator Wheeler knocked on Roxy's door. When she opened it he boomed, "You are hereby served!" and thrust a document into her hand. He said it so solemnly that she laughed. "I don't feel served," she said. "In fact I feel that I have been badly served." The senator was impatient and not in the mood for weak jokes. "Are you ready?" he demanded.

He carried her suitcase to the Washington Court House station after she carefully tucked into her handbag the subpoena to appear before a Senate committee. Once they were settled into a private compartment after changing trains in Columbus, Wheeler's sister Maude handed him a sheaf of papers from her valise.

"I have been making a study of the attorney general," he said. "A most interesting man. Did you know he once gave a speech saying we have to uphold respect for the rule of law? Really. Harry Daugherty said that."

Roxy, seated across from Wheeler and Maude Mitchell, could read the title page in his hands. *Respect for Law*, an address to the American Bar Association, September 1921. Soon after Harry became attorney general. Wheeler riffled the pages, put on his glasses, and read a quote:

"If laws are obnoxious to the people, it is their province to repeal them. Until they are repealed they must be observed and enforced without fear or favor. The government will endure on the rock of law enforcement, or it will perish in the quicksands of lawlessness."

Maude shook her head and laughed; Wheeler scowled while Roxy looked thoughtful. "Maybe," she said, "it's a, what do they call it in the navy, a false flag operation. He's bragging on his own righteousness so people don't look too hard at what he's actually doing. Not a false flag, I take that back, a smokescreen."

Wheeler took off his glasses, placed them in a lapel pocket, and assumed a long-practiced look of grave wisdom. "Sure, that's part of it, but I think it's more that he wants to delude his own self. Like, 'I'm not as crooked as people say I am. They're just a bunch of Bolsheviks anyway.' Do you know what he called me? He called me 'the Communist leader of the Senate.' "

"Well, he's called me some things too. He doesn't fool me one bit," Roxy said.

Harry had been smearing her as a slut. Members of the Senate Judiciary Committee were getting anonymous letters from Ohio about what a wicked and dishonest woman she was. Harry also sent one of the deviated septums to check into a hotel in Cleveland, then doctor the registry to look like he had spent the weekend there with Roxy. Copies were sent to senators and the press. Wheeler said, "Listen, Miss Stinson, I went to law school. I know how this is done. You turn any statement of fact into a question of motive." He considered denying these poison-pen accusations in an official statement, but he and Roxy decided to wait to answer them in sworn testimony.

Maude said, "I hope you are aware, Miss Stinson, of the horse-whipping you are going to take from Democrats and the press too."

"Oh, well," Roxy said, "it's not as bad as being dragged down a gravel road behind a buggy." An expression she had overheard as a girl in Jess's store. She reached into her handbag and handed a letter to Wheeler. When Jess died the Duchess had sent her a sympathy note, so out of politeness Roxy sent her one when Warren died. She did not expect that the Duchess would reply to it or even read it. But the letter, on White House stationery, said:

"Dear Miss Stinson, How kind of you to share your memories of dining with Warren and myself and wishing blessings upon me during my time of sorrow. I can only hope that you will show the same sympathy and compassion for Mr. Daugherty in his time of troubles."

Jess had been right, Roxy thought—well, actually, Harry had been right and Jess repeated it. To the Duchess, it was her small family against the world. Harry was family even if his corruption might falsely besmirch Warren's historical reputation. She would stand against the detractors. She always had.

Wheeler said, "I'm not surprised that she is still using White House stationery. Hmpf. The empress dowager."

Maude repeated, "You are a brave woman, standing up and telling the truth about those people."

"I'm not a saint," Roxy said. "I'm furious with Harry and Mal. Not only are they fighting me over Jess's will, but they are trying to cheat me out of a separate, eleven-thousand-dollar account that Jess set up for me."

"Fair enough, and don't put me on a pedestal either," Wheeler said. "I'm not a saint. I'll tell you a little of my life story. You've heard of the Anaconda Copper Mining Company? It rules the state of Montana like a dictatorship and it's not a benevolent dictatorship either. So I ran for governor against the copper trust, promising to return power to the people. I even found a Negro and a Blackfoot Indian to be my running mates. We were going to be populist heroes and save the Republic.

"Well, Anaconda beat the tar out of me. So two years later when I ran for senator, I made my peace with the powers that be. I promised to represent Montana's business interests in Washington and they put money in my campaign fund."

"Well then," Roxy said, "I should ask, what exactly is your motivation in holding these hearings?"

"Do you know how hurt this country is by all this lawbreaking? Really, I don't think the country ever got over the Black Sox scandal of a few years ago. Fixing the World Series! And now we have all this open flouting of Prohibition."

"I'm not a baseball fan," Roxy said. "All I know is that where I grew up I was supposed to root for the Cincinnati Reds and hate the Chicago Cubs."

Wheeler waved away this irrelevant comment. "There's a fine old word from the Greek, iatrogenic. It means something caused by doctors. Like if a doctor gives you pills that make you even sicker, that's an iatrogenic illness. Well, my thinking is, all this criminality under Prohibition is iatrogenic illness, caused by the doctor—that is, by democracy itself."

Roxy said, “My thinking is, if the people are stupid enough to outlaw alcohol, I’m not stupid enough to stay poor when I could get rich.”

Another impatient flick of Wheeler’s wrist. “The thing is, democracy is much more fragile than people suppose it is. Let’s say you are called to serve on a federal jury. Knowing what you do about the Justice Department, would you trust what any government agent testified to? You see? Now, what if the crooks keep getting away with it—nobody stops them? The country would lose its faith in its own democratic institutions.

“Oh, I’m sorry, I can see that you think I’m lecturing you. What I’m saying is, justice must not only be done, it must be seen to be done. It’s a cliché but like most clichés it’s true. So these hearings will inform the public of just how much corruption there is and that the wrongdoers will be found out and punished. We’re not just going to hold hearings until the problem goes away—which is business as usual, I know.” He frowned, took a puff from a cigar. “I suppose it’s possible that we won’t get anybody indicted, but the lesson is, the A.G. and his cronies will be hauled before the court of public opinion.”

“Sounds like you’re doing it just to be a symbol.”

“My dear lady—nothing *less* than a symbol, don’t you see? It’s democratic rituals, open and above-board, that keep democracy alive.”

He paused a minute and then went on, “I must confess to an element of self-interest too. Like I said, I’m not a saint. Even as we speak, Mr. Daugherty is trying to get me indicted as a Communist agent. Why? Because as the U.S. attorney in Montana during the war I didn’t indict a single person for sedition.”

Maude said,“I tell Burton, that’s a badge of honor.”

Roxy, tiring of this portentous discussion, nodded in agreement. They debated whether they should risk going to the dining car for lunch. Somebody might recognize them and that somebody might tell a reporter.

"Oh, hell, I'm not famous enough to be recognized," Wheeler said. "Miss Stinson, has your picture ever been in the papers?"

"Not since I was singing, but that was years ago."

In the dining car, in deference to Prohibition, none of them ordered a drink. They decided that the dear departed president was a topic safe enough to be overheard if anyone cared to listen.

"I haven't told you enough about meeting the president up in Butte," Wheeler said. "He had the gift, that gift of playing a crowd like a violin. You have to be born with it, it can't be learned and it can't be taught. But any politician would cut off his left nut to—excuse me, Miss Stinson—to somehow acquire that gift."

"I knew him when he was still in the Ohio legislature," Roxy said. She lowered her voice. "I thought he was an awfully nice man but he allowed himself to be controlled. Controlled especially by the Duchess and Harry Daugherty."

Wheeler raised his own voice a little. "Whatever you want to say about him, he did many good things as president. The United States budget is on a rational basis now. That's the kind of thing that doesn't get much publicity but it's appreciated by people who understand how the government works."

Roxy thought Maude was going to stay silent but then she offered, "The president and the first lady both did many good things for women's rights." The other two nodded approvingly.

When they reached Washington that night Wheeler went to his home while Maude checked into the Hotel Washington with Roxy. Maude's job was to keep an eye on her and guard against any of Harry's thugs trying to intimidate her. Roxy could not even call Leland out of fear of wire-tapped phones. Nor could Leland see her on her big day tomorrow lest his picture appear in the papers: BOYFRIEND OF STAR WITNESS IS COOLIDGE BODYGUARD.

Before the dressing room mirror, Roxy looked through the black-framed glasses provided by Wheeler to make her look less sexy. She stared at her face and rued the crinkles starting to emerge at the corners of her eyes and mouth. Don't worry, senator, I won't be sexy. Various puffy hats were tried on until the one that hid the most of her hair was selected. She laid out a dark grey dress with a high neckline and removed all jewelry.

To her own surprise Roxy thought, I'm not nervous. In fact, I'm sleepy. I know more than any of those senators who will ask me questions. I'm going to bed with a clear conscience.

March 12, 1924

Gaga was the prose of the press. SHAPELY EX-WIFE OF DAUGHERTY AIDE RIPS JUSTICE DEPARTMENT. "A statuesque redhead with the figure of a showgirl shocked the nation's capital with testimony about widespread crookedness in the highest levels of government." ATTORNEY GENERAL A BOOTLEGGER, GIRL WITNESS TELLS SENATE. "Former professional singer Roxy Stinson stunned senators yesterday with detailed stories about Attorney General Harry Daugherty's allegedly illegal sales of bonded government liquor." DAUGHERTY A GONER IF COMELY WITNESS'S CHARGES HOLD UP. "A tall, beautiful witness before a Senate committee provided such damaging testimony against Harry Daugherty that even Republican senators privately said the attorney general must resign." CALM, COLLECTED CUTIE COOLY TELLS COMMITTEE ABOUT CRIMES. "Miss Roxy Stinson, never losing her composure despite sharp questioning from Republicans, testified that the officials charged with enforcing Prohibition are bootleggers themselves."

Reporters sent copy boys to the Government Printing Office for the official transcript of the hearing. Reading it after filing their first stories, they underlined passages such as these:

Senator Wheeler. How would you describe Mr. Jess Smith's relationship with Mr. Daugherty?

Miss Stinson. Jess loved Harry. They were closer than brothers. Jess followed him around like a dog.

Senator Wheeler. Mr. Smith was one of Mr. Daugherty's partners, was he not?

Miss Stinson. In law?

Senator Wheeler. No. In crime.

Miss Stinson. Yes.

Rather than have Republican senators bring up Daugherty's smears, Wheeler got them in the open himself.

Senator Wheeler. Are you aware of allegations received by this committee from the state of Ohio concerning your morals, your rectitude?

Miss Stinson. That is ridiculous, that I am a vicious woman, a disappointed woman and all that stuff.

Roxy was not asked whether she thought Jess had killed himself. However:

Senator Wheeler. Were you permitted to view the body of your former husband Mr. Smith before his burial?

Miss Stinson. I was not. . . .

Senator Wheeler. Did Mr. Smith have a fear of guns?

Miss Stinson. Yes. In fact, I once saw him faint at the sight of a revolver.

Senator Brookhart. Senator, what is the possible relevance of this?

Senator Wheeler. Please, this is not a court of law, as you well know, senator.

What amused the press most of all were descriptions of "the little green house on K Street."

Senator Wheeler. Were there drinks served at parties at that location?
Miss Stinson. Yes.
Senator Wheeler. How were these drinks supplied?
Miss Stinson. Well, Mr. Smith always had some in his valise, and sometimes trucks would pull up to unload the cases. And there were always many bottles kept in the cellar.
Senator Wheeler. Trucks? What kind of trucks?
Miss Stinson. Armored trucks. With an armed guard.

At that point Wheeler had to bang his gavel for order in the hearing room.

Senator Wheeler. Were these liquors legally permitted?
Miss Stinson. They were authorized for medicinal purposes, if that's what you mean, senator.
Senator Wheeler. Who dispatched these trucks of quote, medicinal, end quote liquor to K Street?
Miss Stinson. Mr. Daugherty.

That caused such an uproar that Wheeler had to call a ten-minute recess. Wheeler thought, when Washington hides its evildoing the facts eventually will come out—facts that will shock even the cynics.

During the recess a feeble old man walked in with a cane and slowly took a seat in the rear of Room 410 in the Senate Office Building. His eyes were cloudy but he watched the hearing intently once it resumed. At times he nodded slightly, at others he removed a leather-bound notebook from his coat pocket and scribbled something. Everyone around him nodded deferentially to Henry Cabot Lodge, the lion of the Senate.

Once the day's proceedings were gaveled to a close, reporters hurried to the Justice Department to get Daugherty's reaction. His public relations man Ed Beiter had prepared a written statement but Harry insisted on answering questions. Like the Duchess, he had the fault of overdoing things and talking too much.

"General, do you have any plans to resign?"

"I would not have given thirty cents for the office of attorney general but now I would not surrender it for a million dollars."

"Do you think you still have the confidence of President Coolidge?"

"Oh yes, he has all the facts, unless he is being lied to, as I suspect, by certain persons whose malicious activity and deceitful treatment I am surprised have not been detected."

"General, did you have knowledge of the allegedly illegal activities of Mr. Smith?"

"Certainly not. Now, I'm not one to kick Jess Smith or any man when he's down, but if the Senate had any honesty they would have the doctors who treated Mr. Smith testify. He was very nervous and agitated and sickly the last two years of his life and, frankly, his mind was sometimes not all there."

"General, are the Democrats conducting these hearings for political purposes?" (A reporter from Ned McLean's *Post.*)

Harry rose from the seat behind his desk and stood stiffly, then sidestepped to stand below an American flag on the wall for a nice shot for the cameras.

"The Justice Department has abundant proof of the plans, purposes, and hellish designs of the Communist International. Senator Wheeler and others spent last summer in Russia with their Soviet friends because they are part of a conspiracy to capture, through deceit and design, as many members of the Senate as possible. They intend to spread throughout Washington city and the cloakrooms of Congress a poison gas as deadly as that which sapped and destroyed brave soldiers in the late war."

The reporters took a breath and wrote frantically and happily in their notebooks.

"General, if you have this proof as you say, will you release it to the public?"

"I will do so when the country is willing to hear and in condition to comprehend it. But for the protection of innocent persons, much of it now must be withheld."

The only element their stories now lacked was a quote from Jess Smith's friend Florence Harding. Unfortunately, she was sick again and under the care of Doc Sawyer in Marion.

March 13, 1924

Roxy awoke to find herself a national celebrity. When she was singing she would have cut off an appendage, as Wheeler put it, for such publicity but now she was indifferent. Wheeler had dispatched a plainclothes officer of the Capitol Police to accompany her out of the Senate Office Building and through the throng of newsmen the day before. The grainy, half-tone photos that ran on front pages all over the country looked as if a gangster was hustling his girlfriend by the elbow through an unruly crowd.

Men claiming to be Hollywood agents called Wheeler's office seeking to contact Roxy to offer her a screen test, the opportunity of a lifetime. All these callers were rebuffed.

Maude so far had managed to keep Roxy's presence in the Hotel Washington secret. She ordered breakfast from room service but Roxy, not hungry, barely forked the scrambled eggs. She wore a floor-length dress of navy blue and, just from whimsy, a "Harding Blue" neckband in honor of the Duchess.

The same plainclothes cop met her in the lobby and took her a roundabout way to a back door of the Senate Office Building. The three Republicans on the five-man committee opened by casting doubt on Roxy's credibility. They established that she resented Harry's and Mal's blocking her from getting $11,000 from Jess's estate. But she was so forthright about it, Wheeler thought, that maybe the damage is minimal. Then Wheeler's turn came.

Senator Wheeler. I quote in part from Senate Resolution 157 stating that this special committee was empaneled to investigate and I quote, "the neglect and failure of Harry M. Daugherty, Attorney General of the United States, to arrest and prosecute Albert B. Fall and his coconspirators in defrauding the government, as well as the neglect and failure of the said Attorney General to arrest and prosecute many others for violations of Federal statutes," end quote. Miss Stinson, did Mr. Daugherty or Mr. Smith ever discuss with you the activities of Secretary Fall in regard to oil leases when he was Secretary of the Interior?

Miss Stinson. No.

Senator Wheeler. This question is also predicated on the language of Senate Resolution 157. Did Mr. Daugherty or Mr. Smith ever discuss with you the activities of Charles R. Forbes when he was Director of the Veterans Bureau?

Miss Stinson. No. Well, Mr. Forbes's name might come up in conversations about politics, but not about the actual functioning of the Veterans Bureau, no.

The whole room seemed to sigh in disappointment, except for the Republican senators. Things perked up, though, when the subject turned to films of the Dempsey-Carpentier fight.

Miss Stinson. Mr. Smith declared that we had a big thing if this could be put over as a concession—I mean the rights to display it, that it meant a lot of money; he even mentioned a sum of money.

Senator Wheeler. When he said it was for "we," you understood it to mean it was for Harry Daugherty?

Miss Stinson. There might have been others involved in it, but whenever he discussed anything of that sort, it referred to Mr. Daugherty.

When the proceedings closed for the day the Capitol Police kept Roxy away from the press but Senator Ashurst of Arizona, a politician of merely average venality, was happy to speak to them. "Why, what have we got under Republican rule? We have coal thieves and oil thieves and timber thieves and land thieves and ship thieves and other kinds of thieves. You can enumerate them here until you grow hoarse reciting the list." The reporters eagerly transcribed his words and went off to find Harry.

Late that night Maude contrived, against Wheeler's advice, to sneak Roxy into the Wardman Park to see Leland in his room there.

"Jeez, Rox, I never imagined I'd be going with a world-famous dame."

"You silver-tongued devil you."

"I mean it, darlin,' I'm proud of you."

She waved him off. "Tell me this, Leland, why doesn't President Coolidge just fire Harry already?"

"Aw, he says there ain't any proof against him yet and he wanted to keep the Harding Cabinet on board to show the country that there's continuity in the government. That's what Teddy Roosevelt did when McKinley died."

"Well, at least you get inside the White House now."

"Yeah, it's nice but, you know what? It's smaller inside than people think."

They were silent for a minute. Leland kept turning his cowboy hat in his hands, having complained that the Secret Service wouldn't let him wear it on duty. Roxy wanted to smoke but was trying to quit cigarettes because of what they did to her voice. She sounded raspy from testifying all day anyway.

"What do you think of the new president" Roxy finally asked.

"He's boring but you know what, I think the country is ready for boring. The Harding administration was quite a show. Lots of sickness and death when you look back on it."

Roxy said the hell with it and lit a cigarette. "Well, boredom would suit me for a while. You think I enjoy being on stage like that? Those senators always looking like they either want to strangle me or fuck me. Sometimes both in the same sentence."

"Can't blame them for that, darlin.' "

"I didn't say anything about blame. I'm just saying this is taking a toll."

After another half-hour Roxy said she was too tired to make love. Leland protested but, if she could read his signals, actually seemed relieved. Maude drove her back to the Hotel Washington. The manager had given them a key to the service entrance and they took the fire stairs to their suite.

March 19, 1924

For five full days Roxy testified. Harry and Jess sold liquor permits. They sold liquor itself. They sold paroles. They sold the awards of foreign-held assets. They bribed U.S. attorneys. They took kickbacks. They tried to manipulate the stock market. Toward the end even the Republican senators tired of challenging her assertions. Brookhart of Iowa roused himself to ask:

Senator Brookhart. With all due respect, Miss Stinson, you are aware that your testimony here is based mostly on hearsay? I am not questioning your veracity, but I think it appropriate to note that most of what you have told us would not hold up in a court of law.

Miss Stinson. Senator, I was advised by counsel that my task was to answer each question truthfully, not to provide evidence, and that the United States Senate is neither a law enforcement agency nor a court of law.

[Laughter.]

Senator Wheeler. We will have order. Quiet, please.

Roxy was dismissed and the hearings recessed for the weekend. Gaston Means was the next witness. Although under indictment for mail fraud and Prohibition violations, Gaston was having a jolly time for himself. He grinned a lot and, busting protocol, sometimes leaned forward from the witness table to try to whisper to Wheeler.

Senator Wheeler. Mr. Means, the record shows that you have had many, shall we say, unsavory clients.

Mr. Means. Yes, sir, I will gladly work for anyone with money. Just like a lawyer.

[Laughter.]

Means upset Republicans and Democrats alike by confirming that Billy Burns's Bureau of Investigation agents had ransacked the offices of members of Congress, seeking dirt that Daugherty could use against them.

Senator Wheeler. You haven't been through mine, have you?

Mr. Means. No, but I will, if someone will assign me to it.

[Laughter.]

The next witness was George Remus, furloughed from the Atlanta penitentiary to appear before the committee. He testified that he paid Jess Smith more than $250,000 for immunity from prosecution or imprisonment. Together with the three dollars he paid per case of whiskey, the money he handed over exceeded a half-million dollars.

Senator Wheeler. Did Mr. Daugherty or Mr. Smith apologize to you for their failure of protection?

Mr. Remus. Are you kidding?

Senator Wheeler. Just answer the question, please.

Mr. Remus. No.

Senator Wheeler. Is it true that while incarcerated in Atlanta, you enjoy a private room with a bath and that you are served your dinners privately? The witness will answer the question.

Mr. Remus. Yeah.

Senator Wheeler. Who arranged for these privileges?

Mr. Remus. Who do you think?

Senator Wheeler. The witness will answer the question.

Mr. Remus. Mr. Votaw.

Senator Wheeler. Mr. Votaw is the Director of the Bureau of Prisons? And he is married to the sister of the late President Harding?

Mr. Remus. You know that as well as I do.

The groans of the Republicans were not recorded by the stenographer.

By this time President Coolidge had had enough. He fired Harry Daugherty. Coolidge thanked him for his service to the nation and shook his hand goodbye. Leaving the White House, Harry told his driver to head east on Constitution Avenue. He glanced up and saw the Capitol on his right, uphill from the Washington Mall, then returned to the contents of his briefcase. Something told him to look again.

The white dome gleamed in the westering sun. He looked back over his right shoulder to the Washington Monument. As he swiveled his head back to the left, the dome looked even larger, more glorious. An unexpected and shocking thought came to him: *These will make great ruins someday.*

No, that's crazy. We just won a world war. The United States is throwing its ships and automobiles and locomotives all over the world. And our movies, too. We are the greatest power the world has ever seen. Why on Earth would I think of ruins maybe a thousand years from now?

But it's true, isn't it? We've been here about 150 years, that's not a bad run as democracies go. What people like to call a democracy anyway. Maybe after the Communists take over these times will be looked back on as our best times, the good old days. So—Warren, then? Maybe Warren will go down the way the emperor Trajan did, as the man who happened to preside at the height of the empire. Ha! Who would ever have thought that?

Harry was physically sick and emotionally distraught, but he half-smiled and chuckled at that thought. His driver looked at him in the rear-view mirror. He wondered why his boss was muttering to himself.

A week later, Daugherty's holdovers in the Department of Justice indicted Senator Wheeler in Montana. He was accused of taking bribes from his legal clients who sought federal oil and gas leases.

Wheeler and Leland had asked Roxy to hang around for these daily sensations in Room 410, but she caught a train home as soon as Wheeler was done with her testimony. She had a sleeping berth to herself but her thoughts were too troubled to allow sleep. Had she blackened the memory of Jess Smith, a man she loved? The only man who had really loved her, just for herself? But then, how could you taint the reputation of somebody when everybody always knew he was a crook? And now the entire country knew that she was a crook as well. Wheeler and even the Republicans were careful not to ask questions that might force her either to incriminate herself or take the Fifth Amendment. Even so, her complicity with Jess and Harry was obvious. Well, screw the people, I don't care what they think, I never have. But didn't I let myself be used by Wheeler? He might be a Progressive but after all he is just another senator who wants to be president.

And the nerve of Harry, sending that ribbon clerk Ed Beiter over to plead for sympathy. He says Harry has moved his crippled wife Lucie into Jess's old room with twenty-four-hour nursing care and if I slander Harry in my testimony it will only add to Lucie's distress and might even kill her. Hell, I don't owe anything to Harry Daugherty. He always just tolerated me, ever since he used to call me "Punkin" when I was a girl. If not for Harry, Jess and I would never have got mixed up in all this. And Mr. Beiter, you soon will be out of a job. Too bad for you.

In the morning she went to the dining car, not bothering with makeup or brushing her hair. She ordered coffee and stared out the window at the rain on the steep green hills of West Virginia. With fascination she observed how raindrops collected on the pane. They started out motionless or maybe dropping slowly down the glass. But vagrant winds when the train traversed curves or tunnels through the hills caused the drops to zip backwards or sometimes even zigzag.

A large drop toward the bottom right corner of the window seemed to await a merger with its siblings. Sure enough, two drops above it joined and then fell to make a triple-sized drop. Roxy was not a romantic soul; she went through life interpreting it in prose, not poetry. At this moment, though, she knew that the aquatic trio represented Harry, Jess, and herself, their fates ineluctably combined.

A fourth drop skittered to the right above the trio. It dropped a half-inch. It was Leland. Roxy was not surprised or disappointed when it disappeared in the wind.

June 22, 1924

By mid-June Leland was back from Northampton, Massachusetts. Coolidge had gone to his home there while the Republican National Convention met in Cleveland to nominate him for president. Presidential candidates never attended the conventions that might nominate them. To show naked ambition for the highest office was considered bad form.

Leland took some time off after Northampton and wired Roxy suggesting a weekend in New York, see a show, eat at Barbetta's. On the eastbound train she wondered if something might be going wrong with her vision. No matter the scenery out the window—town, forest, or cornfield—the colors were washed out and flat. However broad the horizon, the landscape seemed to contract into a map, a map of desolation. On a good night she got four, maybe five hours of sleep.

She was much richer than Leland but he insisted on paying for the hotel and meals. As they unpacked he was unusually talkative, more proud of guarding the president than he would admit. "Calvin's got two teenage boys, they're really nice," he said. "They don't put on any airs at all. Neither one can beat me at tennis, though."

"Mmmm," Roxy mumbled.

Leland stopped hanging up a shirt and turned to look at her. Something was really bothering Roxy if she showed no interest in political gossip.

"You'd never guess what's the poem that Calvin's got hung above the fireplace there," he said. He took a note from his pocket and read:

A wise old owl lived in an oak;
The more he saw, the less he spoke.
The less he spoke, the more he heard.
Why can't we be like that old bird?

"Can you believe a politician would hang up a saying like that? Some of them, you can't shut them up. But with Calvin it's the other way around."

Roxy tried to perk up. Being perky around your boyfriend was part of the job of being a woman. "That's really an extraordinary motto for a politician," she agreed.

She wore dark glasses when they went out, lest somebody recognize her from the Wheeler committee newsreels. That was unlikely, she knew. The public quickly jumped from fascination to fickleness to forgetfulness in this new age of newsreels and radio. The truth was, even Leland hardly recognized her. He had believed that if there is a heaven, men will be compensated there for all the time they spent waiting for women to get ready. Now he wished she actually would attend to her personal appearance. Beyond basic hygiene, she did nothing. As a result, fewer men ogled her. That fact would have pleased her had it been her intention, but she could hardly form any concrete intention.

They saw *Runnin' Wild on Broadway*, "The world's Greatest all colored Entertainment." Leland chose it because, although nearing middle-age, he liked to be au courant and the show had launched a new dance, the Charleston. He laughed at the broad racial humor while Roxy grunted a few times to indicate that she knew a joke had been made.

Back in the hotel room she sat in a brocaded armchair, giving no indication of getting undressed, ever. Leland stood before her and leaned slightly forward.

"Damn it, Roxy, what's wrong with you?"

"I don't know. I'm sorry. And anyway that's an awful question to ask anybody."

Leland relaxed a little, tried to sound placating. "Look, girl, you always have a letdown after a big show. That was your biggest show of all so it's your biggest letdown. That's all that's going on here. You'll come out of this real soon and we'll be having swell times."

Roxy did not reply. Damn it, women always expected you to put up with their moods, their storms of emotion, but this exceeded any man's forbearance. He said with some asperity, "You feel like you stabbed a dead man in the back, is that what this is about? Listen to me, Jess was a goner anyway. The Senate gumshoes had stuff on him that would have put him away for the rest of his life. Believe me, I know what I'm telling you."

Still getting no response, he leaned in to grab her shoulders and started shaking her. "Roxy, honey, you've got to get this black mood out of you! Get it out of you! Get it out! It's killing me! Let it go!" He shook so hard that her teeth clattered.

Roxy realized that she felt . . . nothing. That wasn't quite true; she felt a wish that Leland would stop shaking her. Beyond was nothing but that vacancy of soul, that oblivion of emotion.

"Baby, you don't have things so bad," Leland said in a let-us-be-reasonable voice, letting go and backing off. "You're still young and pretty and healthy. You don't have any worries about money. You're doing swell; just think of all the people who would trade places with you in one second if they could."

Never has any human being felt better for long by meditating on all the people who are even worse off. Roxy did not become the first person to do so.

Leland stopped, suppressing an outcry, and stood her up. He removed her dress and took her by the hand to the bed. She seemed to be sleep-walking. He laid her face down and massaged her back, methodically and steadily, until she fell asleep.

Roxy had her first decent night's sleep in weeks. When awake she stretched and said, "I'm feeling better today. I'm sorry I've been such a pill."

"Hey, nobody's happy all the time. Or hitting on all their cylinders. You'll get your pep back, I know it."

She brushed her hair, counting a hundred strokes, and put on lipstick. Staring at her eyes, she concluded that they needed no makeup.

On the train to Washington Leland burbled, "Let's do something fun!" in the common misbelief that nobody could stay depressed if only they would do something fun.

"Leland, I know I'm not being fair to you. Just be patient with me for a little while longer, okay?"

"Sure, baby."

The next day they rented horses at the stables in Rock Creek Park. Leland bought her a souvenir straw cowboy hat with "Ride 'Em Rock Creek!" printed on the crown along with a silhouette of a bucking bronco. Roxy agreed to wear it.

The stable boy received a look that could slice sheet metal when he asked Roxy if she preferred sidesaddle. "Women have been riding astride for years now," she said.

"Ain't it the truth, lady, but my boss says I have to ask first."

Leland, already mounted, whooped and slapped his cowboy hat against his horse's flank. The horse, unaccustomed to cowboys, snorted its disapproval. Roxy smiled for the first time in days as she climbed into the saddle.

The day actually was something fun, even for Roxy. Leland showed off his expert Oklahoman horsemanship and his mare, long used to amateur urban riders, seemed to enjoy it. Roxy had not ridden for years but had a placid horse on well-worn trails.

Leland kneed his horse into the middle of Rock Creek but it balked at stepping on all the sharp, slippery rocks. He kiyi-yayed like a man launching a cattle drive in a Western movie, scampering up the bank with a wide grin. Roxy was happy for him. They had rented horses for an hour but stayed out for two and gladly paid the extra charge.

Leland held her tenderly that night and did not ask for sex.

June 24, 1924

Roxy awoke with sunlight through the window on her face. Sunshine is critical to how you feel, Roxy mused. Eskimos live up where it's dark for half the year. How do they stand that?

Leland had gone, working the early shift on the Coolidge detail. He left yesterday's clothes wadded on the floor by the bed where he had taken them off. A typical man, Roxy thought. I'm not picking up after him.

Turning on her side, she happened to notice a sock peeking out from under a pants leg. A grey silk sock. What? As long as she had known him, Leland always wore black Lisle cotton socks.

She sat up, reached down to pick up the sock, and examined it. Brooks Brothers was woven on the bottom. Suddenly she felt chilled.

She went to the hotel room's bureau of imitation maple and opened the top drawer. Underwear. The second drawer. Socks. She counted. Fourteen pairs of grey silk socks, each wrapped in tissue paper stamped with the Brooks Brothers symbol of a sheep. The same kind of socks that Jess wore, having a standing order for monthly shipments.

An invisible giant's paw grabbed Roxy's heart and squeezed. It hurt. A roaring was in her ears. She staggered back to sit on the edge of the bed. She remembered that she needed to breathe.

Leland had shot Jess.

The absurdity of the revelation made her want to disbelieve it. A human life. A pair of socks. The disproportion was so extreme, the clue so preposterous, that she should not dare to draw an inference. Any detective would laugh at her. Yet her feminine intuition—something in which she had placed little credence—confirmed that Leland had shot Jess. He had the motive, the means, and the opportunity, as cops liked to say. The motive no doubt was money. Somebody paid him to do it.

Roxy shuddered and noticed again a tremor in her right hand. A familiar numbness returned to her soul. She could not formulate thoughts. She rose and tossed her robe on the floor by her side of the bed. In the bathroom she splashed cold water on her face. She brushed her teeth in a mindlessness of habit.

What she knew for sure was that she had to get out of that room. She opened the closet door, reached in and withdrew the first clothing that came to hand. It happened to be a cinnamon-colored silk dress. She put it on, started to select a hat, then thought, why do I need a hat, the hell with it. It was a bright June day and she did remember her sunglasses.

Normally she walked through hotel lobbies with the serenity of a woman who knows her beauty is admired by men and resented by women. This time she passed through the Wardman Park lobby oblivious of other people. Like an automaton she obeyed the traffic signals as she walked down Connecticut Avenue until she reached the long bridge over the chasm of Rock Creek far below. She leaned against the railing to stare at the waters tumbling over the rocks.

It had been a wet spring and the water, usually lazy by June, was still swift.

Like the water, Roxy's emotions flowed. Shock turned to grief, grief to anger, anger to rage, rage to elaborate scenarios of revenge. This progression might have taken fifteen minutes or two hours; time did not exist. Roxy did not realize it but rage had displaced her depression. Rage requires energy; depression is its absence.

Might as well walk back up and see the National Zoo, she thought. In the great apes house she watched a famous orangutan swing through artificial trees. We think that apes look funny and stupid but they don't shoot each other, she thought. So who's stupid?

She knew where she could get a drink—numerous places, in fact—but she wanted to be stone sober when she confronted Leland. She advanced through the reptile house, the large cats house, the small mammals house as she tried to remember the seven deadly sins from Sunday school. Greed was one of them, for sure, but they might have called it avarice back then. Greed, that's what is wrong with this whole fucking town.

Well, aren't you a fine judge, girl. You're the one who jumped up and down on the bed in ecstasy when Jess first threw those thousand-dollar bills around. You—I—never thought I was doing anything really wrong—legally wrong, but not morally—but now I see how I was enticed into riding the Washington gravy train. This city contaminates everybody. Even good people. Especially good people.

At least I never was really in love with Leland, that's one good thing about all this. He had his good points but mostly he was just a convenient man.

Slowly Roxy made her way back to the Wardman Park. She sat in the coffee shop drinking tea. A couple of men thought to approach her but were daunted by her scowl.

At mid-afternoon Leland returned to the hotel room, throwing off his summer-weight jacket and complaining about the heat. Then he noticed Roxy sitting stiffly on the edge of the bed.

"You shot Jess," she said calmly and coldly.

Instinctively he started to deny it, but then caught her glare and closed his mouth. She could see thoughts playing rapidly across his face. Before long he loosened his tie, unbuttoned his collar, and sat in the armchair facing her.

"I was worried you'd figure it out sooner or later."

"You son of a bitch," she said with the small jolt of pleasure that comes in telling someone that it's all his fault.

He stood right back up and started pacing. For a taciturn man he suddenly was voluble. "Roxy, listen to me," he pleaded, beseeching with open arms. "I'll tell you exactly how it happened. And you've got to believe me! Jess wanted it! I mean it! He knew exactly what we were there for. He was sitting on the bed in his pajamas and he didn't offer any resistance at all, he just sat there calm as all get-out. He didn't even say anything—well, wait, you know the only thing he said? He said, 'Get it over with.' That's all he said, four words, get it over with. He hardly even moved. I tell you, he wanted it! If we hadn't done it, he'd a-done it himself and it really would have been suicide."

He took a step toward her, still with a pleading, earnest expression. "And I promise you, he didn't suffer. It was quick and painless. Who'd you rather have done it, me or one of the deviated septums?"

"Why? Why did you do it?" She sounded bloodless and clinical even to herself.

"Why, to protect Harry, what do you think? Jess was going to make the usual deal, turn on his boss in exchange for a light sentence. You of all people should know how much Wheeler wanted Harry's scalp. Well, Jess was going to give it to him."

"But Jess loved Harry, he would never be a traitor against him."

"Yeah? Well, love has a way of burning out when you're looking at ten to twenty years in Leavenworth. Jess was human, he was thinking, if somebody's got to take the fall, better Harry than me."

"I'll never believe that Harry wanted this."

"Naw, he knew nothing about it, you're right about that."

"Then who?"

Leland took a long drag on his cigarette. It was a nicotine fix, not a ploy to evade an answer. "It was Billy Burns's operation."

"That's what I thought. I always wondered, what happened to Jess's gun that your Mr. Burns said he misplaced?"

"What do you think? That was a brand-new .32. Billy wanted it for himself."

"You mean he just stole it?"

Leland made a what-else-could-you-expect gesture. After a minute of silence he smashed his cigarette in an ashtray and said, "I reckon this means you won't see me no more."

That remark did not deserve a reply. Roxy said, "I'm turning you in, you son of a bitch."

At that, Leland took two steps backward, nonchalantly sat back down and elaborately lit another cigarette, waving his hand vigorously to blow out the match before flicking it on the carpet.

"Well now, baby, I'm afraid that would be a big waste of time for both of us. There's no evidence—I tossed my gun in the Potomac. It would just be your word against mine."

"I'll get the cops to reopen the case."

"Now, there's an empty threat if I ever heard one. To the cops, the case is closed. Suicide. I could go into the cop shop myself to confess and they would tell me, case closed, go away. You think they'd want to take on all that extra work?"

"All right, but you know that I have friends in high places. God, I never thought I would ever say that. But I can get Senator Wheeler to call hearings and put you and Billy under oath."

Leland looked at her with something like pity. "Come on now, baby, you know better than that. Jess, I mean no disrespect, but Jess was not even a federal employee. He was just a civilian that a lot of people knew and that went and killed his own self." He took another drag and considered. "They might be interested if a murder scandal could still be used against Harry, but Coolidge has already fired Harry so it's all water under the bridge. And anyway the senators are all out of town campaigning until after the election. And your great friend Burton K. Wheeler wants to be vice president. You think he cares about Jess Smith now? Or you? . . . And now I've got a question for you. How'd you figure it out?"

"Socks. What kind of man wears a dead man's socks?"

Leland raised his brows in puzzlement.

"You've picked up the grey silk Brooks Brothers socks that Jess used to wear."

"Oh for Christ's sake. I knew you were smart but that's not even smart, that's just spooky. Really, that was your clue? Picked up his socks? Jeezus. Look. We went through all his drawers looking for papers. And we got a lot that Jess hadn't burned yet. Anyway, you know that Jess was always the best-dressed guy around, and I opened his socks drawer and I thought, hey, those are pretty swell. I think I'll get those myself. So I called up Brooks Brothers and put in an order. I only wear them at work and like when we went to the restaurant last night, you know. It's not like I wear spats too." He shook his head, incredulous.

"How much did Billy Burns pay you?"

"Now that, Rox, will have to remain my own business. He knew that I would do a professional job and that I would keep my mouth shut, which is just as important."

"Well, aren't you proud of yourself."

"Goddamnit, I tell you he wanted it! You might even say that I did him a favor."

Roxy stood and walked to the door. She turned around to say, "Goodbye, Leland. I'll have my things sent over to the Hotel Washington."

As she turned down the hall Leland muttered, "You always did think you was too good for me." She did not hear and he did not try to follow her.

June 30, 1924

She had to nag Wheeler's secretary to get an appointment with him. When she finally got into his office she told him that Leland Jackson had confessed to murdering her ex-husband.

Wheeler puffed a pipe—he thought it made him look wise—and pondered before saying, "Roxy, you know I think the world of you and I'm sorry for your loss, but what do you want me to do about this? It's a local criminal matter for the District police; it doesn't come under federal jurisdiction."

"I guess I wanted your advice. I want to see justice done—he shouldn't be allowed to get away with murder. It might be a local crime and Jess was not a federal employee but Leland certainly is."

Wheeler nodded and put down the pipe. "It's true that the case does have political implications. Your Mr. Jackson is on the presidential detail, so any scandal would reflect on the Coolidge administration—fairly or unfairly, but that's how politics works."

"Well? Why should that bother you? You're going to be the candidate for vice president on the Progressive ticket. So let it fall to President Coolidge, let him fend off the wicked rumors about his own Secret Service."

Wheeler looked wounded. "Roxy, please, you can't think that I am that cynical. I don't play dirty politics, you know me better than that." He looked at her until she muttered, "Sorry." Then he clasped his hands behind his neck and leaned back in his chair.

"You want my advice? All right. There's a crusty old reactionary bastard in the Senate, Henry Cabot Lodge. We disagree on almost everything politically but he's been around forever and knows more about how things work in this town than anybody. Just because I detest him, I think he's the man you ought to go see."

Roxy saw the irony. She had always disdained social conventions, resented authority. Now here she was seeking guidance from two pillars of the establishment.

In Lodge's office the first thing she noticed was a framed *Time* magazine cover portrait of him. The artist had given him a twinkly-eyed, benevolent expression with a white mustache and beard like a thin-faced Santa Claus.

The second thing of note was a stuffed caribou trophy on the wall behind Lodge's desk, shot by his good friend Theodore Roosevelt. God, Roxy thought, when will the country ever rid itself of all these beasts slaughtered by Teddy?

"Welcome, my dear. My esteemed colleague Senator Wheeler has briefed me about your concerns. Please have a seat. May I offer my condolences for the loss of your former spouse."

Roxy was not the first to wonder how, with a mustache so bushy, the old man could sip tea or kiss a woman.

"Thank you, senator. I consider it a privilege to be here."

"My dear, allow me to begin by asking a question of you. Do you know the name, Chester A. Arthur?"

Roxy needed a few seconds. "In school we had to memorize all the presidents. He was one of the nonentities that followed Lincoln in the last century. I'm sorry but I can't recall anything else about him"

"Hmmpf," Lodge chuckled, "nonentities, just so. Mr. Arthur succeeded James A. Garfield from your state of Ohio. President Garfield was one of the most intelligent men ever raised to the presidency. He had invented a new proof of the Pythagorean theorem. Did you know that?"

"No sir."

"Well, Mr. Garfield was elected in 1880. I was just starting out my career in politics as a young whippersnapper in the legislature of Massachusetts. And then Mr. Garfield was shot by a damned anarchist. Excuse my language, Miss Stinson."

"That's all right."

"Poor Mr. Garfield lingered for four months before succumbing. I think his doctors should have been tried for negligent homicide, but I won't go into that.

"Now Mr. Arthur, the vice president, was just a courthouse machine politician of the sort you can find by the thousands in cities all over the country. We put him on the ticket as part of a political deal at the convention, but you needn't care about that. Hell, after all these years, I don't even care any more.

"The point is, Mr. Arthur was a political enemy of President Garfield. I don't mean they disagreed politically, I don't mean that they were on the outs personally. I mean he was an enemy. He went home to New York all the time to plot against the president with his cronies.

"And so when the president was shot, the rumors flew that Mr. Arthur and his cronies were behind it. That they had conspired to do away with Mr. Garfield to put Mr. Arthur in the White House. As a result Mr. Arthur's presidency was poisoned from the start. Actually, in my judgment he became at least a satisfactory, and in some respects a good, president. But the rumors destroyed his health and well-being and he died not long after leaving the White House."

Another thing about politicians, Roxy thought. They never tire of explaining things to you.

"I see by your face, you are wondering why I am giving you this history lesson. But you see, my dear, any allegation that a member of President Coolidge's Secret Service committed a murder would redound to the discredit of President Coolidge. The rumors would hold that Coolidge's men got rid of Mr. Smith as a way of forcing Mr. Daugherty out of office. They knew that President Harding was a sick man and likely to die soon, and they didn't want Mr. Daugherty hanging on as an embarrassment to the new president when he took over. Now, maybe none of that makes much sense when you look at it hard, but the rumors would come anyway. At the very least, the Democrats would ask why President Coolidge harbored a murderer in his Secret Service. You see?" Lodge relaxed in the chair behind his desk with an air of having completed a performance.

"Mr. Lodge, I appreciate your sharing with me the wisdom of your experience. But I came here for advice and what exactly are you advising me to do?"

"Oh, my child, why, put away your desire to take revenge on Mr. Jackson. It could not possibly succeed and it could only besmirch the reputation of a new president just as he is starting out. Why, it's your patriotic duty to let it go. Really, Miss Stinson, you have no choice."

"No sir, senator, choice is exactly what I have."

The old man lit up one of his benign smiles. "Senator Wheeler told me you were a woman of honesty and grit and I can see how right he was. Yes, you have a choice, just so. But satisfy my curiosity. If you decide to proceed against Mr. Jackson, how would you do so?"

"There's always a civil lawsuit for wrongful death."

"It would be a hard case to win, but merely filing a complaint would create the publicity that I pray to God you will not seek."

The interview ended with Lodge wishing her well and assuring her that she could call on him for help at any time.

August 3, 1924

Back in Ohio, Mal Daugherty took back the car that Roxy and Jess had used because it had belonged to Harry. Roxy decided to treat herself to buying a new 1924 Cadillac. Men were always made happy by having new machinery to play with, so why not her?

She took a train to Columbus and a taxi to the largest General Motors dealer there. The salesman was startled by a single woman car-shopping by herself and shocked when she offered to put the cash on his desk right now in return for a twenty percent discount. They settled on fifteen percent off the $3,085 price. Roxy selected a black four-door sedan with a convertible top and a hand-painted blue pinstripe on the lower body. The general manager emerged and insisted on scrutinizing her drivers license before handing over the keys. Roxy wondered whether they were more discombobulated by a female car-shopper or by the fact that she did not wear a cloche or any hat at all. She was not dressed as a flapper but even so, they probably suspected she was a call girl.

Her anticipation was fulfilled—she thrilled to the eighty-three horsepower of the new V-8 engine, speeding down Route 62 to Washington Court House. A paved road! Why should men have all the fun? Passing motorists honked and waved at the beautiful woman in the beautiful car. She loved the boxy styling, the drum-shaped headlamps, the new-car smell, the wind through the open windows, the smooth hardness of the gearshift knob, the contented meshing of the gears.

When she arrived home the children of the tenants of her building on Court Street ran out to greet this marvel. She gave them a ride around town, smiling at their squeals as they waved and hollered to people on the sidewalks. Soon Roxy became known as the "Cadillac Lady," with kids of all ages from all over town clamoring for their time in the holy chariot. A couple of times she drove them out past the Shack, wondering whether she would see Harry there and what she would say to him if she did, but he never appeared.

Sadly, all new toys turn stale in time. Roxy loved the car but the car did not give her peace. She didn't even see the kids any more. Their mothers now forbade them the company of a woman of such notoriety. She openly smoked cigarettes on the sidewalks—that sin alone was enough to exile her from respectable company.

This small instance of bigotry got Roxy to wondering why she still felt at home in her small town. The city lights of New York or Washington did not draw her. Having read Sinclair Lewis's novel *Main Street*, she knew the kind of revenge a smart kid could take on his hometown. And she knew men who would not brook any insult to their boyhood hometown but privately thanked God for having gotten them the hell out of there.

What is more, she understood the hair-trigger sensitivity of any bumpkin to any hint of condescension from a city slicker. Maybe that was her problem. Maybe she had spent so much time in Washington, even Columbus, that the local biddies suspected her of putting on citified airs.

No, the problem was theirs, not hers. She decided that she did not mind small-town conformity because the pressures to conform did not apply to her. When you are the smartest kid in class you will be lonely and set apart, unless you make arduous efforts to fit in. She had not made such efforts. Yet she did not look down on those who did. She took people as they came, that is, ordinary people just trying to make the best of things. Not the Harry Daughertys of the world.

The fact remained that whatever makes you exceptional also makes you lonely. She had no confidante except Evalyn McLean and she was in Maine. A letter arrived from Leland but she tossed it away unopened. Leland had been fun and the sex eventually was good but they never became "one flesh," no matter what the Bible says. She had more of a confluence of souls with Jess but for all that they remained a mostly lonely pair. No matter the circumstances, we are forever by ourselves. In Washington Court House or Washington, D.C., or wherever, we all try to deny our essential solitude.

Roxy stood sipping coffee in her kitchen in a bathrobe. Maybe someday she would be less lonely. A new man was not unthinkable. For now, she needed to decide what to do with her life and her money.

As the weeks passed, the more she reflected the more she realized the disadvantages of being female. She would have made a better banker than Mal Daugherty, a better coordinator of grifters than Jess Smith, a better director of veterans affairs than Charles Forbes, a better . . . hell, come to think of it, Florence Harding could have made better president than her husband, at least a smarter and a tougher one. Even though the Duchess was a dumb Dora about the stars. But when you thought about it, even calling her the Duchess was condescending. A way for men to sneer at a bossy woman. If she herself were male, Roxy was sure, she would not have been kept out of the White House and she could have saved Mr. Harding a lot of grief.

She rehearsed her regrets over sitting out the fight for the right to vote. When she was young and foolish she believed that women did not go to war and shed their blood for the flag, so how did they deserve to vote? Now she believed that men did not deserve to arbitrate what women deserved. She knew men who were ashamed of having failed to serve in the Great War, even if they had medical deferments from the draft. She had never understood why, but now she felt abashed because she had been absent from the march for women's suffrage. She had something to live up to, amends to make.

The more she thought about it the more she got mad, not so much at men as at the government. Look at Harry, he would have been a crooked small-town lawyer, maybe bribe a couple of judges, tamper with a couple of juries, loot an estate or two. Put him in government and he corrupted the entire justice system of the United States.

Or consider that Warren and Florence Harding sincerely swore to take care of our veterans. An insane man who despised the military could hardly have done more harm to veterans than Charles Forbes did.

And it wasn't just a matter of a few villains like Harry Daugherty and Charles Forbes and Albert Fall. Nor could it all be blamed on Warren Harding's poor judgment of people. Government itself is an instrument for screwing people. I know things about the government that hardly anyone ever gets to see, Roxy thought. I found out early in the war that they were tapping my phone. How could the senators have been surprised to learn that Bureau of Investigation thugs were snooping in their offices? That is what government agents do.

Think of Senator Wheeler, the Progressive hero, ha ha. He told me that the Senate investigators had put a tail on Florence Harding, just because she was close to Harry Daugherty and might lead them to some evidence. Wheeler volunteered this as merely an interesting fact, with no betrayal of irony or regret. At this very minute there probably were federal agents tapping telephones and opening mail and breaking into offices. Because they could and because that was the kind of people they were. And these outrages are on top of the normal pathologies of bureaucracy, the waste and incompetence.

And even if all the bureaucrats were able and honest, the system passed stupid laws. Never mind Prohibition;

Congress had decreed that you can't show interstate movies of prizefights. Just because a colored boxer had whipped a white one. Of all the scams that she and Jess pulled, Roxy was proudest of bootlegging the Dempsey-Carpentier movie.

She wondered whether Florence Harding had known about that scam and what she thought about it if she did. Her thoughts kept coming back to the Duchess, a woman she did not know well and never liked very much. But Florence had taken a battering from life and tried to give it a battering back. She had her faults, such as endless rancor toward people she thought had snubbed her (a large group). She was inflexibly faithful to her friends, though. What was most important, she was brave enough to stake out policy positions and a public role as first lady.

The government had sent American boys to fight a foreign war for purposes still unclear. Florence Harding made the care of wounded soldiers a sacred passion. In that cause she probably did more tangible good for more people than any male magnifico in Washington.

The things that happen to you in life raise questions, Roxy decided. You try to find answers but what if life doesn't want to play along? Life was not like it was written in novels, where every opportunity is promising, every coincidence beneficial. But the Duchess . . . maybe enough years had passed that the Duchess had found some answers.

September 22, 1924

The first thing that Florence Harding saw, the first thing she hated, was the large sign at the entrance to White Oaks Farms: DON'T STARE AT THE PATIENTS. On 130 acres outside of Marion, Dr. Sawyer and his son Carl had built White Oaks as the first private mental hospital in the country. They insisted that Florence stay there for treatment of her heart and kidney ailments.

Florence had established a residence in the Willard Hotel in Washington. She returned to Marion for a summer visit. On Wednesday evenings Carl's son Warren (named for the president) took her for a drive in the country. Soon he understood why she insisted on Wednesdays. That was the night that Marion's Protestant churches rang their bells for prayer meetings. The tolling reminded Florence of how they rang for her husband's funeral.

As the anniversary of his death approached Florence wrote a poem and had it engraved to send to friends:

> In the graveyard softly sleeping,
> Where the flowers gently wave,
> Lies the one I loved so dearly,
> And tried so hard to save,
> Husband how hard I tried to keep you,
> Prayers and tears were all in vain,
> Happy Angels came and took you
> From this world of sorrow and pain . . .

She caught a summer cold and succumbed to the Sawyers' entreaties that she move into a bungalow at White Oaks. She wrote to Evalyn about visiting her later that summer in Bar Harbor, Maine, before returning to Washington.

The elder Dr. Sawyer tended to her often. Florence worried about him—he seemed to have taken Warren's death as hard as she did. White Oaks had its own cows, chickens, orchards, and vegetable gardens. Each morning after collecting the eggs and milking the cows, Sawyer visited Florence.

"I am afraid I can give you no encouragement about traveling to the East, Duchess," he said.

"But soon it will be too cool for me to be in Maine. And I feel fine."

"No, ma'am, I must insist that your condition is too weak."

Sawyer, always a small man, seemed to have shrunk even more. Like many short men he always had maintained an erect posture but now he slumped and shuffled. He looks awful, Florence thought. Sawyer wished her a good day and went out to rake the gravel in a driveway. He fell over and died.

After attending his funeral Florence made plans to go to Washington. Carl Sawyer was even more dictatorial than his father and said he could not allow it. True enough, she was getting sicker. She told a reporter that she was starting to work on her memoirs. She knew it was a falsehood.

Evalyn took her private train car from Bar Harbor to Marion. They had dinner in the car as Evalyn tried to pry Florence away from her doctor. "Carl Sawyer is not the only doctor in the country," she said. "You know you always have a home with us wherever we are."

Florence looked around at the railroad yard where she and Warren had come and gone so many times. "I will never see you again," she said.

"Now, now, you are going to get better and visit me."

"Evalyn, this is the end."

From the gossip in town Roxy knew that Florence was sinking fast. She drove to White Oaks and confronted Carl Sawyer. "Mrs. Harding is gravely ill and I will not permit her to have visitors," the doctor said.

"I will not permit you to keep me out," Roxy said, shoving him aside. The doctor followed her into the private room. "Leave us," Florence said, nearly a whisper, with a feeble wave of her hand. Sawyer glowered and said, "You may have a ten-minute visitation" before leaving.

Florence was propped up on pillows in a leather Morris chair with the back reclined a bit. Roxy sensed once again that unmistakable yet indefinable smell of a sickroom. A bedside table, the usual repository of flowers, instead held a radio and a carved elephant statuette. During her travels

Florence had collected hundreds of elephants, symbol of the Republican Party. This one was made of some kind of rare tropical hardwood and probably had been given to her by some colonial official.

Florence wore a silk robe of, Roxy was pleased to see, Harding Blue. She did not look as surprised to see her as Roxy had expected. "Well, hello, Miss Stinson," she said. As imperious as ever, she demanded that Roxy admire the elephant. "Everyone who comes here admires him. I picked this one out because of the way its trunk points up. I don't like all the ones with their trunks down so much. Look up, not down, is what I always say." By following her eyes Roxy knew that she was supposed to pick up and stroke the damn thing.

When she put it back, Florence gestured for her to move an armchair closer to the bed. Roxy pushed it across the floor and started to say something when Florence said, "Let me turn this off." She reached over to click the radio dial. "I like to listen to jazz music on KYW in Chicago. It comes in fine at night but in the daytime I just get this scratchy static."

Neither woman wanted much small talk about elephants or jazz. For her part, Florence was too weak just to chat.

"I am glad to see that you are looking better than Dr. Sawyer led me to believe," Roxy said. "You're going to come out of this the way you always have."

"Miss Stinson, I am too old and too sick to listen to any lies."

"Very well, Mrs. Harding, I will take comfort in your honesty. You know we were never close friends but I always admired you."

"Thank you for that. You are here because you want something. What do you want?"

"I want to wish you a full recovery. I mean that. But here is what I came for. I am giving my money away to take care of our veterans. I want you to tell me which charities are worthy of my support."

A single tear appeared under each of Florence's eyes. Defying gravity, they stayed there and did not dribble down her cheeks. Moments passed before she said, "Anything else, my dear?"

"Yes. I am going to work for peace so that we never again send American boys off to fight foreign wars."

Historical Note

Even after a century of constant political scandals, the corruption of the Harding administration still strains credulity. This book is a work of imagination but I have scarcely exaggerated the venality of Harry Daugherty, Charles Forbes, and others.

Leland Jackson is a fictional character. All other major characters are historical figures. Incidents in this novel are based on the historical record but I made up most of the figures' thoughts, speech, and actions. Also there are some minor adjustments in the chronology.

Violence and tragedy continued to follow many of the persons in this story.

Roxy Stinson. In 1926 she married an auto salesman from Columbus, Phillip Brast. The couple moved into a modest house in Washington Court House and lived quietly. Roxy always refused requests from reporters and historians for interviews. She died on New Years Day in 1973 at age 83.

Florence Harding. She died at White Oaks Farm on November 21, 1924, at age 64. Her grandson George Warren De Wolfe, an alcoholic, committed suicide in 1968 at 54.

Harry Daugherty. His wife Lucie died in the same week as Florence Harding. Daugherty was indicted on corruption charges in 1926 and tried twice. The first jury deadlocked 7-5 in favor of conviction, the second 11-1 in favor of conviction. Daugherty died in 1941 in Columbus at 81.

Charles R. Forbes. His wife divorced him in 1923. The next year, Forbes was convicted of defrauding the government, fined $10,000, and sentenced to two years in prison. He spent later years trying to excuse President Harding while blaming Harry Daugherty. Forbes died in 1952 at 74.

Albert B. Fall. In 1929 he was found guilty of taking $385,000 in bribes for granting no-bid leases on federal oil reserves. Fall was fined $100,000 and sentenced only to a year in prison but he was the first Cabinet office to be incarcerated. Fall died nearly penniless in a Catholic charity hospital in El Paso in 1944 at 83.

Edward McLean. Evalyn McLean filed for divorced in 1931. McLean claimed he was already remarried to a sister of a Hollywood star but his story was false. He moved to Latvia, where a divorce was granted in 1932. His mental illness caused a court to force the sale of the *Washington Post*. In 1933 a jury found McLean to be legally insane, whereupon Evalyn withdrew her divorce case. A court committed McLean to a psychiatric hospital in Maryland, where he died in 1941 at 52.

Evalyn Walsh McLean. She wrote a column, "My Say," for the *Washington Times-Herald*. She continued her philanthropic efforts for soldiers after World War I and during World War II. Her daughter Emily Evalyn "Evie" McLean, the fifth wife of Senator Robert Rice Reynolds of North Carolina, committed suicide in 1946 at 24. Evalyn died of pneumonia in Washington in 1947 at 60.

Alice Roosevelt Longworth. Nicholas Longworth became Speaker of the House in 1925, the same year that Alice had a daughter, Paulina. Senator Borah was widely believed to be the child's father. Nicholas died of pneumonia in 1931 at 61. Alice published an autobiography, *Crowded Hours*, in 1933. Paulina committed suicide in 1957, after which Alice raised her granddaughter, Joanna. Alice died in 1980 at 96.

Carrie Phillips. She returned to Germany after Mrs. Harding's death and allegedly became the mistress of a German prince. With her husband James she went home to Marion before Hitler took power. She kicked James out of their house shortly before he died in 1939 at 73. Carrie died in 1960 at 86. Love letters between her and Warren Harding were not made public until 2014.

Nan Britton. In 1927 she published *The President's Daughter*, describing her affair with Harding. The book was attacked as incredible. She did not release love letters that would have proved her case. Nan raised her daughter Elizabeth Ann in Illinois and the family later moved to Oregon. In 2015 DNA tests proved that Harding was the girl's father. Nan Britton did in 1991 at 94. Elizabeth Ann died in 2005 at 86.

Gaston Means. Means was convicted of perjury and sentenced to two years in federal prison. In 1930 he published *The Strange Death of President Harding*, which suggested that Mrs. Harding had poisoned her husband. After Charles Lindbergh's son was kidnaped in 1932, Means bilked Evalyn McLean out of $104,000 by falsely claiming to know the whereabouts of the victim. Means was sentenced to fifteen years for grand larceny in that scheme and died in federal prison in Leavenworth, Kansas, in 1938 at 59.

George Remus. In 1925 Remus was sentenced to two years for Volstead Act violations. While at the Atlanta penitentiary he told another inmate that his second wife, Imogene Holmes, had control of his money. That inmate was an undercover federal agent who then quit his job, found Holmes, and began an affair with her. In 1927 Remus shot Holmes to death. Remus was committed to an insane asylum but released after seven months. He remarried and died in 1952 at 73.

William J. Burns. President Coolidge forced his resignation as chief of the Bureau of Investigation in 1924. He was succeeded by J. Edgar Hoover; the agency later became the Federal Bureau of Investigation. Burns moved to Florida and wrote detective stories based on his career. He died in 1932 at 70.

Burton K. Wheeler. The Progressive Party ticket in 1924 with senators Robert M. La Follette for president and Wheeler for vice president won 17 percent of the vote. In 1925 the Senate and a jury cleared Wheeler of charges brought by Harry Daugherty. Wheeler served twenty-four years in the Senate and died in 1975 at 92.

About the Author

James L. Merriner is the author of five nonfiction books about politics and history, specializing in issues of corruption and reform. A graduate of Harvard University, he has served as the James Thurber Writer in Residence at Ohio State University and as president of the Society of Midland Authors. Mr. Merriner covered presidential politics as the political editor of the *Chicago Sun-Times* and the *Atlanta Constitution*. *Stumbling in the Public Square* is his first novel. He lives in the Chicago area, where he is also an arts photographer. Visit him at www.jameslmerriner.com.